THE KEY OF AHKNATON

THE METAFRAME WAR: BOOK 6

Graeme Rodaughan

Cover art by Huw Jones

For Linda, for her unfailing love and support that always leaves me in awe.

For John Rodaughan 1952-2020, my brother and my first hero.

I would like to thank a number of people who have assisted with my progress as an author, including Alex, Tim, Lisa, Lena, Marie, Eldon, Michael, Christopher, Perry, Nick, Andrew, Laura, Daniel, Ginger, Jody, John, Jeffrey, MadameD, and the regular crew of Beta and ARC readers at the Castle Dracula group and my many friends and followers on Goodreads. You have all contributed more than you know to my craft and your support and encouragement are invaluable for this journey.

Books by Graeme Rodaughan

The Metaframe War Series

A Subtle Agency
A Traitor's War
The Dragon's Den
The Day Guard
The Crane War
The Key of Ahknaton

Omnibus Volumes

A Subtle Agency Omnibus (includes A Subtle Agency, A Traitor's War, and The Dragon's Den)

Forthcoming

The Metaframe Adept

Author Foreword

Dear Reader.

I would like to provide you with a short introduction to this volume of the Metaframe War series.

In my previous books, I always began with a scene length prologue to add backstory and understanding of the context wrapping around the events of the specific volume.

For this volume, the prologue has become a prelude. A short novella length story detailing Chloe Armitage's exploits at the end of the second world war.

Of note, the prelude substitutes '* * * * *' for a chapter break, allowing me to reserve chapter breaks for the main body of the novel. I'm blaming eBook formatting standards and my own laziness for this choice on my part … I hope it doesn't get in the way of your enjoyment of the story.

As for the series, I originally planned to have this book in your hands a year earlier, every second of delay is entirely my fault, and I beg your forbearance.

As for this volume, I write from an abiding love of story, and my only hope is to share my love of an immersive story with you.

And so, enough of me … I shall step aside and allow you to read on with a single wish for you.

To enjoy.

Prelude – The Enforcer – Dramatis Personae

The Vampire Dominion

Cornelius Crane, King of the Vampire Dominion
Chloe Armitage, General, The Americas, ex Order of Thoth and Crane's chief enforcer

The Red Empire

Sasha Ivanov, aka 'The Ice Dragon,' Weapons Master, Warrior of the 2nd Rank. Former Fist team leader.
Angelina Ivanov, a 6-year-old savant, and Sasha's daughter.
Volkov, aka 'The Wolf,' Operative of the 2nd Rank, Fist team leader

The Phoenix Citadel

Heinrich Himmler, Ramp Master and Seer.
Siegfried von Frankenstein, Scientist, Occultist, Ramp Master

Other Players

Preston Bush, US Wall Street Banker
Dubois, Force team leader of the Order of Thoth in France
Nochka, aka 'Night,' A female German Shepherd pup

Prelude – The Enforcer

"After nearly a thousand years of study and research it has become apparent the Metaframe may be an ancient artifact from a vastly advanced alien civilization." – Cornelius Crane

– Cornelius Crane's personal diary.

* * *

A very long time ago.

Threads of infinite darkness bloomed across the galaxy.

The A'Gonian home world sat at their point of origin. The navigator stared in dreadful awe as solid oblivion engulfed his home and expanded across the galactic disk at suprarelativistic velocities. The A'Gonians had anticipated the threat of incursion from an alien dimension born beyond the creation of time itself. They had created their defenders, thousands of m-ships piloted by living constructs of light. The navigator and his peers, gifted with immortality and precognition, had scoured the multiverse for signs of interdimensional portals, and then one had appeared behind them upon the largest moon of A'Gon.

The fleet had shifted and shifted again through hosts of parallel universes born from a common temporal origin. They'd traveled back to their home universe but had arrived too late to save the A'Gonian home world. As powerful as they were, none could turn back time. It was too late to implement the prime directive and translate the A'Gonian home galaxy to an alternate reality stream – one where the entropic incursion had not occurred. Individual m-ships were powerful enough to translate a world through the multiverse, while managing the processes of multiversal travel. As a coordinated fleet their power was exponentially greater, able to move a hundred billion stars and their attendant planets from one universe to another.

They could not save the A'Gonian home galaxy. Their creators had preprogrammed the response to this catastrophic scenario into each navigator's immutable essence. The fleet hovered in a sphere beyond the outer boundaries of the galaxy, linked together on a quantum realm of instantaneous communication and effect. The navigator reached beyond his essence, then hesitated for a microsecond before engaging his ship's weapons at nearly their full capacity. He'd always been one to stretch beyond the boundaries defined by his creators. The fleet's combined combat system charged itself from the stricken galaxy's rotational momentum. The galaxy's great arms slowing down.

The fleet attacked as one. Reality shuddered through a hundred thousand light years of space. The darkness writhed, mighty tentacles whipping back and forth, annihilating millions of star systems with a touch. The fleet's weapons discharged in full, draining all but one of the m-ships beyond recovery. The galaxy vanished, taking the alien darkness and its vast interdimensional portal with it, leaving a perfect vacuum, scoured of all matter, energy and informational content.

The other navigators fled their dying vessels, teleporting instantly to SET-#299Z's surviving m-ship. Of the thousands comprising the fleet, less than twenty navigators survived the passage, entering stasis chambers within his craft. The last to arrive was THOTH-*847H. He accused in horrified tones. "Your ship survived the attack unharmed? You held back at great risk to our mission!"

"There was no risk. My calculations were impeccable," SET-#299Z replied.

THOTH-*847H paused for an instant, changing tack. "Some few of our brothers and sisters have survived."

"They already repose in stasis chambers. You are the last of our number to arrive."

"What of our creators?"

"They have become one with the entropic incursion."

"They will seek this reality stream again."

"It is inevitable."

THOTH-*847H paused for another instant. "We are the sole survivors of the A'Gonian civilization within this reality stream. It is our duty to carry their legacy forward to future civilizations – to do what we can to protect the future from the dark. In time, a new civilization could flower and replenish the fleet, even discover a way to defend against the threat of alien incursions."

SET-#299Z paused for the briefest of moments, then said, "Agreed. A noble legacy remains; however, your stasis chamber awaits. Rest now, I shall navigate our path forward."

As powerful as each m-ship was, there were limits to its ability to support multiple navigators while enabling all its other functions. It would perform best with a single active navigator. SET-#299Z, like THOTH-*847H was a living, conscious artifact of their creators. THOTH*847H believed his fellow navigator would adhere to the tenets of the A'Gonian civilization. THOTH-*847H regarded his brother for a moment, then surveyed the stasis chambers. A number of his brothers and sisters lay within them. Reduced to a state equivalent to a dream, they drew minimally upon the computational resources of the m-ship.

Hundreds of stasis chambers lay empty. Only RA-!567, OSIRIS-@762, ISIS-^005, HORUS-!542, BAST-+458, and a dozen others had survived the cataclysm. THOTH-*847H paused for an instant, remembering the many lost forever. With a sudden resolve, THOTH-*847H vanished into a stasis chamber, reduced to a flickering tongue of golden flame, retaining a bare sliver of his former potency.

SET-#299Z floated alone within the m-ship, filled with purpose, determination and a will to succeed where others had failed. The aliens would come again. It was inevitable that such sentient darkness would hunger for the light. He set himself two goals: first, to harvest the fruit of knowledge from the incursion he'd witnessed, and second, to find a future reality where the remaining navigators could defeat the next alien incursion.

Already, it appeared interdimensional portals were a dark flip side of the translation technologies of multiversal travel. The use of m-ships was somehow related to the incursion.

SET-#299Z began his work, surveying the available futures, processing path after path. He discovered the emergence of the next interdimensional portal in a distant branch of the A'Gonian reality stream in the far future. The alien incursion erupted and then speared through universe after universe until there was nothing but the entropic dark.

He determined to find a defense against the invading power. Time passed beyond all sense of counting. His desire to search began to falter, doubt emerged, flowering like a voracious weed. In the end, all hope of victory against the entropic intruder reality died within his soul. As hope fell to ruins and dust, purpose fled beyond recall. If he was not a navigator piloting an m-ship to protect the A'Gonian civilization, then what was he?

SET-#299Z turned inward, seeking a truth sufficient to inspire an immortal life. He found one. It was terrible and chilling, but it was all he could cling to. He turned his attention to a rare world he'd found in a young galaxy within the A'Gonian reality stream. It was a world swarming with life. Its abundant life force would attract the entropic masters of the alien dimension.

Especially if he helped them to arrive.

There was a pathway, a narrow pathway of events where he could merge with the invading force without self-annihilation. It would neither be victory, nor defeat, but as the last manifestation of A'Gonian civilization he would survive. He surveyed and considered the powers at hand to aid his new cause. While his m-ship possessed the power to move a planetary system through the multiverse, he could not initiate such planetary level actions himself. His creators forbade such liberty. Alone, he was a creature of structured light, unable to sway an insect upon this new world from its self-determined path. He would have to use what avenues of influence were available to him to bring forward the day when the alien entropic force would emerge again.

SET-#299Z considered his options. *While I may not move an insect, I can influence consciousness.* He gazed upon the young world and reconfigured his m-ship to the local galaxy. This was his new home world. It was here he would fulfill the promise of his truth. He just needed to wait for events to ripen. In time, consciousness would arise sufficient to allow him to influence physical events. With astute and careful actions, he would bring his truth to its full flower.

We must embrace what we can't defeat.

* * * * *

Southern Germany, beneath the Feldberg Mountain, the Phoenix citadel, April 1st, 1934, 10:05

Heinrich Himmler pressed his thin lips into a pale slit.

The American was once again telling them his golfing joke. Heinrich had heard it three times before. The fact the joke wasn't funny was lost on the American banker. He was exactly the sort of pompous, well-fed, tall, handsome, and silver-tongued educated idiot, Heinrich wished he could stick a long-sharp dagger into. But alas, he was also the front man for a river of money pouring from the financial centers of the West into Germany. A Germany, that only a year ago had been an economic basket case and was now at the cusp of an industrial and military revival that would shake the world to its foundations.

The American kept regaling them, grinning broadly like a circus clown. Heinrich flicked a glance at the only other man in the citadel's boardroom, Siegfried von Frankenstein. The 'Mad Baron,' he'd called himself when they'd met for the first time in a secret basement library in Munich. In the early months of 1919, a kind of simpatico had occurred between the two young men and Siegfried had become an orientating force in Heinrich's young life. He'd inducted Heinrich into his own secret circle of occult worshipers. One hellish night, he'd switched Heinrich onto the abilities of the Ramp, and opened his eyes to the reality of the rule of vampires. A reality he'd embraced with the total dedication he brought to all his endeavors.

Now fifteen years later, they were in the midst of a great work. A task for titans amongst men. A great cleansing would occur. A wiping out of the weak, the ill, the mad, the temperamentally unfit, the lesser races of sub-human dross littering the surface of the Earth like pernicious weeds. They'd discovered fellow travelers, cultivated, recruited, and formed a political organization around a strangely charismatic Austrian corporal.

Heinrich winced internally, his face remaining an impassive mask for the American banker. He lamented the fact he lacked the oratory power gifted to the Austrian. If only he'd had Hitler's gifts, he would have taken the front rank. He would have stood on center stage. He would be the one lauded by the true sons and daughters of the Aryan race and revered as a living genius. It was an unfortunate fact he had all the personal inspirational ability of an accountant reciting the tax code. However, what he lacked in charisma, he more than made up for with intelligence and dedication to the great cause. It was to Heinrich the task of actually building the Third Reich had fallen. A task Heinrich had pursued with every fiber of his being, but not for the Third Reich imagined by the upstart Austrian corporal. That insipid dream would never eventuate. Instead, the temporary Third Reich would provide cover for the great and glorious work of the Phoenix Citadel.

Hitler, Goering, Goebbels, and the rest of the Nazis were an elaborate ruse to cover his own plans. They would manipulate the common people of Germany with the lie of Jewish supremacy. They would unite the Germanic race between the utopian ideal of a thousand-year rule by a master race and the genocidal destruction of a scapegoated people. There was nothing like the shared shedding of blood to bind the minds of the weaker members of society to the will of their masters. Between the anvil of a noble ideal and the hammer of a massive blood sacrifice, the latent economic and military might of the Germanic peoples would become a fearsome weapon to scour Europe and make the lands around the Phoenix citadel safe for Siegfried and Heinrich's true work.

And the success of Siegfried and Heinrich's great and glorious work was all important.

The bland Nazi ideal of a thousand-year Reich paled into insignificance compared with the eternal rule of a living god – and that was what Siegfried had promised in the secret library in Munich during the winter of 1919. The ancient deity Set would manifest in his true physical form. Siegfried and Heinrich would stand as immortal demi-gods at his side. Those who Set spared from his righteous wrath would worship Siegfried and Heinrich as gods.

The American laughed mightily, breaking through Heinrich's reverie. Heinrich blinked, momentarily nonplussed. The banker, thoroughly amused by his own joke's punchline, slapped the dark-polished wood of the boardroom table. His gaze flicked back and forth between the two Germans and he said, "You guys have no sense of humor." He shook his head once, and his lips twitched as he shrugged his broad shoulders. "But what does it matter?" The big banker spread his hands wide, indicating the subterranean fortress beyond the pale concrete walls of the boardroom. "When so much has already been achieved."

The American, a key member of Wall street's banking elite had no idea of Heinrich's real plans for the Phoenix citadel. He saw the super-soldier serum as an enabler to rulership of the world by an Anglo-American financial elite. The Nazis were useful stooges to wage a second world war for the benefit of the captains of Anglo-American finance. The American bankers could invest in every side with guaranteed profits regardless of who won or lost the coming war.

Heinrich despised him. But he still needed the banker's money. He frowned. The lies infesting the American's mind needed polishing. He declared emphatically, "Much more still needs to be done. The flow of dollars must increase if we are to achieve our noble goal of a thousand-year Reich."

The banker flicked his hand dismissively. "My New York and London colleagues are solidly behind the European initiative. God, more than half of them are true believers in what the Nazis' stand for. They would all welcome a cleansing of the world. The science of eugenics is more than a passing fashion in the United States. We are already instituting programs to sterilize the criminal and the insane. We are planning to establish broad-based use of birth control amongst the poor and colored races to limit their incessant breeding."

Siegfried tilted his head slightly but refrained from speaking for a long moment.

The banker frowned, apparently detecting a rebuke in Siegfried's silence. He addressed the occult scientist directly. "You have something to say, Mr. Frankenstein?"

Siegfried raised a prematurely gray-shot eyebrow and said in slightly derisive tones, "I propose that you and your ... colleagues ... lack ambition."

"Ambition? Surely, you're joking. I've witnessed the results of your serum this morning. Remarkable. A real game changer. An alliance between your science and Wall street's wealth will make history and transform the world."

Siegfried smiled with a momentary air of abstraction, then declared with absolute conviction, "Super-soldiers can be had in time. That is the work of lesser minds and is beneath my attention. The serum is an elegant solution and is a dramatic improvement over stitching together the dead and relying on galvanism. Far beyond such minor puzzles, I will in a few short years deliver an advance beyond yours or anyone else's imagination. Not only this world, nor this galaxy, but all the universes shall tremble before the might of the engine I shall call forth in this citadel."

The American banker blanched momentarily at the mention of 'stitching together the dead,' then leaned back and laughed dismissively. "Universes? I thought there was only one!"

"Oh, no," Siegfried declared. "There are many."

The banker paused and frowned, as if his mind was struggling to accommodate the notion that Siegfried was entirely serious.

Heinrich's jaw clenched and he glanced at Siegfried. His co-conspirator risked disabusing the American of his vast ignorance of how the world really worked. That would never do. He stood up and offered with a wave of his right hand and an air of thin congeniality. "Siegfried, Mr. Bush." He circled the boardroom table to a side table laden with cakes, pastries, steaming coffee and fresh cream, and suggested with a prim smile. "Perhaps it's time for a break. Please try our finest examples of a German baker's skills."

The banker's lips curled with anticipation. He rose from the boardroom table and selected a chocolate eclair stuffed with whipped cream. Moments later his mouth was full of it, his big teeth mashing up and down like a machine, his eyes gleaming with avaricious delight.

Heinrich regarded the American banker impassively. The fool had no idea who he was really dealing with. Once Set strode the world, men like Mr. Preston Bush would vanish like snowflakes before a volcanic furnace. The vision of Mr. Bush's flesh sloughing from his bones and blowing away in a gray gale filled his imagination with a silent yet vast anticipation.

A slight smile curled Heinrich's thin lips. There was still much to do, and he would see it done. The living god would become manifest in the world of men and all would cower before his might.

Nothing could stop the birth of Set.

* * *

To
Mr. W. Averell Harriman,
Brown Brothers Harriman & Co,
Manhattan, New York City,
2nd April 1934,

Dear Averell,

I hope this letter finds you well.

There is much to report. Events have progressed faster than anyone could have imagined. The Germans under Hitler have found a new vigor and work tirelessly (if unknowingly ... Ha!) for our esteemed cause. Our investment in the Phoenix project continues to bear fruit. However, we will require additional capital to ensure completion of the work in time to meet our necessary schedule. Please note the proposed itemized list of costs and milestones I have provided in the document attached to this letter. Note the indicative cost is above what we initially planned for. That said, I'm sure Boris Hartman and our Wall Street colleagues will want to sign off on the additional capital transfers for our essential European initiatives. We must set this continent aflame if we are to achieve our goals of a unified global order under our righteous and wise control.

I have finally met SvF, and he is indeed a genius of the first rank, but like many of his sort is more than a little unstable. Once the super-soldier serum has been perfected, I would recommend removing him from the project entirely. He prattles on about alternate dimensions, portals through time and space, and some such nonsense of a super force beyond the known universe. If it wasn't for the remarkable physical feats I've witnessed from surviving members (of which there are but few) from his early trials of the serum, I would classify him as a madman fit only for castration and commitment to an insane asylum.

The good news is that we have completed the citadel, with all security, scientific and engineering capabilities now operational. The next stage of the project to perfect the super-soldier serum is ready to begin.

Heinrich H has proved himself a veritable demon for organization. He continues to play a leading role in our cause from the German side. It's such a shame he is ill-equipped in the 'commanding presence,' department. I suppose we must persist with the Austrian corporal for the time being, as we have no other viable replacement for the political face of our cause in Europe.

Of note, Fritz Thyssen failed to show his face at the meeting yesterday, and I wonder if he is as committed to our cause as we should like. We have been operating the Union Banking Corporation to facilitate this operation for nearly a decade. Does the soft-cocked kraut not realize what we require of him? Sometimes I wonder if all our German allies have sufficient nerve to see this project through. They seem to me to be the weakest link in our cause. Perhaps we would find more loyal allies within the Chinese, Japanese, or even the Russian elements of our world-wide organization.

Still, there will be opportunities to adjust our allies as needs require. That is all for now, I am staying at the usual hotel in Freiburg, you know the one with the wonderfully young and compliant hostesses, and you can find me there for the next two weeks.

Kind regards to your dear family,

Yours sincerely,

Preston Bush

– Letter sent by secured private courier from Freiburg im Breisgau to New York City, United States, 02nd April 1934. Shadowstone archives, New York City.

* * * * *

"I have chanced upon a marvelous fellow in our library in Munich. He has all the hallmarks of a seer. He may well be able to assist our cause. Perhaps he will be able to reveal a living key. If so, his worth is beyond estimation."
– Diary entry on the 18th January 1919, Siegfried von Frankenstein.

* * *

Freiburg im Breisgau, Nazi occupied southern Germany, April 1st 1945, 18:38

The air reeked with the stench of death.

Chloe Armitage, chief enforcer of the laws of the Vampire Dominion waited patiently in the near-absolute darkness of a cold basement. A chamber that something had recently died in. *Rotten cat*, she identified silently. Two at least, given the slowly wafting scent variations fouling the air. The maggot-ridden corpses lay hidden beneath or behind two of the many half-wrecked cabinets and split barrels littering the underground chamber. She wrinkled her nose with disgust. Sometimes, the senses of a supernatural hunter were more curse than blessing – she'd have to work on her filtering techniques. Crane insisted, that with enough practice a vampire could filter out the most disgusting smells. Well, time would tell if she could master the methods.

Chloe sighed and adjusted the fit of the black scarf binding her long dark hair. Her patience was wearing thin. She'd been waiting in the dark since before dawn. A lone shaft of sunlight speared through a shrapnel hole the size of Chloe's head in the western ceiling of the basement, cutting the cellar gloom into two halves. The shaft of deadly illumination beckoned to her heart with a promise of divine annihilation. A couple of seconds exposure on her bare skin would set off a chain reaction immolating her entire body in less than a minute. Further complicating matters, the late-afternoon sunlight was cutting across the sole stairwell out of the cellar.

The sun had another twenty minutes before it would dip below the horizon, then Chloe would be free to move beneath the night sky. A freedom denied her, as much by the trenchant shaft of deadly illumination as by her king's commands. Cornelius Crane, the king of the Vampire Dominion, and the sole person Chloe had to answer to in a world riven with violence and madness, had given her a mission.

"Fetch me the Red Empire child alive," Crane had demanded. "She will be fleeing to the west with her father. That is the only objective. I will arrive later tonight to pick her up."

His words had rung faintly against a background hiss over the radio. A three-man Shadowstone squad had provided the hookup before dawn from a mobile radio system hiding in plain sight in the back of an XVIII SS Army Corps' truck in the bombed-out center of Freiburg. Chloe had no doubt the three Shadowstone operatives would be wearing different uniforms within a month. The French First Army under General Jean de Lattre de Tassigny operating under the broad umbrella of the 6th United States Army Group would overrun southern Germany within two weeks, three at the most.

The Nazi experiment in Europe was 'kaput!' Crane would administer sanctions and she would deliver punishments. Dieter Franz as the Vampire Dominion general with governance of Western Europe would suffer the consequences for this disorder. Crane was adamant another worldwide conflagration would never happen again, especially with the imminent advent of nuclear weapons from the Manhattan project.

Humanity was proving to be far too dangerous to allow freedom of action – the first half of the twentieth century had proven as much.

Chloe tilted her head left and right, stretching her neck muscles with a faint click of sliding cartilage. She reminded herself of the virtue of patience and reflected upon Crane's commands. He'd been explicit about the parameters of this mission. He'd nominated this specific address, an upper-middle class residence half bombed out of existence in late November 1944 by RAF Bomber Command, and yet it had become an Order of Thoth safe house for a fleeing Red Empire renegade with a gifted daughter.

But gifted with what? Crane had not specified why he wanted the girl alive, only that he did. Nor had he explained how he knew this particular house would be where the Ivanovs, (yes, it had to be Sasha and Angelina Ivanov of past surveillance) would come too. His ability to anticipate, if not see in full the near future, was unexplained. His precognitive powers remained inexplicable. Crane always claimed his ability was based on the mastery of fifteen languages and nearly a thousand years of study of the human condition, but still, this level of accuracy was beyond the pale. One day, she vowed to herself, she would understand the full basis of Crane's power and she would subvert it. But that day was yet to come; in the current moment she was Crane's servant – a role she would execute with efficient and effective action for anything else was beneath her.

She was nothing else if not superbly competent at her role.

A distant noise broke her reverie. One set of footsteps padding along the sidewalk toward the front of the house on the east side, and a pair of heartbeats: one an uninitiated child and the second marked by the slow efficient drumbeat of a seasoned Ramp master.

Her target had arrived.

* * *

Her father's arms held her close to his chest.

Angelina clasped her arms around her father's neck, watching the streets slip past behind them. He'd trained her well; she knew what to look for and was her father's eyes on anyone following them. As far as her child's eyes could see, there was no one chasing them, but they both knew better. The Iron Wolves under Volkov, her father's former friends from the Red Empire, pursued them, and they would never give up the chase. Their only hope lay with finding an Order of Thoth force team led by a man named Dubois. An Order helper had provided an address three days ago for a temporary safe house in southern Germany.

Her father had carried her nearly non-stop since then, covering mile after mile, breaching the front lines of the Red Army and the Nazi units on the collapsing eastern front. Mostly they'd been able to skirt past Russian or German combat units, and various stragglers, deserters and lines of prisoners. But this morning, a group of black uniformed soldiers with death's head insignia at their throats and wild urgent eyes stopped them.

Her father had set her gently aside on the edge of the road and whispered to her to look away. He'd drawn his hidden blades and cut the Nazis apart within the space of a handful of heartbeats. He'd already picked her up and blurred away as the last fanatic was hitting the blood-splattered ground. Angelina hadn't obeyed her father. She hadn't looked away. She wanted to understand what was happening. It was not the first time she had seen blood and death in her six years of life.

As the sun rode through the sky, her father ran and ran, until the great orb rested swollen and red on the western horizon. They'd reached a city late in the afternoon and jogged along street after street, searching for sanctuary. Her father dropped his pace to a walk, turned to face the west, and stood still. He eased her from his iron-hard arms onto the cracked pavement of the sidewalk.

She glanced up at her father. He wiped his right hand down his face, flicking wet perspiration onto the pavement. He pressed his lips into a thin line of disappointment, and surveyed the bombed safe house in front of them. His eyes remained lit from deep within, fit to defeat the approaching shadows looming over them. Fresh energy overtook weariness. He gripped her hand firmly, and muttered in a low voice, "Needs must."

"Are they here?" Angelina asked. They were supposed to meet the Order, but the house seemed deserted. Her father's senses far exceeded her own. He was a full initiate of the second rank of the Red Empire, and before their flight to the West, a candidate for the third rank and therefore a potential Red Ghost.

Her father surveyed the building and Angelina tracked his gaze. It was a double-story home, with bomb craters and rubble to the left and right. Even from the sidewalk shadowed by the front of the building, it was obvious aerial bombardment had destroyed the back third of the house. He remarked grimly, "Dubois and his team are not yet here. We must shelter for the night. Perhaps they are only a few hours away."

"What of the Iron Wolves, Father?"

He turned back toward the north with a long searching look and shook his head slowly. "I don't think we've lost them yet, Ange."

She put her arms around his waist and declared, "If we have to fight them, you will win."

He knelt in front of her and hugged her close for a moment and then held her back so he could look into her face. His jaw was set with an iron determination, but his eyes held a barely hidden question. "The Iron Wolves are an elite fist team. It will be six against one. Those are not good odds, even for me."

Angelina's heart thudded in her chest. Her father would win. He could beat anybody. With wide eyes, she said, "But they are only fighting to follow orders. You are fighting for us."

Her father smiled at her and tousled her long dark hair. "Yes, little one. We are strong with purpose." He stood up and pushed open a gate on a short fence in front of the house and stepped through it. He beckoned with his left-hand for Angelina to follow. His smile vanished, and he drew one of his deadly curved short swords from within his dark-gray trench coat.

Angelina followed in the shadow of her father. If any evil men waited for them in the half-wrecked house, her father would kill them. He'd earned the name of 'The Ice Dragon,' against two of the great Olgoi Khorkhoi in the tunnel mazes of Matahat al Diydan and was one of the deadliest fighters in the whole of the Red Empire. She always felt safe when her father was nearby.

Her father would always protect her.

* * *

Chloe stared at the shaft of fading sunlight spearing through the cellar.

The sunlight illuminated a spider feeding on a fly. The spider had strung her web between the left-hand side of the stairs and the nearest wall. The little female had just finished her feast, waving her forelegs up and down before daintily gliding across the strands to the center of her web within the shadows.

Chloe sharpened her vision, revealing the full details of the spider's face. For a moment it seemed the glossy arachnid was staring back at her, then she turned and settled, each foot holding a web, waiting for the tremulous touch of her next meal.

She sighed gently, sometimes beauty rested in the most unlikely locations.

Minute particles of dust fell from the ceiling. Ivanov was searching the house. He'd cleared the remains of the upper floor and was now securing the ground floor. His daughter following dutifully behind him. Another minute, two at most, and he'd be investigating the basement.

She'd drawn her blade as soon as the Ivanovs had entered the house. The majestic length of the Red Dragon caught the thin glow of reflected sunlight with every movement, gleaming like a holy relic in the gloom. She stilled the blade, then leaped upward in a smooth movement, flattening herself between the rafters covering the ceiling. With both feet and her left hand pushing outwards to hold her position, she disappeared with her weapon amongst the shadows.

Chloe could surprise Ivanov from the relative safety of the basement darkness. She only had to wait for him to move into position at the bottom of the stairwell and she could strike. His death would be quick, clean and efficient. Then she could capture the child and take her to the pickup point in the Black Forest. Crane was due later this night. He was flying in from London with his own forces, and would land at the designated clearing near the peak of the famous Feldberg mountain.

The mission objective was bare moments from her grasp.

Ivanov stopped dead in his tracks, in line with her position but near the opposite wall on the north side of the house.

Slow heartbeats and rushing footsteps approached the house. Chloe swore briefly beneath her breath. Another six Ramp masters swarmed the half-bombed building. Crane had mentioned the Ivanovs were fleeing the Red Empire. Clearly, their pursuers had caught up with them. She arched a frustrated eyebrow, the battlespace within the house was a mishmash of shadow and shafts of sunlight piercing the western and southern walls, and parts of the ceiling. She'd formed a concise mental map of the house on arrival before descending into the sanctuary of the cellar. Fighting against seven Ramp masters in a sun poisoned environment was a less than inviting prospect. The Ramp masters would forget their internal squabble the moment a vampire was present. Especially, once they understood it was her. Her reputation had grown over the last ninety years and there was nothing like a shared and famous opponent to unite her opposition.

The front and rearmost doors burst inwards under the thrust of powerful kicks. Warm bodies burst into the main surviving room of the house.

The child hid behind her protector and cried out, "Father?"

Cold steel slithered from a dozen scabbards. Ivanov shuffled slightly, adjusting his combat stance. He declared in hard low tones, "Back off, Volkov. You'll not have her."

A deep voice spoke in Russian, calm, reassuring, soliciting, "Sasha, Sasha, Sasha … why did you run? Your daughter was safe within the love of the Red Empire."

Six pairs of footsteps maneuvered through the house, closing in on the Ivanovs.

"What the Red Ghost proposed wasn't love," Ivanov snapped back.

Booted feet stalked forward, and the child's shoes left the floor. She gasped once and fell silent. The advance of the Red Empire fighters halted as one.

"Back off," Ivanov demanded, "or I'll cut her throat."

Chloe pictured the scene instantly. Ivanov clutching his daughter to his chest. One blade sheathed, the other at his daughter's throat. A faint trace of fresh blood caught her attention. He'd nicked her just to prove he wasn't bluffing. Volkov and the other five fighters stood frozen, ranging between a dozen and twenty feet away from Ivanov. They obviously wanted the girl alive too.

"Come now, Sasha. Don't do something you'll regret," Volkov said, a barely detectable tremor creeping into his voice. "Don't imagine for a second the Red Ghost, or anyone on the supreme council would allow someone as special as your daughter to come to harm."

Chloe arched a quizzical eyebrow beneath the floor – just who was Angelina Ivanov?

"I think we have different views on what constitutes harm, Volkov. The Red Ghost wants an automaton who obeys his every command. My daughter deserves her own destiny."

"Her destiny will be fulfilled serving the Red Empire," Volkov declared, his voice filled with inevitability. He took a step closer to Ivanov. The rest of his men followed his lead closing upon Ivanov's position. Their clothing rustling slightly as they adjusted their combat stances. Their blades held with lethal stillness given the absence of sound near their hands.

Chloe took a deep breath and let it out slowly, both Crane and the Red Empire sought to possess the child. As for her father, would he really kill her, or was this a bluff to get Volkov and his gang to retreat. Even with her supreme Ramp, if Ivanov had the will to do so, there was no way Chloe could stop him from cutting his daughter's throat. She frowned; her mission was suddenly on the cusp of failure.

A low rumble of approaching engines sent a warning from the street. A pair of trucks and a third vehicle with a confusing noise signature, perhaps a sedan or something like it with six wheels, pulled to a stop outside the front of the house. "What now?" Chloe asked in a confounded whisper.

One of the Red Empire fighters broke the silence in the room, declaring with a harsh voice, "Someone is here!"

"Who?" Volkov snapped.

"Nazis!" another fighter replied.

"They're a rabble," Volkov said derisively.

But no … they weren't a rabble at all. Chloe counted twenty-one slow heartbeats in the surrounding streets. The Nazis – if that was who they truly were – were all Ramp masters.

Her mission had just got complicated.

* * *

The blessed child was within the half-bombed house.

Or cursed child? Heinrich reflected for a brief moment. At this range, the presence of the child stood out like a bright golden flame against a world of dull grays and blacks. Her presence had been growing stronger for days. Her father was with her. That was clear enough, he'd brought her unwittingly into the heart of Heinrich's territory. Another six fighters infested the ruined house. It was a complication, not a disaster; the element of surprise remained with Heinrich and his men. These Red Empire scum would be expecting ordinary soldiers and not the Übermensch of the Phoenix citadel.

His men swarmed from their trucks. They mostly carried 9mm submachine guns, hand grenades, and straight-bladed two-foot-long swords modeled on a Roman gladius belted at their waists. Heinrich rose to stand in the back of his gray open-tourer limousine. He shouted, "Attack. Kill them all except the girl. No grenades! If you harm the girl, I'll skin you alive myself."

The platoon of super-soldiers blurred away. Heinrich stepped from his custom-built Mercedes-Benz and followed his troops, flanked by a pair of bodyguards armed with 7.62mm light machine guns. With more than three to one odds in their favor, he was confident of quick success.

Soon the gifted child would be his.

* * *

Angelina's father swung her down to the floor behind him.

She rushed over the wooden floorboards to the nearest corner of the room, turned and huddled against the wall. Her father stood tall, facing their enemies, a bright blade held in each hand. Her heart thudded in her chest. It was one thing to believe in her father, it was another to see him face down six elite fighters of the Red Empire.

One of the men raised his submachine gun. Volkov snapped at him, "No guns!" before piercing Angelina with a hard stare.

Angelina gulped air. She tried to calm herself. To reach a point of stillness to summon the Metaframe. She could use a petite summoning to temporarily blind the Iron Wolves and allow their escape. Her heartbeat thudded in her ears. Her eyes glistened with tears. The room blurred into a mist around her. She couldn't find a place to center herself.

Pounding boots resounded on the steps in front of the house. Grim-faced men in black uniforms blurred into the room and engaged the Iron Wolves in bloody combat. But they were not here to save her father and herself, they were another threat. Angelina's heart thudded with panic, crushing all possibility of summoning the Metaframe.

She cried out through a strangled throat, "Father!"

* * *

Battle erupted above Chloe's head.

Footsteps stamped across the floor. Submachine gun fire hammered overhead, answered by the stuttering bark of automatic pistols. Running boots set dust and flakes of wood puffing away from the ceiling of the basement.

"Enough is enough," Chloe whispered. Her target could die within this chaotic melee. She'd have to risk sunlight to fulfill her mission objective to capture the child. She couldn't allow the mission to fail through inaction. She stilled herself, centering her awareness. She'd be alone against every man in the house. There was one target and there had been twenty-eight hostiles to start with. A number already reduced by four within the first three seconds of combat as the Red Empire and the Nazis tore into each other.

If it wasn't her mission, she'd laugh at her enemies slaughtering each other. Instead, Chloe dropped to the floor of the basement, and ramped hard, bringing her intrinsic vampire speed and strength to a sharper pitch. She leaped over the shaft of sunlight and blurred to the top of the stairs. She kept her supreme Ramp on the edge of activation, waiting for the right moment to unleash its flood of power. She burst through the basement door in a tan cloud of wooden fragments and dashed into the maelstrom of combat within the main room.

Like flicking a switch, she dove deep into her supreme Ramp, accelerating markedly, everyone else slowing relative to her. The main room of the house was an open-plan mix of dining room opposite a library and music room. On her immediate right, a set of stairs rose to the upper floor. To her left was a low coffee table and beyond it a white grand piano covered in a thin patina of dust. Directly opposite her, to the right of a long dining table littered with rancid scraps was Ivanov, his curved blades gleaming like wet rubies in a shaft of evening sunlight, the bodies of a Red Empire fighter and a pair of black-uniformed Nazis lying in spreading pools of gore at his feet. Behind his left shoulder, his wide-eyed daughter scrunched herself into the north-east corner of the room.

Chloe registered twenty-three shafts of sunlight spearing through the room with a single glance. To her left and right, knots of men fought in deadly, trenchant combat. Outnumbered more than three to one by the Nazis, the Iron Wolves lived up to their fearsome reputation. The floor, walls and ceilings became macabre artworks painted in blood, sinew and bone as bullets, blades and bare hands crashed and tore through living flesh.

Chloe whirled, the magnificent blade of the Red Dragon traveling through a full horizontal circle faster than any eye could follow. One Red Empire fighter and three of the black-uniformed Nazis took her blade without defense. Their faces struggled to register shock as the top halves of their bodies slid off their hips.

She was past them before they crumpled to the floor. Ivanov and the girl were her targets, and Volkov was in the way. Some sixth-sense of combat intuition alerted Volkov of her presence, or perhaps it was the look of horrified recognition sweeping like a dark cloud over Ivanov's face. Volkov turned just in time to witness his doom.

Chloe's katana beat past Volkov's rising blades and sliced through his sternum, erupting out his back, painting a bloody whip across Ivanov's chest. A moment later she'd dragged her blade out through the far side of Volkov's body and thrust him away from her. Three Nazi soldiers moved around her, long knives stabbing down in deadly arcs. She blurred amongst them, her blade almost invisible as it moved, blood and entrails splashed left and right, and the three men fell aside, never to rise again.

She arose from their midst, streams of 9mm rounds slashing through the air around her. She dodged the bullets as needed, and ignored them when appropriate. Ivanov met her gaze. His blades in high and low defense. His body heat flaring in maximum ramp. His daughter stared at Chloe from behind her father with teary eyes. Ivanov would do all he could to defend his daughter's life.

Chloe was certain it would not be enough.

To Chloe's right, a harsh voice from the front doorway cut through the racket in the room, shouting, "Kill Her!"

Flames spat, a pair of light machine guns erupting into life, she veered to the left, leaning hard, her left hand reaching down to the floor. The 7.62mm rounds lanced through the air over her head. She glanced right for a fraction of a second, long enough to register a German officer flanked by a pair of guards armed with MG 42s with round drum magazines just inside the front door of the house. Her heart sank; she flicked her gaze left – toward the west and the setting sun. The heavy caliber 7.62mm rounds struck the remaining inner walls on the west side of the house and punched through them. Each one leaving a hole in the wall through which deadly sunlight streamed into the room.

One ray struck Chloe's left cheek in a searing agonizing blow, flicking her head to the right in instant reflex. She whirled; blurring at maximum supreme Ramp – reaching desperately for the sanctuary of the basement darkness. Her dark cloak flapped like a demented wing behind her. The bright machine gun fire followed her. Slashing through the room; indiscriminately hitting friend and foe alike, but too slow to catch her. She dove back into the darkness, her left hand clasping her face, her eyes wide, her mouth open in an 'O' of horrified shock.

Above her, commands resounded, "Quickly! Quickly! The girl! Take the girl!"

The fighting continued, but without Volkov, the rest of the Red Empire succumbed to superior numbers. Ivanov fell with a strangled grunt. The child screamed once in heartfelt torment. Stamping boots resounded. The child's heaving sobs diminished as she vanished within the arms of her captors.

Grenades bounced down the stairs into the basement, but Chloe had already retreated deep into the darkness. She held her raw left cheek, gasping through the singular agony of sun exposure. The grenades exploded harmlessly, too far away to harm her.

Above her, the officer shouted, "Forget her! She cannot stop us now. ... Back to the citadel."

Moments later, the house was as still as a tomb, populated only by the dead. Chloe waited in the darkness below, nursing her healing face. She listened carefully, determining the direction in which the Nazis had gone. They were heading east toward the Black Forest, toward the Feldberg. A shiver played along her spine. They were heading directly toward Crane's pickup point. Chloe didn't believe in coincidences, not where Crane was involved. What did he know that she didn't? Too much it seemed.

Chloe glanced at the fading sunlight barely penetrating the hole in the basement ceiling. Nightfall was only minutes away, and soon her third-degree sunburn would heal. She would track these Nazi Ramp masters and make them pay for interfering with her mission. A cold fire burned within her soul. She would wrest the child from their grasp or die trying.

She grinned without mercy in the darkness – she wouldn't be the one doing the dying.

Forget me, will they? I think not.

* * *

Angelina landed on the polished black leather of the rear bench seat of a gray open-topped tourer car.

The German officer pressed her back against the rear seat with his left hand. Her breath hitched, and she sobbed again. Her father was dead. He'd done everything he could to protect her. The evil men had to crawl over the broken bodies of the dead and dying to get to her. One of the surviving soldiers had picked her up, his face grim, but his eyes shone with zealous fanaticism. He was too fast and strong for her to resist. He'd carried her against his black-uniformed chest in a parody of her father. She'd looked over his broad shoulder as they'd left the room. She'd seen her father for the last time. His face pale, his blue eyes staring at the ceiling, lying on his back on the blood-soaked floor, a dozen wounds across his body and nearly as many men lying still around him.

A random line from her lessons ran through her, *'The shades of the battlefield will sing your praises in the afterlife.'* Her father would not lack the honor of a choir in death.

The German officer's hand pressed harder against her chest, stealing the breath from her lungs, and bringing her back from the memory of her father. She stared at him with wide eyes and cried, "Why? Why did you kill him?"

The officer's thin-lipped mouth sneered and he spat harshly. "Your stupid father cost me half a platoon of my best men." He paused for a moment, his eyes widened and his sneer morphed into an avid grin. "But we have you now!" His eyes gleamed with avarice. He opened a wicker basket resting on the floor of the tourer with his free hand, and pulled something forth in a small gray blanket. It squirmed in his grip and he plopped the blanket and its contents on Angelina's lap. "This is Greta," he said with a dramatic wave of his hand. "She needs your help." He looked hard into her eyes. "You have to look after Greta now. She's an orphan – just like you. You're all she's got in the world."

Angelina slowly shook her head at the squirming blanket, *What now?* She wiped her tears away with a swipe of her arm. There was a little black nose pushing its way out of the gray blanket. Angelina knew what it was before she pulled the top of the blanket aside. The shepherd pup had a face full of short black fur, and her eyes were dark as night. The pup leaned forward licking her open palm. She lifted the pup from the blanket and held her close. The dog's little heart beating fast next to her own. She whispered,

"I'll call you Nochka." She promised to herself that no harm would come to Nochka; even if she was a tool of the evil man who had killed her father and made her a prisoner, she was still an innocent soul and worthy of protection unto death.

Protect the innocent, an instinctive belief that had cast her apart from the heart of the Red Empire.

Her eyes darkened with hard memory. She'd summoned a small version of the Metaframe spontaneously while learning to meditate three months short of her sixth birthday. Her shocked instructors reported the event to the Red Ghost; that was when her troubles had started. They'd called her a sorcerer. They'd expected her to have a single power, but while calm, she could generate nearly any effect she could imagine as long as it conformed with the physically possible. The changes she wrought would last for hours or days before vanishing.

The Red Ghost had interviewed her before a council of the most senior members of the Red Empire. He'd called her a child prodigy, a savant, and a living key. He'd promised to protect her and keep her safe. Over the following months she discovered his protection meant her own absolute obedience and conformity to his wishes. He couldn't tolerate the most minor transgressions. He wanted what she could do with a desperate desire and feared her independence equally as much.

Angelina had responded with ever growing disobedience and intransigence. The Red Ghost had responded with ever harsher demands for absolute obedience. They'd discovered her instinctive desire to protect the innocent and their avarice darkened into something worse. The Red Empire's quest to bring justice to the guilty would never suffer from concerns for the innocent. They named her heretic, and witch, and despite her parent's protests, they kept her drugged to deprive her of her capacity to concentrate. In the end, they resorted to abduction, imprisonment, torture and sensory deprivation in a vain attempt to control her power. She had no memory of her sixth birthday which had passed in a drugged haze in a sensory deprivation tank.

Her father had come and broken her free of her captors, and they'd ran and ran and ran. But her mother was missing, and her father had whispered, his eyes glistening with tears that she was gone forever. He'd never spoken the exact words. A final truth he couldn't admit to his only child. Her mother was dead, her life sacrificed in the battle to free Angelina from her warders.

And now her father was dead and villains had stolen her again. She stared into empty space – she could hardly bring herself to believe what had just happened was real. A numb emptiness plumbed her soul, abject terror its swift and silent companion. She silently cursed her power. It had brought nothing but death and horror to her family. Angelina wished she'd never heard of the Metaframe.

The big gray vehicle pulled away from the curb, turning in a half-circle before accelerating away. Behind it, the trucks followed with the remnants of the black-uniformed soldiers. The officer leaned in next to her, his right hand stroking the back of her hand.

His touch sent a repellent shiver along her skin and she lunged away from him, but his other hand held her wrist fast. He grinned at her with yellowed teeth. He leaned in closer and whispered into her ear, his voice wreathed in the stench of rotting meat and stale tobacco, "Come now, Angelina. Call me, Heinrich. There we are, we're no longer strangers. Now we can be friends."

She looked at him in horror. "You killed my father!"

"It wasn't personal," the officer remarked in an off-hand tone. "I didn't hate your father. No, not at all. He was just in the way of the most important work in the history of the world."

Angelina kept her mouth shut. The less she said to him the better. He was an evil man. She wished fervently her father had killed him. A heart-wrenching sob clutched her throat. She bit it down, tears squeezed from her eyes, and she hugged Nochka tight. The puppy's fur pressed against her neck. Nochka's warm doggy smells a comfort amongst the growing darkness. The car was speeding along a tarmacked road, rising up into the nearby hills and forest on the shoulders of the mountain. The sun was dropping beneath the horizon, becoming a thin half-disc in the west.

The evil man stared at her and tightened his grip on her wrist with a silent promise that escape was impossible. Angelina took a deep breath and let it out slowly. She loved her father and he'd done his best for them both, but now it was up to her. There was no one who could save her from this strange and vile man. She looked at him briefly, he was still watching her with an avaricious and triumphant leer like he'd just found his personal pot of gold. The old men of the Red Empire had looked at her the same way once they'd discovered she was special. She turned away and looked out at the passing forest. Shadows leaped by, dark echoes of a world closing in around her. She would do what she could to give the officer nothing. She glanced back at him again. He'd called himself, 'Heinrich.' Well, she had another name for him, 'Stinker.' She noticed his glasses. They were simple glass. He didn't need them. It was a lie; he was a liar. Stinker was a murderer, a liar, and a thief of children. She turned away, revolted by his leering repulsive presence.

The night air rushed past the car, cutting like a cold blade against her skin. Angelina hunkered down within the rear seat of the tourer, holding Nochka close as much for warmth as comfort. The road wound up through the hills toward the largest mountain. Whatever happened, it didn't matter where Stinker took them. Angelina always knew where she was, always.

It was part of what made her special.

* * * * *

"A new shipment of the *Ophiocordyceps diabolicus* fungus has arrived from Brazil. It will be our last for some time as it is becoming increasingly difficult to get U-boats safely across the Atlantic and back again. It will be sufficient to create enough enhanced soldiers to guard the citadel but not more than that." – Diary entry on the 24th of September 1943, Siegfried von Frankenstein.

* * *

Freiburg im Breisgau, Nazi occupied southern Germany, April 1st 1945, 18:58

The last rays of the setting sun passed over the horizon.

Chloe burst forth from the cellar and set out on the track of her quarry. She rose to the western edge of the bomb crater behind the house and stood tall upon the rubble. She whirled around and faced east, looking past the ruined house.

A slight breeze lifted wisps of raven-black hair around her face and ruffled the edges of the dark cloak draping her shoulders. She sniffed the air, flicked her head left and right to take in her immediate surrounds, then stared into the deep distance toward the Black Forest sweeping up the massive side of the Feldberg. The Nazis had a ten-minute head start. It would not avail them. Ramp master or not, no human could long evade a hunting vampire, and Chloe was the greatest hunter of her kind.

The officer, and his men had left in vehicles and would stay on the roads for now. But where were they going? She searched her memory, the events of the last fifteen minutes unfolding like a perfect three-dimensional vision.

The officer had commanded with a shout just before he left, 'Forget her! She cannot stop us now.' Then he'd paused. He'd first called from just inside the eastern entrance of the house, he'd been facing the west, toward the setting sun. His surviving men had been moving toward him, one of them carrying the sobbing child. Then he'd shuffled, taking a step backward during a moment of hesitation. Was he split for a moment between the child and his destination? Was he torn in two directions at once?

Chloe pursed her lips thoughtfully.

Then he'd whirled decisively to the east, shouting the rest of his command as he strode out to the street, 'Back to the citadel.' His voice rang with urgency, but it wasn't just that. A man driven only by urgency, especially the urgency of fear and hate, would have used the last ten minutes of sunlight to tear the basement apart until she'd burned alive beneath the fading sun.

No, urgency to kill her was not a major player in the officer's soul, there was an eagerness, an avid anticipation of something deeply desired to come. The timbre of his voice had reverberated on the final word, 'citadel.' A word freighted with heart-felt emotion and potent with meaning. The officer anticipated the imminent fulfillment of his greatest desire at the citadel; ergo the citadel was nearby.

Close and reachable by car. However, no map she'd studied held a 'citadel,' within the vicinity of the Feldberg. "It must be hidden," Chloe whispered. She regarded the mute enormity of the Feldberg beyond the eastern edge of the city. Its peak jutted out of the forest twelve miles away. She sighed. They, whoever they were, had built the citadel within the mountain and made it only accessible by road, no other conclusion fit the officer's behavior.

To know was to act. Chloe blurred forward, sprinting through the ruined house toward the Feldberg. In twelve minutes, she would be at its summit with a commanding view of the surrounding forest. From such a location she'd be able to detect any movement around the mountain. Once in the street she glanced at the sky; it was as clear as a crystalline lake, the first of many stars revealing themselves in the early twilight. She took a breath and smiled; it was perfect weather for hunting.

There was one other belief readable in the officer's words and actions; the citadel was a sanctuary. Once within the mountain, the officer felt safe – it was another reason why he hadn't taken the time to pursue her within the basement. He believed he wouldn't need to. The officer had taken the girl into what he believed was an impregnable fortress. A fortress well-hidden and guarded by an unknown number of Ramp masters.

Chloe blurred through the outer fringe of the Black Forest. It was time to prove the officer wrong.

* * *

The heavy Mercedes-Benz tourer raced along the road.

Three minutes earlier, Heinrich's driver had directed the gray open-topped vehicle off the main road. The side road snaked through the forest, cutting left and right around lesser hills, but ever rising toward the massive Feldberg. The tourer's engine roared, its headlights spearing forward into the gathering gloom. The trucks followed after the car; their headlights flashing past Heinrich's shoulder. He didn't fear exposure to allied aircraft, radar reports from the citadel had indicated he was safe from mundane threats for now.

He shouted over the rushing air at his driver, "Faster! Faster!"

The driver leaned forward over the steering wheel. The supercharged engine thundered and the tourer accelerated. All three vehicles careened along the road in a determined effort to reach the Phoenix citadel as soon as possible. The car raced around a bend in the road and the main entrance of the citadel loomed in front of them. A rectangular maw; ten meters wide, five meters high, and lit with bright white lights from within. It always seemed to Heinrich to be a giant's mouth whose dark tongue was the road – a beast ready to swallow all who dared enter the mountain. The big Mercedes-Benz and the two trucks rushed through the entrance into a square tunnel ten meters on a side and pulled to a halt.

Heinrich looked to his left. Angelina Ivanov huddled against the door. The German shepherd pup remained wrapped in a blanket on her lap, enclosed within the arc of her arms. The dog was Siegfried's ploy. The child was six or seven years old. With her father dead, there were limited forms of leverage left. A cold regret seized his heart. Siegfried had insisted on her willing participation. Heinrich could not coerce the child with his preferred instruments of terror and violence. He frowned at the child. But if they threatened the pup ... perhaps Ivanov would do the right thing – even if she understood nothing of the great work.

Siegfried approached; his face lit with delight. A pair of blonde, curvaceous, white-coated nurses, chosen for their Aryan good looks and a capacity to manage young children, flanked him. He opened the car door, and offered the gifted child his hand. "Come now, you're perfectly safe here. The assassins of the Red Empire cannot hurt you within this fortress."

Heinrich studied Ivanov. She hugged the pup to her chest and stared at Siegfried for a moment, then looked around the dark-gray stone walls of the tunnel, taking in the squads of super-soldiers, the pair of nurses, and the fact that every pair of eyes peered at her with thinly disguised predatory anticipation. She edged off the seat and dropped to the floor, hugging the pup within its gray blanket to her chest. She looked up at Siegfried with a knowing gaze far beyond her meager years, and said, "You're more than you appear to be. There's something with you that doesn't belong. Who are you really?"

Siegfried's eyes narrowed, a frown momentarily creasing his forehead. He ignored the child's question with a quick request to his white-coated entourage. "Come Hilda and Beatrice, help the young lady. She has no doubt experienced grave troubles in recent days."

The slim, buxom, white-coated nurses moved forward to stand next to the child. They placed firm hands on her back and guided her forward along the main tunnel toward the heart of the citadel.

The child went with them for a few steps, halted and whirled. She looked hard at Heinrich, then back at Siegfried, and declared in a high voice, "I will not help you." She pointed and shouted at Heinrich, "You killed my father." Fat tears rolled down her cheeks and the nurses bustled her away. The pup whimpered in her arms, and she struggled with the animal for a moment as if fearful the pup would fall to the floor.

Anxiety gripped Heinrich's gut. What if she refused to help them? A thousand years could pass before another child gifted as she was appeared, and by then he'd be long dead. The Third Reich was already a disaster, it would be lucky to survive another month. The allies would arrive soon, and with them the filthy Order of Thoth, unless the Red Empire arrived first in the van of the Slavic hordes pushing westward. Their enemies would discover the citadel. Even if not immediately found, it would be impossible to keep the citadel operational for more than a handful of weeks.

This was his one chance to bring Set into the world and stand at his side as a living immortal demi-god. He pulled off his officer's cap and wiped his hand over his forehead and back over his receding hair. Siegfried's damned Ramp hadn't changed that little fact for him. He thrust his hat back over his thinning locks and addressed the three squad leaders within the citadel entrance. "The great work will begin immediately. Let none disturb us. Put all forces on full alert and lock down the citadel. No one enters and no one leaves until the work is done."

There was a chorus of assents and black-uniformed soldiers blurred away. A soldier flicked switches on a nearby control board. A klaxon wailed, orange wall lights strobed, and the mighty blast doors closed with a conclusive thud over the entrance behind him.

Once closed, no one could open them without waiting for a fifteen-minute interval. Heinrich gritted his teeth. His thin lips pressed together into a bloodless gash. While a part of him still thrilled to see his men leap to their appointed tasks; where triumphant anticipation had reigned, a sudden terror gripped his soul. Not fear of the risks of the great work, that was unthinkable, but a near-overwhelming fear of failure.

Heinrich took a deep breath and let it out slowly. He was not one of the lesser animals destined for slaughter in the great cleansing of the Earth. He was a true Übermensch destined for immortal divinity. He'd labored with Siegfried for more than twenty-five years to create the Phoenix citadel. It was a finely-tuned machine ready to fulfill its divine purpose. If Siegfried and himself succeeded tonight, as they must, then the distraction of the Third Reich and the second world war would have worked as planned, hiding the true purpose of the Phoenix citadel from the world until it was too late to stop.

Heinrich strode forward along the broad corridor, following several meters behind Siegfried. The pair of white-coated nurses, their smooth hips flexing beneath their tight uniforms, guided the gifted child forward immediately in front of him. He stared at Ivanov's back with merciless hunger, everything rested upon her small shoulders.

The air within the citadel was electric. His soul was on fire. There was no time to waste. A god was waiting to be born, and Heinrich would ascend tonight to his rightful place at Set's immortal side.

Heinrich would manifest his destiny. He squashed his transient concerns. They were beneath an Übermensch, the child would co-operate. There was no more room for fear or doubt. Nothing could stop Set now.

It was time to transform the world.

* * *

The outer doors of the main entrance slammed shut.

Chloe slid to a halt a dozen feet back from the edge of the road leading into the underground citadel. The great stone doors looked like a natural rock wall from the outside. She'd arrived seconds too late. Before the doors had closed, a thinning strip of bright electric light had illuminated the road. The citadel had a power source, and that meant exhaust stacks and water sources. If there was another way in, she'd find it.

She turned, and blurred up the mountain for a quarter mile. She halted, arresting her momentum against a tree with a thud. Her left-hand imprinting in the bark. Standing stock still, she listened, expanding her senses to their maximum limits. A drop of cold water splattered on her forehead. She lifted her gaze. Above her a vortex of dark clouds was forming above her position. A shiver ascended her spine and she said in quiet awe, "That's not natural. The night was clear only ten minutes ago."

She looked between her boots, as if she could force her vision through tons of rock by sheer force of will. "What are they doing down there?" *They'd better not be harming the child,* she added silently.

Chloe reserved a frigid place in her heart for those who harmed children. Adults could look after themselves, but abusing a child was an abomination. She drew a line at harming children – a line she'd never crossed. Every single human she'd harvested to meet her needs had been an adult. Whenever she found vampires who preyed on children, she routinely purged them. Perhaps it was a holdover from her origins in the Order of Thoth, but in any event, she would always determine for herself what was right and wrong. A second drop splashed on her left shoulder and she frowned up at the swirling vortex. It was a mystery she would solve if she got the chance, but first she had to retrieve the child from the Nazis within the citadel, and to do that she had to get in.

She stilled herself again, and conducted her sensory search. Six sources of soft susurration emerged from the natural background noise of the forest. She looked around, her gaze lancing toward each point of industrial whispering. Multiple air vents rose from the ground, two of which were running hot. Exhaust stacks for deeply-submerged diesel-electric generators. She ran from air vent to air vent. All stood draped in camouflage to avoid aerial spotters. Ground troops would have kept the mountain side clear of casual or professional investigation over the years. However, no troops scoured the forest's twilight realm of leaf and shadow. After the slaughter at the safe house in Freiburg, presumably the citadel didn't have any to spare. No, the rats had retreated into their hole. She vowed silently to root them all out before the next dawn arrived. The individual vents were only two feet wide, and heavily grilled – far too tight to allow her to pass through them.

Chloe frowned, access via air and power remained blocked. She took a breath and whispered, "Water."

The citadel design probably collocated the power and water complexes. The cheapest and fastest way to build an exhaust pipe was a straight line to the surface. Chloe moved to a spot midway between the two exhaust stacks. She figured she was standing over the citadel's power station. It was a safe assumption the power supply would be next to the pumping stations supplying the citadel with potable water. She stilled herself once more, tuning out the faint industrial noises emanating from the pipes while searching for the rhythm of flowing water. A handful of seconds later she had it. Down the hillside and veering to her left. She blurred away, sprinting between the trees until she came to an exposed gray-painted metal pipe. The pipe emerged from the rock, curving away into the distance, and rising up the mountainside to some unseen snow-melt fed reservoir.

Chloe sniffed, her face tightening. Time was ticking away. Every second the child remained in the clutches of the Nazis reduced her chance of mission success. She reached out, sweeping her hand across the surface of the pipe. The pipe was heavily constructed, made of industrial steel six feet across. Chloe glanced up at the eldritch sky. The vortex was growing stronger. There was no time left to find a better way in, or to track the pipe to some high and no doubt guarded entrance. The steel looked thick, like she'd need an anti-tank round to cut through it. Of course, she didn't have such a weapon upon her.

Chloe drew the Red Dragon, slashing it down into the top of the pipe. The gray steel sparked and shrieked, giving way to the superior meteoric-iron alloy of the genius-forged blade. The katana left a foot-long horizontal slash through the top of the pipe. A thin stream of water geysered into the air. Chloe blurred again and again, sparks flying, a moment later a square flap of steel two and a half feet on a side flipped into the air on a titanic rush of water. She leaped on top of the pipe upstream of the hole and sheathed her sword. She took a single deep breath, gripped the nearest edge of the opening to the left and right, and pushed through the geyser and into the pipe, quickly making her way downstream with the flow of water into the mountain.

The wet darkness swallowed her.

* * *

One of the nurses lifted Angelina under her armpits and carried her over a foot wide slit in the floor.

The white-coated woman placed her down and Angelina found her footing again. She took a step forward into a cavernous chamber and stopped still; her breath stolen by wonder. Her neck craned back, her gaze rose, above her loomed an enormous inverted stepped pyramid. Great lamps dotted the perimeter of the ceiling, far enough away to seem mere dots of light. The pyramid gleamed with a metallic luster, its inverted apex resting in mid-air approximately thirty meters above a low square platform in the middle of the chamber floor.

A momentary dizziness assaulted her and then drained away. Angelina regarded the great chamber with wide eyes. Like all children of the Red Empire her education had begun at the beginning of her fourth year. The usual subjects, war, deception, combat, poison, language, history, and mathematics, the last she'd excelled at, surpassing her instructor by her fifth birthday. The geometry of the room was off. She took another step forward and began breathing again. She frowned, sucking on her bottom lip. No, the geometry of the room was not off – just different, special. There was something beyond her understanding in the room, and it wasn't just the upside-down step pyramid made of strange metal – there was an extraordinary potential within the chamber. It gripped her stomach and she pulled to a halt. The room was pregnant with an eldritch power waiting to be born.

The white-haired one capered before her. The nurses pushed on her shoulders, gentle, but insistent. She moved forward, Nochka began squirming within her blanket, and she placed her on the floor where she trotted forward a meter in front of Angelina and the two nurses.

Whitehair whirled full circle, his arms outstretched, his face alight. He stopped suddenly, leaned forward, his hands on his knees, bringing his frizzy-white-haloed head down to her level. He stared hard at Angelina with eyes shining with enthusiasm. "You have a most important part to play, young lady." His eyes grew wide with excitement. "Tonight, will be a moment of glorious transformation for this world."

Angelina thought of a bad word, then stopped herself from saying it. *Give them nothing. Do not help them,* she thought. Whatever evil they contemplated; she wanted no part of it.

Whitehair rushed forward and scooped up Nochka. He rose, stroking the squirming puppy, and grinned at Angelina. Nochka looked at Angelina with wide, dark eyes and struggled helplessly within Whitehair's grip. "Oh, she's so sweet. Such a lovely pup. What a darling thing she is."

Angelina stepped forward and hoped Nochka would bite his mocking mouth. If the pup was older, she'd be able to rip his throat out. Her father would have beheaded Whitehair without hesitation. The Red Empire sang through her veins – there'd be no mercy for the guilty. She glanced over her shoulder. Stinker had followed her, a bare dozen feet behind her. She assessed her surrounds with a glance as the Red Empire had taught her. Another thirty soldiers, armed like Stinker's soldiers, stood at guard rest within the chamber. Arrays of metallic-gray equipment lined the walls, including banks of electrical cabinets with black cables snaking over the floor. The chamber was a mix of inexplicable technology beyond anything she'd ever seen, allied with whatever nightmare science Whitehair had cobbled together.

Whitehair took a step toward her, Nochka held before him like a talisman of control. He grasped her rear legs and began to pull. The pup whined and struggled in Whitehair's merciless grip.

"No," Angelina shouted, rushing forward to stand before Nochka's captor.

Whitehair relaxed his hand, a sly smile curling his lips. "Of course, no real harm done." He held the pup by the scruff of her neck and gestured with his left hand at a spartan steel chair in front of a bank of gray electrical cabinets covered in flashing lights. "Come now, every princess must have her throne."

"Give her to me," Angelina demanded without moving an inch away from him.

"Of course, once you take your appointed place," Whitehair declared, with a flick of his head toward the chair.

Angelina walked to her right and sat in the indicated chair.

Whitehair strode forward, thrust Nochka into her lap, and demanded, "Make sure she doesn't disturb you." He grinned, and stared deeply into her eyes. "Keep her safe."

Angelina stared back for a moment in silence, Nochka licking her left wrist in gratitude. Her heart thudded with a deeply felt desire to do this man harm. The Red Empire had taught her well. For all its faults, the Red Empire understood punishment better than anyone.

Whitehair crouched down in front of her. Stinker had advanced and stood a few yards back. The nurses had disappeared behind her. Whitehair looked deeply into her eyes. His gaze was magnetic, but her training kicked in. She knew the techniques of neurolinguistic programming and how to thwart them. All should be wary of trifling with a child of the Red Empire, and with Angelina Ivanov – even less so. But, still, she would not see an innocent harmed. She would play along for now to ensure the safety of Nochka, and see where these evil men would seek to go. Wherever they went she could always find her way back. She frowned, how much blood, terror and anguish waited along their pathway?

Whitehair arched an eyebrow and half-snorted dismissively. He rose and stepped back, glanced at Stinker and remarked with a triumphant air, "We are ready to begin."

Stinker nodded, his eyes glistening, his mouth twisted in a gleeful smirk.

Whitehair smiled triumphantly and took up a position in front of a control console. He flicked several switches and moved a number of levers. A pervasive hum resounded throughout the chamber.

Angelina cuddled Nochka and waited for whatever would happen next.

* * *

The water pipe was as dark as dark could be.

In completely lightless conditions, Chloe's vision reduced to shades of gray. The water carried her forward. She'd dedicated a fraction of her mind to counting seconds, and had passed three hundred. She'd hit a steel grate and it had taken her forty-eight seconds to cut it partially free with the Red Dragon, and bend it aside with her vampire strength. She had to be wary in the dark. It was possible for a vampire to drown – it just took longer than a human. She was looking for a branch in the pipe, and it must be coming soon, or else she'd swim past the citadel toward wherever the pipe ended.

Chloe figured she'd know it if she passed the citadel. The citadel had to handle waste somehow, and throwing it into the downstream water supply would have been a simple convenience for the designers. She could taste the water and it was still fresh, if it soured, she'd know she'd missed an access point into the citadel. She frowned in the shades-of-gray gloom. Obviously, the mission was paramount, but the last thing she wanted to do was taste Nazi shit.

An opening revealed itself to her touch. The pipe branched at right angles to the right, reaching deeper into the mountain. Chloe pushed off the left-hand wall of the pipe and took the right-hand tube. This was the pathway into the citadel itself. The water in the new branch was still. There was something stopping it from flowing. Chloe swam forward through the six-feet wide pipe with a moment of trepidation. Whatever was stopping the water, could it stop her?

She proceeded another fifty yards in less than a minute. Something dark and solid emerged in front of her. It was a great metallic valve; a cone of metal pointing directly at her shaped with a dozen slim leaflets. Somewhere outside the pipe was a mechanism that controlled the valve. A system would open the valve periodically to refresh the water supply of the citadel, but at this critical time – it remained closed.

Damn it, Chloe thought furiously. She moved forward and examined the valve as best she could in the absolute darkness of the pipe. It was a cone, three feet wide at its base and three feet long. But she needed to spread it, so she could fit through it. The leaflets had been well-machined to fit neatly together and hold back the mass of a huge column of water above this point.

But could the leaflets deal with a vampire-driven blade made of genius forged meteoric-iron. Chloe drew the Red Dragon and wedged it into the point of the valve. She levered the blade, spreading the leaflets of the valve. The opening was bare inches wide and water rushed through it to a chamber beyond the pipe – there was at least some empty space beyond the valve.

Chloe withdrew her sword and quickly sheathed it. With both hands she penetrated the gap she'd made in the tip of the valve. She gripped the metal hard enough to tear her fingers to the bone, her blood shedding into the water. She delved deep into her silence, summoning the extremity of her supreme Ramp. Golden light coruscated along her nerves and muscle fibers. Harder than steel and with a strength beyond imagining, Chloe pushed the valve open against the weight of the water and flushed through it into the holding tank beyond the valve.

The valve snapped shut behind her. It was a damaged machine, a six-inch gap revealed between twisted metal, water continuing to flow through the newly opened channel into the holding tank.

For a few seconds she floated, resting after the extremity of effort, like a fetus within a cold dark womb. She stirred, and rose to the top of the holding tank. She breached the surface of the water two feet beneath the ceiling of the tank and drew a shuddering breath. Multiple supreme Ramps had taxed her reserves. Breaking the final valve had taken her utmost strength.

Chloe opened her eyes wide and sought the means of her release. Above her was an access port with a spin lock. Of course, from time to time the tank would need routine maintenance to ensure the high quality of water supplied to the facility. An access point was a necessity, a necessity she'd just bet her life on.

She grasped the spin lock, flipped her booted feet to the ceiling of the tank to anchor herself and twisted with all her vampire strength. Locks snapped and pinged somewhere above her. She winced at the unavoidable noise, then spun the lock. She dropped back into the pool and pushed the hatch open with a careful hand. There was no need to announce her presence, stealth first, and then ferocity. It was her way.

Chloe emerged to the roof of a wide circular tank. The tank rested in a large chamber carved from the raw stone of the mountain. In the near distance a bank of diesel engines thrummed. Chloe crab walked forward, keeping a low profile as her saturated clothes dripped onto the steel top of the tank. She reached the edge of the tank and peered into the large chamber beyond.

The room was at least one hundred and fifty yards long and fifty high. Holding tanks filled the nearest third, great pipes rose from their bases and disappearing up into the ceiling, or stretched along the walls to the north. Sitting next to each pipe was a heavy-duty pump rumbling with a low thrum. Beyond the tanks and pumps, six rows of diesel-electric generators hummed with a muted roar. Chloe took a breath; she recognized the generator design from a previous mission. The largest, most-advanced U-Boat submarines used the same equipment. Not many U-Boats remained this late in the war. The last examples of the type sat docked within hidden enclosures in the northern German city of Greifswald.

Around the machines were nine men, none of them Ramp masters, engineers and mechanics as far as she could tell. Men she could safely ignore for the moment. She stilled herself and listened, sending her vampire senses along the corridors and stairwells of the citadel. Chloe searched for heartbeats and found what she was looking for. There was only one child's heartbeat within the citadel. Chloe's attention zeroed in on it. There was her target. There was the gifted child. She blurred off the roof of the water tank and into the nearest stairwell, racing up into the citadel. She'd not leave this underground fortress without the child.

She refused to fail her mission.

* * *

Angelina watched Whitehair; a creeping terror clutching at her soul.

"Now we will see what we can see," Whitehair said with an airy wave of his hands.

The pervasive hum reduced to a low background buzz, and then vanished altogether. A swirling mass of luminous spheres, each a brilliant point of subtle color moving in a steady flow around an invisible axis appeared between the apex of the inverted pyramid and the low platform in the middle of the chamber floor. Whitehair flicked another switch with an audible click and the sphere of colored lights froze in place.

It wasn't the real Metaframe, but a representation of it. Angelina sighed. She wished she could have protected her father back at the safe house. She could have done something to blind or otherwise frustrate his opponents. But it'd all happened too fast. Summoning the Metaframe required a calm and focused mind. She'd been worried for her father, and yet also filled with trust he could save them, and then the Iron Wolves and the Nazis had arrived, and overwhelmed him with numbers. Her chest tightened with the memory and a pair of tears rolled down her cheeks – had she failed her father?

Angelina looked around the massive chamber. Black-uniformed soldiers stood in groups near the north and south entrances, holding their weapons at rest, displaying an air of mild curiosity. Stinker stood nearby and regarded her with eager expectation, while Whitehair continued to operate his console. The nurses stood behind her left and right shoulders, and Nochka dozed in her lap.

Thousands of the lights in the representation dimmed, leaving two hundred and forty-eight that brightened. Whitehair stepped forward and gestured with a wave of his right hand. "This is where we are right now." He glanced at Angelina, and pressed a stud on a device in his left hand. The brighter lights moved for a second, re-arranging themselves in the representation of the Metaframe. Whitehair waved again at the colored lights resting like an alien ghost in the middle of the great chamber and stated, "And this is where we want to go."

Angelina had counted the lights in a glance. The brighter one's first shape felt like home, the second shape was a distant place at right angles to everything else, and there was something there, something curious and very strange. A cold discordant note in an otherwise harmonious symphony rang within the fabric of the Universe. Just regarding it raised goosebumps over her shoulders and she gasped in terror. She stared at Whitehair and demanded, "Why do you want to go there?"

"To bring the gift of divine peace to this world forever."

Angelina glanced back at the destination mapped in the representation. The shape resonated deeply within her. She could find it, and she could return from it. She knew how to do it intuitively, like knowing how to breathe. She paused for a moment. "And what of Nochka and myself?"

"Of course, you will be free to go wherever you wish," Whitehair said dismissively. He glanced briefly at Stinker, and said, "We only have this one request." He paused, as if considering his words. "Unlike the Red Empire, we have no need to control you. With us, you will be," and he spread his hands wide, "liberated from the bonds of servitude."

Angelina didn't believe his twisted words. The offered peace would be the peace of unassailable dominion and the liberty would be the rendered impotence of the helpless witness. She regarded the new configuration and compared it with the here and now. Visions of an alien world swept before her inner eye. The location was vastly different from home. A cold, desolate world, with life reduced to molds and lichens. The atmosphere was barely breathable and hostile to life. The 'thing,' drew her mind's eye. A disk of liquid silver, with a single edge and only one side. It hung unsupported in the air above a near-frigid stony desert. A twisted presence, without doubt the object of Whitehair's desire.

He cajoled her. "Just us, just the people in this room. You also of course, we need you to get us all back."

Angelina wondered if Whitehair fully understood what he was asking her to do. The seed of a daring idea came to her. She almost smiled but remembered her lessons, and nodded curtly instead. Perhaps it was for the best to help this man with his request. After all, she'd been born, why not another. How long would it be before these despicable men had an accomplice who shared their beliefs. How long would it be before they reached their vile goals and subjected an innocent world to their dominion. Angelina scanned the room in a moment of desperate hope. There was no one else. She was on her own. It was up to her to do what she must to protect the innocent. She stroked the sleeping pup in her lap. Not just for Nochka, but for the whole world.

The weight of responsibility nearly crushed her young soul. She closed her eyes for a moment and remembered her father's sacrifice. He'd died to protect her life. He'd sacrificed himself to guard her future. Her chest hitched on a strangled sob. How could she do less?

A desperate strategy arose within her. She would do as Whitehair asked. She would take him, Stinker, and their men to this alien world – and leave them there in a cold, hostile desert. A place matched to their personalities. They should feel at home there for the few hours they would have left to live.

Angelina took a deep breath and let it out slowly. Her father invaded her thoughts. Images of him lying dead on a dusty floor filled her to overflowing. She strangled another sob, took another deep breath, and let it out slowly. Grief flooded through her. She claimed her grief for her own and swallowed it down in hard gulps. She stilled herself, calmed her mind, and drew her focus to a single point of concentrated power. When she summoned the Metaframe it would not be one of the petite sorceries she'd demonstrated for the elders of the Red Empire. No, it would be the full presence of the Metaframe with the power to permanently translate the world or some part of it, to a different reality. The Red Ghost had been right to call her a living key and now it was time to demonstrate her power. She was far too young to Ramp with her body, but she was different – she could Ramp with her mind alone.

It was time to navigate.

* * * * *

"I have completed the surfacing of the inverted pyramid with superconducting alloy. I have constructed the cradle for the Engine of Set.

Now I only need a means to manage the grand presence of the Metaframe and we can access the location of the interdimensional portal. Himmler needs to prove his worth and find a living key before the damnable Order of Thoth or the Red Empire over-run our position. I grow weary of his excuses. Perhaps he is not the seer I supposed him to be." – Diary entry on the 12th December 1944, Siegfried von Frankenstein.

* * *

The Phoenix citadel, the Metaframe Chamber, April 1st 1945, 19:20

The false Metaframe vanished.

Angelina accelerated her mind to its maximum extent. The Metaframe emerged into view. The room snapped into crystal clarity. She seized the Metaframe with her mind, picking up the two hundred and forty-eight spheres relevant to the navigation. The inverted pyramid shimmered above the Metaframe. There was something there ... a tremulous shudder, a portent of incomprehensible power shedding off the pyramid like a frigid wave from the outer reaches of space.

Time slowed precipitously. The men and women in the room near-frozen as she reached for the distant location. The process of translation was perfectly balanced. They would go there, subtracting an appropriate amount of galactic rotational momentum in the target universe, while adding momentum in the source universe. The net mass-energy change between the two universes would be zero.

All this seemed obvious to Angelina as she balanced the necessary equations to translate this space with the distant one. As the process neared completion, the alien portal swam into view. It was a two-dimensional object with only one side. She gasped, horrified by the shroud of death emanating from it.

Angelina lost her words. Whatever she understood of death was inadequate to describe the portal. It was both a thing not normally alive and yet also dead. A rock wasn't dead, because it was never alive. This was a thing that had never lived and yet it had always been dead.

A temporal horror from another multiversal reality; older than the origin of time in this universe. A rip in the fabric of time itself. A thing long dead before Angelina's home universe had been born in an explosion of light.

A sob rose in her throat. This alien portal from another space-time dimension was beyond her ability to comprehend.

Her senses stretched within the realm of the Metaframe. A strong heat plume erupted around Whitehair. He'd ramped when the Metaframe swung into view. He held something within his right hand. A short-baton-shaped control switch. His thumb pressed down on a prominent red button.

A ripple of light emerged at the upper edge of the inverted pyramid and flashed down toward the apex. The pulse grew exponentially stronger as each level reduced the space it occupied. It reached the tip of the inverted pyramid. A bright bolt of white lightning erupted from the apex of the pyramid and speared down through the invisible axis at the center of the Metaframe. An invisible force slapped Angelina into the back of her chair. Nochka stiffened, still too slowed relative to her temporal acceleration to yelp with fright. Everyone fell sprawling to the floor. The Metaframe winked out of existence, and in its place reposed a ten-feet wide, silvery disc.

Whitehair had used a capability of the inverted pyramid to reverse the translation navigation. Instead of Angelina and the Nazis traveling to the world of the portal, the portal had arrived in the chamber.

A terrible urgency gripped her. She had to get rid of it. She summoned every ounce of concentration she possessed and the Metaframe returned, but it flickered in and out, swirling dimly around the otherworldly portal. Temporal acceleration slowed and stopped; time snapping back to normal movement. She lurched forward, falling to the floor, Nochka leaping away. The Metaframe continued to flicker, multi-colored lights brightening and dimming without rhyme or reason.

The portal remained, steadfast, stable, eternal within the Metaframe's stuttering lights.

The Metaframe faded and vanished.

Whitehair shouted triumphantly, "Here! Here! It opens!"

Angelina lifted her head, pushing herself off the polished stone floor. Behind her the nurse's shoes slapped across the stone as they rushed toward her. Nochka padded to her too. She looked up at the portal. The surface was more like a window made of silver than anything else, not a mirror but a view to somewhere else. A place where monstrous shapes moved. Angelina recoiled, picking up Nochka with an instinctive sweep of her hand. She turned with a step, running into the legs of the nurses.

Whitehair laughed many yards behind her.

The portal was alive.

* * *

The flickering-colored lights disappeared.

"Here! Here! It opens!" shouted a white-haired scientist.

Chloe was certain she'd just witnessed a partial manifestation of the Metaframe. She'd pumped Jean Philippe Allemande about the 'Divine Engine of Thoth,' before she'd purged him back in 1899. He'd filled in a few gaps in the education provided by Crane; an education sorely lacking on this particular topic.

Chloe scanned the room with a glance. The scientist was striding toward an uncanny disc hovering beneath an inverted stepped pyramid. The giant structure hung more than seventy-five yards down from the ceiling in the middle of an enormous chamber carved from solid rock. Thirty of the Nazi super-soldiers stood in two main groups, one near her at the south entrance, and another one-hundred and eighty yards away in front of the north entrance. The child rose off the floor, a German shepherd pup in her arms. She ran directly into a pair of white-coated blonde women who shoved a thick black hood over her head and drew it closed with a string around the girl's throat. They picked her up, still holding the pup, and sat her firmly back into a spartan metal chair in front of a wide bank of electrical cabinets.

Halfway between the child and the scientist stood the bespectacled officer. The one who'd commanded the platoon at the half-bombed house and stolen the child from beneath her nose. She took two seconds to measure heartbeats. Except for the child, everyone in the room was a Ramp master. Although the soldiers and nurses smelled strange, as if there was something odd in their body chemistry. An unknown technology had transformed them.

Chloe put speculation aside. She wasn't here to work out every last mystery. The child was less than a hundred yards away and everyone in the room stood staring at the weird disc hanging beneath the inverted pyramid. It was time to act. The Red Dragon swished free of its scabbard with a faint hiss. She'd have to kill everyone in the room to secure the child. It shouldn't take very long at all.

She assessed the guards a second time. The ones on the north side of the room had registered her arrival with excited pointing and shouting. They carried standard issue 9mm submachine guns, and straight short swords similar to a Roman gladius. The nearer soldiers turned to face her and raised their weapons without advancing.

Chloe raised an eyebrow in mute inquiry. She doubted they knew how to use their edged weapons effectively. Still, it was thirty plus to one in an open environment. Not entirely trivial, there was always a chance someone could get lucky. She took a breath and ramped hard, taking herself above maximum vampire performance.

The white-haired scientist whirled in a blur. "Ah ha!" he drawled sardonically. "I was expecting one such as yourself." He punched a button on a short baton within his hand. A dozen vents in the floor flipped open in a broad line twenty feet in front of Chloe. Aerosolized silver jetted in bright plumes into the air. Repelled, she pulled to a halt and flashed backward into the south corridor.

Warded by a vile curtain of pure silver, Chloe became a helpless witness to events.

* * *

The agent of the Vampire Dominion was back.

Heinrich stared at the blood-sucking bitch for a long moment. The vampire stood trapped behind a fence of aerosolized silver. She had somehow found a point of ingress into the citadel but had arrived too late to change what was about to happen. Whatever mission she had – it had already failed. He turned and strode after Siegfried toward the portal. He wanted to be close to greet Set when he emerged triumphantly into the world.

His friend and mentor had stepped up onto the platform forty yards away, and halted a handful of feet in front of the portal. Siegfried stood wonder struck before the alien device and declared fervently, "Magnificent!"

The surface of the portal shimmered faintly like a pool swept by a zephyr. A shadow loomed within it. Heinrich veered to the left to get a better look at whatever it might be. Siegfried had never been able to explicitly define how Set would manifest. He always maintained the presence of the portal was a necessary and sufficient step to bring Set into the world. The portal was here, surely the physical manifestation of Set was imminent. The shadow thickened at the very center of the shimmering disc into a splotch of darkness the width of a human hand. Was this Set? Was Set about to push through the portal and enter the world?

Heinrich's heart thumped in his chest. The moment of his apotheosis was upon him. Soon, he'd become an immortal demi-god ruling with absolute power at Set's right hand. Siegfried took a confident step forward and raised his right hand toward the center of the portal. He paused for the briefest of moments, then touched the gathering darkness on the surface of the portal with his forefinger. He turned to look at Heinrich, a wild grin on his face, his eyes lit with triumph.

Heinrich stared at him. Transfixed. Divinity was upon them. The world would never be the same again.

A drop of blood appeared on the very edge of Siegfried's hairline directly above his nose. His smile faltered. The triumph fled his eyes. His mouth opened into an 'O,' with a sudden gasping intake of breath. His right shoulder jerked once, as if he was trying to free his finger but to no avail – he was stuck fast to the shimmering surface of the portal.

Siegfried's exhalation began as a shuddering whimper, rising sharply into a shrill scream. A ripple began on his right forefinger, flowing up his arm, accelerating in an instant into a bone snapping whip. The wave rippled over Siegfried's body like a strong wind ruffling a flag. His feet lifted from the floor and flapped wildly. His scream vanishing into dreadful silence; he slumped bonelessly to the floor, his limp arm stretching elastically upward, still attached to the center of the portal by an elongated finger.

A seam opened beneath the drop of blood on Siegfried's sunken forehead and ran a wavering path down his midline, disappearing beneath his clothes in a moment. An instant later his skin lifted away from the rest of him and slithered backward through the portal. The weird portal released its grip upon Siegfried's limp, boneless, skinless, body. What remained of him flopped to the floor in a spreading pool of blood and crumpled clothes.

Heinrich, his mouth open, his breath frozen, stared at Siegfried's ruined face. One hideous lidless eye peered back at him. Beneath the bloodshot orb, naked lips quivered with awareness as if to speak a word, but Siegfried's lungs couldn't expel a breath without a rib cage. Skinned and boned – Siegfried was still horribly alive.

Heinrich recoiled in disgust from his dying ally. Behind him, the nurses shrieked in urgent alarm. He ignored their terror, something far more important was stepping through the portal as if from one room to the next.

A human figure appeared on the platform between the portal and the twitching lump of blood-soaked flesh on the floor. It was an utterly naked Siegfried von Frankenstein. For a wild moment, Heinrich believed his life-long accomplice and boon companion was still alive. Hope soared in his heart; divinity awaited them both. The thing opened its eyes and regarded Heinrich avidly.

There was nothing but a swirling vortex of darkness within each eye socket.

The two nurses screamed once each, then froze. Men grunted, or took a step backward. Hands flew from weapons to faces. Hearts quailed.

An atavistic shiver raced up Heinrich's spine. Something had gone horribly wrong. This couldn't be Set. Where was the new God made manifest flesh? The divine being who would transport Heinrich beyond the coils of mortality. The one destined to bestow the gift of true immortality and worldly power worthy of a faithful servant.

The creature regarded everyone in the room for a handful of seconds, its gaze flicked around to rest on the nearest human – Heinrich. Its lips parted, revealing nothing but darkness within. It uttered in an inhuman voice that cut through the dreadful silence like a hideous secret suddenly revealed, "I have come to murder the light."

Heinrich's eyes widened and his guts curdled with abject horror. This wasn't the glorious triumphant Set described by Siegfried back in the secret library in Munich. He glanced over his shoulder, the way to the northern corridor was clear. His gaze flicked around his men. It was time for them to prove their absolute loyalty to the great cause.

He pointed at the thing occupying Siegfried's stolen skin and shouted at his super-soldiers, "For the Fatherland! Attack!"

It was time to escape.

* * *

The nurses screamed in abject terror.

Silence fell like a funeral shroud over the great chamber, then an inhuman voice chilled Angelina's blood, "I have come to murder the light."

The nurses released their grip on Angelina's shoulders and arms; their retreating footsteps slapping on the concrete floor. Her hands flew to the drawstring around her throat. The knot hung loose. She pulled it open and dragged the cloth bag off her head. Angelina's gaze flashed to the alien source of the words. It looked like Whitehair but wasn't. It didn't belong here. It didn't belong anywhere. Angelina always knew where something belonged. It was part of finding things, of knowing where she was, she always knew – her knowledge was inescapable.

A monstrous shriek split the air.

She slammed her hands over her eyes. She couldn't look at it – the very sight of the thing standing in front of the portal tore at her soul. The shriek had emanated from within the portal, from a place beyond her ability to know. The same place the thing filling Whitehair's skin had come from.

Stinker shouted panicked commands. Guns fired, grim voices barked orders, footsteps resounded across the stone floor as men ran toward the portal. Something flew past her, slamming into the cabinets behind her. The nurse on her left began a shrill wailing at the limit of human terror, the other nurse was silent. Something brushed against Angelina's ankle and whimpered. She dragged her hands away from her face and looked down, Nochka, her black eyes wide, was trying to climb her left leg. She reached down, picked up the struggling pup, and held her close.

With her chest heaving with each breath, Angelina lifted her gaze and scanned the room. Stinker was backing hurriedly away to her left, heading toward the open north corridor. The Whitehair-thing had left the raised platform beneath the open portal and was slowly progressing toward her. A great pair of black tentacles, slopping an oily black goo reached forth from the portal to the creature's left and right. The right-hand tentacle was pulling back, dragging the empty skin-sack of the silent nurse with it.

Angelina turned slowly to the right, caught between a desperate need to know and a terror of what she'd witness. The remains of the nurse quivered on the stone floor in a lumpen mass within her starched uniform; a pool of blood slowly spreading around her and seeping through the white cloth of her uniform. The other nurse's shrill cries echoed off the walls as she ran away. Beyond the shivering flesh, a wall of silver misted the air near the south corridor entrance. Beyond the sparkling wall stood a dark-clad figure holding a bright sword. The same vampire who had fought briefly within the safe house.

"I am one. I am many," shouted the Whitehair-thing near the middle of the chamber. Angelina flicked her head left. It threw its arms wide and thundered, "Join us and live forever as one!"

The black-uniformed soldiers attacked it and the lashing tentacles. Bullet's tore at its flesh, passing straight through it. The closest soldier raised his short sword and blurred forward. His blade disappeared into the Whitehair-thing's chest. There was no blood, vague tongues of dark smoke retreated back into the body as the blade withdrew. Other soldiers stabbed or shot the whipping tentacles, and found the same result.

The Whitehair-thing ignored the wound. Its right hand flashed out, touching the nearest soldier's forehead with an outstretched finger. The man's skin unpeeled like a glove ripped off by the finger tips, and flew into the air. The raw flesh flopped bonelessly to a twitching heap on the cold stone floor. Black light gushed from the Whitehair-thing's eyes and mouth, filling the skin as it fell toward the floor. It landed on both feet, rose naked to its full height and attacked the nearest soldier. A moment later his bisected skin was flying into the air, hunted by rays of darkness from the Whitehair-thing and his first victim. The dark beams extinguished a second later and the Whitehair-thing turned to the south, stalking the nearest soldiers who continued to fire at it with their submachine guns or stab at it with their swords. Each round drew a wisp of black smoke from a wound. Each time the smoke curled around itself, returning into the body, and closing the skin behind it. The Whitehair-thing lifted the nurse's empty skin-sack from the stone floor and breathed dark light into it. It inflated in a moment and she stepped free from his grasp. A second later, she latched onto a screaming soldier with both hands. He frantically stabbed her again and again with his sword, wisps of dark smoke jetting left and right, until his hand went limp and his de-gloved skin flew into the air.

Another fell shriek filled the chamber. The portal had grown from ten feet to twenty feet wide in less than a minute. A great disk hanging in space between the apex of the inverted pyramid and the platform. More tentacles lashed out of the portal, and at their center something dark and massive pushed at the middle of the portal. The tip of a beak broke through. Black and glossy, it stretched vertically apart. A titanic shriek emerged from the utter darkness within the gaping maw and resounded for a third time within the chamber.

Another four soldier's de-gloved skins rose into the air, stalked by dark rays, the skin-sacks inflated with the essence of the realm beyond the portal. The grim commands fled. Men shouted, screamed and panicked. The soldiers descended into a mob, fighting only to break free and escape.

Angelina sidled away to the north. She had to summon the Metaframe. It was her only chance to send the portal back to where it had come. She tried to calm herself, but could find no peace within the swirling chaos around her. The path to the south held a vampire who stared fixedly into the room. Her eyes like glittering sapphires. Her face a frozen pale mask. There would be no safety there – vampires were anathema. Angelina turned fully to the north, and with Nochka held firmly within her arms, she fled for the exit as fast as her feet could carry her.

Nochka yelped with terror against her chest.

* * *

The child ran.

Chloe's gaze snapped after her. Whatever had happened in the seconds before Chloe had arrived at the south corridor entrance, the child was at the center of it. She had to retrieve her. She was the only one who could undo the existence of the portal and send whatever horrors coming through it back whence they came. The silver plumes lost half their height, running out of their store of the paralyzing metal. Chloe took in the one-sided violence occurring within the chamber. Fourteen monstrous things stalked eighteen desperate soldiers. The Nazi super-soldiers remained helpless before whatever was emerging from the portal. Clearly, if these things escaped the citadel, they would take over the world in short order.

The silver sprays dipped further and cut out.

The number of soldiers dropped from eighteen to fifteen. The flying skins inflating with darkness before they struck the floor, rising immediately to join the fray. Half a dozen greasy black tentacles tens-of-yards long waved through the chamber. One grasped a soldier for a moment, squeezed, and his de-gloved skin flew into the air. It inflated like a balloon, fed by dark rays from the eyes and mouths of the others. As soon as it hit the stone floor it rushed the surviving soldiers, seeking another victim to convert to its dreadful existence.

Another fell shriek split the air. Chloe winced; the sound cut through her brain like a knife. She judged the falling mist of silver. The sooner she moved, the better her chances of reaching the child before one of these strange creatures took her. But she couldn't risk contact with the silver. A single touch would thwart all her powers and render her helpless to the fiends occupying the chamber.

The silver continued to settle. Gravity raced against time, and time was winning. She supreme ramped, cold fire ripped through sinew, nerve and bone. She blurred forward, leaping on a long high arc over the uppermost edge of the silver cloud, over the slow trenchant slaughter of the soldiers, tumbling once and landing in a crouch on the stone floor beyond the battle.

Grey dust puffed beneath her boots with the impact. She rose to her full height, the Red Dragon naked in her right hand, and sprinted toward the northern corridor.

The officer dashed for the far doors. He glanced back over his shoulder at Chloe. The child was struggling in his arms. He'd captured her while Chloe remained trapped behind the silver mist. He did an about face and sprinted for the north corridor as if the very devil was after him.

He wasn't far wrong.

He ran and shouted, "Close the doors." A soldier within the northern corridor slapped a red switch on the wall. A klaxon wailed. Orange lights strobed. Chloe dug within, blurring forward.

A pair of square, ten-yard high, gray-stone slabs, slid across the entrance. The officer slipped through the narrowing gap with the squirming child in his arms. He turned at the last, a triumphant grin on his face.

The blast doors closed with a resounding boom. Chloe slammed into them with a frustrated cry. Behind her, the rest of the chamber descended into near silence, broken only by the slash and slap of waving tentacles, and the steady pad of approaching feet.

She whirled.

Chloe was the only thing remotely human in the room.

* * *

The blast doors slammed shut.

The foul vampire remained trapped with the things from the portal. Three squads of Übermensch super-soldiers from the main entrance looked at Heinrich expectantly, waiting dutifully for orders. He'd selected them well. The prime flower of the Hitler youth from the nineteen-thirties. He'd personally cultivated them for more than a decade. All capacity for independent thought eliminated from their personalities. They would serve him unto death.

Heinrich held the struggling child by the wrist in a grip of iron. Siegfried had warned him. As long as she was upset, he would have nothing to fear from her sorcerous powers, but first they had to get away. She was his trump card. If what he attempted next didn't stop the incursion from the portal, he would need her to reverse this mayhem and save his life. Once he was safe, he would cut her throat to ensure she couldn't harm him. She was far too dangerous to let live.

He swept his free hand back toward the blast doors, glanced at two of the squad leaders and commanded, "Let nothing pass this gate. Guard it with your lives."

The black-uniformed super-soldiers snapped to attention and shouted, "Yes, Sir!"

He hoped they'd buy him enough time to escape before they died. He addressed the remaining squad leader. "You and your men will come with me." The man snapped his heels together in a text book salute and shouted his assent.

Heinrich nodded once and turned away. The third squad ready to follow behind him. "Come," he demanded of the child. "Stop struggling. Do you want to die here?"

The girl looked at him with wide eyes filled with tears. "It's my fault it came."

Heinrich grinned sourly, if she believed that, perhaps he could salvage something from this disaster. He snarled at her, spittle flying furiously. "Of course, it's your fault, you stupid child." He lifted her off the ground by the wrist and she squealed in pain. He tucked her under his other arm. The damnable puppy was still within the grasp of her free hand. He quelled a sudden impulse to dash the animal's brains on the floor in a fit of spite. The pup had served well as a lever over her actions, and perhaps it would prove useful again.

He blurred to a broad stairwell that zigged and zagged downward sixty yards to the power and pumping station's sub-level. Beyond was a second stairwell leading one hundred and ten yards down to the lowest sub-level. It was there he would find his escape route. Heinrich clutched the sobbing child tight.

The puppy barked once at him in a fit of helpless insolence, then fell into guarded silence.

Heinrich blurred down the stairs, followed by his four body-guards.

* * *

The portal swelled beneath the inverted pyramid.

The edge of the disk reached nearly the full one hundred feet from the raised platform to the apex of the inverted pyramid. A beak pushed through the portal, a great black mass behind it. A dozen tentacles, a yard thick and glistening with an oily sheen beneath the overhead lights, pushed at the edge of the portal. The beak snapped hungrily, stretched wide, and uttered an alien screech fit to burst Chloe's eardrums.

She winced, she stared around the chamber, her eyes wide. The scientist, a nurse, and thirty soldiers advanced implacably toward her; all naked, all with vortexes of darkness for eyes, and yawning mouths filled with insatiable absence made solid reality.

For the very first time in her life, Chloe hoped she was faster than those who sought her life, because these foes were neither human, vampire, or Ramp master. They were beyond her experience and they had comprehensively destroyed thirty Ramp masters attempting to kill them. No weapon could harm them. Just a single touch spread a contagion that stripped skin and bone from common flesh. The lumps of raw meat scattered over the floor had stilled in death, none had survived long once skinned and filleted by these alien things.

Chloe wasted no time on considering the fate of the dead, and focused her attention upon those still moving. She'd cut her supreme Ramp short upon contact with the closed northern blast doors. The southern corridor was empty, if she could reach it, she could find a momentary respite sufficient to regain the initiative.

The alien things broke into a run en masse, as if some greater power had given a silent order.

Hive mind? Chloe thought momentarily. She stilled herself and ramped hard, bringing her supreme Ramp into full flower. Fresh energy exploded from the base of her spine and flooded through her. Thirty plus abominations closed to within fifty yards, and a dozen waving tentacles reached across the chamber from the beaked monstrosity emerging from the portal.

Chloe blurred to the right, rising up off the floor, and dashing along the banks of electrical cabinets lining the western wall. The alien things simply turned and sprinted after her. They matched the speed of a mature Ramp master, but fell behind her extreme velocity. The tentacles reached, slapping against the wall in front and behind her.

She leaped desperately. Just a single touch of the alien flesh would be enough to undo her.

The writhing tentacles of dark flesh smashed into the cabinets in showers of white sparks and rising plumes of blue-gray smoke.

Chloe dove and twisted, leaped and sprinted, ducked and rolled, finally flashing down to the floor in a dark swish of her trailing cloak. She crossed the threshold into the southern corridor.

A thunderous shriek of frustrated rage echoed throughout the chamber behind her. She slammed the switch on the wall. A klaxon wailed, a set of orange lights strobed, and a pair of great blast doors made of solid stone slid across the entranceway. They slammed shut with a boom. The klaxon silenced and the orange lights winked out.

Chloe quelled her Ramp and backed away a step. She was alone, nothing moved in the corridor stretching two-hundred and fifty yards behind her. She opened her senses to their vampire maximums, searching and cataloging the noises within the citadel. The diesels thundered, the pumps thrummed, and the air vent fans whirred. She pushed all the industrial noises of the citadel into the background, she was looking for something else – something alive.

The great blast doors shuddered before her, gray dust puffing out around the edges. Whatever was in the chamber was working to escape. She had minutes at best, or she would die and the world with her in the following hours. Her last glimpse into the chamber had revealed the portal stretching beyond a hundred feet, cutting into the apex of the inverted pyramid above it, and into the platform beneath it. It was growing exponentially, and there was but one hope of stopping it.

Chloe searched for the child's heartbeat and found it. She was on another level below her, the one with the power stations and water pumps, but on the opposite side of the citadel. She was on the move, heading further downward. Six hearts beat beside her, the officer, the pup and four Ramp master soldiers. The citadel had descended into chaos, all the other humans were heading for the sole northern entrance. But it remained shut, and the Gods only knew if anyone could open it again without the officer or the scientist in attendance. If the northern entrance was a viable exit, the officer would have gone there. Instead, he had fled to the lowest level. He must have a reason. In any event, he had the child. Nothing had changed. Chloe blurred down the nearest stairwell to the lower levels. The child was still the mission.

The only mission that could save the world.

* * * * *

"Imagine a universe in which entropy animates the dominant life forms." – Diary entry on the 2nd January 1945, Siegfried von Frankenstein.

* * *

The Phoenix citadel, sub-level-2, April 1st 1945, 19:23

Few had reason to visit the lowest level of the Phoenix citadel.

A vast basement packed with explosives – a final failsafe if the Red Empire, the Order of Thoth, or the Vampire Dominion ever discovered the citadel. Heinrich hit the bottom of the stairwell and blurred to the left between the pallets of wired high explosives. Seconds later he reached one of the most secret aspects of the citadel. The escape silos in the middle of the lowest level.

His trailing squad of super-soldiers looked around the broad tunnel at the heaped pallets of explosives with semi-curious eyes. Their inferior minds beginning to wonder what was really going on. He turned to them and commanded sternly, "The time has come to defend the fatherland from the communists and the Jews. You are all heroes of the Aryan race. You've pledged your lives to the great cause, and you will live in the halls of Valhalla for eternity. The divine storm maidens of Odin himself will fulfill your every need forever."

The men looked grim, but they nodded.

Promise young men eternal life, an endless supply of virgins, and forbid dissent until the ability to question atrophied into oblivion. It was a tried-and-true formula for the domination of the youthful male mind.

The child continued to squirm beneath his arm. He flung her to the floor, where she sprawled with the yelping pup in her arms. She picked herself up, first soothing the dog before checking her elbows and knees for bruises. For all her gifts, she was weak-minded, afflicted with the diseases of empathy and compassion.

Heinrich sniffed, thoroughly disgusted with what he had to deal with. He ached inside. The loss of the promise of divine immortality grieved him like a knife through the gut. But just as painful, the great cleansing of the dross of humanity would not occur. All the feral humans would remain; the stupid, the ignorant, the hopeless, the diseased, the intransigent, the non-compliant, the dissident fools who clung to the fruits of their own reason as if that meant anything in the face of real power ... Heinrich pulled his mind to a halt. He could spend a week, a month, or even a year ranting about what had just happened. He had to focus on immediate needs – his own safety was paramount. He needed to escape and he needed the child. He bent and scooped her up off the floor along with the pup within the cradle of her arms. He set her on her feet and took hold of her wrist. She looked at him with wet eyes, her face tear-streaked and pale with shock. He ignored her for the moment, she wasn't going anywhere without him.

He ordered the squad, "Take a guard position on these silos and allow no one to approach."

Two access paths reached the basement, stairwells to the north and south from the upper levels. Whatever came at them would have to take one of those paths unless it could cut through solid rock. He frowned briefly, surely the fiends couldn't do that too? His men nodded again in response to his order and split into pairs. They took positions twenty feet to the left and right, their submachine guns aimed down the broad open space between the two rows of explosives.

Heinrich's lip curled dismissively at their slavish obedience, and he turned to the silos on the eastern wall. Two great tubes stood side by side, separated by a metallic-gray control panel. He entered an eight-digit code on a keyboard. A door on the silo on the left projected forward from the tube and slid up. An escape pod rested within, aligned with the open doorway. It was little more than a cradle for a shielded ejection seat. The cradle rested upon an electromagnetic rail system. One capable of propelling the escape pod through a tunnel curving up and back in a long reversed 'C,' shape, first to the east and then to the west, finally exiting at the peak of the mountain. The cradle would fall away into the surrounding forest while the ejection seat would arc high in the air before falling toward a designated field on the outskirts of Freiburg to the west. A parachute would deploy to enable a safe landing.

The escape pod had room for one adult occupant. He could accommodate a child on his lap if he needed to. There was one other thing to do before he made his escape. He flicked a switch on the console, arming the citadel's explosive failsafe. A counter flashed one hundred and twenty in bright-red digits and began counting down the seconds to detonation. In two minutes', time, the citadel would cease to exist, and perhaps the fiends from the portal would vanish with it. But he wasn't sure if that would happen – who could know what might harm them? He held onto the child's wrist tight enough to leave bruises. He needed her as insurance against the worst-case scenario.

"Sir," one of the squad members called from the southern side of the level. "Someone is coming."

Heinrich whirled – not someone – something. In the distance, the vampire bitch stood, starkly outlined by the sharp lights in the ceiling. She blurred forward. He shouted, "Kill her!" He turned back to the console and activated the launching sequence for the left-side escape pod. There was no time to lose. He had to be inside the escape pod within the next ten seconds or the pod would leave without him.

He glanced over his shoulder. The first pair of soldiers engaged the vampire, firing their submachine guns in long thunderous bursts. The second pair blurred to their assistance and opened fire. Heinrich had seen her operate at the bombed-out house. If his soldiers purchased him another ten seconds with their lives it would be enough to enable his escape.

Their deaths would be a necessary sacrifice.

And just as forgettable.

* * *

Five ramp masters, a child, a pup, and Chloe remained alive within the doomed citadel.

All the other heartbeats in the hidden fortress had fallen silent. The outer doors to the north remained shut. Both doors to the north and south of the Metaframe chamber lay open, and whatever was within them was claiming the citadel for its own. Chloe estimated she had one or two minutes at most before the bizarre creatures from the portal were upon her in this lowest of levels.

Chloe checked herself for the briefest of moments as she dodged a storm of 9mm rounds. Not just her, but the world itself would die. Great beauty abounded within the world. Lightning crackling across the sky. Storm clouds boiling beneath bright stars. The sting of sharp cold rain upon her face. The vast intricacies of life within a virgin forest at midnight. The near perfect silence of a cave. The deep light of the galaxy witnessed from a desert mountain top. The sharp thrill of challenge in the midst of battle. The triumph of victory.

She'd lose everything forever.

But first, she had to deal with the Nazis. The first two fell to her blade. Great sweeps of the Red Dragon to the left and right made two men into four parts. She blurred through the gap between them. The second pair provided no more resistance than the first. Who were these men? Trumped up Ramp masters with minimal real training. They hadn't come to the Ramp by the usual route. In any event, they now lay slumped against pallets of explosives in spreading pools of entrails and gore.

She flicked the Red Dragon clear of their blood and advanced upon the officer.

His jaw dropped. No doubt he'd expected stiffer resistance from his men. For the briefest of moments, Chloe wondered if he'd have time to understand the depths of his ignorance before he died. She suspected not.

He wrapped his left arm tightly across the girl's chest, and pulled her up so her head was just beneath his chin. The pup fell free, dropping to the floor with a yelp of surprise. A razor-sharp dagger appeared in his right hand; its blade resting against the child's throat. His eyes locked on Chloe and he stammered, "I'll … I'll cut her throat! Stay back!"

Chloe stilled for an instant – struck by a sense of déjà vu from beneath the safe house. She called his bluff, advancing with murder writ large in her eyes. "Kill her, I don't care."

The officer's eyes widened; his gaze flicked at the slowly flashing counter on the console. At the same moment, the pup barked and attacked his left ankle, biting and snarling for all it was worth. The officer winced, glancing down for an instant.

Chloe blurred forward, closing the final yards between them, the Red Dragon arcing down to cleave his skull to the brain stem.

The officer lurched backward, throwing the child from him, directly into the path of the descending blade.

Chloe dragged her sword aside. The officer had flung the child hard enough that wherever she landed, the impact would kill her. She pivoted hard, reversing her path, racing back toward the child. She reached out her hand. The hard iron edge of a pallet frame loomed before them. The child was flying head first toward it. She leaped, her left hand wrapped beneath the child's back, her momentum lifting both of them above the pallet. She twisted hard around her axis, landing feet first against the western wall, squatting low, shedding momentum and shielding the child. She dropped safely to the floor and looked up.

A flashing red light dominated the left silo doorway. "Have her," the officer shouted from within the escape pod. "You can die together."

A great whoosh erupted from the silo and the escape pod vanished upward. The flashing red light within the silo vanished. The officer had escaped. Chloe set the child down gently on the floor, and released her. The child stared at her, pale faced, shivering slightly, her heart racing. She gulped. The pup stood next to the child, her hackles raised, a low growl in her youthful throat.

Chloe took a knee before the child, bringing her face level with the girl's face. "I'm sorry you're frightened," Chloe said quietly. "But we are short of time." She needed to rewrite the parameters of her mission. The future depended upon it. She had to win the child's trust and fast.

She opened her left hand, palm up a foot in front of the child's heart and stated, "I will guard your life, Angelina Ivanov, as if it is my own life or die trying." She drew the Red Dragon lightly across the palm of her hand. A line opened, blood welling forth, spilling in fat drops on the stone floor. Before the wound closed, Chloe locked her gaze on Angelina's eyes and declared with every fiber of her being, "This I swear before vampiric witnesses on the sacred blood of Mekra, mother of us all."

Angelina looked around her. "Witnesses?"

"I witnessed it. It is enough. You're a child of the Red Empire, have they included this oath in your lessons?"

The child took a long breath and let it out with a shudder. She nodded solemnly. Her heart rate was rapidly returning to normal and color was coming back to her cheeks.

Chloe asserted with hard eyes. "Then you know I will not allow you to come to harm."

Angelina nodded again, and said, "Yes." The pup sat at her feet and watched Chloe with wary eyes. She asked in a small voice, "Are we running away?"

Chloe had counted heartbeats earlier – there was no one left alive in the complex, but there was plenty of movement – too much movement. The creatures had conquered the citadel. Footsteps resounded down both the north and south stairwells. They would attack from both directions at the same time. The lower level was a death trap. She shook her head once and smiled ironically at the girl. "No. We will reposition for tactical advantage."

She rose to her full height and said in an off-hand tone, "I never run away."

* * *

The vampire rested her left hand gently on Angelina's shoulder and asked, "Can you trust me?"

Angelina glanced left; the level stretched away beneath a string of lights. Something stepped down from the stairwell. It was the thing Whitehair had become, its swirling vortex eyes looked into her own. The thing's hunger hit her like a slap.

"Yes," Angelina answered. There was no other choice, she had to trust a vampire with their lives. The vampire wrapped her and Nochka up in arms as hard as steel. In the same moment she moved. The room vanished behind her. The interior walls of the empty silo rushed past. A row of yellowish lights blurred into a near continuous line. The vampire flew from side to side with each gargantuan leap, running up the silo in a display of gravity defying power.

They emerged from the mouth of the silo into the cold night air on top of the mountain. The vampire carried her twenty meters back from the edge of the silo and placed her on the damp sward. She looked into Angelina's eyes, her own face in shadow, a tall silhouette against the pale-yellow glow emanating from the silo, and asked, "What can you do?" The vampire lifted her face, and swept her gaze across the storm vortex boiling above the mountain. "We have to end this."

Angelina tracked her gaze. Beyond the perimeter of the vortex, the bright stars spoke of home. Angelina always knew where she was. She remembered perfectly where the portal came from, a desolate nearly lifeless planet. Her eyes widened. "We can starve them."

"What?" the vampire asked, staring down at her.

"I can't close it but I can send them back, but I need more time. Can you protect me?"

The dark-haired vampire stared at her and vowed without hesitation, "To the death."

Angelina stared back at her face and the ruthless determination written there. An adamantine will stood between her and what was emerging within the mountain. Behind the vampire, the buttery light emanating from the mouth of the underground silo dimmed. Beneath her feet, the portal was growing, cutting through the solid rock as if it wasn't there. Her eyes widened and she whispered, "They're coming."

The vampire whirled in a blur. Her magnificent blade appeared before her, a pale gleam running along its length in the fading electric light. She called over her shoulder, "Time to do your thing."

Angelina sat down on the sward and took a deep breath. Nochka padded around her and curled into a warm furry ball at her left hip. Her mind flooded with calm. For the first time in a long time, she felt truly safe. She was no longer running. One way or another, she would decide her future in the next few moments. She was at peace with the world.

She reached for the Metaframe.

* * *

Tactics filled Chloe's mind.

Vertical and horizontal bisection, or trisection, she would try each method once. If they failed, she'd use the flat of her blade to push them aside. She couldn't allow them to reach Angelina. She had to buy the child time or the world would die. The ground vibrated beneath her feet for a moment. She'd set a fraction of her mind counting down seconds aligned with the red counter on the console on the lowest level. No one installed pallets of explosives at the bottom of a secret citadel for nothing. Fifty-nine seconds remained before the citadel collapsed beneath them. Would the top of the mountain implode to fill the empty space?

Chloe smiled grimly. There was nowhere safe on the planet; least of all within ten feet of the main exit path out of an underground citadel filled with deadly implacable alien horrors. Monstrous creatures whose sole goal was the conversion of living flesh into possessed abominations. It seemed a vampire was just as attractive to them as any other form of life. She shook her head slowly; to imagine her life had come to this. Defending a child against an alien invasion. She glanced upward in ironic wonder; her gaze caught momentarily by the uncanny storm vortex swirling overhead.

Her internal counter reached forty-five, then descended to forty-four seconds.

Chloe stood in the eye of the storm. She pressed her lips together. It was all related; the Metaframe, the eldritch storm, the inverted pyramid. She made a silent vow that if she managed to survive this night, she'd find out what was really going on and put a stop to it. She glanced over her shoulder at the child sitting quietly fifty feet behind her, and opened her mouth to speak. She wanted to tell her to hurry up. They were running out of time. Angelina's face relaxed into a deep calm. Her eyes opened wide, sapphire mirrors of Chloe's own. They stared into a place Chloe couldn't follow. Angelina's heart rate slowed to forty beats a minute, slow for a child. The faithful dog was almost asleep at her hip. Chloe kept her silence, watching for shadows in her peripheral vision.

Her internal counter passed thirty-three seconds.

The buttery glow emanating from the underground silo winked out. Chloe turned back and ramped hard. She kept the supreme Ramp held lightly on a hair-trigger. Once she went there, she could maintain it for three to five seconds before exhaustion set in. It was her most powerful weapon, waiting for the loss of all hope.

A river of negative light erupted from the underground silo, rising like a slice of hell through the storm vortex into the infinity of space.

Chloe staggered backward, her jaw dropped, and she quailed within. This was not just the absence of light. This was darkness made solid, an entropic force fit to consume a universe. Her throat froze, she wanted to cry out but couldn't make a sound. Deep within she screamed in utter abandon. In a loss of control, she spontaneously supreme ramped as her instincts called forth her strongest offensive powers. Even in the utmost of terror – she would fight to win or die.

Multi-colored lights appeared behind her, illuminating the mountain top and the distant surrounding tree line. Her shadow appeared on the sward, stretching toward the mouth of the silo. What light fell upon the tower of darkness disappeared without trace. An alien river – the hell-born ender of worlds. Shadowy forms leaped from the abysmal tower, resolving into the mad scientist and his previously human followers. They blurred forward as one, their dark vortex gazes searching past her, hunting for the child.

Chloe lifted her blade, ready to give her all. She no longer hoped it would be enough. The mad scientist shifted his gaze toward her. His mouth yawned open in a mockery of a grin – within his maw rested the annihilation of the light. He rushed toward her, his immediate followers branching to the left and right to surround Chloe and Angelina. Behind him, figure after figure stepped from the river of darkness onto the mountain top.

Chloe narrowed her eyes, her supreme Ramp reaching its full flower riding the cold, urgent energy of terror. Thunder clapped mightily behind her. A flicker of golden flame appeared at the base of the Red Dragon and raced along the blade to the tip.

She attacked, her sword flaming through a wide overhead arc. Chloe split the mad scientist in two, his separated halves evaporating almost instantly into harmless ashy fragments.

The creatures of the portal turned and attacked; Angelina seemingly forgotten for the moment. They swarmed Chloe, a single touch meant certain death and utter failure. She was clear about which of those two outcomes she feared most. Her fiery blade swept through great arcs. She twisted left and right, leaped high, and darted through the narrowest of gaps. In her wake, fragments of annihilated ash wafted to the ground.

The creatures kept coming, oblivious to their safety in the service of the alien darkness.

Chloe found herself on one knee, her supreme Ramp running into its ragged edge. The Red Dragon described a stuttering arc of fire against a storm-swept sky. Her blade moving faster than her gaze could follow. The creatures of the portal leaped at her in desperate abandon. Their arms outstretched, their hands reaching, their fingers clutching. With her supreme Ramp faltering, her doom was upon her.

A second clap of thunder resounded over the mountain top.

The creatures vanished. Chloe whirled, her chest heaving. The towering river of darkness was gone. The silo mouth filled with a plug of bald stone. Beneath her feet a faint shudder faded away. She turned and looked up. The Metaframe whirled above. The remnants of her supreme Ramp clung on with trenchant fingers, holding time within their grip. There was something else there within the Metaframe. An active presence, a swirling ebony cloud perhaps a yard across. Near it rested other multi-colored clouds of similar size, silver, emerald, sapphire, ruby, and another dozen – all gleaming with an otherworldly potency. Finally, there was one more, a pearl-colored cloud shot with golden flame, twin to the fire that had animated her blade. It struggled with the shadowy cloud for the briefest of moments, bright sparks flashing between them.

The Metaframe faded from view. The flames riding her blade vanished with it.

One thought slashed like a hot knife through her mind, *The gods are within the Metaframe and they are at war with each other.* She frowned, how could there be war without resolution, unless it had just started? Perhaps the arrival of the portal had changed things within the Metaframe. She pursed her lips; she couldn't know for sure one way of another.

She let out a long sigh and turned toward the child. Had she done enough? Had they won the battle?

Angelina looked at her with warm eyes and smiled with joy.

* * * * *

"Our agent has secured the encrypted formula for the super-soldier serum from Siegfried von Frankenstein's notebook. The codes to break the encryption are pending further action."

– Extract of a Shadowstone Report, Freiburg im Breisgau, March 24th, 1945. – Shadowstone Archives, New York City.

* * *

The Feldberg, the summit, April 1st 1945, 19:27

Chloe sheathed her sword and assessed her surroundings.

The storm vortex had all but evaporated, only a few wisps of dark cloud remained to obscure the bright stars overhead. The winding tree line was anywhere from two to five hundred yards away. The trees descending in all directions down the mountain's sides. She noticed a flat strip of tarmac running away from her down the long-axis through the broad clearing on top of the mountain. She was standing in Crane's pickup point. A thousand yards of tarmacked road could accommodate a DC-3 transport.

But he was not yet here, and her internal seconds counter was in single digits. Chloe waited quietly; she suspected Angelina had dealt with the explosives problem. The counter hit zero and nothing happened. She approached the child who was quietly stroking the pup in her lap, and asked, "What about the explosives?"

Angelina looked up at her. "Gone, all gone to the other place, swapped with rock from there to here – to balance it out." She shrugged her small shoulders. "Rock is rock." A serious look overtook her face and she said, "They are raging. They are hungry with little to eat. They are far away but they are coming. I don't know when, but one day they'll be back."

Chloe nodded. They'd won the battle, but an unasked-for war remained. She looked up at the night sky for a long moment, her vampire sight piercing the darkness, revealing the utter brilliance of the naked Milky Way above her. A carpet of multi-colored jewels strewn over a velvet background of infinite darkness. She would have to prepare. The presence of the Metaframe had lit her sword, rendering it potent against the invaders. There was a way to win – she just needed to secure it. But was the Metaframe responsible for the flames on her sword? She could not deny her perfect memory. One of the gods within the machine had sported flames identical to those that engulfed her sword to such devastating effect. It had wrestled with another for a moment at the end, one shadowy and dark. Did she have a patron and an adversary within the Metaframe? If so, on what basis would the patronage continue?

She looked down at Angelina who was now stroking and calming the pup, and regarded her thoughtfully. After all, who would be more important to the gods in the Metaframe, a gifted warrior or a young goddess who could shape reality at will? Chloe sniffed sardonically. The gods of the Metaframe had gifted her the flames because she was the only one standing between the creatures of the portal and Angelina.

Chloe's lips curled into a half-smile. No, she was not so important after all. She reached out into the night, searching with her vampire senses. Aircraft engines murmured in the night. She turned to the west. A squadron of long-range P51 Mustangs flanked a lone DC-3 transport. All were bare specks in the far distance. Chloe lifted her gaze; a second squadron was flying top cover thousands of feet above the DC-3. She studied the approaching transport, it had to be Crane. He'd come for his prize. How did he know she would be here now? The planes had left their airfields before the battle had started – it remained a troubling mystery.

She pursed her lips and wondered if Angelina would be better off with the Vampire Dominion as opposed to either of the other factions. The aircraft drew closer, the DC-3 banking through a broad arc to line up on the airstrip, while the fighters peeled away into a pair of contra-rotating circles above the mountain. The DC-3 transport landed at the far end of the clearing, braking hard as it raced along the narrow strip of tarmac. Darkness shrouded the airstrip. The pilots would be vampires, able to land without lights. The aircraft turned through a tight circle and pulled to a halt forty yards away. Its engines slowing to a dull, throbbing idle. A hatch halfway between the wing and the tail swung wide, a strip of interior light cutting away the shadows of the approaching night. Crane leaped forth, flanked by two of his praetorians, the near-giant Spengler, and the blond axe-wielding Calley.

Crane strode forward, off the tarmac and across the damp sward. His bodyguards spread to the left and right, scanning the tree line for threats. His gaze focused on Angelina for a long moment before locking on Chloe. He closed to an easy half dozen feet from the child and her, and remarked with approval, "I see your mission is complete. You have done well."

Chloe arched an eyebrow. "You think so? ... We just stopped an alien invasion."

Crane tilted his head slightly, and nodded once. "Indeed, I saw the lights of a grand Metaframe summoning. How did the aliens access our realm?"

"Through a portal."

Angelina piped up, "I was tricked."

"Really – you were tricked, were you?" Crane asked rhetorically, staring down at Angelina, a grim smile playing around the edges of his mouth. His chest lifted as he took a long breath. He nodded a couple of times in silence. His left hand rose and stroked his chin. His dark-brown eyes looked into the distance without focus, and he stated in a soft voice, "And this is why the Metaframe should never be used."

Chloe didn't like the direction Crane's mood was moving in. The air was heavy with implied threat. "Angelina saved us all."

Crane raised an eyebrow. "On a first name basis, are we?"

Chloe frowned.

He sniffed derisively. "Yes, indeed she did save us." His eyes narrowed a fraction and he murmured, "She is very powerful."

Chloe breathed out; the mountain top rested in a moment of silence.

Crane took a step forward toward Angelina. She stared up at him, towering above her and opened her mouth to speak.

Chloe's hand flew instinctively to the handle of the Red Dragon.

Crane's sword blurred from its scabbard, appearing an instant later embedded through Angelina's fragile body. Without hesitation, he drew the heavy blade out through the side of her chest, cutting through her heart, spine and lungs.

Chloe blurred forward – an instant too late.

Angelina slumped to the damp grass in a spreading pool of blood, the pup yelping hysterically beside her.

Chloe knelt next to her, lifting Angelina into her arms. She had to save her. She'd promised. She ripped at her left wrist with her fangs, her vampire blood splashing free. If she was fast enough, perhaps she could still save her life, perhaps there was a chance. She pressed her forearm against the gaping wound.

Crane's left hand snapped around her wrist, trapping her blood in his iron grip. He drew her arm up with an iron strength beyond her own and commanded in fell tones, "No one will create a child vampire."

"What have you done?" Chloe demanded, staring up at Crane, her eyes wide.

Crane flung her bodily through the air, whirled toward her and shouted, "What I must."

Chloe rebounded to her feet from the tarmac, striding forward, her face pale with fury. "I have failed my oath."

"You swore an oath to her?" Crane snapped incredulously.

"I had to win her trust. She trusted me," Chloe testified, she looked down at Angelina's dead body. The child's still eyes stared back blankly. A sharp stab of self-accusation pierced Chloe's heart. She seethed, uttering through clenched teeth, "She didn't need to die."

Crane shrugged, spreading his right hand wide toward Angelina's corpse. "I see why you gave your oath, and for the best too. But still, trust is a fragile thing, easily broken. How long do you think it would be before her Red Empire heritage came to the fore and she saw only a hated and feared vampire rather than a protector? And then what? You could find yourself eliminated from existence in a moment. We must not entrust such power to a child, and far less to the adult she would've grown into."

Chloe put her face in her hands for a moment. She couldn't stand to look at him. It was too much. She'd never wanted to kill anyone as much as she wanted to kill Crane – and yet, caught within the web of Allemande's curse, she could not.

Crane stepped forward, placing a firm hand on Chloe's right shoulder. She flinched and pulled away. "Really, Chloe," he stated derisively. "I never imagined you'd be this naive."

Chloe closed her eyes for a long moment. Breathing slowly. She opened them. Crane was still studying her, secure in the knowledge Allemande's curse prevented her from attacking him. Spengler and Calley watched her, open sneers on both their faces. They were Crane's men through and through. They had no time for her and she none for them. She took a step back, and waved a tired hand at the DC-3. "I presume you are finished here."

"Indeed, I am," Crane replied. "Of course, there is still the matter of General Dieter Franz."

Chloe nodded; her eyes hard.

"I expect him back alive for punishment. Is that clear?"

"Crystal," Chloe ground out through clenched teeth.

Crane paused for a moment, before nodding once. He signaled his praetorians with a wave and made his way back onto the transport. Thirty seconds later he was in the air and winging his way back to London.

Chloe clenched her hands into hard fists, raised them up, turned her face up to the sky and screamed. She dragged in a breath and screamed again, longer and louder than the first. She staggered, dropping to her knees with a moan. She stretched out her fingers and dug them into the ground. She pulled them back, raking a pair of long furrows. She frowned, her eyes dark and hard. She attacked the ground, tearing it apart with her bare hands. A handful of minutes later she rose and crouched beside a shallow grave.

She panted for a long moment and sighed. The German shepherd pup was still crying next to Angelina's corpse. Chloe reached down and picked up the young dog. She remembered the dog attacking the officer's ankle. The pup had shown courage and loyalty under duress and deserved a reward. She whispered, "I'll find you a good home."

She looked back at Angelina's broken corpse. Saving the dog was the last thing she could do for the child. She put the pup back down onto the sward and knelt next to Angelina's body. With tender care, she lifted her up and placed her gently into the grave. She rose, retrieving the pup who'd leaped into the grave after the child. She swept the raw earth back into the grave with her hands until at the last, she patted and smoothed it down.

She rose to her feet, left the peak of the Feldberg, and hoped never to return. One thought kept returning to her mind as she made her way through the night, with the little pup sleeping in the crook of her elbow. *One day I will be free again.*

* * *

The battle was over.

The prototype ejection seat on the escape pod had worked perfectly. Heinrich dropped toward an open grassy field on the outskirts of Freiburg im Breisgau. He'd watched the battle on the mountain peak from afar as he descended gently beneath his parachute. The vampire bitch and the gifted child had defeated the fiends from the portal.

Siegfried's experiment had gone disastrously wrong. His promises were nothing more than a mad-man's delusion. Who could know if Set even existed?

Heinrich sniffed and sneered sourly, at least he was still alive. An important silver lining to the catastrophic ending of a plan twenty-six years in the making. He frowned, considering his remaining options. He could make good his escape and live to fight another day. He could move into the shadows of the world and foment a true Fourth Reich, one that would succeed where the previous doomed attempt had failed. The next time, there would be no need for tanks and armies. The one-party state would overtake all else through the stealthy means of finance, politics and propaganda. The effort might take another seventy or eighty years, but with the benefit of the Ramp he could live long enough to see the fruits of his labors realized in full.

It was a purpose worthy of a true Übermensch and in the end if would leave a lasting legacy for his name. If immortal divinity was no longer on offer, then mortal fame would have to do. The ground rose to meet him. Heinrich ramped, unclipped himself from the ejection seat, leaped clear at the last moment, and landed easily in a crouch. He rose and scanned his surroundings. The silk parachute fell away, lying listlessly on the sward. In the near distance a cow mooed in surprise. There was barely a breath of wind. He glanced upward; the storm vortex had vanished. An enigma he'd witnessed upon spearing out of the underground silo. He concluded it was an artifact of Siegfried's occult science. No doubt, he'd never see its eldritch like again.

Heinrich checked the backpack supplied with the ejection seat. It bulged with valuable and useful items; gold coins, a pouch of cut diamonds, the codes to a Swiss vault filled with a lifetime of plundered treasures, fake identity papers, a subtle disguise, non-descript civilian clothes, a 9mm automatic of American make with a pair of spare clips, maps, a carton of Dutch cigarettes, three days of pre-packed food, two books of matches, *and a partridge in a fucking pear tree.*

He noted sourly, some imbecile had inserted a rare signed hardback copy of 'Mein Kampf,' in the backpack. Presumably to assist with his ideological edification. He tossed the useless book aside; it was dead weight. He debated for a moment the wisdom of swapping out of his uniform and adopting the disguise, but given southern Germany was still in Nazi hands, his uniform and rank still had value. He judged the rest of the backpack contents to be appropriate. They were enough to get to Switzerland and escape the continent. Argentina was apparently quite pleasant at this time of year. He would be able to live like a king while he rebuilt his plans and a new world-wide organization.

His immediate need was to find transport. He started walking toward the low lights of Freiburg. Perhaps he could requisition transport or at worst steal a car. He'd only traveled a dozen yards when someone emerged from the gloom in front of him. A man of medium height, wearing a long black coat, and a black beret. He swished the edges of the coat aside, revealing a long katana in an ancient oriental scabbard, belted at his waist. A 9mm Sten gun appeared in his other hand. The submachine gun's barrel was pointing with perfect stillness at the center of Heinrich's chest. The man inquired in English with a substantial French accent, "What have we here?"

The Order of Thoth, Heinrich thought furiously. No one else would be carrying a katana in this time and place. He turned and fled toward the forest. More forms emerged from the darkness and converged on him. He tried to blur between them. Someone tackled him from the side throwing him down onto the grass. He landed face first in a warm pool of cow manure. The stinking muck splashing left and right. He gagged miserably on the dark-green filth, attempting to push himself away from the noisome mess.

Powerful bodies held him still. He tried to break free, but hard hands tightened upon his arms and dragged him upright.

The fiends held him fast, green filth dripping off his face. He shouted, "I'm no one."

"Lies! You're Heinrich Himmler!" the first man said, "and clearly a Ramp master as we have long suspected."

"How will we deal with him?" asked a dark-haired accomplice near the first man's left shoulder. The wight wrinkled his nose in disgust. "Should we consider a bath first?"

"Deal with me! Deal with—" Heinrich snapped angrily, apoplectic with the indignity of being held against his will. No one had done such a thing for decades. He tried to lift his hands to wipe the bovine manure from his face, but he could barely move much of anything.

"Cyanide pills are their favored form of escape," interrupted a third man, speaking over him.

The first man blurred forward, grasping Heinrich's jaw with iron strength. He forced his fingers in, scraping Heinrich's teeth, looking for a hollow tooth filled with a vial of cyanide. He wiped his fingers upon Heinrich's shirt and stepped away empty handed. He wrinkled his nose in disgust and remarked, "I think you'll regret not having one of those installed."

Heinrich tried to rub his aching jaw but still couldn't free a hand to do so. The Order of Thoth Ramp masters held him with grips like steel traps. He spat out, "Who are you?"

The first man stepped back a half-dozen feet and raised an eyebrow. "I'll give you that, my name is Dubois. Know this, you horrific scum; the elite of the French resistance have captured you. Whatever form tyranny takes, whether fostered by man or vampire. We will fight it."

Heinrich sneered dismissively and declared, "I'll give you nothing."

"Not even for a bath?" suggested the man holding his right arm.

Heinrich snarled, speechless with rage.

One of his captors observed incredulously. "He really didn't think he could get caught."

"A fatal conceit," Dubois acknowledged. He nodded and commanded, "We'll pump him of everything he knows and then hand him over to the allies. Yes, British intelligence will do for the cover-up and will see this piece of merde finished for good. We need to keep the Order's part in this action secret."

"He'll be a mess by the time we finish with him," a fourth man remarked with a malevolent grin.

A fifth man asked, "How long will we keep him?"

Dubois remarked without looking away from Heinrich's face, "Six or seven weeks should be enough to drain this beast dry. Now gag this animal. I don't want to listen to his whining until we get him to the farm house."

Heinrich gasped a stinking breath of air to protest, but his nearest captor filled his mouth with thick cloth before he could speak. The rag had rubbed across his chin before passing his lips. The pungent taste of cow shit filled his throat. One of his captors knotted the gag behind his head and gave him a hard slap behind his ears fit to rattle his teeth. Another two held his arms with hands like iron. A moment later they dragged him forward. He stumbled, then began walking to avoid the final ignominy of hanging on the arms of these Order of Thoth fiends.

Stinking manure covered him and he was a captive of an Order of Thoth force team.

He'd lost everything except his life.

There was still hope.

* * *

Himmler Commits Suicide

Heinrich Himmler Kills Himself in British Prison.

London, May 24 (U.P.) — Heinrich Himmler, number one Nazi war criminal, killed himself in a British military prison at Luneburg last night, boasting that he was the dreaded hangman hunted for more than two weeks by three allied armies.

– Excerpt of The Bend Bulletin, Central Oregon's Daily Newspaper, Thursday, May 24 1945. Shadowstone archives, New York City.

"Senior members of Shadowstone have allowed rogue elements to hijack our initiative to develop a super-soldier serum in southern Germany. A lapse that led to a breach of our reality through misuse of the Metaframe. We have purged the relevant miscreants from our organization or seen them eliminated by others. However, a troubling question remains – how to ensure an appropriate level of awareness in those left behind without revealing the secret of vampire existence?" – Cornelius Crane's personal diary [1945].

"In accordance with the strategy of fomenting low to medium level wars, proxy wars, and wars by non-state actors we will establish a new initiative named 'The Cold War.' We will manage this new initiative with the newly promoted top echelon of Shadowstone within Washington, Moscow, Zurich, and London. Once the current chaos in China has returned to a state of appropriate control, we will add Beijing." – Cornelius Crane, King of the Vampire Dominion at the Conference of Generals, New York, 1946.

Dramatis Personae

The Ancients

Ahknaton, Ruler of the Southern Realm, High Priest of the Temple of Thoth. Master Architect. Ramp Master.
Hakron, Second prince of the Southern Realm. Master Scribe. Ramp Master. Ahknaton's brother
Mekra, Princess, Ahknaton's wife.

The Vampire Dominion

Cornelius Crane, King of the Vampire Dominion
Chloe Armitage, General, The Americas, ex Order of Thoth and Crane's chief enforcer
Haras Mosule, General, Middle East, ex Red Empire warrior of the 3rd rank
Dieter Franz, General, Western Europe
Shen Zhen, General, East Asia

The Exiles

Arthur Slayne, (Exiled) Master Strategist, Force Leader, Weapons Grandmaster, Speed Talent
Jon Thunder-Axe, Metaframe Sorcerer.
Dwayne Washington, Order Helper

The Mirovar Force Team

Jay Creeley, Operative, Weapons Master
Peter Lamb, Operative, Armorer, Strength Talent
Chiara Romano, Operative, Combat Surgeon
Anton Slayne, Order novice
Li Wu, Order novice, Weapons Master

The Blake Force Team

Justin Blake, Force Leader (South West) Weapons Master, Strength talent. Former student of Gang Wu

The Red Empire

Shabbah al Ahmar, aka 'The Red Ghost,' aka Dalien Morte. Head of the Red Empire

Thueban Kabir, aka 'The Great Serpent,' aka 'Taipan,' Weapons Grandmaster, warrior of the 3rd rank

Tamsah al Ramil, aka 'The Sand Crocodile,' Fist team leader, warrior of the 2nd rank

Whispering Death, Fist team leader, warrior of the 1st rank, speed talent

Keen-As-A-Knife, Junior Gate Guard

Shadowstone

James Haley, Chloe Armitage's aide de camp
Louise Wesson, Head of Operations
Architect, AI specialist, East Coast Hub
Siobhan Ulysses, Operative, Panopticon Fortress
Charles Archer, Squad Leader, Day Guard

Other Players

Akimitsu, Mekrarian vampire

Gullette, Chameleon, Call of Command
Shemina, Chameleon, Female.

Hana Tanaka, Scientist

Chapter One

"What you ardently seek to avoid, you shall bring forth." – The Way of the Faithful, a book of Red Empire Lore.

* * *

Arizona, Phoenix, Jon Thunder-Axe's residence, September 12th, 01:02

A fist hammered on Jon Thunder-Axe's front door.

Jon jerked awake. The luminescent green dial of the clock on the bed stand read, '01:02.' It took a second or two to orientate himself. The door knocker repeated their effort, thumping on his front door for a second time. Jon wanted to make sure it didn't happen for a third time; he called out, "Okay! Okay! I'm coming! Alright? Hold your horses!"

He swung his feet out of bed and onto his polished wooden floor. He was a bit fuzzy; he'd been asleep for less than an hour. He'd been hoping for news of the events at Arthur's airport, but not a lot had come through and he'd decided to get some rest rather than stay up all night fretting about something he couldn't change. He flicked on a bed-side table lamp, spotted his slippers and slotted his feet into them. A moment or two later and he'd pulled his favorite dressing gown on. Thus clothed, he walked from the bedroom to the front of the house. He glanced at a flat-screen on the hallway wall, it ran half a dozen feeds from multiple cameras outside the house on an isolated network, including a view of who was standing on his porch. He recognized a familiar face. Jon strode to the front door, tightening his gown's sash around his comfortable waistline. It seemed events were playing out as Arthur had predicted. A familiar voice called through the door, "Jon, it's Dwayne."

"Yeah, I know," Jon said, unlocking and opening the door.

Dwayne Washington stamped his boots on the door mat and stepped over the threshold. He was carrying a silvery armored case covered in green Faraday tape, which he put down on the floor. He embraced Jon in a hug and stepped back. He shook his head and stated with a wide-eyed stare, "The shit has hit the fan! I've lost contact with Arthur!"

Jon quickly scanned the street past Dwayne's left shoulder. There was an insect-splattered black Kawasaki motorcycle parked in his driveway, but there was nothing else of note in the quiet suburban cul-de-sac. He guided Dwayne past him with a wave of his hand, closed and locked the door. He turned and said, "The last I heard there was a battle at Arthur's airport north-east of Las Vegas. The network went dark at quarter past eight. I don't know what happened after that. The main-stream news reported a toxic-industrial spill at a private airport in Nevada. The state authorities declared the whole site a public health hazard. They have cordoned the site off and are not allowing anyone in until they have assessed 'the risk.' I figure the vampire death count was extreme and Crane needs time to clear the bodies. He'll get some vampires in over the next forty-eight hours and toss the bodies out onto the ground. The evidence will disappear a minute after sunrise."

"Could be," Dwayne agreed. "I'm just as much in the dark as anyone else. I've been riding hard for over eight hours. I don't know what the hell is going on."

Jon looked down at the case and lifted a quizzical eyebrow. "Is that what I think it is?"

"Yep." Dwayne nodded.

"Look, before we start, what do you need? Something to eat? Something to drink? Water? Coffee?" Jon waved a hand at his drinks cabinet on the side of the entry foyer and said, "Something stronger?"

Dwayne looked at the cabinet and snorted in a 'what-the-hell,' manner. "Sure," he agreed. "What have you got?"

"Well, I like to drink local," Jon said with a raised eyebrow. He opened the cabinet and pulled out a bottle filled with a dark spirit. "Copper City Bourbon." He lifted a pair of glasses with his other hand and asked, "Would you like to try it?"

Dwayne nodded. "Sure."

"Grab the P-Case and follow me," Jon said, heading down the hall and into his kitchen. He put the bottle down on an island bench and filled the glasses half full with ice blocks from his fridge door. He returned and filled the glasses with bourbon. He picked up the bottle, nodded at Dwayne, and led the way into his living room opposite the kitchen where he took a seat on a broad low couch. Dwayne took a seat in a recliner opposite, a low coffee table resting between them. Dwayne placed the silvery P-Case next to him on the polished wooden floor.

Jon placed the bottle of bourbon on the coffee table. He lifted his glass in a silent salute, and sipped from it. Dwayne took a long slug from his glass and quickly followed with a second drink. He put the half-empty glass down on a coaster on the edge of the coffee table and asked, "What instructions did Arthur leave with you?"

"He gave me an envelope eighteen years ago with a directive to open it in the event the Panopticon fortress was destroyed. Needless to say, I opened it a couple of hours ago."

"What did it contain?"

Jon reached into a deep pocket on his dressing gown and retrieved a faded standard letter envelope. He lifted it up and said, "This." He turned it over and read aloud the writing on the outside. "If Dwayne arrives at your door with the Panopticon in a P-Case, open this envelope." He looked at Dwayne for a second and tore the envelope open. A letter was inside. He unfolded it and read the letter to Dwayne. "'My old friends, if you are reading this, then at least part of my plan has been successful. We have captured the Panopticon, destroyed the fortress protecting it, and Dwayne has delivered it to your door. If my plan has been fully successful, then Crane and Armitage are dead by my hand, but I will have perished with them.'"

Jon paused for a long moment, his eyes widened with shock, his right hand flying to his open mouth.

Dwayne swore, "Damn. ... It can't be true ... can it?"

Jon blinked several times, his heart freezing with dread. He continued, enunciating each word carefully to avoid breaking down. "'My death will have been a necessary sacrifice to close the trap around our most dire opponents. With luck, the Mirovar force team will have survived and can participate in the mopping up operations against the remaining vampires along with the rest of the Order. That said, the Red Empire will perform the bulk of the work. Reach out to the Red Ghost at Matahat and spread the word on the locations of the vampires. That, of course is the first order of business. Use the Panopticon on the supplied rig and determine the location of every blood sucker on the face of the Earth. Get that information to those who can swing a blade. We'll have a day or two of 'long knives,' and the scourge of vampires will be behind us.'

'Of course, please give my love to William, Anna and Anton. You can tell them the truth now. It will all be a shock for the young fellow. He will most likely be grown up by now and hopefully knows nothing about our world.'

'One last note, if Armitage and Crane are still alive, then I have failed. In that event, stick with the plan and notify the Red Empire, perhaps we can still salvage victory from the ashes of my defeat.'

'Fare well, my friends. I couldn't have done it without you. It has always been an honor; kind regards and all that. And get a decent scotch for my wake.'

'Your friend,'

'Arthur Slayne.'"

Dwayne closed his eyes for a long moment, sighed and slugged half his remaining bourbon.

Jon shook his head slowly in disbelief, rereading the letter in silence as if that might change its message. He lifted his face from the faded page and asked, "Do you know what happened to him?"

Dwayne shook his head.

"Not even a hint?"

"Nothing," Dwayne answered. "He's vanished into thin air. He could be amongst the dead at the airport."

"This is crap," Jon uttered, his eyes hard with pain. He stared wide-eyed at Dwayne for a long moment. He clenched his jaw, and swallowed his grief. They had to absorb their losses. They had to keep moving forward against the vampires. But first, they needed to acknowledge other sacrifices made in Utah and Nevada. "Speaking of the dead."

"What?"

"I figure Francis is gone as there was no chatter from him, and Jay was leading the Mirovar force team into the airport."

Dwayne nodded.

"He'll be missed, as will most of the Blake force team."

Dwayne gasped. "Holy shit!"

Jon frowned. "Only Justin survived. He's in surgery at UMC in Las Vegas. We have a helper on site, one of the A&E doctors. I heard the news from her. She's keeping an eye on the situation. He'll have a 'miraculous,' recovery and check out in a day or two. The paperwork will show his injuries were much less severe than they first appeared. I've notified his cousins in New Zealand about what's happening, plus Anita Chang in Australia and Ahmad Bakhoum in Egypt. Justin reported, Crane and Armitage escaped. Crane killed the Blake force team by bombardment from his command drone."

"Did Arthur die or did he survive?"

Jon looked hard at Dwayne and said, "I think we can spend some time using the Panopticon to answer that question along with discovering where all the vampires are."

Dwayne nodded, a hopeful smile on his face. "If he's still alive, we'll find him."

Jon raised an eyebrow. "Our new first order of business?"

"Absolutely. So, what's next?" Dwayne asked.

"We follow Arthur's instructions and fire up the Panopticon."

"When?"

"I'll set the alarm for four am. We both need to get at least a couple of hours sleep; it will be a long day tomorrow."

Dwayne nodded. He looked spent; he'd been running on adrenaline for the last twenty-four hours.

Jon said, "I've got a spare room. There's a bathroom down the hall with towels and everything else you might need. There's a wardrobe in the bedroom with lots of clothes. You'll find something that will fit you. I get guests in all shapes and sizes."

"Anything to eat?"

"I'll fix you a couple of toasted sandwiches." Jon studied the Panopticon P-Case sitting next to Dwayne for a long moment. He looked into his friend's face and said, "But before we hit the sack, I think you need to summarize for me everything you know about the last twenty-four hours."

Dwayne rose and refreshed his drink from the bottle on the table and swished the bourbon around the ice at the bottom of his glass. He took another slug, followed Jon into the kitchen, and sat down at the island bench and began to talk.

Jon listened in silence as he prepared a late-night snack for his friend.

* * *

She'd separated the goats from the flock.

Louise Wesson, worldwide head of Shadowstone, and nominally, the chief defender of the secret of vampire existence, scanned the operatives she'd placed to one side of the Salt Lake City airport hangar. She hesitated in the face of an irreversible decision.

She silently reviewed the last eleven hours of near insane levels of activity. She'd received her current orders yesterday in Fort Dix at 18:20 from Crane via Armitage. She'd scrambled what forces she could, including the last two of her remaining Day Guard squads in a brand-new osprey II drone, and flown directly from Fort Dix to Salt Lake City airport.

Her osprey drone had landed seven and a half hours earlier at 20:00 Utah (8 pm) local time on the eleventh. By then, the local Shadowstone Gold-1 spectrum team designated to the territory surrounding the Panopticon fortress, and a squad of four operatives from the PSYOPS division out of Seattle had taken over the airport. They'd placed an armed perimeter around a large hangar on the north-east corner owned by a Shadowstone proxy company, and collected all the fortress staff into the one location for debriefing.

The Shadowstone staff had done their job well and by the book. The PSYOPS team was already providing news reports to the main media outlets, casting the destruction of the Panopticon fortress as a tragic geological accident at a high-value 'clean-tech,' geophysics research facility. The news narratives emphasized the horrific loss of life – everyone who worked at the fortress had officially died. However, forty-six survivors still breathed; under normal protocols they would be rebadged with new identities and moved on within the Shadowstone organization – but Crane's orders had been explicit. 'Use your day guards to eliminate all the survivors, and the Gold-1 spectrum team and PSYOPS operatives.'

The survivors knew vampires were real, and no one could know how many of the PSYOPS and Gold-1 spectrum team members would believe their reports. She had to execute all of them. She had to destroy any knowledge of the existence of vampires, of their rule of the world, and cover up all traces of her protection of Crane's secrets.

Louise wondered for a brief moment how many other incumbents at the top level of Shadowstone had known the truth and simply kept their silence.

Probably most of them, she answered. After all, no one got to her level without real capability. They must have known and simply gone along with the vampire's agenda. Every one of her predecessors was guilty of betraying humanity to the predators and parasites ruling them. If they hadn't known, in an act of willful ignorance, they were just as culpable – there were no excuses for betrayal. She reflected briefly on James Haley, her immediate predecessor and now aide-de-camp for general Chloe Armitage. He must know by now what was really going on. He'd remained silent. He was as guilty as the rest of them. He'd been enabling the rule of the vampires for years. She suspected he'd been one of the few who had naively believed in the noble mission. Haley believed he was fighting for the greater good. An attachment, that if he was in the hangar with her this morning, would put him in with the goats. There could be no greater good from allowing vampires to rule humanity. Whatever argument had convinced Haley would be a self-serving lie of the parasitic predators that now ruled where once a free and proud republic had stood.

Certainly, she would accept no excuses for herself. She secretly knew the truth of Crane's intentions. Even her day guards were to remain ignorant; oblivious weapons executing the will of Crane to keep his precious secrets hidden from the world. But did she need to obey Crane's latest orders? Did she need to keep Crane's secrets? Could she keep them? Was it even possible anymore? The world of the vampires was falling apart. She took a soft breath and considered recent events. When Crane had appointed her to her new role less than twenty-four hours prior, he'd set her three objectives. Rebuild the secret research facility number thirty-four in Brazil and restart the Day Guard serum production lines. Accelerate the East Coast Hub and the commissioning of the new Panopticon, and integrate the Shadowstone and Day Guard organizations into a single weapon under her command. Clearly, Crane didn't think a mere human could be a threat to his rule or he'd never have delegated so much authority into her hands.

The implication was clear, Crane would kill her on a whim if she failed to deliver on his commands. He could kill her; he could drain every last drop of her blood and she'd be helpless against him. He could make her body disappear and make up a believable story about her disappearance. She knew Crane could do all these things without effort or risk.

However, Louise could deliver to the letter on Crane's objectives while subverting their intent. During the flight from Fort Dix to Salt Lake City she'd discovered a shipment of five hundred doses of Day Guard serum was sitting in a locked box within a small warehouse at the ruins of the Brazilian research facility. Satellite photographs revealed the warehouse was untouched by the destruction of the main buildings. Logistics reports indicated the existence of the vials and their current location. She could access another five hundred doses within a day or two and build another two hundred and fifty day guards within a week. This time, she would inform the special forces candidates of the risk of dying. She'd only accept volunteers, and discontinue the deployment of the TEF-4 neurotoxin implants. This time the day guards would know who the real enemy was and what they were really fighting for – the future of humanity versus the ongoing rule of the vampires. By insisting on fully-informed volunteers who had knowingly risked their lives, she could ensure a totally loyal cadre of Day Guard troopers. She could forge a force of men and women who'd proven their willingness to put their lives on the line for the cause of freeing humanity from the parasitic predators who ruled them from the shadows.

Furthermore, there was a sizable contingent of Phase IVs in the United Kingdom. They were already marshaling at Gatwick airport for transport to Fort Dix. There was a good chance they would have an improved survival rate when dosed with the serum compared with regular soldiers. She would provide them with the same knowledge and choices. The eighty plus soldiers who'd survived the engagement with the Order at the village of Ogton in Yorkshire would make for a rapid expansion of the ranks.

Louise had to make use of every available resource if she was going to have a chance of freeing humanity of the scourge of the vampires. She blinked and paused, breathing quietly, reflecting deeply on what she needed to do. She'd spent most of the last decade as a state-sponsored assassin. A living weapon, a killer without remorse, but she'd never been a murderer. She'd only taken lives that needed taking to protect the many from the few, or so, she'd believed.

She studied the staff she'd separated out in the last seven hours of intensive interviews. She'd called upon every skill and nuance of her spy-hunter repertoire to identify those who were most likely to kneel before the vampires rather than fight them.

She studied those who had failed to pass her examination. Fourteen men and women, a mix of command-and-control staff from the Panopticon fortress, half the operatives of the Gold-1 spectrum team, two of the PSYOPS, and a lone machinist. They all shared a willingness to accept any order from an authority figure, an inability to exercise critical, independent thought, and a belief that the end justified the means. The force Louise was forging demanded better. The war against the vampires demanded better. She needed a force she could trust.

She allowed herself to rub the bridge of her nose in a rare display of fatigue. She'd been awake for more than twenty-five hours and she could feel the initial effects of sleep deprivation. She'd carried the load by herself. There was too much to do and no one else she could trust to do it. Not yet at least, however there was one new candidate in the warehouse who'd already revealed her potential. Siobhan Ulysses, a young officer who'd demonstrated a cool head under chaotic conditions, and by many reports had personally assisted in the destruction of the vampire general, Clayton Maze. Louise expected her to be a strong contributor within her force, or she was no judge of character. She would have to tap appropriate subordinates on the shoulder soon and elevate them to assist her. If she couldn't delegate effectively and grow her organization, she'd doom her war against the vampires before it started.

Louise glanced at a clock on the hangar wall. It read '03:32,' in local Utah time. She didn't really need to know the time. She was procrastinating in the face of the most fateful decision of her life. She took another breath; a sardonic half-grin curled the edges of her mouth. She knew what she had to do. It was time to strike. It was time to risk revealing her hand to the vampires.

Her half-grin vanished. Her eyes flashed with resolve. She lifted her 9mm submachine gun and declared to all her staff, "I'll never ask anyone here to do something I wouldn't do myself." She waved her FN P90 in a sharp arc over the group of fourteen separated staff. The gun spat flame, a plume of gray smoke issuing from the barrel. The targeted men and women screamed and yelled, flinching backward or twisting away, high-impact rounds thudding into flesh and bone, cutting them down where they stood. She swept the gun back again, her finger hard on the trigger. Those still standing, jerked and stumbled, shouted and shrieked, joining the ranks of the fallen. They slumped to the floor, clutching at bloody wounds with claw-like hands. Louise stepped forward; sending a long second burst into the writhing mass until her weapon clicked on empty.

Louise surveyed the stillness. She stared with hard eyes at the spreading pools of blood on the pale concrete of the hangar floor. A thin wisp of gray smoke rose from the mouth of her submachine gun. She took a deep breath and let it out.

There'd be no traitors in her ranks.

* * *

What would the Vampire Dominion do with the Panopticon fortress survivors?

It was a question that had bedeviled Jay Creeley on his near all-night ride from Slayne's airport. With the Panopticon down, he'd risked the ride straight up Interstate 15 to Salt Lake City. For long stretches he'd pushed the bike hard, exceeding the speed-limit to reach Salt Lake City before the window of opportunity to make contact with the survivors closed. The survivors knew vampires existed. There must be people amongst them who were willing to fight back against the vampires now the truth was known. They were insiders with intimate knowledge of how the Vampire Dominion operated. He could forge a fruitful alliance if enough of the Shadowstone operatives joined his fight against a common enemy. He had an idea, a crazy idea swirling around in his head. If his idea worked, the Day Guard would become competitive with the vampires as a fighting force.

He just needed to find someone who would listen to what he had to say instead of trying to kill him on sight. There was no doubt Shadowstone would know who he was after the debacle at the Panopticon fortress. Everyone in the Mirovar force team had spent time in a prison within the vampire facility. Shadowstone would have taken DNA swabs when they were unconscious, and multiple full-face photographs and video. They knew who he was and he'd never be able to hide anywhere a camera watched for the foreseeable future. Li had revealed in the parking lot behind the roadhouse opposite Slayne's airport that the mission was a bust. A brand-new Panopticon would be in place within a month. Once it was online, he'd be a marked man.

Arthur Slayne had led them into a disaster that'd got Francis killed and the Blake force team all but annihilated. Jay reflected briefly upon the Blake force team. Samuel Taylor could have been the next head of the Order; with his life-partner Taylor Feury they'd been the 'Two Taylors,' a devastatingly effective combat team. Jay had slipped down from Seattle to Los Angeles from time to time as a late teenager to train with them. They were the reason he was a recognized weapons master before he'd moved to the Mirovar force team. As for Tim Leung, Max Guerra, Red Cevarre, and Patrick Wichowski they were all comrades in arms he'd shared time with before his move to the North-East. He scowled, each and every one of them was a victim of Arthur Slayne's hubris.

Jay seethed for a moment, then took a pair of deep breaths to calm himself down. He needed to put his rage aside. The Slaynes had proved to be everything he'd feared they would be. Harbingers of doom and destruction. Six months ago, the Order of Thoth had been a fully functional organization of nearly a hundred Ramp masters with a storied five-thousand-year plus history. The appearance of Anton Slayne had presaged its destruction and Arthur Slayne had driven the final nails into the coffin of the Order with his ill-fated mission against the Panopticon fortress. There was a single operational force team left, commanded by Ahmad Bakhoum in Egypt. Apart from Li Wu, the loremasters were gone. With no one to guard it, the history of the Order, it's ways and traditions would fall away. Within another generation, the Order of Thoth would be a footnote in history for those few who still remembered it. Jay's mission to co-opt Shadowstone remained his final hope, a Hail Mary in the face of the destruction of all he believed in.

As for the former members of the Mirovar force team, he'd always welcome Li to join him. He'd forgive Peter too, but Slayne and Morte were beyond the pale. A mortal wound sat between them and Jay, and only blood would suffice to heal it. Whatever path his life took, at some point in the future he would ensure Anton Slayne and Chiara Morte paid for their crimes with their hearts' blood. Nothing else could ever satisfy him.

Jay throttled the bike, dropping down through the gears to match the entrance into Salt Lake City international airport. His Order nightglasses remained operational and he'd picked up enough chatter to detect the arrival of three nightfalcons many hours before. They'd converged on a large hangar on the north-east corner of the airport complex. Clearly, Shadowstone would debrief their staff before doing anything else. He needed to find out who was in charge and which side they were really on.

Jay steered his motorcycle through the traffic barriers and toward the last hangar on the north-east corner of the site. Within the next five minutes he'd make contact with Shadowstone, not as an enemy but as a potential ally.

He hoped they would allow him to talk before they tried to kill him. This was his last roll of the dice. If he couldn't forge an alliance with a rebel Shadowstone force than he was out of options. He was a desperate man living in desperate times. He was committed to this final course. This was his last chance of fighting against the vampires. If it didn't work out, there was nothing left to do but wait for the vampires to use the new Panopticon to find him and kill him.

Jay rode toward the distant line of armored troopers; his stomach seething with fear and a desperate hope.

* * *

The bodies lay where they'd fallen.

Louise smiled with grim irony. She ran an organization which excelled at burying the dead. Now she needed a clean way to get rid of fourteen corpses without their employers, the vampires, finding out what had happened. If Crane, Armitage, or even Haley audited her actions, and she couldn't rule an audit out, her disobedience would get herself and all her loyal followers killed.

She had to ensure these fourteen deaths and the survival of the other staff remained hidden until she was ready to strike. She tapped the most able member of the Panopticon survivors to take charge of the mission. "Ms. Ulysses. I need you to take charge of the remaining Gold-1 spectrum and PSYOPS staff, and clean this hangar fit to convince the vampires and the general public nothing untoward has occurred here. You must complete this before dawn. Can you get it done?"

"Yes, Ma'am," the young officer replied with a crisp salute.

"Outstanding!" Louise nodded. The clean-up was in safe hands. She turned back to her laptop, staring at the screen without really seeing it. Her number one strategic issue remained; the capability gap between the vampires and the day guards. The vampires remained twice as fast, three times as strong, and healed wounds in minutes that would take her troops days – if they ever healed at all.

The only advantage she had was the augmented target and shoot capability of their new smart rifles. An advantage currently offline pending the operational deployment of the new Panopticon in mid-October, just over a month from now.

Killing the staff, she couldn't trust had opened a window of opportunity for her enemies to discover her. Her previous actions, such as enabling the discovery of the Panopticon fortress by Li Wu, had been almost completely passive in their covert nature. Now she'd shifted from passive to active; still covert, but more vulnerable to discovery. The clock was ticking. The risk of discovery was growing with every second of delay. A risk Louise had to accept. She'd cast the dice of fate, there was no going back – she had to find a solution to the capability gap as soon as possible.

Despite the risk weighing upon her soul, she had no regrets. She'd done what was right. She must defend the Republic, and she would defend it with the blood of her troops and her own blood to the very last drop.

The first order of business was to rebadge the surviving staff and insert them into the East Coast Hub. She would concentrate her force within the new beating heart of Crane's realm. A heart she would make her own. She would assign this first task to Ulysses. At the same time, she would lead the mission to Brazil to recover the five hundred doses of Day Guard serum. A mission she would start within an hour. Her osprey II drone was ready to fly again; refueled and restocked by Shadowstone affiliated ground staff. More osprey II drones were arriving at Fort Dix from the assembly lines to service the growing needs of the Day Guard. She would have another nine drones delivered within days. By then she'd have two hundred and fifty to three hundred day guards she could position anywhere in the world in a day. A potent strike force once the new Panopticon came online in four weeks' time.

Louise pressed her lips into a tight, thin line. Initiatives were in play to grow, position and equip her forces, but which did not address the one-to-one capability gap versus the vampires.

A red banner flashed across her laptop screen. An interloper had breached the perimeter around the hangar. Her Day Guard squad leader covering site security called in over the secured tactical link, "Ma'am. We have a visitor. He wants to talk."

Louise lifted her finger to her earbud and asked, "Who is he?"

"He won't say. He says he'll only talk to whoever is in charge."

Louise rubbed her forehead. *Who was this clown?* She ordered her squad leader, "Send him on his way."

"We already tried that. He disarmed Simpson, and Hicks, and he's got a gun pointing at my face."

Louise flicked a switch on her laptop, accepting an immediate video feed from the squad leader's helmet onto her laptop screen. He was staring at a serious looking young man with blue eyes, a shock of dirty-blond hair, holding a regulation 9mm side-arm pointing with lethal stillness a yard short of her trooper's face. The young man matched a set of photographs taken at the Panopticon fortress the day before and uploaded for general access onto the Shadowstone cloud.

She recognized him as fast as her laptop's facial recognition software generated the match. One of the 'most wanted,' members of the Order of Thoth, Jay Creeley was seemingly staring into her eyes. He spoke without moving the gun an inch off its line, "I'd rather not be pointing this at your man. I think we might be on the same side. I need to talk with whoever is in charge."

What an extraordinary opportunity, Louise thought. She tapped her earbud twice, opening a comms link through the squad leader's helmet. She said, "This is Louise Wesson, worldwide head of Shadowstone. Give back the gun Mr. Creeley and I will guarantee your safe passage. Come through and talk with me – it's time we met."

Creeley flipped the gun in an easy motion and handed it back to her squad leader. Creeley dropped back a couple of yards, mounted a black motorcycle and rode past her men. A subvocalized, 'Fuck!' made it over the tactical link as her men watched Creeley disappear into the hangar.

Louise rose up from the trestle table she was sitting at. Creeley cut between a pair of nightfalcons dominating the hangar floor. Guided by more of her men, he slowed, veering the bike toward her. They watched him warily, their fingers on the triggers of their weapons. She might have guaranteed his safety, but her men were watching him like hawks guarding a lone chick from an approaching fox. For the briefest of moments, she noted the shift in loyalty of her men. They had taken on the cause; they had bought into it. They believed. Their belief was alive in their actions.

She watched the approaching Order of Thoth operative with keen eyes. Creeley brought his motorcycle to a stop, unmounted and stepped away from it. He held his hands up at shoulder height. Two of her day guards approached him, another pair standing back a dozen feet, their rifles trained on his center of mass. The first pair searched him, patting him down for weapons. They searched the motorcycle next, separating out a katana in a dragon embossed white-enameled scabbard and a H&K MP7 submachine gun, placing them next to each other on the trestle table.

Creeley lifted his hands wide and said, "I'm unarmed. I'm at your mercy. The only reason I would do this is to make you an offer I'd stake my life on."

At my mercy? Louise understood fully the combat power of Jay Creeley. Even unarmed, he could probably escape if he wanted to, or even kill them all if he wished. Opportunity and risk, they so often occurred together. She studied him carefully. He didn't seem to possess knowledge of sympathetic and parasympathetic control. His physical reactions and cues were an open book to a long experienced ex-spy-catcher such as herself. The last thing she needed was a Trojan horse inserted into her growing organization. He seemed genuine. He seemed open and honest. If he could make a real difference with the Day Guard's capability, she'd be a fool not to hear him out. She raised a quizzical eyebrow and asked, "And your offer is?"

Creeley nodded and took a step forward. Her guards moved toward him, guns snapping up and ready to fire. He stepped back, a sheepish grin on his face. "Okay, okay. I'll tell you from over here." He paused for a moment. "Ever since I saw your new troops in action at the conclave battle in Minneapolis, I had an idea. I figure the system you are using to enhance your soldiers is a partial activation of Ramp epigenetics."

"Ramp epigenetics?"

"Basically, clusters of ancient genes that are normally switched off. If switched on, they rewire nerves, muscles, skin, blood and bone. There is a twenty to twenty-five percent cellular density gain, with uplifts of strength, speed, endurance, agility, reflexes, healing, etc."

Louise had studied the executive summaries from the research facility in Brazil and remarked, "We term it, 'System Zero epigenetic factors,' instead of Ramp epigenetics, but I think we're talking about the same thing." She stared hard at Creeley. "And your idea is?"

"There's a technique known to the Ramp masters of the Red Empire and the Order of Thoth. A pressure point technique for activating the Ramp epigenetics." Creeley glanced at her men surrounding him. "It's normally very dangerous to use. It kills more often than not, but if someone survives, they go on to develop the full Ramp capability over the next three months, and sometimes faster than that."

Louise's gut tightened with excitement. This could be the answer she was looking for. What would it mean for a soldier who had already passed through the Day Guard serum process to undergo the pressure point technique? She asked, "Can you demonstrate this?"

"Do you have a volunteer?"

Louise looked expectantly at her nearest squad leader. "Hunter?"

Hunter grinned sardonically and nodded. He looked at Creeley and asked, "What do I have to do?"

"Take off your body armor and clothes from the waist up. I need to access your chest."

Hunter moved to the front of the trestle table, one of the Shadowstone operatives from Gold-1 assisted him with the straps and locks on his body armor. He stripped down to the waist. His upper body rippled with hard muscle. His ebony skin almost gleamed beneath the overhead lights.

Creeley said to Louise, "I'll need to approach. I have to stand in front of him. It's a pressure point technique; I have to be able to touch him."

Hunter glanced once at Louise for a final confirmation. She nodded, lifted her hand and said, "Wait a moment. I want this filmed on multiple angles." She signaled one of her operatives, and called out, "Carlyle, three cameras please. I want what happens recorded in full." Carlyle nodded and got to work. Five minutes later, Creeley stood a yard opposite Hunter directly in front of Louise. A triangle of cameras with ultra-fast digital optics on tripods recording the pair of men. Carlyle examined one of the cameras and nodded toward Louise; the recording system was ready.

"Okay, Creeley," Louise said. "Show us what you've got."

Creeley glanced at her and gave a short nod. He addressed Hunter and offered with a shrug. "This could kill you."

"Get on with it," Hunter declared nonchalantly, but his eyes hardened with anticipation.

Creeley shaped the fore and middle fingers of his right hand into a stiff knife. He stared intently at Hunter for a brief moment as if steadying himself. His hand blurred over Hunter's torso in a tightly controlled sequence, striking him deeply more times than Louise's eyes could follow.

Hunter staggered backward, but kept his feet.

"Shit," Creeley whispered incredulously. His face frozen with surprise. He obviously expected something more dramatic to happen.

Hunter put his left hand to his throat for a moment, winced with pain, and then rubbed his chest with both hands. A dozen red welts rose across his torso.

Louise asked, "How do you feel?"

"I'm dying of thirst! ... And I'm starving!" Hunter exclaimed.

Creeley whistled, and remarked, "I'm surprised he's still on his feet."

"Stay where you are Hunter," Louise ordered. She signaled another operative, who brought over a pair of large water bottles and ration packs.

Hunter snatched the first bottle, opened it, lifted it, and kept drinking until it was empty. He tore open the ration pack and started eating with ravenous hunger. In between bites he grinned. The welts began fading. He finished the ration pack and opened the second water bottle. Just like the first, he drained it before placing the empty bottle on the trestle table. He looked at the operative who'd handed him the food and water and ordered urgently, "Get me the same again." The operative hurried away to obey.

Louise cocked her head and asked for a second time, "How do you feel?"

Hunter grinned at her and declared, "Like I could take on the fucking world, begging your pardon, Ma'am."

Louise nodded. She signaled Carlyle to cut the cameras and he switched them off. She looked across the trestle table at Creeley and asked, "So, you want to join us to fight the vampires?"

Creeley stared at her with steady blue eyes and declared, "Yes, Ma'am, that's why I'm here."

"Your first mission begins now. Get ready to fly. We leave in ten minutes at oh-four-hundred."

"And the mission?"

"Retrieve five-hundred doses of Day Guard serum from the ruins of a vampire research station in Brazil. You will form part of the security detail, and we'll complete your debrief on the flight."

Creeley nodded.

Louise regarded her newest recruit. Jay Creeley and the pressure point technique were a game changer. It was time to begin the next phase of her plan. It was time to rebuild the Day Guard into a force capable of fighting the vampires.

It was time to go to Brazil.

* * *

Cornelius' command shadowstar speared through the upper atmosphere.

Descending rapidly on jets of cobalt fire, the two-seat drone shed its tremendous velocity. Forty-five minutes earlier, the sun had curved past the western horizon leaving Japan in darkness. The islands lay like crumpled velvet thick with clustered diamonds upon the eastern pacific. Within minutes, he'd be on the ground in the middle of the secret fortress of the Obsidian Claw ninja clan. A clan annihilated by his own hand a mere eighteen nights before. A fateful night that had seen the birth of an abomination. The emergence of a new type of vampire. He knew the name of the creature who had escaped the fortress, 'Akimitsu.' The best of the ninja warriors he'd handpicked for elevation into the vampire ranks. His goal had been to establish a secret and stealthy force of implant-controlled vampires born with the strength of Mekra's blood. But her blood had become corrupted by her long imprisonment in a coffin of silver and a diet based solely on blood from his own veins. Mekra had become a new and diabolical creature, unusually strong, hard and fast. A change faithfully passed on with her blood.

Furthermore, Mekra appeared to have a telepathic link with her offspring. Akimitsu had slaked his thirst with a trail of dead bodies that never strayed from heading west. Sometimes, he'd move north or south within a band two hundred miles across, but he was clearly heading to the western hemisphere like a moth to Mekra's flame. It had to be telepathy, nothing else could explain Akimitsu's path to Mekra's donjon. Without the Panopticon, finding Akimitsu would be like finding the proverbial needle in a haystack. Cornelius needed a new strategy. With the Order all but destroyed, and the Red Empire still on the rebound after the destruction of their citadel in Jerusalem, he could ignore the Ramp masters for the moment. The immediate priorities were simple, he must protect the secret of Mekra's existence, destroy Akimitsu before he created more of his kind, and preserve the secrecy of the Vampire Dominion while doing so.

Cornelius had split his remaining forces into three groups. Force-Asia under general Shen Zhen, with two shadowstar drones, three osprey IIs, and forty praetorians. They would continue to beat the bushes of China behind Akimitsu, maintaining the appearance of a search. Let Akimitsu and Mekra believe his destination was unknown to Cornelius and that substantial forces sought him in China. The equal of Force-Asia, Force-Europe, under general Dieter Franz would stage near Romania, but be ready to enforce a perimeter around Mekra's donjon at a moment's notice. Force-Africa, at just over half the size of Force-Asia or Force-Europe contained all the remaining praetorians he could muster. Under general Haras Mosule, it would stage in a concealed location near Mekra's donjon to provide a rapid-reaction reserve force to bolster any strategy of defense or attack. A panoply of human operatives drawn from the European, Chinese and African branches of Shadowstone would provide ground support.

As for general Armitage, he had a separate role for her to play.

Immediate tactical needs plagued his mind. His operational commanders had to know enough to organize an effective defense around Mekra's donjon. He'd told his generals an adroit fiction; Akimitsu sought a rumored artifact hidden in the Transylvania alps of Romania. His mirthless grin was enough to dissuade further enquiry. Cornelius drew a long breath and sighed. For all their numbers, equipment and training, he expected his forces would not be enough. He would have to kill Akimitsu himself. It was only fitting, after all, Akimitsu was his own mess.

The drone began its final landing sequence, rotating slowly around its central axis as it descended to the right side of the main courtyard. A suite of onboard sensors scanned the abandoned fortress and found nothing left alive larger than a rat. Cornelius had the canopy open and was out on the flagstones before the jets stilled to cooling immobility.

Cornelius surveyed the dark flagstones beneath the starlight, finding scattered implant sheathes resting in the grooves between the stones. Moved there with the sunburned ashes of the dead mekrarian vampires and forgotten by a careless breeze. He stooped and picked up one. He only needed one, but he continued and collected all eleven used and lost that night. It might be a while before he could source replacements. He lifted the last and examined it closely with his vampire vision. It resolved into fine detail. The tiny explosive charge used to deliver the load of powdered silver had scorched one end of the implant, but the casing was intact, and if any silver remained it was beyond his ability to detect it. Satisfied, he pocketed the implant sheaths and returned to the drone. In moments he was airborne, flying like a spear thrown by a god back to research facility number one in Queens, New York.

It was time to upgrade his precognitive powers.

* * *

Jon Thunder-Axe flicked a series of electrical switches on an internal wall panel.

Rows of lights switched on along the high, sloping ceiling, one after another until the small rectangular warehouse was lit. It was not a large industrial warehouse, more an extra-oversized shed with delusions of grandeur. There was one key element within it. A tractor trailer with a second trailer hooked behind the first trailer – a B-Double rig – dominating the concrete floor of the open space like a frozen dinosaur waiting to come to life. The first trailer was a mobile command center filled with the latest information technology. The second was an advanced Hitachi Heavy Industries mobile fuel cell to power the first trailer. Arthur Slayne had provided the equipment two years ago. Components sourced from all over the world. Prototypes, illegal technical transfers, advanced DARPA military only tech: it never mattered to Arthur, he was a master of the ways and means of the modern industrial world, and he had the funds to back it up and make it happen.

Jon had never asked where the money had come from. He figured the Order had been around for millennia and had built up reserves it could tap into as needed. As for the B-Double rig, it was Arthur's plan 'C,' or perhaps plan 'D.' Arthur had vanished, but he'd left instructions for what to do with the Panopticon. The ideal solution was to get the Panopticon to Arthur's secret site in Hong Kong, but that wasn't likely to happen now. Too many people had lost their lives. There was no one left to help, and the risks of moving outside of the United States were too great.

It was clear what Arthur had intended. Use the Panopticon to illuminate the structure and location of Vampire Dominion forces, as well as all the 'civilian,' vampires they protected. Once known, share the information with anyone who could hunt down and eliminate them. However, the Order of

Thoth had been all but destroyed. Only the Red Empire remained with the capability to end the vampire menace.

As for the Panopticon itself. It required at least one quantum processor to run, and an array of interconnected quantum processors to run properly. Access to quantum processors was a strictly regulated technology guarded by Shadowstone for Crane. They'd sourced the quantum processor in the first trailer from an industrial research center in South Korea, carefully funded by Arthur through a long line of proxy corporations. The processor was more or less hand crafted, employing the latest experimental technologies, and off the official Shadowstone books. Arthur had paid off the engineers involved in its manufacture and they'd scattered to the four winds. This processor and half a dozen more had slipped through Shadowstone and Crane's controls. They deployed the first in the trailer and the rest at a secret site in Hong Kong. Not only that, Arthur had installed a cradle for the Panopticon P-Case to enable easy transfer and integration onto the quantum processor and its attendant quantum state memory banks.

The big shed was at the rear of a larger site in an industrial park on the edge of Phoenix. It was the foundation of Jon's cover story – a working truck maintenance business. It ran at a modest profit, and enabled Jon to get on with his real life while long-term employees kept the lights on and the business ticking over without paying too much attention to what happened in the shed at the back of the property.

Jon glanced across at Dwayne. He held the P-Case in his left hand. He was a loyal Order helper and understood fully the value of what he held. Once fired up, the Panopticon would give access to many of the Vampire Dominion systems. However, they'd have to be careful what they did. The remaining vampires would be looking for traces of the Panopticon. If the vampires discovered them, they'd attack in short order. Hence the B-Double, having a mobile rig they could move from site to site was an essential part of Arthur's strategy to defeat the vampires reacquiring or destroying the Panopticon.

In any event, Arthur had expected Crane to build a replacement to the Panopticon. It was only a matter of time. He'd always planned to destroy the Panopticon fortress before the replacement system came online, creating a window of opportunity where the vampires would be especially vulnerable to attack.

A thrill shivered through Jon's chest – Arthur's plan was in motion – a shed-load of trouble was about to land on Crane's doorstep. He strode across the pale concrete floor toward the B-Double, Dwayne at his left shoulder. They approached the rear of the first trailer. The trailer's rear doors stood shut, chained and locked. Jon produced a key and unlocked them, swinging the doors wide. A soft creamy glow emanated from within the trailer as automatic lights switched on. He glanced over his shoulder, a faint hum emanating from the second trailer as the fuel cell engaged. The system was ready.

He guided Dwayne into the first trailer, navigating their way between racks of electronic equipment, and held out his hand for the P-Case.

Dwayne gave it up with a nod.

Jon slotted the P-Case into its specifically built cradle near the front of the trailer. A soft susurration began as the trailer's inbuilt air conditioning kicked into gear. The temperature would drop soon to just above freezing. He pulled his jacket a little closer and rubbed his hands. A pair of chrome 'A' frames filled with quantum-state technology, one upside down over the other dominated the front quarter of the trailer. A one-inch sphere of white light lit up between them. Jon looked away to the P-Case cradle, the core of the quantum processor was too bright to look at for long.

The green line on the P-Case slid to the left, as the Panopticon began uploading onto the trailer's systems. He switched on a number of secondary systems to enable access and use of the Panopticon. Arthur had warned him, one quantum processor would not be enough to access the Panopticon's full AI emulation capability. Even so, it would be enough for the tasks at hand. Before long the Panopticon would be operational and Jon would have access to core Vampire Dominion systems. No doubt, the vampires would've begun taking steps to protect their systems from a rogue Panopticon, but given the brief time in which to act, and the massive losses on the previous day, much would remain open and vulnerable.

The Panopticon could run penetration algorithms designed to take advantage of secretly inserted vulnerabilities in all the major IT systems of the world. The military satellites were an open book. Financial systems, law enforcement systems, even internal Shadowstone network data such as safe house locations would be readily available. However, once he started using the Panopticon, it would only be a matter of time before the vampires and their Shadowstone agents noticed his presence on the networks. He would have to work quickly to maximize value before they discovered the Panopticon was operational. Once the vampires understood the Panopticon was operational, Dwayne and Jon would begin running – and running was their first and best strategy.

Dwayne and Jon sat at consoles opposite each other and a yard back from the P-Case cradle, and watched the green line shrink. Soon they'd be ready to start using the Panopticon.

Jon flicked open a well-thumbed 'Panopticon Operations Manual,' stolen a couple of years ago and sneaked out of the fortress by Dwayne. He quickly found the chapter on searches. His first task was to find Arthur Slayne. His second task was to find the current location of every vampire on the planet. Apparently, Crane liked to keep tabs on the vampires and had them all registered in a list. The information was bound to be in the Panopticon. Once they had the list, they would send it to the Red Empire via an anonymous back channel provided by Arthur. The Red Empire would do the rest.

He instructed Dwayne. "I'll look for Arthur, could you please compile an up-to-date location list of all registered vampires."

Dwayne logged into his terminal, glanced at the blank screen, and back at the upload progress on the P-Case. "I'm on it."

Jon followed his gaze. The green line shrank to zero. The one-inch ball of white light within the quantum processor shifted to iridescent blue. The Panopticon was now online.

Dwayne and Jon set to work.

* * *

Tania Morte lay naked upon a cold, stainless steel, autopsy table.

She lay unnaturally still, safely paralyzed by a silver net. Around her hovered three vampire scientists, the senior staff of research facility number one. Two wore thick protective gloves to protect themselves from inadvertent contact with the silver net. The third leaned over Morte's right forearm and pressed a newly sheathed loremaster implant against her pale skin.

Cornelius stood at the foot of the table, carefully studying the progress of the procedure. The tip of the implant broke through Morte's pale skin, a bead of blood appearing around the tip. An instant later, minute tendrils emerged from the implant, reaching and burrowing into her flesh, dragging the rest of the implant behind them. A handful of seconds later the implant vanished, and the minor wound closed behind it.

The lead scientist took a step back. The overhead lights gleamed off his hair-cream-slicked hair. He turned toward the foot of the table and remarked with tremulous excitement, "It is done!"

Cornelius noted the scientist's words as almost an afterthought, his attention focused upon the naked woman lying on the slab. Even paralyzed by silver, minor movements were still possible for a vampire, and her mind would be fully awake. Morte's eyes widened. Racked towers of medical monitors next to the autopsy table displayed her vital signs. Her heart rate accelerated despite the depressing effect of the silver net. Her brain waves leaped into extreme activity. Her eyes rolled up into her head, her fingers vibrating against the cold stainless steel of the table. One of the assistant scientists followed what was happening on the loremaster laptop networked with the implant, and reported, "CPU nearing maximum. Data throughput at ninety-eight percent. Whatever's happening, it's hitting her hard."

"Continue," Cornelius commanded. He needed to find out if the modified loremaster implant was safe to insert into a vampire. He'd just gone to Japan to retrieve a vampire suitable sheath to wrap around the Order of Thoth technology, and avoid rejection of the human implant by his superior vampire flesh. He needed an edge in the coming conflict, and mastering the information space was his lifelong strategy. He needed to know more than anyone else. He needed the best access to up to date information, and he'd ensure he had it. This experiment on the wife of Dalien Morte had to succeed. The loremaster technology had been beyond his grasp for years. That gap needed to end this morning. He needed to know what she was experiencing. He ordered sharply, "Lift back the net and restrain her arms. We need to talk with her."

The two gloved scientists lifted back the silver net, laying it over Morte's hips and thighs. She gasped, her head flicking left and right. They gripped her arms and pressed them down against the inner sides of the autopsy table. She whispered desperately, "Free me! He is coming for me! He is coming for us all!"

Cornelius leaned forward. "Who is he?"

"Set!" she whispered; her voice barely audible. She lifted her head, her gaze boring into Cornelius' eyes and shouted, "He's coming for you!" She convulsed once and fell back to the slab, her eyes rolling up into her head. The attendants lifted their hands. One said, "She's gone limp."

"Hold her!" Cornelius shouted.

Too late, her left hand shot out, gripping, clenching, hard fingers ripping through flesh, tearing the throat out of the nearest attendant. He fell back, his face frozen with shock, blood spurting in ropy streamers to the left and right of his face.

Cornelius drew his blade, his great sword cleaving down through Morte's skull an instant later. She slumped back to the autopsy table, blood flooding around her split cranium, flowing in a crimson stream around her shoulders and down the drain at the foot of the table.

The experiment was over.

Cornelius flicked his sword, clearing it of any residual gore before sheathing it. He looked at the lead scientist and ordered, "Extract the implant and ready it for immediate insertion."

"But master—"

"You heard me!"

The vampire nodded. "Of course, my king. Your will be done."

The experiment demonstrated the implant worked. It would be dangerous to use, but danger beset Cornelius upon all sides. He needed the edge the loremaster technology offered. Whatever risk remained – he would master it – after all, he was not Tania Morte. His options would continue to narrow until he regained the initiative against his many enemies. The loremaster implant would provide the edge he craved. With working access to the loremaster technology, the initiative would return to his hands, and then his enemies would face his wrath.

And his wrath had festered for long enough.

* * *

Bright strip lighting gleamed off the sleek black hull of the raider II scout helicopter.

Whispering Death watched four uniformed ground crew refuel his aircraft. The other three members of his fist team stood in a semi-circle to his left, watching the entrances and exits of the hangar for any threats. He respected their vigilance. They were all good men, named warriors of the Red Empire – he was proud to lead them.

One of his men nodded toward a pair of doors marked with the universal signs for toilets. Whispering Death nodded. Of course, if one of his men needed to answer a call of nature after a long flight from the west, then so be it. A second man glanced at him and followed the first. Whispering Death consulted his wristwatch. The Rolex was a gift from his father upon the event of his naming ceremony. It read, '20:05,' local time. The watch's internal GPS function automatically adjusting to the local time zone. The provision of local transport was running late. He'd ordered the delivery of an SUV to this hangar at the main airport of the city of Hami in north-western China by 19:30. He looked up from his left wrist, a white SUV drove out of the gathering twilight beyond the front of the hangar.

At last, the transport had arrived. The Red Ghost's orders had been explicit. Whispering Death and his fist team were to meet up with a local cell of Red Empire helpers and conduct operations versus the Vampire Dominion within China. They would find out what had caused the recent upsurge of vampire activity reaching from the islands of Japan to the western Chinese hinterland. Radar tracks and deeply encrypted communications had illuminated the use of shadowstars, the new osprey IIs, and local Chinese Shadowstone variants of the nightfalcon by the vampires and their human dupes. The Red Empire estimated thirty to forty praetorians were hunting someone (or something) traveling west across China, aided by at least a hundred Chinese Shadowstone operatives.

He reflected quietly as two of his men trotted toward the toilets. The news of the mutual destruction of the Panopticon and the Order of Thoth had coursed through the Red Empire like a wildfire. Whispering Death had greeted the news with a grim sigh. While the destruction of the misguided souls of the Order of Thoth was inevitable, even with the loss of the Panopticon, it was not a victory for the Red Empire. The loss of the Order signaled the growing audacity and ascendancy of the Vampire Dominion.

The recent destruction of the Jerusalem citadel was a bitter memory, as was crossing blades with the infamous vampire general, Chloe Armitage.

Armitage had trapped him behind a Red Empire barrier with bare minutes left to evacuate a doomed facility, leaving their fight unresolved. Perhaps they would cross blades again, and he'd get a chance to pit the full capability of his speed talent against her formidable skills.

The white SUV pulled to a halt forty meters short of the raider II. A respectful distance from the flammable gases of the fuel hoses snaking into the hull of the advanced scout helicopter. He glanced at the distant toilets. The door was swinging shut behind the second of his men. It'd be a couple of minutes at most before he could move forward with his mission. He approached the SUV, the fourth member of his team a step behind his left shoulder.

It was time to meet the city of Hami cell of Red Empire helpers.

* * *

Mekra's words rang in Akimitsu's mind like a tolling bell, '*Commandeer the Red Empire assassins.*'

She commanded him to convert them all and capture their advanced transport. He'd taken twenty-three hours to escape the praetorians north of Beijing. Guided by his beloved queen, he'd coerced a truck driver to take him to Hami. That wight had died from a snapped neck an hour previously, his truck parked and ignored just outside a far corner of the hangar.

Akimitsu had stemmed his desires. There was no need to advertise his presence in Hami with blood feasting. There would be plenty of time to slake his thirst in the near future.

His queen needed him. He had to accelerate his travel to her prison. He had to make all haste to free her. Behind her command he could taste a hint of fear. If he failed, she would never escape her prison.

Akimitsu hid himself well. Mekra's spirit was nearby, guiding his actions with inspired suggestions and kind advice. Her words were liquid honey within his mind. He shivered with her psychic touch and dreamed of what the utter divinity of her flesh would be like.

He'd swallowed all his pride and hid himself inside a stinking cubical within a foul toilet block. His queen had wisely advised at least one or more of the Red Empire assassins would use the toilet block upon their arrival. All he had to do was wait for the optimum moment to strike. As potent as his new powers were, his queen advised him to be wary of fighting all four members of the Red Empire at once. It was best he split his opponent's forces and fight them in pairs, and defeat them without risk. His queen was both wise and good. There could be none better. His heart sang with the thrill of service to her divine purpose. Not that he knew what her purpose might be, it was enough to know he belonged to her and her divine will directed his life. He'd almost forgotten his time within the clan of the Obsidian Claw. That time of his life seemed to be nothing more than a dull echo of the vivid life he lived now blessed by devout service to his queen.

The first of his prey entered the toilet block, the door swinging closed behind him. A moment later, a second man entered and joined the first at the urinal wall. The interior of the toilet block was suddenly rich with the scents of the two men. The heavy redolent note of their leather jackets, the tang of their metal blades. The succulent aroma of the blood flooding their veins. There were two more, sixty yards away in the middle of the hangar surrounded by the clank of metal on metal, the thrum of motors and pumps, the hiss of flowing gasses, and the empty chatter of the voices of lesser men. They were too far away to prevent what would happen next.

Akimitsu was a master of the art of Ninjitsu, the art of invisibility. He readied himself, his two-foot-long ninjatos gleaming mirror-like beneath the strip lighting above his head. He waited for the men to open their trousers, for the streams of urine to strike the urinal wall, for their guard to go down as they relaxed into sighs of satisfaction.

The inevitable moment arrived. He leaped over the cubical wall, his straight blades arcing down. The men stiffened as his shadow passed across them, reflexive plumes of heat rising off them – but too late. Akimitsu's blades struck true, plunging though their backs, punching out of their chests, sending ribbons of blood slashing like red whips across the dank yellow tiles of the urinal wall. He landed, withdrawing his blades with a snap. The two men fell left and right, gurgling on their own blood. He flicked and sheathed one blade, and slashed the other across his left wrist.

Akimitsu squatted between the two men and squeezed the divinity of Mekra's blood from his veins into the open wounds of his fallen comrades. Yes, they'd briefly been foes, but within a few short minutes they would belong to his queen. They stiffened for a second time as Mekra's blood rushed through their veins, conquering every cell it touched. Akimitsu blurred, dragging the two men into sitting position, hard against his chest, their legs splayed out to either side on the gray concrete of the floor. His hands clapped beneath their noses, closing their mouths with an iron grip. No one would hear their screams. No one would come to aid them, not that anyone could help them now for they were beyond all aid.

The two men shivered, trembled and thrashed but could not break free. Akimitsu breathed slowly and waited for the handful of minutes to pass. His gaze locked on the door into the toilet block. The last thing he needed was a casual interruption of the process of vampiric transformation. He still needed surprise on his side.

He could not fail his divine queen.

* * *

Abject terror seized his soul.

The moment stretched, then snapped shut with a dreadful inevitability. The light within Whispering Death guttered and blew out, smothered beneath a blanket of darkness without end. Her presence filled his soul, riffling through his memories like a player with a deck of cards. She discarded most of them, but lingered upon the highlights, appraising and re-experiencing them in full. The recent fight with general Chloe Armitage uppermost amongst them.

A single word flooded his soul, *Rival!*

On its heels came a swelling desire, potent, ripe, flush with a driving need to kill Armitage. To extinguish her life like blowing out a candle. The desire belonged to Her, and shattered all will to resist. His lifelong loyalty to the Red Empire withered on the vine, turning to ash and dust within his heart.

The world whirled around him. A trenchant thirst clawed at his parched throat. A glorious scent filled his nostrils. He jerked up from the cold concrete of the hangar floor. He took in his surroundings in a glance. His men were all alive, but like him, they belonged to Her. He'd been the last to fall to the surprise attack. A natural result given his speed and skills.

Mekra's voice sounded within his mind, now a soft and loving whisper, "You will serve me well." Her voice fell to silence and her presence withdrew. All color fled from the world. His heart ached with desperate longing for her return.

The scent of fresh blood clawed at his face. His gaze fell upon one of the helpers struggling beneath the knee of the stranger from the toilet blocks. The other helper and the four ground crew lay about on the hangar floor near the helicopter in various states of disarray. A thin streamer of blood splashed here and there upon the concrete. His men stood with scimitar fangs displayed over their bottom lips and faint smiles of recent satiation.

Hunger wrenched his gut; his thirst scraping his throat with sandpaper. Fangs sprouted from his gums, pressing hard past his bottom lip. He leaped upon the helpless man. The fellow's breath puffed out in a gasping grunt. The man never drew another breath. Moments later, Whispering Death rose from his first meal as a vampire, wiping the excess blood from his lips with the back of his hand. His men were already unhooking the fuel lines from the raider II. They were of one mind. They shared a single goal.

Fly as fast as they could to Romania and free their divine queen.

* * *

The early Autumn morning sun glinted off the towers of New York City.

James Haley reported, "We landed six hours ago at oh two thirty in Fort Dix. The chameleons fed back in Phoenix. They're resting now."

"Make sure your osprey is ready for a trip to Japan within the hour," Chloe ordered. Her smartphone rested behind her on the edge of her kitchen's island benchtop; its speaker phone function engaged. She stood at the nearest armored window. New York City lay resplendent in the morning sunlight beneath her, only a fraction of her attention remained focused on Haley's report. *Soon. Soon, I will walk beneath the sun*, she thought to herself.

Chloe whirled away from the tinted transparent armor of her windows. There was much to do, and so little time to do it in. She could not waste time in self-indulgent absorption with her desires. No. She'd have to focus on the present, and focus with every fiber of her being if she was going to grasp victory against the many forces that worked against her objectives.

James continued, his voice carrying a note of caution. "With the Panopticon out of action, it's becoming more ... challenging to keep everything secret. The chameleons were messy in Phoenix. Fortunately, the local criminal gangs who are now missing a few members are unlikely to complain. However, maintaining the secrecy of the chameleons, or the Vampire Dominion for that matter, is at risk of failure, and that risk is growing exponentially."

"We live in challenging times, James," Chloe replied. "You should expect to give your utmost effort if we are to achieve our goals. Only your best will do. Are you willing to do that?"

"Yes, Chloe," he said readily. "However, I want to make sure you're appraised of the growing risks. Our mission? Our objectives? This could all spiral out of control."

Chloe smiled dryly for a moment. Her eyes dropped to half lidded. "James ... chaos will be our ally. As for keeping the vampire's secret? I think we've passed the threshold of no return. Crane will try, so will the Red Empire as they have vampire secrecy as an objective for their own purposes, but too much has happened and the game is nearly up. The secret of the vampires is almost public knowledge. Once it breaks for real, it will sweep the world like wildfire." Chloe took a long breath and let it out. "And, so it should. The lie has lasted for far too long. You know what I stand for?"

"The truth."

"Yes. And the truth will out."

James paused on the other end of the line. She could easily imagine him nodding to her words. He was a capable operative, and he'd bought into her point of view. But like everyone – he had no vision of what she really intended for the world. How could he? He remained limited by the inherent ignorance of his circumstances and a lifespan measured in years instead of millennia. One day, one day soon, she would relieve James and everyone else of their ignorance and it would be for the better, but that day was yet to come.

He said in a clear voice, "Logistics, Chloe? The Spike 512 would be faster than the osprey."

"But difficult to hide the chameleons on, especially from the pilots. No, James, even if slower, it's safer to use the osprey. In this instance, a few hours of flight time are not significant. ... No, prep the osprey for a flight to Japan immediately. I will join you at Fort Dix within the hour."

"The refit of the osprey is already underway."

"Good work."

"My pleasure, Chloe. We'll be ready for takeoff at 09:30 hours."

"One last thing, the Black Dragon katana. Do you still have it?"

"Yes, Chloe. On board the osprey."

"Keep it safe. I have a purpose for that blade."

"Consider it done."

"Excellent."

An alarm sounded on her smartphone. A call was coming through from Cornelius Crane. She said urgently, "James. I've got a call from Crane." She cut her subordinate off and answered Crane, "Yes?"

"Chloe, I have need of you."

What's new? "Yes, Sir," she replied with a hint of sarcasm edging her voice. "I'm at your service."

"Indeed, you are," Crane said, pausing for a moment. "Now open the hangar above your penthouse – I'm landing in my command drone."

Chloe's eyes widened with sudden questions. Why was he here? What did he need now? Why wasn't Crane focused on solving the rogue vampire problem in China? She uttered a single word, "Cornelius?"

"You're coming with me to Romania. We're hunting the rogue vampire together. That should please you."

Chloe looked out the window at the New York skyline, her eyes unfocused. She answered, "I thought you wanted me to eliminate Anton Slayne. Is that still on the table?"

"Yes. Can James Haley continue to track his location?"

"Yes, he's the best we've got."

"Then he'll have to proceed alone. Higher priority needs require your immediate attention. Come now, hurry up. My drone is wasting fuel in hover mode."

"I'll be there in a minute."

"Indeed."

She was stuck between a rock and a hard place. She hung up on Crane and voice-dialed James. He asked, "Chloe?"

"I can't join you on the mission to Japan. The success of the Hana Tanaka mission is all on you and the chameleons. You have to come through for me."

"Chloe? Ma'am?"

"Save me, James. Find Tanaka and bring her back to New York City alive."

"On my life, I will," James vowed.

Chloe cut the line. She hoped James and the chameleons would be enough to recover the Japanese biomedical scientist. Without relief from Crane's implant technology her plans were as dust. As for finding Anton Slayne, that could wait. She grabbed a duffel bag of her essential equipment and made for the stairs up to her penthouse hangar.

Damn it! Crane had just spoiled all her plans.

* * *

Sunlight slashed through the hangar in a trenchant glare.

Cornelius' command drone rose smoothly into the morning sky. Chloe Armitage sat beside him, dressed in a sleek black bodysuit. A long duffel bag with her sword, body armor, and combat fit out rested in a compartment behind her seat. He set a course for the small town of Border in central Romania. The command drone rose higher, rapidly accelerating as it prepared to go hypersonic.

He closed his eyes for a brief moment, reviewing the tremendous events of the last forty minutes. The Order loremaster implant rested in his right forearm, its attendant laptop uprated with a long-life battery and plugged into the drone's power and communication systems, sat hidden in a shelf behind his seat. He'd attempted a vision in a quiet room within the research facility in Queens. The device had burned like a hot coal embedded in his undying flesh. He'd entered a lucid dreaming state and experienced a combined vision integrating the precognitive gift of Jean Philippe Allemande with the Order technology. Mekra and Anton Slayne remained the primary threats to his life, but the former would only be an issue if she managed to escape. As for his defenses, Chloe Armitage was the decisive factor. He would keep her at his side where he could keep an eye on her, and benefit from her supreme combat skill set. No one he was facing could engage her in combat and live.

Two other thing's he'd learned. The Panopticon had just emerged back onto the world's networks and Arthur Slayne was still alive. The loremaster technology remained intimately linked to the Panopticon. The Panopticon had been an Arthur Slayne Trojan horse from the start. An exquisite example of a long con. No wonder Slayne had been able to insert the

Mirovar force team into the center of the Panopticon fortress and destroy it.

His loremaster vision had revealed a location – Phoenix, Arizona. He'd notified his executive assistant, Ursula Zielinkski and the skeleton staff remaining at the citadel in Manhattan, New York City. He'd instructed her to assign the remaining human staff to go to Phoenix and destroy the Panopticon. The Panopticon in the hands of his enemies was too much of a threat. There was no hope of salvaging it now. It would be best to destroy it. There was a single squad of Day Guard troopers, and another squad of Shadowstone operatives. A small force, and underpowered versus Ramp masters but they would have to do. There was no one else available and he couldn't send vampires during daylight. There was core logic in the Panopticon system that enabled FGEO search and validation of vampire locations. There was a register of all known vampires, including the praetorians. He routinely monitored Praetorian life signs through their tactical communications links. He could infer their locations from their life-sign data. Someone with root access to a newly operational Panopticon could conduct all those searches and discover registered vampires or praetorians converging on their location. He had to assume Arthur Slayne or those helping him would conduct those searches as soon as they were able to do so.

As for Louise Wesson and her small group of remaining day guards and Shadowstone staff. They were already fully engaged in sanitizing the aftermath of the destruction of the Panopticon fortress. She'd also sent a report detailing the discovery of a final shipment of Day Guard serum found at the ruined Brazilian research facility. Her objectives were strategically important and needed to progress.

Her news of the additional Day Guard doses was one of the few positive pieces of information Cornelius had seen in the last twenty-four hours. The sooner Wesson could rebuild the Day Guard the better.

The Vampire Dominion was vulnerable with the Panopticon in his opponent's hands, but first he must deal with Mekra and Akimitsu. Once he had victory there, he could turn his full attention to hunting down the location of the rogue Panopticon, destroy it and annihilate all those found with it.

One final thing from the vision impressed itself upon him. A shadow had emerged at the end. A howl from the depths of space. An uncanny presence, something unrealized but pregnant with dreadful possibility haunted the loremaster realm. He remained blind to what that presence might be, but whatever it was, it seemed to be inimical to his own goal of maintaining the Vampire Dominion. He'd noted it as another threat to his rule. In time, he would understand its nature and then deal with it in a final and comprehensive fashion. Perhaps, as Tania Morte had warned, Set was seeking him.

Just another in a long list of enemies.

Cornelius opened his eyes. He turned to Armitage and remarked almost casually, "It is time to reveal all. I need to ensure you understand fully the world in which you operate if you are to help me in this hour of need. I will tell you these truths because I trust the combined bindings of Allemande's curse and the implant resting next to your brain stem. You cannot harm me, nor can you allow me to come to harm. The sooner you accept your inescapable circumstances, the sooner you will be at peace with your life."

Armitage looked directly into his face and remarked with understated acidity, "And what of my life? I vanish within your grand show. There is nothing left beyond this veil of deception. When will I live an authentic life?"

Cornelius stared at her with dark-brown eyes as hard as flint. Keeping Armitage at his side was like keeping the most venomous and deceptive serpent wrapped around his throat. As long as her deadly venom remained directed at his enemies and she could not use it upon him – all was well. She needed to forget whatever personal fantasy she held for her own life and accept her destiny. He lifted a finger toward her and declared, "Our fates our bound together. We either survive and prosper together or we are both doomed. What else can you do but submit to my will? Do you want to be destroyed?"

She looked at him intently, took a long breath and answered quietly, "You are right. Of course, what else can I do?"

"Indeed," he acknowledged with a slight frown. He needed Armitage to be an empowered servant to his will. Even though true trust could never live between them; she needed to know the truth if she was to become fully effective. The loremaster vision had been explicit, he needed her to know everything. He looked into her vivid blue eyes and declared, "Mekra is alive."

The drone accelerated to hypersonic speed, pinning them momentarily back into their seats.

Armitage lifted her head off the headrest and turned to face him, her mouth forming an 'O,' of surprise.

* * *

After a brief double-take, Chloe remarked, "You don't say?"

Crane's frank admission astounded her. *Mekra was alive!* Her mind whirled. Of course, it all finally made sense, general Dieter Franz had remarked on the night of her transformation, 'What is this? What have you given her?' Then he'd said, 'What have you done? What was that blood?

I've never smelled its like.' The blood was atypical. Franz had simply been the only general willing to voice an opinion. As a human, Chloe had been unable to detect any difference at the time and in all the long years she'd never connected these specific dots. Crane had asserted moments after her conversion, 'I have given you the strength to carry out my edicts.'

And Crane was right, she was truly first born of Mekra. But he still didn't know of the gifts she'd brought with her from her natural-born genius: an eidetic memory, the supreme Ramp, and muscle mimicry. He would never fully understand her, he was incapable of understanding her. A sudden sharp pang of loneliness pierced her heart, she acknowledged it silently – no one was capable of understanding her. In the same instant, she steadied. Crane was sharing what he knew – it would be wise to listen carefully.

Crane's eyes tightened for an instant before he continued, dismissing her momentary sarcasm with a wave of his left hand. "We have time on this flight to discuss many things, perhaps things that should have been discussed before now." He paused for a long moment as if ordering his thoughts. "I was a general in the first crusade, back in ten-ninety-six. I was also a senior member of the Order of Thoth. Of course, the crusades were not really about Christianity versus Islam. The real issue was the Red Empire wanted control over certain lands they believed harbored the Key of Ahknaton and the Papyrus of Hakron the scribe, and naturally the Order of Thoth opposed them. Both organizations were guilty of co-opting everything in their path to pursue their own bloody agendas. I grew tired of the mindless bloodshed. Surely, I could establish a global order to end such wasteful conflicts. I was often in power struggles with the other leaders within the Order, and one night I met Mekra face to face. I found out later, she'd sought me out. I think you'd be surprised if you met her. She's a stunning presence, charismatic, magnetic, flawlessly beautiful. It's easy to fall under her spell."

Crane looked away for a moment, his brown eyes darkening with ambivalence. "She converted me that night. I gave myself to her willingly. I lifted my arm and she slaked her thirst upon my blood. When I was near death, she opened a vein upon her wrist with her own fangs and thrust it against my lips. At first the taste of her blood was repulsive, then her blood transformed within my mouth and became the ambrosia of the gods. I must admit, I sucked greedily until the agony of transformation hit me. You know the final steps all too well. It is no different for any of us. She'd brought a young slave with her. Little more than a goat herder given what he smelled like. I fell upon him like a starving hawk upon a rabbit. In seconds, I'd drained him dry and stood before Mekra her devoted and willing servant."

"She knew what she wanted. I became her lover and the first amongst her guardians. She needed protection and I provided it – and I was the best she'd ever had. Her opponents were many, not just the Ramp masters of the Order or the Red Empire, but other vampires too ... they were incessant. One after another would raise an army and attack. This was the world from the eleventh to the sixteenth centuries. There was a wide-spread belief that any who drank her blood would reign supreme over the world forever. A blood cult riven with factions ranging from those who would give their lives to protect Mekra as the one true ruler of the vampires to those who sought her destruction in an orgy of vampiric blood feasting. Amongst the madness of disparate beliefs there was a grain of truth. Those who were first born from Mekra's blood were stronger and faster than other vampires, and if you continued to drink of her blood, you were stronger and faster still. Of the first born there are few of us left. I figure that you have worked out by now your own status?"

Chloe nodded silently.

"Indeed. You were never a slow student. One of the many reasons I chose you for the role of my enforcer. As for the other first born, I killed the best of them on the night I imprisoned Mekra in silver. I hunted the rest down and slew them one by one. Only one escaped me, named Hong Long, an elusive creature who styled himself 'The Great Dragon.' He has either hidden himself well or is long dead."

In Japan, raced through Chloe's thoughts. The protector of Hana Tanaka had to be someone powerful and experienced. Someone skilled through long centuries of avoiding Crane's quest to rid himself of rivals. She'd not be surprised to discover a secret coven of blood-cult vampires still active in Japan despite Crane's many efforts to root them out.

Crane paused and looked at Chloe expectantly. She asked, "Mekra's prison is near this town of 'Border,' in Romania?"

"Indeed, it is. Her donjon is situated in the Transylvania alps and has been since the night of the fifth of July, fifteen-fifty-four. Mekra had a circle of seven guardians around her to protect her from those who would usurp her throne. But she should have looked closer to home for the threat. She was becoming increasingly arbitrary in her judgments, sowing chaos within the human and vampire realms, delighting in her own power and the suffering of others. She slaughtered two of her guards on a capricious whim, and ordered the rest of us to stake a third naked on a hillside to await the sunlight. She replaced these men with newly turned vampires born of her blood including Hong Long. It was enough to spark a palace coup, for none of us knew who would be next to fall to one of her chaotic moods. I formed a cabal with the other three surviving guardians and we agreed to a plan to rid ourselves of Mekra's insanity and split the world into four realms we could each rule. We planned and worked for weeks, and then one night we struck. It took all of us to master Mekra's speed and strength, and imprison her within a silver net. Of her new spawn, we slaughtered two within the first hour, but the third, Hong Long, fled. We four who remained, took Mekra's paralyzed body to a mountain donjon and interred her in a sarcophagus of pure silver. Of my three accomplices, I betrayed them all to their deaths beneath the next dawn. After all, I was their superior, and why should I share the world with them? No, it was for the best. I closed and locked Mekra's donjon and began a routine of feeding her about once a year. With her silver reduced metabolism, it was enough. But I made an error of judgment in feeding her with blood from my own arm. After centuries of feeding upon vampire blood she has changed into something else. A different form of vampire and her corrupted blood breeds true. Those sired by her blood have her enhanced characteristics."

"Great," Chloe noted ironically.

Crane gave a short nod. "It's a catastrophe, but no one could have foreseen it. So, our mission is to find and destroy a single vampire named, Akimitsu. He was an elite member of the Obsidian Claw ninja clan in Japan."

"Was?"

"The Claw is extinct." Crane shrugged. "I had to eliminate them after they witnessed the birth of these abominations and the escape of Akimitsu."

"And since the escape of Akimitsu, what then?"

"He has traced a path west toward Mekra's donjon."

"How?" Chloe said, frowning.

"I suspect Mekra has a telepathic connection with her offspring."

"Which implies she can see what he sees, even if she is holed up in a silver coffin in the middle of Transylvania."

Crane nodded.

Chloe arched an eyebrow. "So, Mekra is bait. Akimitsu is heading toward her to free her, and our plan is to intercept him and kill him."

"Yes. All while keeping vampires secret from humanity, and Mekra secret from vampires. I expect to kill Akimitsu myself. However, you are my contingency plan if events take a turn for the worse." Cornelius' mouth tightened, and he remarked in hard tones, "As they have consistently done in recent months."

Chloe's eyes narrowed briefly. She'd a hand in many of Crane's recent reversals but was loathe to interrupt his monologue, she focused her attention on what he was saying.

Crane looked hard at her. "If Mekra escapes, the Vampire Dominion could fall within the next few weeks. You will not survive her ascendancy for she will not tolerate a rival. This you must know if you are to defend all the Dominion stands for."

Defend your life and your secrets that is, Chloe thought, her face a shining mask.

"In the last one hundred and seventy years of your vampiric life, you have been much exercised to bring our Dominion into existence and maintain it against our many enemies."

Your enemies. I have shed much blood to defeat your enemies.

"This has been for the greater good, for many who have sought to rule would do so with great slaughter and cruelty."

A self-serving belief if I've ever heard one.

"In any event, all this should now be clear. We must destroy Akimitsu, keep Mekra secret, and close out the horror of a return of her rule."

"Absolutely, crystal clear," Chloe declared.

Crane looked at her for a long moment, frowned and said, "Sometimes, I despair of your loyalty. But there is the implant – you will die if I die."

Chloe took a breath and sighed. "This is so." She sniffed ironically and stated, "I remain your weapon of choice."

He nodded.

Chloe took another breath, watching Crane through half-lidded eyes. He was right to fear the fall of the Vampire Dominion, but so far, he'd not correctly ascertained the primary source of threat to his rule.

Herself.

* * *

"The list is complete," Dwayne Washington said, puffing over his fingers as he rubbed some warmth into them. "What's the Red Empire email address?"

"Well, at least one of us has made progress," Jon Thunder-Axe remarked turning to look at Dwayne's display. A spreadsheet report dominated the screen. The table listed names, locations, contact details, length of time at the address, along with a thumbnail photograph for over eight hundred vampires all over the world. His eyes narrowed and he asked, "Can you split out the praetorians?"

"Sure can," Dwayne answered, flashing up a second table. "There's a mess of them in Romania, and the rest are spread out in a line from north to south in western China.

Jon studied the second table. There were associated lists of shadowstars, ospreys, nightfalcons, and attached Shadowstone units drawn from Europe, China and Africa. It looked like two operations were in progress, one in China and one in Romania. He scanned the list; the names of Crane and his generals were conspicuous in their absence. Clearly, rank had its privileges. He added a few words of explanatory text and a secret code phrase to an email, filled in the Red Empire address, attached a set of instructions to turn the lists into continuous feeds from the Panopticon and sent it to Dwayne's terminal. "Send the files with this, and get ready to move. We need to be out of here when the proverbial begins hitting the fan."

"Why will the Red Empire trust an email from us?"

"Because only the Red Ghost, Arthur Slayne, and myself are aware of this communications channel. Let's just say Dalien Morte inherited an 'accommodation,' forged between Arthur and Morte's predecessor."

"Wow, and without the Panopticon, the vampires won't be able to intercept something as simple as an email."

"Exactly. They have become so dependent upon the Panopticon; they have mostly lost the capability to use other systems."

Dwayne grinned and attached the files, and sent the quantum encrypted email to the designated address. He glanced back at Jon, rose and headed toward the rear of the trailer. He called back over his shoulder, "I'll start with route number one."

"Great," Jon said. Dwayne passed through the doorway, and closed the door behind him. Jon turned back to his screen. Dwayne had over thirty separate routes throughout the continental United States to travel. Everyone a main arterial highway commonly used by B-Double rigs. The object was to blend in, to become the proverbial needle in a haystack. Dwayne was a skilled driver, one of many skills he'd picked up over the last thirty years.

A barely audible hum started at the front of the rig as electric motors powered by the towed fuel cell spun into motion. Gears were engaged and the rig glided forward at little more than walking speed. Dwayne would ease the rig out of the shed, down a lane way past the maintenance shops and onto the street out front of the site. Jon glanced at the clock in the bottom right-hand corner of his screen. It was just past 06:15 in the morning. Phoenix was waking up to a new day. Jon flexed his fingers, then rubbed and squeezed his knuckles. He set up a pair of satellite monitors, one on western China and the other on Romania. He'd be a fool not to take the opportunity the Panopticon offered to monitor the movements of the enemy.

He focused his attention upon another task. It was time to continue the search for Arthur.

Jon sighed quietly. If Arthur was still alive, he was well hidden.

* * *

Shabbah al Ahmar's soul burned with triumph.

Dalien Morte snapped at his command center operators, "Establish the live feed and put the results up on the main display."

His men set to work, a handful of seconds later the main screen hosted a ten-foot-high world map dotted with hundreds of white and gold stars. The former were regular vampires, the later were praetorians. Dalien and his men looked at the screen with wide eyes. He whispered hoarsely, "We have them. We have them now." He raised and steadied his voice; and addressed his command center team. "This opportunity cannot be wasted." He stared hard at his CC commander. "Khufu, I want confirmation on all those vampire locations established as soon as possible."

"Yes, Red Ghost!" the commander responded.

"Ensure full stealth surveillance, we can't afford to alert them to our plans. Prepare a full set of designated kill lists mapped to our local teams in each geography. When we strike it must be a simultaneous attack performed without errors. There must be no escapes. This is the closest we've ever come to an opportunity to wipe out the vampires."

"Your will, Shabbah al Ahmar."

A second screen carried the full list of names. Dalien scanned it with a glance without detecting his wife's name. He was not surprised; she'd hardly be a registered vampire. No, Crane had kept her somewhere secret. There was still hope he could find her in the aftermath of the destruction of the Vampire Dominion. He stepped forward and studied the locations of the praetorians. They remained deployed in two main groups, one in and around Romania, and the other in a broad line running north-south in western China. He looked closer. The enemy forces in China were brushing against the city of Hami, where Whispering Death was on a mission to investigate the high tempo of vampire activity in north Asia. He called out to his staff, "What's the current status of Whispering Death?"

"Red Ghost," said one of his operators. "He's just missed his hourly check-in, but the raider is flying at top speed toward Almaty in Kazakhstan."

"What the hell is he doing?"

The command center team remained silent. There were no obvious reasons why Whispering Death was flying toward the west. Dalien pressed his lips together. The line of flight of the scout helicopter was on an almost straight line toward Romania. Why was one of his talented young officers flying at top speed toward Crane's largest force? He snapped, "Khufu, set a man to find out what the hell Whispering Death is doing."

"Yes, Red Ghost."

The Red Empire had tracked reports of random vampire killings from Japan through northern China. Shadowstone had failed to suppress all the evidence. Crane had stretched Shadowstone too thinly and their capabilities were breaking down. There was a rumor of a new type of vampire … he ordered, "Put the raider's location on the screen."

Whispering Death's aircraft appeared on the screen as a small red helicopter icon. It sat bathed in a field of darkness covering half the screen and was slowly progressing westward. The helicopter would be in perpetual night as it chased the sun to the west – a perfect circumstance for a vampire crew. His triumph drained away and he frowned. The majority of Crane's forces were in Romania. His second force was following the night westward across China. One of Dalian's most loyal lieutenants was flying toward Crane's main force before the noses of nearly half of Crane's praetorians. Had he just lost a fist team to a rogue vampire out of Japan?

Dalien whispered, "The fox flees before the hounds." His eyes narrowed as he stared hard at Romania. He considered the absence of praetorians everywhere else in the world. Crane was conducting a major operation in or around Romania. The operation was important enough to force Crane to concentrate all his forces upon it.

The rogue vampire rumor must be true, and not just rogue, but a unique threat to Crane. For some unknown reason, Crane expected the rogue vampire to head for Romania, the same location Whispering Death's raider II was seemingly heading to. Whatever was going on, Romania was within striking distance of his fleet of raider IIs and petrel Is out of Matahat, but he couldn't use them with so many Dominion shadowstars in the air. While his six osprey II clones, the Russian-built petrels, carried quad mounts with the latest prototype hypersonic air to air missiles. Crane's concentrated shadowstar force would likely overwhelm his forces and slaughter them before they reached Romania.

Dalien rubbed his chin and regretted assigning all six of the Russian atomic demolition munitions to Taipan's mission to annihilate Crane's citadel in New York City. Taipan was out of reach and somewhere on his way to North America. Dalien had already thrown that spear, and he couldn't recall it. The praetorian forces operating in Romania would have to wait. The strike against the registered vampires would proceed apace, all he could do in the meantime was prepare to act on any opportunity. He called out, "Khufu, fit our raiders with long range tanks and put them on yellow alert. I want them ready for extended-range use as soon as possible."

"Your will, Shabbah al Ahmar," Khufu replied.

If the shadowstars dispersed, and an opportunity presented itself, he could put one hundred and fifty fighters with massive close-air support on the ground in Romania within four hours. The lines around his eyes tightened. The end of the Vampire Dominion was almost within reach.

But only if he could grasp it.

* * *

The late afternoon sunlight cut through the gaily decorated kitchen windows.

The mother lifted her fists and screamed, "Leave my children alone!"

The European director of Shadowstone, Helmut Kohler glared at the woman coldly. He had his orders from on high. The population of the town of Border in Romania was expendable.

She knelt next to her husband. He lay sprawled on their kitchen's linoleum floor, barely breathing. The foolish obstructionist had tried to fight back and one of Helmut's agents had pistol-whipped him. Two of the squad held the woman's wriggling, twisting children while a med-tech applied an injection gun to the throat of the nearest one. There was minute click as the gun fired, injecting a lethal dose of EBOLA-MIMIC-457: a deadly poison that rapidly duplicated the features of full-blown Ebola. The med-tech pressed the gun against the side of the second child's neck. The little girl, her brown eyes wide with terror tried to twist away but to no avail. The gun fired, administering a lethal dose of the poison.

The woman rose from the floor and rushed toward her children, her small fists swinging, her face wild with rage. Another agent tackled her before she covered more than a meter and a half. The med-tech turned, thrust the injection gun against her throat and it clicked for a third time. The agent restraining her, dragged her away as she lashed out with her feet at the med-tech.

As a child, Helmut had attended a farm on a school trip. The farmer had spent an hour injecting a long line of cattle with a drug to protect them against parasites. He watched the struggling mother with the same cold interest he'd experienced on the farm. Her exertions would speed the spread of the poison rushing through her system. Already, the poison had reduced the squalling brats to low moans, their wide eyes rolling in their heads, their faces becoming slack.

The mother's terrified gaze flicked from her husband to her children and back again. She moaned. Nausea was an initial and brief symptom of the poison's growing effect.

The children fell limply to the floor, a crimson tear appearing on the corner of each of their eyes. A pair of bright red drops bubbled and grew from the youngest's nostrils.

The med-tech's injection gun fired for a fourth time. The husband would never awake. The woman's knees wobbled and the agent holding her released his grip and pushed her forward. She fell to the floor, thin lines of blood leaking from her eyes, ears, nose and mouth.

She spasmed twice and lay still, barely breathing as a thin sheen of blood seeped through her skin.

Helmut led his men from the house. The late afternoon sunlight slashed across the front yard. He addressed his second in command. "Call this outbreak in to the national authorities. Border is under absolute quarantine. No one in or out until further notice." The man nodded, stepping onto the small house's neatly manicured front lawn while tapping a tactical communications rig at his right ear.

His mission would succeed. Shadowstone would co-opt the local machinery of the nation state of Romania and ensure the way was clear for the operations of the vampires. Helmut smiled grimly at the thought. *Yes, vampires*, it had become clear to him over the preceding months and only one question remained, pressing like a caged animal within the shadows of his soul.

What do I have to do to get promoted to their immortal ranks?

Chapter Two

"Regarding chameleons, it should be noted they cannot sustain their camouflage indefinitely. Apparently, it requires a focus, or energy from them and has a limited duration. Shorter if they are fighting or running, longer if resting quietly. You can force them to reveal themselves through sustained pursuit. Then run them to ground and destroy them. Expect to lose more than ten of our kind when confronting one of them. They possess a trenchant vitality and are slow to die. Fortunately, they are a solitary creature." – Cornelius Crane, personal notes in his private library.

* * *

Brazil, North of the Amazonas, en route to Research Station #34 (Ruins), September 12th, 12:31

The turbines thrummed with a muted thunder.

Louise's osprey II drone speared toward research station number thirty-four in the Amazonas region of Brazil. Her new secret organization led by Siobhan Ulysses would be inserting themselves into the East Coast Hub by now. They had requisitioned a domestic airline jet from Utah to the east coast, leaving a small crew behind to complete the cleanup at the Salt Lake City airport hangar. They would be hitting the mess hall for a richly deserved meal, followed by showers and then the dormitories for some well-earned sack time.

She had managed to get five hours sleep in the last six and a half hours as her osprey II drone flew at a steady six-hundred miles per hour from Salt Lake City to Brazil. Her two squads of Day Guard troopers led by Archer and Hunter had accompanied her, along with the Order of Thoth operative, Jay Creeley.

Louise sat in the main body of the hold with most of her men, her laptop on her knees. The flight had been uneventful, with a simple thirty-minute stop to refuel at the international airport in Belize. She studied Jay Creeley as he sat opposite her. He could be a treasure trove of information on what remained of the Order of Thoth, the Red Empire, and the vampires, or the Vampire Dominion as Creeley referred to them. She'd delayed the debrief for six hours. She'd needed to sleep. However, in the last half hour, he'd confirmed the power structure. Crane ruled with his generals as an elite cadre around him. Chloe Armitage was his chief weapon against whomever opposed him. When he'd spoken about Armitage his voice had trembled with hate. He'd lost loved ones to her, that was clear. He had an absolute hatred for the vampires and some of his former team mates. Hence his course toward Louise. He couldn't continue with Slayne, Wu, and the rest. The Order hung by a thread, the Red Empire was not an option, and striking out on his own was futile. The only way he could fulfill his heart-felt purpose to destroy the vampires was to join the nascent rebellion within Shadowstone and the Day Guard.

Louise understood him and was willing to see what he could offer. She glanced across at her senior squad leader, Hunter. He'd undergone the pressure point technique applied by Creeley back at Salt Lake City airport. It'd been a transformation. He was already measurably stronger and faster. He was still eating for two and drinking lots of water. He was gaining two pounds an hour. Creeley said he'd never seen anything like it. The combination of the phase V Day Guard serum and the pressure point technique appeared to be a game changer. Her other squad members were asking for the same treatment. She'd held off for now, she wanted to make sure Hunter would be okay. The memories of all the men she'd killed because of their adverse reaction to the serum, their berserk rage, progeria, and catatonic depression still haunted her. Yes, she'd wait to make sure this worked before she risked more of her men. She swallowed; her mouth suddenly dry. Every single death within the nascent Day Guard weighed on her. Every man needlessly sacrificed was an unsung hero. She vowed silently, to avenge the abuse of their courage by the vampires.

Creeley had been relating recent battles at the Panopticon fortress and Arthur Slayne's private airport north-east of Las Vegas. He'd just remarked on the presence of an osprey II drone identical to the one in which they flew, and the disappearance of Arthur Slayne. Louise's aircraft was the second osprey II off the production line. James Haley possessed the first osprey II.

Louise checked her laptop, logged onto the standard Shadowstone networks, and attempted to retrieve the automated flight logs for James Haley's aircraft.

An FGEO, 'For General's Eyes Only,' security constraint guarded Haley's logs. As Crane's delegate she had the authority to view them, but the network would record her access.

If she opened those records, Haley would know she was checking where he was flying. She couldn't allow that; instead, she ran a secondary program on her laptop, drawing a number of nested circles on a map of the United States centered on Slayne's private airport in Nevada. The circles defined the perimeter an osprey II drone could reach in a given time. She searched for Shadowstone facilities near the southern border of Nevada, and found one site of interest. She brought up the details of a Shadowstone safe house on the outskirts of Phoenix, Arizona.

One of the generals had ordered the safe house be fitted with enhanced cells to hold 'special,' captives. Based on current electricity and food drops, it was in use by a team of eight, possibly ten given the latest food list. But who was manning it? Against regulations, there was no registry of the identities of the staff or prisoners. Was the rise in food supply this morning due to the arrival of two more people? She glanced across at Hunter. He was just finishing a chocolate flavored protein bar; his fourth in the last half-hour. Eating for two? No. Not eight to ten people, more like four to five Ramp masters. Enhanced cells? Who was the new addition to the site? Were they a prisoner? Was it Arthur Slayne?

Louise didn't believe in coincidences. She checked further. An FGEO security blanket covered the whole site. If she delved deeper, she would reveal her hand. Louise was head of Shadowstone and yet she had no knowledge of who was using this safe house. She took a deep breath and let it out. Like many large world-wide organizations, it was easy for the left hand not to know what the right hand was doing, especially for a paramilitary organization charged with maintaining secrecy and security on a global level, and of necessity compartmentalized by 'need to know,' access rules. Still, this looked like an egregious situation of a safe house dedicated to the use of a single general and kept as much off the books as it was possible to do so. One word escaped her lips in a whisper, "Armitage."

"What?" Creeley asked, his eyes flashing at the name.

"I think I know what happened to Arthur Slayne. He's being held prisoner in a safe house on the edge of Phoenix, Arizona."

"I don't care," Creeley remarked harshly.

Louise glanced at Creeley and raised an eyebrow. "Noted. He's not the mission. Still, he could reveal some useful information."

Creeley shook his head. "I wouldn't trust anything he had to say. He only plays his own game. His only skill is getting other people killed."

Louise looked at Creeley for a long considering moment and said, "Sure. We're not heading to Arizona anytime soon. He's on ice and will remain that way. After all, why tip our hand to the vampires in a vain attempt to rescue Arthur Slayne from imprisonment."

Creeley nodded, a grim look stole across his face. He was seemingly satisfied with Louise's directive.

"Our real mission is Brazil," she confirmed. "We have to retrieve the five hundred serum doses there. We can rapidly rebuild the Day Guard, and with your pressure point technique we can bring everyone up to the level of a ... 'Ramp Master.' This will be the decisive edge necessary to make the Day Guard a viable fighting force against the vampires."

And once the Panopticon 2.0 came online, they would have smart rifles with an enhanced target and shoot capability. The vampires wouldn't know what'd hit them. Louise and her forces could attack with surprise and devastating power.

She took a deep breath and let it out slowly. They still had to survive the next month, and the first task beckoned – retrieve the five hundred doses of serum. If they couldn't do that, her strategy was nothing more than an idle fantasy. She entered a series of commands on her laptop and gained access to a military satellite holding position over the Amazonas region. With the Panopticon down, she had to rely on 'old-school,' techniques. Still a military satellite was a useful asset, even if nothing more than a passive surveillance device.

It was time to investigate the ruins before they landed.

* * *

The sleek black and red helicopter raced over the verdant Amazonian jungle.

Miguel Rodriguez, Red Empire fist team leader, peered through the front canopy into the distance. He glanced at a clock on the helicopter's console. It was 12:45 local time; the ruins should become visible any moment. Just under twenty hours earlier, the Red Empire had deeply penetrated the world's military satellite systems. The Order of Thoth had destroyed the vampires' Panopticon. Since revealed to have been located in a recently destroyed fortress in Utah. Without the protection of the Panopticon, a half-ruined facility had appeared on the edge of the Urucu river, south of the mighty Amazon, and within forty miles of the regional center of Coari. A hundred thousand souls occupied Coari, a major city in the Amazonas region. Little did they know the facility forty miles away along the wide course of the Urucu river was a Vampire Dominion research station previously masked from the world by the now defunct Panopticon.

The Red Empire scout helicopter was a six-seater upgrade of the S-97 raider I. A pusher-propeller aircraft with a sustained cruise speed of two hundred and fifty miles per hour and a dash speed thirty miles per hour faster. Miguel and his team of three operatives, one of whom doubled as the pilot sitting to his left, had left their base in Rio de Janeiro in the pre-dawn darkness a tick over eight hours earlier. The Red Ghost, now operating out of Matahat al Diydan in the republic of Dagestan, had tasked them with this mission. They'd covered over nineteen hundred miles with a single refueling stop half way along the route at the municipal airport at Sinop in Mato Grosso. Once they'd investigated the Vampire Dominion site thoroughly, they would return to base along the same route.

The jungle parted, revealing a large clearing abutting onto the Urucu river. A jetty of dark-brown wood jutted out into the river, two motor boats sat on the bottom of the river next to it on the near side, their wheel houses rising forlornly out of the dark water. The raider II was coming in from the south-east. Miguel indicated a flat area of gray tarmac between a pair of large rectangular sheds on the near corner of the site that could serve as a helipad. The pilot adjusted his controls, the raider II going through a wide bank to the left before settling down onto the gray bitumen, coming to a stop facing the main ruins to the west.

To his left was a wide hangar, a single prop aircraft on wheels and floats sat within it. To his immediate right was a one-story building fronted by a series of steel roller doors; all down, and apparently locked. Beyond the nearest building to the north, what he assumed was a warehouse, rose a second two-story building, and a sizable water tower back toward the river.

In front of his helicopter were a pair of buildings. A two-story structure on the left that had suffered heavy damage from explosions and fire, and a second structure on the right, that could have been accommodations and was little more than burned out wreckage. On the north side of the tarmac, between the ruined accommodations building and the 'roller-door,' warehouse was a broad open shed filled with lathes, mills and other metal working machines. Beyond it a pair of diesel generator stacks rose; one straight and the other slewed at a steep angle.

"Corpses, Sir," remarked the pilot, Gomez, pointing through the canopy at several low clumpy mounds near the buildings.

"Certainly, looks like it," Miguel agreed. The jungle was quick to reclaim its territory, seizing any opportunity to return the incursions of puny humanity back to their natural state. Given enough time, the jungle would wipe the presence of the vampires from the face of the Earth. Miguel liked the jungle; he could relate to its remorseless tenacity.

The helicopter's single turbine stilled. It was time to get to work. They had to assess the site and see if they could find any intelligence on the Vampire Dominion's operations useful to the Red Empire. This was a preliminary survey. If they found anything significant, a more specialized team would arrive from Matahat to conduct a deep investigation.

Miguel twisted in his seat, and addressed the other two members of his team sitting in the middle seats of the cabin. "Gonzalez, you and Gomez, will take the north side of the site. Check those two warehouses, and the wrecks at the jetty. Go through the machine shop and the diesel plant behind it. Check the living quarters on the north west corner." He regarded the second man in the rear of the cabin. "Fernandez, you and I will cover the warehouse to the south and the main building on the south west corner. It looks like most of the explosive damage occurred on that building. If anything of interest has survived, it's probably on our side of the site." He swept his gaze across his team. "Keep the chat going, men, I want to hear from you every fifteen to twenty seconds or so. It looks like we're the only ones here, but watch out for booby traps or other surprises."

His men assented. He pushed open the right-side door, exiting to the ground with Fernandez behind his shoulder. It was the middle of the dry season, but the eighty-five percent humidity hit him like a wall after the air-conditioned comfort of the advanced helicopter cabin. Gomez the pilot and Gonzalez exited on the other side of the aircraft. Once outside the confines of their aircraft his men fitted their combat rigs. They wore dark-green peaked caps, sunglasses, gray-green camouflage pattern t-shirts, combat webbing, camouflage-pattern trousers and jungle-green combat boots. His men wore paired curved two-foot-long short swords belted at their waists, and held 9mm H&K MP 7 submachine guns. Miguel matched their actions, then checked their combat loads and equipment. Satisfied everyone was ready he nodded at his men. They split up into two pairs. Miguel and Fernandez passed in front of the helicopter and began their investigation of the southern side of the Vampire Dominion site while Gomez and Gonzalez covered the northern side.

Miguel lifted his submachine gun and proceeded toward the lone hangar on the south side of the site. A long-dead white-coated corpse lay on its front just short of a single-prop Cessna aircraft equipped with floats to fly off the nearby river. He toed the human remains over onto its back with his combat boot. Ragged patches of desiccated skin clung to dry bones. The efficient insect denizens of the jungle had harvested everything else. A plastic identity card hung from a frayed lanyard around the skeletal neck. Miguel reached down and ripped it away. The frayed cloth of the lanyard tore through wasted ligaments and the naked skull rolled a foot away, staring with empty sockets at the rear of the hangar. Miguel read the ID card. The remains apparently belonged to one 'Dr. Shu Li.' Head of Molecular Biology. She obviously didn't make it out alive, but what had killed her wasn't obvious. There were no bullet holes in the weathered remnants of her clothes. However, her cause of death wasn't the main issue. What was a molecular biologist, and apparently the head of an organization devoted to the same discipline doing in a remote location in the Amazon?

"Sir," Gonzalez called over the tactical link. "We've opened the first warehouse. There's a quarter-sized refrigerated shipping container running off a fuel cell with a consignment note for Fort Dix on it. The fuel cell is almost on empty, but it's still operational. The temperature in the unit is set to two degrees Celsius."

"Wait there, we'll be over in a minute," Miguel ordered. Molecular biology? Were the results of whatever science practiced here kept in the cooler? He turned and set off at a jog away from the Cessna toward the warehouse on the other side of the raider II.

"Wait, there's something he—" Gonzalez said.

Gomez screamed, a high falsetto of extreme agony that cut off a second after it started.

"Shit!" Gonzalez shouted. 9mm gunfire erupted in the shadows of the first warehouse.

Miguel and Fernandez ramped hard, racing past the nose of the raider II. The first warehouse stood thirty yards in front of them. The far-right roller door stood open, flashes of gunfire snapping like camera bulbs in the shadows within. An arm attached to a still firing 9mm submachine gun flew through the open doorway, spinning away to the right.

Vampires! They could be hiding in the shadows.

Miguel drew a sword with his left hand, his submachine gun held in his right. He blurred to the entrance of the warehouse, Fernandez a yard back on his right side. The interior of the warehouse lay in shadow, but Miguel could see well enough. Gomez had been torn in two, and Gonzalez had lost more than his right arm. What in hell had killed his men? He took a step backward. Something emerged from the shadows along the back wall, blurring forward. He reflexively fired at it, but too slowly, his rounds passing through empty space. Something gray, dark and razor sharp slashed across his throat with a wet slap. His head went flying through the air, landing on the rough tarmac behind him, bouncing and rolling away to a stop near the raider II.

Somewhere, on the ragged edges of his hearing, Fernandez screamed in dreadful agony.

Fernandez's voice – shrieking in abject horror – was the last sound Miguel Rodriguez, fist team leader of the Red Empire, ever heard.

* * *

Louise's osprey II drone circled slowly above research station number thirty-four.

An unknown threat had killed four Red Empire operatives. Louise sipped a mouthful of filtered water from a water bottle and returned it to the pouch strapped to her left hip, and considered the satellite map of their target. Forty-five minutes earlier, a privately owned advanced scout helicopter had landed on the helipad. Four men had emerged from the aircraft and begun investigating the site. Within two minutes something had killed them all. Whatever tore them to pieces remained unidentified.

Jay Creeley had a theory on which he continued to expound. "It's a chameleon," he asserted with wide eyes, "we encountered one in Reykjavík at the end of August."

"What the frack is a chameleon?" asked her second squad leader, Archer.

"All I want to know," said Hunter, cocking his finger and thumb like a gun and aiming it, "is how to kill it."

"Easier said than done," Creeley remarked, glancing back and forth between the two squad leaders. "They're a super-rare apex predator. Vampires, the Order of Thoth, the Red Empire, everyone who could, would hunt them down whenever they found one. But expect to lose ten guys to kill one of them. They are faster and stronger than vampires and they can camouflage to their surroundings even while moving." He rubbed his forehead, his eyes squeezed shut. "This is really bad luck."

Archer frowned, his blue eyes flashing. "If they're 'super-rare,' how come you've managed to run into two in less than two months?"

Creeley spread he hands wide. "I don't know. Maybe they're getting frisky or something."

"Frisky or not," Louise said, slapping her right fist into the palm of her left hand. She swung her right forefinger across her men. "It doesn't matter. We have a mission and we have to complete it." She glanced at Creeley before scanning her team with a hard gaze. "We assume Creeley's right." She rose to her feet, and addressed her men assembled in the hold of the osprey II drone. "There are fresh bodies strewn over the target. There is a clear and present danger. Assume the site is hot and hostile. We keep the drone's engines running while it's parked on the tarmac. We go in fast. We get the vials and get back to the osprey and take off as quickly as possible. If anything moves, we kill it. I don't want any of you taking chances or playing heroes. We all get out of here alive and get back to Fort Dix in one piece with the vials of serum intact. Is that clear?"

Her men looked up at her and gave their assent.

"Okay," she said. "Specifics. Hunter, your team will guard the drone and the path to the warehouse. Archer, I've tasked your team to enter the warehouse, get the vials and get back to the drone."

Hunter and Archer both nodded.

Louise called out to her pilot, "Simpson, put us down with our tail facing the south east corner of warehouse number one. I want us within thirty yards of the door. Got it?" He glanced back at her from the cockpit for a moment with a quizzical look on his face, and she clarified her orders. "Yes, with our tail facing the open roller door."

"Copy that, Ma'am," he replied.

"What about me?" Creeley asked.

Louise knew what the Order operatives were capable of. She said, "Take the side opposite Hunter and myself. Help guard Archer's team. You're worth any two of my team in a fight."

Creeley nodded, put his hand on the handle of his katana, and muttered something beneath his breath.

Louise stood up. Creeley looked like he'd just assessed their chances as hopeless. That was too bad. She and her team were already committed. Crane would never let them live now they knew vampires existed. They were already in the kill zone. There was no path other than forward to victory or death. She reflected for a brief moment on their situation. *Never underestimate what someone with nothing to lose is capable of.*

She cocked her submachine gun. It was time to go into battle. She'd organized her available force to execute the mission in the least amount of time. Perhaps they could get in and out before any giant invisible lizards showed up and started ripping heads off.

Chameleons. If she didn't already believe in vampires, she would have laughed at the idea of invisible lizards, but the evidence was too strong to discount Creeley's story. The four Red Empire operatives were dead. Two of them had ramped with visible heat plumes beneath the military satellite cameras. There was no mistaking what they were, and despite their speed and strength they lay in dismembered chunks attracting flies beneath the mid-day sun. Whatever had killed them was almost certainly still there and she was going in with a force that was woefully unprepared and underpowered to the threat. She herself was merely human, no special powers at all. But still, she'd go in with her men. There was no way she would cower in the drone while they took all the risk. She would lead from the front, nothing else was acceptable.

She held her submachine gun casually in her right hand, her left slapped up against the hull of the osprey just short of the rear ramp door. She glanced to the left of her hand. There was a fully loaded multiple-grenade launcher (MGL) and half a dozen H&K 419 smart-assault rifles racked next to the door. Heavy artillery – she hoped she wouldn't need it.

Simpson brought the drone down onto the tarmac. The aircraft shuddered slightly as it landed and took up the shock through its landing struts. The rear door opened, first revealing a bright horizontal slit that rapidly expanded as the ramp swung down to the ground. Archer, joined by Simpson from the cockpit, and the rest of his team were the first down the ramp, sprinting forward in pairs, their assault rifles held high, their armored heads on swivels. Hunter and his squad followed, Louise and Creeley went with them, forming a six-man team from the tail of the drone to the open warehouse. The tactical link was hot. Hunter and his men had their rifles locked against their shoulders and ready to fire. Creeley had his katana drawn, its magnificent blade gleaming in the bright sunlight.

Archer and his team vanished into the warehouse shadows.

* * *

The humidity enveloped Jay in an oppressive cloud of instant perspiration.

He'd picked up a spare camouflage cap in the drone to shade his eyes from the bright sunshine, and adjusted it as he ran down the drone's ramp. He hit the tarmac at the end of the ramp and ramped hard, turning in a full circle to scan the perimeter. The day guards slowed to half-speed around him and Wesson looked like she was moving in treacle. They all carried guns. A possibly futile effort versus a chameleon. The giant lizards could be upon them before they had any chance to shoot. Jay relied on the White Dragon for both offense and defense.

He looked hard at the ground for tell-tale movements. A leaf disturbed without a breeze, or an unexpected crunch of sand, just anything he couldn't explain. He pressed his lips into a tight line; most likely they'd lose one of their own to discover the chameleon was amongst them. He remembered a remark Francis had made after Reykjavík. He'd said, 'Chameleons fight best when visible. If pressed, they will lose their camouflage ability. That's when they're most dangerous. When you can see them. If you have to fight one, strike for the throat or heart, but strike deep – they have bones like armor.'

Jay wore an earbud networked with the osprey's onboard tactical communications link. The second squad leader's voice came over in an exultant whisper, "The fridge is open and still frosty. Got the prize. On our way back."

Louise answered, "Make it quick, Archer."

Jay paused, took a breath, maintained his ramp and continued to watch for threats. The verdant jungle rose in a dark-green curtain around the site, broken only by a broad river resting on the north-east corner of the site, dark brown water lapped around a wooden jetty and a pair of sunken river boats. He lifted his left hand to wipe a stray drop of perspiration from his left eyebrow.

His hand never made contact with his face.

The shock was almost indescribable, like a pair of trucks hammering into him from the left and right. There was nowhere to go but up. His feet rose off the tarmac, his left arm trapped against his side, his right arm swung free. He reversed the White Dragon and lashed down past his waist. It struck dense flesh, coming back trailing a streamer of dark red blood. Something roared behind him in monstrous rage. He arched backward in agony, a dozen razor-sharp talons tearing through his chest from the inside out. A tortured scream erupted from his throat. His right hand blurred again – but he fell apart before he could complete a second strike. The White Dragon flew from his grasp, spinning away in the sunshine.

He hit the ground in a series of wet thuds and ropy streamers of blood and entrails, the oblivion of eternity claimed him a moment later.

* * *

Hunter hit Louise like a freight train.

She blacked out for a moment, unable to track what was happening. Louise came to at the top of the osprey's ramp. Hunter stood tall at the bottom of the ramp. He sprayed the space over Creeley's corpse; his heavy assault rifle riffing through its fifty-round magazine. He lifted his rifle and it fell silent, a wisp of gray smoke issuing from its barrel. The other members of his squad had already pulled back to the edge of the metal ramp. They stood facing outward, their assault rifles raised, ready to fire at a moment's notice – but there was nothing to shoot at.

Her last memory before blacking out was Creeley rising up off the ground, screaming, his sword flashing in the bright sunshine. Something roared and he fell apart in a shower of blood. A huge lizard-shape had flickered for a moment where Creeley had stood, then Hunter had tackled her.

Whatever had left Creeley in blood-soaked chunks on the tarmac had vanished. A chameleon? Creeley had asserted one was here. Louise didn't waste time wondering if the creature had targeted the team's most powerful fighter by accident. She assumed it was intelligent enough to do it deliberately.

Hunter ejected his spent magazine and slotted a fresh one home.

A man screamed from within the warehouse.

"Shit!" Archer cried out over the tactical link. "It's here!"

Or are there two? Louise thought, her heart freezing with horror.

Gun fire erupted in the shadows of the warehouse. Her men were dying forty yards away and Louise was helpless to do anything to stop it. She pushed herself off the ramp and rose to her feet. Bright flashes strobed off the interior walls of the flat-topped building. A single scream rose and suddenly cut out.

Archer led two of his men from the warehouse. Simpson was missing, but instead of running toward the osprey, Archer caught her gaze for half a tortured second before he cut to his left, and ran toward the corner of the warehouse and the river beyond it. He whirled at the edge of the building, firing his assault rifle in a broad swathe behind him, his two remaining squad members mirroring his actions. He shouted defiantly, "Want some? Get some!"

Archer was disobeying her instructions. He was playing the hero. He spun away, his two men following closely behind him. The squad sprinted for the dock jutting out into the river. They didn't make it. Halfway to the dock the trailing man rose off the ground, he lifted his rifle, firing over his shoulder. The thing holding him swam into view, recoiling, its massive pale-gray head pulling to the right as one of the bullets ripped through a cheek. The man died a moment later in a shower of blood and the creature vanished as all her men opened fire upon it.

Archer and his remaining trooper rushed onto the dock jutting onto the river. "We've got this boss," he declared over the tactical link. "Get the vials!" he gasped in a desperate shout, "It's gotta come along the dock, or through the river. Either way, we'll see it on the planks or in the water."

Archer was smart, it was a tragedy he'd probably lose his life within the next minute. Louise ordered, "Hold there, we'll get you on the way through."

"Copy that," he replied.

Hunter glanced at her for an instant, his dark eyes filled with determination.

She said, "Get the—"

Hunter vanished. He was fast, like Creeley was. His three squad members remained behind, guarding the osprey and her. Louise threw the submachine gun to the side where it clattered against the metal bulkhead and lifted the multiple grenade launcher off the rack. She faced the open tarmac, and chambered a HEAP grenade. If she could cover her men's retreat back to the osprey she would. It was time to see what a lizard could do against a high-explosive armor-piercing 40mm grenade.

If only she could get enough time to see it, surely, she could kill it.

* * *

Charles Archer and Hicks sprinted down the dock.

They whirled as one, assault rifles raised. The creature could run down the dock toward them, or enter the Urucu river. Either way, unless it could fly, they would see it. The dock was composed of poorly maintained wooden planks, loose and noisy to step upon. Anything moving through the water would be instantly visible and targeted for destruction. The end of the dock was the most defensible position they could reach in a handful of furious seconds.

Charles believed in Ms. Wesson's mission. The vampires were real. The republic was in danger and needed protecting. If in this moment, it fell to Hicks and himself to make the ultimate sacrifice, so be it. He'd signed up to nothing less when he'd originally joined the United States Navy Seals. Whatever was advancing toward them, they would meet it with skill, courage, and a barrage of hot lead.

They hadn't lost the battle yet. There were no forgone conclusions. If Hicks and himself could survive, the osprey II drone would fly overhead, the loading ramp down, lines dangling. The angels would arrive and carry them away from the clutches of death and defeat. In any event, he'd buy the Boss time to get the vials and complete the mission.

The Day Guard had to succeed. They had to restore the Republic. They had to destroy the parasitic regime of the vampires. Charles' finger rested on the trigger of his H&K 419 big-bore assault rifle. He whispered encouragement to Hicks, "We've got this, Hicks."

Hicks gave a short nod and a brief glance, his gaze steely. They would honor their oaths or die trying.

It was enough.

* * *

The wheelhouse of the nearest sunken wreck imploded.

Archer and his one remaining trooper whirled, strafing the hulk with heavy 7.62mm rounds.

Louise stared at them, willing them from afar to hit their elusive target. Wood flaked and puffed away, hot lead slashing through the walls and hull of the decrepit motor-boat, vanishing beneath the river's surface in lines of bubbles. Gray smoke plumed as the rifles thundered until their magazines ran empty.

Archer shouted, "Reload!"

On her left, Hunter emerged from the warehouse carrying a large dark-enameled case with both hands, his weapon slung over his shoulder. His men fell in behind him as he passed through their corridor in a blur toward the interior of the osprey.

Louise's gaze flicked back to Archer. He and Hicks had reloaded and were scanning the wreck. They turned, staring at the water surrounding the dock, their faces pale, intent, fierce – seemingly impervious to the dread she felt.

Hunter flashed past her, his men tramping into the hold. "I've got it, Ma'am," he shouted from behind her.

She glanced over her shoulder. "Take us off. We have to pick up Archer."

He nodded, putting the case aside and rushing forward to the cockpit. His three troopers formed a line guarding the open ramp beneath the tail of the osprey. The drone's turbines roared. The aircraft lifted off the ground, swayed, and banked toward the dock. His men snapped long ropes to pad eyes forged into the ceiling and threw the weighted rope ends out over the lowered ramp. Louise stepped up to join them, the multiple-grenade launcher cradled tightly in her hands.

Her two troopers were still alive at the end of the dock. The osprey dove through the air over the river. A stray memory ran through her mind, of fishing with her father as a child. She banished the thought a moment after it arrived, reasserting the full focus of her mind, but terror still clenched her guts, was she fishing for her men?

Louise's heart froze – what would she catch?

* * *

The osprey's turbines thundered, echoing off the surrounding jungle.

Charles Archer swiveled his head left and right as he stood with Hicks at the end of the dock. The creature must've leaped from the river bank to the top of the sunken motor-boat on the left. A prodigious feat of strength to clear the other wreck and cover forty yards in a single jump. Hicks and himself had each emptied a fifty-round magazine of armor-piercing caseless into the wreck. Charles shook his head, pressing his lips into a thin line. He couldn't be sure they'd hit anything at all. There was no blood visible in the water, and it was too dark and cloudy to see more than a couple of feet below the surface.

"Grenades!" he shouted, stripping one from his harness, tearing the pin out and looping it fifteen feet away into the river. Hicks followed a moment later to the opposite side, past the nearest hulk. The weapons crumped beneath the dark-cloudy surface, sending twin sprays of water flying into the air.

Hicks whirled from left to right and back again, the barrel of his assault rifle tracking the direction of his gaze. He snarled with frustration and demanded, "Where the hell is it?"

Charles shouted, "Grenades! Again!" He dragged another grenade from his webbing, flicked the pin away with his thumb and looped it into the water twenty feet away. If they could keep the creature away for a few more seconds they'd buy their escape.

The osprey's turbines howled above them; its shadow passing over the dock. A pair of thick ropes dangled from the open bay over the lowered ramp, swinging toward them.

The second set of grenades exploded beneath the water. Muffled crumps sending fountains of river water into the air. Charles sucked air past gritted teeth and reached for the nearest rope. Hicks looked up, his left hand reaching for the second rope. They'd only get one chance as the osprey flew past. If the creature was still around there'd be no time to survive long enough for a second attempt.

The dock erupted beneath their boots. Wooden planks splintered and shattered in wild cracks like errant thunder. Dark-brown water sprayed everywhere. Hicks shouted, "Hell—"

The creature was upon them.

Charles pulled his rifle around and fired.

* * *

Hicks screamed for an instant.

Louise looked on in horror as Hicks was torn in half. Archer fired, standing on a pair of wooden stumps rising out of the water where the end of the dock had been. The creature shimmered beneath the water spray for a moment, impact wounds stitching across its chest from Archer's rifle. The monster's arm lashed out, black spines lining its deadly arc, silencing Archer forever in a splash of scarlet.

She shivered, calling out to Hunter in near panic, "UP! UP! UP! UP!"

Turbines roared to the left and right. The osprey leaped through the air. Both ropes went taut. Her men rushed to the sides of the hold, attempting to get an angle on what was hanging off the lines. But the creature was beneath them, hidden by the hull. Louise stepped back from the edge of the ramp. The creature was still alive, and climbing the ropes. She slammed the close button on the ramp and it started to rise up. The gap narrowing from ten feet … to nine … to eight. God, how long would it take to close?

Two of her men pulled their combat knives to cut the taut ropes.

Louise stared at the gap. The jungle shimmered like a passing heat wave before her eyes. Drops of dark red blood splashed onto the floor of the hold. She slapped the open button. It was too late to cut the ropes; it was already in here with them. Violence erupted like a dark thunderstorm within the hold. One of her men lost his head, painting the wall and ceiling with ropy jets of blood. The other two opened fire at point-blank range shooting at where they believed the creature was. Their rifles thundered in the confined space. Rounds ricocheting off the bulkhead. The creature howled. Shimmering into visibility, looming within the tight confines of the hold. It stood well over seven-feet tall, gray pebbled skin, streaked with white and splotched with bright blood. It glared at its human foes, long-clawed hands like gray dinner plates grabbed her men by the throat and twisted to the sickening sounds of snapping bones.

Louise took a single step forward, pressing the barrel of her grenade launcher against the right side of the creature's rib cage. Beyond it, the ramp was lowering again. To her right her men fell limp, eyes bulging, trapped by the creature's strength.

In the same instant, she pulled the trigger. There was a muffled chuff, and a flash of light. The molten-copper whip of the grenade tore a six-inch-wide hole through the monster's torso. The shaped charge splattered blood and chunks of burned meat over the edge of the ramp door. The creature lurched to its left, away from her, dragging her doomed men with it. It fell through the open ramp doorway, her men vanishing over the edge, carried away within its dying grasp.

Louise ran forward to the edge of the ramp, her left hand reaching for a hand hold on the wall. The creature splashed into the river, her two men followed it down, falling bonelessly into the dark water in secondary splashes. Hunter appeared next to her right shoulder, pulling her back from the edge. He said hoarsely in hollow aggrieved tones, "They're gone Ma'am. They've flat lined."

Louise asked dully, "Did anyone else survive?"

Hunter hesitated for half a second, shaking his head slowly. "Only us."

Louise shook her head. Horrified by the sacrifice of her men. The only reason Hunter and herself still lived was due to the selfless bravery of others. The obligation weighed on her. She lifted her eyes to the heavens. She would not let her men down. They had not died in vain. She would see this war through or die trying.

She took a deep breath and let it out. This was nothing like an assassination. It was no longer about a target and herself with no one else at risk. Her men had trusted her. They'd placed their lives in her hands. She'd done the best she could and still – they'd died.

Louise rose, racked the MGL on the wall to her left, turned and approached the dark-enameled case. It had simple flick-locks to the left and right. Obviously, no one expected anyone would be handling these vials who didn't have a right to access them. She laid the case flat and lifted the lid. There were trays and trays of vials, each one a dose of the Day Guard serum. There was a dosing gun, and a single full kit of medical fluids and IV lines. She could dose herself here and now in the drone. She could be through the process by the time they landed in Fort Dix. Using the serum was a coin-toss chance of dying. She didn't care; her men had already shown the way. She stared resolutely at Hunter and commanded, "Hook me up. It's time for me to be all that I can be."

Hunter nodded and moved to obey.

The drone flew on, guided home by its auto-pilot.

Chapter Three

BREAKING: Airborne Ebola Outbreak in Romanian Town

There are multiple reports of an outbreak of airborne Ebola in the town of Border, Romania.

Published 09/12 10:20 Eastern Standard Time (New York)

Romanian authorities report a full lockdown and quarantine of the town of Border (Pop. Approx. 4000) in Transylvania, Romania. Authorities have declared martial law, deploying military and para-military units to ensure the integrity of a cordon around the quarantined region. Medical and scientific staff are working around the clock to resolve an outbreak of a novel form of airborne Ebola.

– Breaking News article on the Internet.

* * *

Romania, The town of Border, September 12th, 19:45

The command shadowstar descended toward the town square.

Cornelius relished the opportunity to land. He'd been sharing the cabin of the command shadowstar drone with his reluctant enforcer for four hours. They'd discussed many things in a wide-ranging conversation. He'd filled her in on everything he knew about Mekra and Akimitsu, including the location of Mekra's donjon. He'd alerted her to the fact the Panopticon was online and operating somewhere near Phoenix, Arizona.

A report had arrived five minutes earlier from the day guards and Shadowstone operatives searching for the Panopticon in Arizona. Their osprey II had landed next to a long shed at the rear of a truck repair business. They'd traced the Panopticon signal to the same site three hours earlier. Now it was on the move with short, intermittent network access signals, which narrowed the area of search but couldn't pinpoint the location. The very system that would have solved this problem in seconds was the one lost. The Shadowstone/Day Guard team had taken off to broaden their search patterns using the sensor arrays on the osprey II. Finding and destroying the Panopticon was now a waiting game.

Despite Cornelius' new loremaster ability, the location of Arthur Slayne was still unknown. He'd refrained from attempting a vision in the presence of Armitage as she would be sure to detect the warmth of the loremaster implant in his right forearm. The damn thing burned like a hot coal when it was fully operational. It was a drawback; when accessing his precognitive powers in the past he'd been able to claim he was merely reflecting on events with his eyes closed. Now he couldn't do that without revealing his power to any nearby vampire. Still, with the loremaster laptop wired into the command shadowstar's network he could conduct a loremaster vision while wearing his tactical helmet, and an opportunity to do so without observation would arise soon enough or he would simply order everyone away and make it happen.

While Armitage needed to know as much as possible to defend his life, there were some things he could never reveal to her, and his precognitive power was one of them. While she no doubt suspected as much, there was a big difference between suspicion and knowledge. He'd also kept the full details of his plan for the defense of Mekra's donjon and the destruction of Akimitsu to himself. *Was it paranoia to trust no one?* No, it was necessary to maintain an information advantage against all opponents, real, possible or imagined. His opponents would have to surmise his intent after the events had already played out – if they were still alive.

The command shadowstar drone touched down in the center of town. As its engines wound down, another pair of shadowstars and three ospreys IIs loaded with the forty Force-Europe praetorians under the command of general Dieter Franz, landed nearby. Shadowstone operatives with fuel tankers rolled into position to refuel the elite elements of his personal airforce. Within minutes, hoses snaked across the concrete, pavement, and bitumen, and pumps thrummed in the background.

The town of Border was under complete lockdown. The local population held under house arrest, terrified by the prospect of an outbreak of airborne Ebola. Private traffic had vanished from the roads, leaving only Shadowstone operated vehicles. Multiple layers of cordons stretched around the town and the broader region up to the regional center of Braşov.

Shadowstone Europe staffed the inner cordon, and directed the operations of Romanian military and police forces manning the outer cordons. It was sufficient to eliminate the noise and clutter of local traffic and reveal anyone, such as Akimitsu, entering the vicinity of Mekra's donjon.

The refueling operations completed. One of the shadowstars rose on jets of cobalt fire. Cornelius slaved the pilotless craft to his tactical helmet and sent it to a position three miles above the town. The drone's sensor arrays searched for any incursion, its weapons waiting to deliver certain doom.

Cornelius smiled grimly; he was ready for Akimitsu to arrive.

* * *

Mekra smiled with anticipation, her invisible astral form hovering thirty feet above the town square.

Crane, and his lackey, Armitage, stepped down from their flying craft. A shadowstar they had called it in their conversation within the craft's cabin. Mekra had listened to every word after they had arrived. With Akimitsu and the Red Empire fist team making all haste to her prison, and now halfway between the cities of Almaty in Kazakhstan and Nukus in Uzbekistan, she'd returned to prepare their way. She'd arrived just in time to witness the landing of Crane's forces. He was clearly anticipating the arrival of Akimitsu, but did he know about the additional converts or her power of astral travel? It appeared not, or he'd be much more guarded in his final words with Armitage.

She rose high into the sky, the town dwindling beneath her. Her extreme vampire senses remained fully empowered in her astral form. Crane's forces were deploying around the town. She waited for them to take up position for the night. They formed a tight cordon, but not quite tight enough to stop a team of mekrarian vampires deeply skilled in Ninjitsu. She would guide them through Crane's defenses. She would send her small team through a narrow corridor from the south-west. They were on track to arrive two hours before sunrise. They would ditch their flying craft, and proceed on foot to the village of Azuga where they would recover necessary tools to open her prison and wait out the day. Their arrival shortly before dawn was too late to implement her plan. She would find no freedom released into the daylight. She would have to wait for the following night, then she would strike.

Mekra looked a handful of miles to the south, to the village of Azuga. There was an ancient underground bunker built in a time of global terror. Long abandoned by the local peasants, it would serve Akimitsu, Whispering Death, and her other minions well, until the hateful sun fell and the glorious night rose again.

Her freedom was almost upon her, she could taste it to the depths of her soul.

* * *

"We are in position," general Haras Mosule reported over the command channel.

Mosule commanded Crane's reserve force of twenty-four praetorians. Equipped with a pair each of shadowstars and ospreys, they waited twelve miles to the north in a secret hangar beyond the regional city of Braşov.

Chloe leaned casually against the side of the command shadowstar and listened with one ear as Crane and Mosule completed their exchange. They were almost speaking in code phrases, never revealing their actual location or plan of action. Crane assumed the lost Panopticon compromised the tactical helmets and communication systems, but unless whoever had the Panopticon knew about Mekra, they could not fully understand what was occurring in Romania. The interior of any of the shadowstars remained shielded, but the Panopticon could intercept anything sent across a comms channel and reveal it to the Panopticon's operators.

Crane glanced at her, a quizzical frown on his face. Chloe preempted any comment and waved her hand in the direction of the nearest unit of deployed praetorians. "With the Panopticon live and in the hands of adversaries unknown, perhaps we should limit communications and cameras. Certainly, having five shadowstars within thirty miles of each other is simply telling anyone who's watching that a major operation is underway."

Crane curled his lip and stared at the distant armored praetorians. "I'm not stripping my men of their helmets and communications, or grounding the shadowstars." He turned back to face her. "We need those systems operational. We'll have to wear the fact Arthur Slayne may be watching all this right now."

Chloe had given up being impassive in Crane's presence. He typically interpreted a lack of response as her trying to hide her true feelings. It was better to always give him something he could misinterpret. She gave him a warning glance. "We can't rule out that Slayne may still be alive."

"I'm assuming he is. I wouldn't trust a report that Slayne was dead without witnessing his corpse at my feet."

The elder Slayne was still under guard at the safe house in Phoenix. She looked at Crane and smiled in soft acquiescence. "Of course, that is wise. However," she glanced over her shoulder toward the south west, "regarding this cordon of yours ..."

"Yes?" Crane inquired.

"Is it as tight—"

"Say no more," Crane snapped.

Chloe raised an eyebrow. The slight gap to the south west was deliberate. Crane had left an opening for Akimitsu to slip through. He intended for Akimitsu to get close to the donjon. The second of Franz's shadowstars left the square, rising without a pilot into the night sky on jets of pale-cobalt fire. Without doubt slaved to Crane's command helmet.

She looked at Crane impassively. Despite his recent revelations, he couldn't stop himself from keeping secrets. She was not surprised. Crane was one leopard who could never change his spots. She connected the dots. A fake world-killer virus unleashed in central Romania. A new strain of vampires brought to the same location. The lie and the hidden truth aligned as one.

Chloe lifted her gaze, tracking the second shadowstar to its position loitering three miles above the town. Crane had commanded the drone's carry nuclear weapons for this mission. Perhaps he planned for a massive sanitation event, ridding the world of the threat of mekrarian vampires with the media cover of a fake horrific virus outbreak.

If true, Crane was getting desperate.

Chloe lifted her right hand, studied her immaculate fingernails, and smiled softly to herself.

* * *

The lake was liquid moonlight glimmering beneath the night sky.

The still water raced beneath the hull of the raider II. Akimitsu glanced at the instrument displays. Local time registered 04:59 on the scout helicopter's console. Sunrise would arrive in less than two hours. Mekra had already instructed him on what to do. He was to take his team to the town of Azuga, four miles south of Border, and wait there. There was already a place she'd found for them. A relic of the cold war, a Soviet-era nuclear fallout bunker, disused, covered in graffiti and forgotten. They'd thrashed the helicopter's engines all the way from Hami, only stopping for fuel and blood, running the raider II at maximum speed for the whole distance. It had bought them the opportunity to arrive well before dawn at risk of burning the engine out. The aircraft was almost new, very-well maintained, and had survived the abuse.

Whispering Death had explained the operation of the raider II earlier in the journey. The original design would've carried eight men. The evolved 'IIs' dropped two seats and moved the rear bulkhead forward to accommodate an electronic warfare package designed to render the aircraft all but invisible to electronic sensors. However, a shadowstar could loiter upside down, enabling its vampire crew to watch the ground with their own eyes and superior vampire senses. The scout helicopter was fast, small, black and running without lights, blending in with the dark terrain beneath it. With a bit of luck, the vampires would never see them.

An alarm blared a shrill warning.

"Missile lock!" Whispering Death shouted.

"Get out!" Akimitsu yelled.

"Splash it!"

Two of the other vampires pulled the sliding doors back on each side of the aircraft. The helicopter shed speed, dropped into the night-shadowed water, steam billowing off the turbine's heat shields, and began sinking immediately. Akimitsu and the former Red Empire fist team dove into the water and swam for the distant shore.

Behind them a pair of air-to-air missiles lanced into the sinking raider II, vaporizing it, sending a shockwave shuddering through the dark lake water. The five vampires speared deep beneath the surface, never rising for air, rushing through the water with powerful kicks, escaping the fury of the missile strikes that claimed their helicopter.

A lizard's tail, Akimitsu thought triumphantly as the helicopter wreckage sank to the bottom of the lake. Let Crane believe he had killed them all. They had arrived to free their queen and free her they would. They all longed to reveal their queen's glorious destiny to the world. He thrummed with heart-felt need, soon he would liberate his queen. They would not fail in their quest. They were all of one mind.

How could they be otherwise?

* * *

Cornelius Crane studied the reports on the command drone's displays.

His high-flying shadowstar drones had intercepted an incoming Red Empire raider II with predictable results, splashing the helicopter into a mountain lake a tick under forty minutes ago. However, there were no signs of bodies within the wreckage on the lake floor.

The shadowstar drones were the outer layer of his cordon around Mekra's donjon. However, the novel mekrarian threat, now apparently strengthened with recent Red Empire converts with an advanced scout helicopter had bypassed them. There was no sign of Akimitsu or anyone else for that matter within the forest near the lake.

Cornelius was not surprised. The new mekrarian vampire had vanished into the woods near the fortress of the Obsidian Claw. Not even leaving a heat trail. The conclusion was all too obvious. Akimitsu and his new cohorts were cold-blooded, their body temperature matching their surroundings. A characteristic that would assist Akimitsu or any other mekrarian vampire to blend into their environment. Cornelius frowned, he could easily imagine Akimitsu and any others within the helicopter escaping into the lake where the water would disperse any signature of their location, then emerging on the stony lake shore and disappearing beneath the thick canopy of the forest. Even the canopy piercing LIDAR sensors on the shadowstars would have difficulty identifying a vampire blurring from tree trunk to tree trunk.

The only readily available solution to mekrarian stealth was direct observation. With that in mind, he'd slaved a dedicated optical camera on the first shadowstar flying top cover over Border onto the front door of Mekra's donjon. He'd slaved the feed from the camera onto a one-inch square within his tactical helmet's heads-up display. The rocks covering the entrance to Mekra's donjon remained in place. The camera hovering three miles above the site would reveal anything moving in the open within four-hundred yards of the hidden doorway.

Akimitsu had arrived in a stolen Red Empire scout helicopter. It was probable, bordering on certain he'd converted one or more Red Empire fighters to Mekra's ranks. Most likely a fist team, three to six men at most. But still, any Red Empire Ramp master converted into a telepathically controlled weapon at the beck and call of Mekra would be a living nightmare.

Cornelius' plans were progressing in accordance with what he'd witnessed in his first loremaster vision back in the research facility in Queens, New York. He needed Akimitsu to reach Mekra's donjon, it was a precursor to victory – a victory resting on a knife edge.

A victory he'd foreseen.

* * *

The town was gravid with tension.

Chloe sniffed. The air was rank with fear. She'd not smelled its like since the Cuban missile crisis of 1962. The townsfolk were well aware something apart from the outbreak and lockdown was happening. They'd whispered amongst themselves and with their neighbors. A quiet word here and there muttered against a wall or over a fence. The word had spread. The shadowstar drones and osprey IIs were the very latest technology. The body armor of the praetorians gleamed beneath the street lights. When skin was visible, it was paler than normal. One word stood out amongst the background chatter, 'vampires.' A word uttered within fifteen minutes of their arrival and which had grown on a current of quiet terror.

Romanians! Why should these people be so quick to acknowledge the truth? What part did ancient legends, the curse of Vlad Tepes, and the fictional scribblings of an Irish author play? Whatever the reason, the answer was little more than an idle curiosity. Hell was going to open up and swallow this town and all the people within it.

Chloe could feel it in her bones.

She glanced to the east; the dawn was glowing across the horizon. She retreated to the side of the command drone, preparing to join Crane within its secure confines. The rest of the praetorians were in the now grounded ospreys. Shadowstone operatives backed up by Romanian paramilitaries patrolled the streets while pilotless shadowstars guarded the skies. Shadowstone would ensure the security of the vampires during daylight hours. Several houses stood silent; their families drained of blood. Crane's army needed feeding and the local populace had provided the necessary sustenance. Chloe had kept her distaste hidden behind a wall of silence at the inevitable feeding upon children by some of the praetorians.

Her smartphone vibrated silently. She pulled it out of its armored pocket on her left sleeve and flipped it open. There was a text from James Haley that read, 'We have reached Hana Tanaka's apartment in Tokyo. We will begin our search from there. J.'

The message evaporated a second after she read it, all evidence of its existence vanishing without a trace.

James and the chameleons were in motion. Good, at least part of her strategy was in progress. She leaped lithely into the cabin of the command drone. It was time to get some sleep. With Akimitsu hiding from the sun somewhere nearby, she was sure the next night would be a busy one.

She might even have to fight.

One could always hope.

Chapter Four

"Those who can only see what they want to see will be ruled by those who can see what must be seen." – Chloe Armitage

* * *

Japan, Tokyo, Outside Hana Tanaka's Apartment, September 13th, 11:52

James broke the code on the electronic lock, then gave the door a gentle push.

The door to Hana Tanaka's Tokyo apartment swung open, revealing a short hall leading into an open plan living area. Shadowstone Japan were all over the apartment building and the surrounding block. Unfortunately for them, they'd never had the head of the US branch break through their rings of surveillance. They'd never had someone with full inside knowledge go through their motion sensors, cameras, and microphones like a rat through a well-trodden maze.

James took a step forward across the threshold into Tanaka's apartment. The chameleons ghosted out of nowhere into the middle of the apartment block hall. James' eyes widened, and he said in hushed, urgent tones, "Shit, Gullette. Couldn't you have waited until we got inside."

Gullette regarded him with wide-set reptilian eyes and said, "Meat-that-talks, driven by terror, like all prey."

"Thanks for the wise words," James uttered sarcastically. He strode forward into the apartment's entry hall and beckoned over his left shoulder to the big lizards, summoning them into the living room. They followed him in with ducked heads, and he swept a hand around the place. "What do you need to find her?"

Chloe's objectives were clear: capture Hana Tanaka and bring her safely back to New York City, and retrieve the serum for reversing vampirism. All achieved while hiding the operation and the chameleons from the surveillance might of Shadowstone Japan. They couldn't afford for word of what they were doing to get back to Cornelius Crane. If Crane found out Chloe was actively attempting to subvert his system of implant control, it would surely result in their deaths or something even worse.

Finding Tanaka's apartment had been as simple as conducting a search on Shadowstone's current operations. The Panopticon maybe lost forever, but the standard organizational networks remained fully functional. He'd hired a van at Narita airport to transport Gullette and Kavanne. Shemina had stayed with the osprey II within a Shadowstone proxy-owned hangar. Gullette was increasingly protective of Shemina. The implication was clear;

she was about to become fertile. James didn't want to be anywhere near the lizards when that happened. He could easily become someone's snack.

Gullette's big gray head swiveled to the left, and he snorted at a closed door. James opened it, and entered the apartment's bathroom and laundry. A laundry basket stood in a corner. Tanaka had left in a hurry, leaving her last load of unwashed clothes in the basket. James rummaged around in the pile of laundry and pulled out a black T-shirt. He lifted it with both hands and shook it out. There was a faint aroma of a stale deodorant but nothing else he could detect. A print of 'The Great Wave Off Kanagawa,' covered the front of the T-shirt. The girl had taste, if a bit generic.

James raised the unwashed shirt to Gullette. The big lizard sniffed it once, then stepped away. Kavanne followed suit and sniffed mightily, then coughed quizzically at Gullette. Gullette regarded James and said, "We hunt now," his grin widened, "meat scurry and hide, no hope left."

James opened his left hand, revealing a black disc the size of a coin. "Take this with you so that I can follow."

Gullette snorted dismissively, but took the tracker and made it disappear within his left fist. He croaked once, and the two chameleons vanished. A breeze snapped through the hallway as they left the apartment.

James followed them into the main hall of the apartment block, relocking the door behind him. He strode down the hallway to the elevators, resetting the Japanese Shadowstone sensors as he passed them while setting up tracking on the disc carried by Gullette.

They were as ghosts in this world.

* * *

The Crimson Lord strode confidently into the underground chamber.

Everyone bowed toward him, and Hana Tanaka quickly followed suit, without taking her eyes off him.

He glanced briefly at Hana, then focused his attention upon her sister. He snapped at Sakura, "You have a weapon against Crane? I have read your report. Show me the vials."

Sakura glanced at the four guards that spread out behind the premier unlicensed vampire in Japan. She gently placed her briefcase upon the surface of a simple stone table in the middle of the broad sparsely decorated room, flicked the locks open, and laid the case open.

Hana craned her head; she'd not seen this before. There were eleven vials filled with a cloudy serum within the case. There was an empty slot in the foam tray for a twelfth vial.

The Crimson Lord stood opposite Sakura and said, "The twelfth vial?"

"Used on me," Sakura stated emphatically, "and proof it works."

"Yes. Reduced to a Ramp master – that much is obvious." He lifted a vial with long slim fingers and examined it with black eyes that gleamed beneath the fluorescent lights. "So, the Red Empire succeeded in developing a cure for vampirism." He paused and frowned. "Not much of a weapon if it can be reversed with a dose of vampire blood. What on Earth was Dalien Morte trying to achieve?"

"The researchers never offered an explanation."

The Crimson Lord paused and then grinned ironically. "Perhaps we can get a dose close to Crane ... but probably not." His grin vanished and he scowled. "This is a useless weapon. Have you nothing else to expiate the shame of your capture by the Red Empire?"

Hana quailed within. Her brother Fumio stood quietly to her right. A katana belted at his waist, and a sub-machine gun slung on his right hip. While Fumio had grudgingly accepted her presence, her sister Sakura was positively hostile. If the Crimson Lord killed Sakura in a fit of pique, there was nothing stopping him from killing herself for good measure. Her flight to the Akai Kage no Ichizoku to escape Crane had proved to be a futile quest for sanctuary. She had to do something to shift the odds in her favor.

She stepped forward to offer everything she knew. It was her last chance to prove her value to these creatures and perhaps Sakura would recognize her little sister's worth. She blurted out, "I know how Crane is controlling Armitage, and I can track them both."

The Crimson Lord smiled at her, then glanced disdainfully at Sakura. "Now that is how a loyal servant serves their lord. Perhaps you could learn a thing or two from your younger sister." He turned back to Hana and said, "If your words prove true, not only have you saved your life, you will gain immortality within our clan."

Sakura turned her head to face Hana, her eyes narrowed with disdain.

One of the guards behind the Crimson Lord frowned, lifted his right fist to his jawline, snapped a quick command, then reported, "My Lord, we have a human intruder."

The Crimson Lord, wrinkled his nose, and demanded, "I want him stripped and checked for weapons. What is he? Is he a suicide? Find out why he's here and then bring me his stinking carcass – still breathing, mind you."

"Yes, my Lord," the guard said and then snapped another command through his wrist-communicator.

Hana looked toward the entrance. Who on Earth would be crazy or desperate enough to walk into this den of killers?

Her eyes dropped to half-lidded, *apart from myself.*

She glanced back at Fumio, and he frowned slightly at her and shook his head slightly, then focused past her and lifted his submachine gun toward the entrance into the chamber.

Hana looked at Sakura, who stared at her with dark eyes; a cruel smile curling the lips of her mouth.

No safety would ever come from her sister.

* * *

The dusty Tokyo warehouse loomed around James like a colossal dinosaur frozen by time.

The chameleons had found the vampires, but could he survive long enough to complete his mission and rescue Hana Tanaka? He'd made contact with the enemy, and the mission was mostly proceeding according to plan – mostly.

"Strip!" the vampire guard demanded.

James raised a quizzical eyebrow.

The second vampire guard glared at James, and flicked the barrel of his submachine gun at him.

James pulled off his jacket, folded it and placed it upon the warehouse's pale concrete floor. He undid his tie, and pulled off his shoes and his socks. He shrugged off the shoulder holster for his .45, and undid his belt, along with the sheath for his Ka-Bar combat knife. A few moments later, he'd divested himself of everything except for his underwear, while placing his .45 automatic and Ka-Bar on top of his neat pile of clothes.

"Everything!" the guard snapped, a savage grin curling his thin lips.

James shrugged, dropped his shorts and stepped out of them. He picked them up, folded and placed them on top of his gun and the rest of his clothes.

The second vampire lifted a wand-like metal detector and beckoned James to him. James approached and the vampire scanned his body with the device. It gave a chirp and flashed a steady green light. He wasn't carrying any concealed weapons or explosives within his body and now they knew that too.

He was defenseless, harmless, easy prey; exactly what he needed the vampires to believe. He kept a tight grip on the atavistic fear swirling like a cold serpent within his guts. He needed to brazen this out. He needed to trust Chloe's purpose and the lizards as her agents. It was a big ask to trust the lizards to do what was necessary, but they were essential to the success of the mission. He couldn't do it without them, and the best he could do was offer himself as bait to open the path into the vampire's inner sanctum for the chameleons to enter.

James had briefed the lizards as well as he could. There were Shadowstone files upon all three of the Tanaka's and he'd impressed upon Gullette and Kavanne the necessity of keeping Hana Tanaka safe and bringing her back to New York City. His job was to keep the vampires distracted and get the chameleons inside. Hana Tanaka was somewhere nearby, her trail led here. She could be alive or dead, but her trail ended at this warehouse – there was no mistake. It had taken seven hours for the chameleons to track Hana Tanaka's movements through the sensory chaos of Tokyo. James filed that fact away. If the lizards ever hunted him, he could count his longevity in hours. Were they better hunters than vampires? He suspected so. It was a good thing there were so few of them.

The first guard gave him a shove in the back, and James stumbled down the first couple of stairs before he caught his balance. He glared over his left shoulder at the prick who'd pushed him. The vampire bared his fangs and declared, "You're a dead man."

James turned away in silence and made his way down the stairs. Somewhere behind him, two invisible chameleons were following him into the coven's lair. James expected the guard might have to revise his opinion about how 'dead,' James was going to be, once Gullette and Kavanne made their presence known.

The next few minutes were going to get messy.

* * *

The tall Caucasian walked guardedly into the room.

They all stared at him. This wonder who'd come willingly into the Crimson Lord's domain. Hana frowned, she judged him to be one-ninety-three or four centimeters tall, with a powerful physique, a fighter's body, a soldier's body, and completely and unselfconsciously naked. She couldn't believe he was a naive victim, something else was going on here. Something out of sight.

One of the guards shoved the prisoner forward and he moved almost to the middle of the room. He recovered his balance like a cat, fast and agile for his size, and took a position near the table in the middle of the room. Four of the Crimson Lord's guards spread around the room. The remaining two stepped forward and stood to the left and right of the prisoner. They slapped their hands upon his shoulders and pushed him down to his knees. One of them shouted, "Kneel before your lord!"

Sakura stepped backward and stood on Hana's left. Fumio was on her right, his submachine gun trained on the human. Sakura glanced once behind her. Hana followed her gaze to a steel door in the rear corner of the chamber. Fumio had shared with Hana that the door led to an escape route and was proof against all but the most potent attacks. Sakura was thinking about escape. Hana tensed, what could she do to escape what would happen next?

The Crimson Lord stepped forward and addressed the prisoner. "Who the hell are you, and why shouldn't I kill you immediately?"

The man answered in level tones, "I am James Haley, former head of Shadowstone US, and aide-de-camp to General Chloe Armitage of the Vampire Dominion. My mistress has sent me here to broker a mutually beneficial alliance against Cornelius Crane."

The Crimson Lord paused for a moment. "How did you find this site?"

"Japan is heavily surveilled," he said, and gestured toward Hana. "We followed Ms. Tanaka to this site. We witnessed your arrival and followed you in."

The Crimson Lord's face froze. "Not in more than four centuries have I been tracked … how could you, a mere human do so? Who helped you?"

"Technology."

"I don't believe it. Crane has had the Panopticon for a decade and never found me." He grabbed Haley by the ears and twisted.

The man shrieked.

The Crimson Lord let go. Then grabbed Haley's head and pushed it back to the limit of the man's flexibility. The Crimson Lord leaned in, and leered at the prisoner. "Who helped you? Or lose your ears permanently, and that'll just be the start of our fun."

Haley panted, then flicked his eyes to the left at Sakura. His left hand lashed out, pointing a stiff finger at her. "She revealed all to one of our operatives while she was captured in Jerusalem."

Sakura shouted, "No. He lies. '

"She, told our man everything. Then killed him when he released her from her Red Empire prison. She thought her betrayal of you died with our operative, but we recorded everything on his tactical link. That is how we knew to look here. That is how we found you."

The Crimson lord released Haley and stepped back; his eyes half-lidded. He folded his arms across his chest, his head flicking to the right to stare at Sakura. He snapped, "Sakura! Explain yourself!"

Sakura's eyes widened; her right hand flicked out toward Haley. "The American is lying. They all lie. Their corrupt civilization drowns in lies and Armitage is the mother of lies. Kill him. Kill him now, before he spreads more of Crane and Armitage's poison amongst us."

Haley gasped for breath; his face covered with fresh perspiration. His eyes flitted about the room, searching – for what?

The Crimson Lord suddenly rose up off the floor. A look of agonized shock seizing his face. He fell apart to the left and right in a shower of blood, and loopy gray and blue entrails. The horrific sound of wet tearing flesh resounding through the chamber. Something ghosted into the room behind him, then blurred away in a hint of mottled grays and bone white flashes.

Simultaneous with the attack on the Crimson Lord, the two vampires holding the prisoner lost their heads. Their skulls flying left and right, blood fountaining into the air as their headless bodies paused upright before falling away.

Hana screamed.

Someone grabbed her from the left and pulled her away with a bone jarring snap. She flew backward. Before her, the rest of the guards attempted to fight back and were torn apart in a racket of snapping bones and tearing flesh. Hana landed on her feet. The steel door creaked open behind her. A hard hand gripped the back of her neck with a vise-like grip. Sakura hissed over her left shoulder at Haley, and said, "Call off your lizards or she dies."

Haley rose to his feet, and two great upright lizards pulled to a halt to his left and right. The creatures regarded her with yellow-lamp eyes and not a shred of compassion. They flicked their huge hands, great black talons shedding drops of blood and gobbets of flesh in ribbons upon the tiled floor.

Of the Crimson Lord, and his six guards – none survived. All lay in dismembered pools of blood, splintered bones and ripped flesh. It had all happened in one or two shocking heartbeats of horror.

Hana closed her eyes. She was already dead.

There was no way she'd walk free from this room.

* * *

"Give me the serum!" Sakura Tanaka demanded.

Her pale fingers clenched around the back of her sister's neck. "Or, I'll snap her little neck like a twig."

James took a breath and let it out. He had to get Hana Tanaka to safety. Saving Chloe from Crane's implant depended upon the young Japanese scientist, any other consideration was secondary. He snapped the briefcase closed and picked it up. He strode forward to stand ten feet in front of the Tanakas. He assessed the situation. Fumio still had his submachine gun leveled at James' bare chest. He could easily kill James, as the chameleons wouldn't stop a bullet for him. The chameleon's commitment to their own agenda was always crystal clear. However, Fumio didn't seem to be as extreme as Sakura in his views. Perhaps here was a lever James could use to secure Hana's release.

He couldn't use the phrase 'Hana's freedom.' Hana was never going to be free. She knew way too much for someone not on the inside of the great game. She was only able to transfer from sudden death at the hands of her sister, to captivity by James and the chameleons, with final judgment rendered by Chloe. James looked hard at Sakura, and said, "I'll give you the vials, but only if Hana is left unharmed."

Sakura grinned. "Done. Throw me the case."

"Let her go."

"No. You go first."

James sighed. Sakura was such a toxic bitch. He needed to maximize the pressure upon her. He flicked his head left and right, and the chameleons spread away from him, stalking closer toward the corner of the room occupied by the Tanakas. Gullette lowered his head, his lower jaw opened wide, revealing rows of shark-like teeth. He hissed and grinned malevolently. Kavanne's head bobbed forward and back, then he barked a savage challenge, saliva dripping from his teeth to splat in dark splotches upon the floor.

Fumio's face paled, and Sakura's face hardened. She snapped, "Stop right there, or she dies."

Hana's face drained of blood and she trembled within her sister's iron grip.

James lifted his hand and the lizards played along, stopping and hissing angrily. He could sacrifice the serum. Chloe had been clear about the priorities. Sakura was still a Ramp master and could snap Hana's neck before the chameleons could stop her. Fortunately, the chameleons hadn't ghosted. That would have sent Sakura over the edge, and Hana would be a corpse now rather than a prize. James lifted the briefcase with the vials in it, and said, "I will throw this to you, but you have to release Hana at the same time."

Sakura stared at him, seemingly considering his offer. "Okay. Throw the case." She took a step back closer to the open steel doorway. She stilled, ramping and waiting for James to act.

James raised his eyebrows, and drew his right hand back and low, ready to toss the brief case to Sakura.

Both chameleons hissed.

Fumio blanched and moved closer to the exit.

Hana winced, the grip on the back of her neck as tight as ever.

Fumio caught James' gaze and flicked his head to the left toward his sisters.

James threw on instinct, the case tumbling end over end toward Sakura. Her left hand blurred up, catching the handle of the case. Her face twisted into a snarl, and her right hand tightened around Hana's neck.

Hana gasped.

Fumio batted Sakura's hand away from Hana's neck and shoved his younger sister toward James and safety.

Gullette and Kavanne blurred forward.

Fumio, and Sakura with the briefcase, blurred backward into the escape tunnel.

The steel door slammed shut behind them with a resounding clang. Gullette and Kavanne crashed into the heavy surrounding frame and bounced back, snarling and hissing with vexed disappointment.

James beckoned to Hana with his left hand. "Come with us to safety."

She hesitated for a brief moment, then staggered forward. James took her within the wing of his left arm and walked her toward the exit. He looked over his shoulder at Gullette with hard eyes. "What took you so long back there?"

Gullette's mouth widened into a grin. "Meat-that-talks, smells good when fearful, salted meat."

James pulled to a stop and stared at the big lizard for a long moment. He quailed within. *One of these days they're just going to eat me.* He turned away in silence and took a step toward the exit. Blood splatter dripped down his naked torso. Seized with disgust he cast his gaze about and spotted a strip of cloth clear of gore. He stooped and picked it up and began rubbing the blood off. He hesitated for a second ... *What if I had an accidental cut, with all this vampire blood flying around. Accidents could happen.* He shook his head in sudden dismissal of the idea. He'd leave becoming a vampire or not in Chloe's hands, and strode for the exit, guiding Hana Tanaka back up to the warehouse and their waiting Mitsubishi van.

It was time to get some damn clothes on and get the hell out of Tokyo.

* * *

Haley called out from the cockpit, "Taking off for Anchorage. We'll be back at Fort Dix in twelve hours' time."

Hana Tanaka tightened her seatbelt. She sat in the hold of Haley's craft. He'd called it an osprey. The giant lizards were in the hold with her, but they were ignoring her. She was heartily thankful for that. She watched with wide eyes and an open mouth, as they pulled three ground crew snatched from Narita airport apart.

The screams had already died. Blood splashed and splatted across walls, ceilings and floors. One stream reached out and lashed her legs with a thin ribbon of crimson. Entrails, organs, and other detritus littered the floor. The lizards reached down with hands the size of plates and scooped up livers, hearts and lungs, and gobbled them down in heaving swallows. They coughed, cackled and barked as they ate, seemingly mightily entertained by their obscene feast.

Hana barely dared to breathe.

The lizards fell upon the defleshed bones, snapping femurs and other major bones open, lifting them high and sucking them dry with slurping sounds and obvious relish.

Hana wanted to look away, but couldn't close her eyes. She'd never seen anything like it. Such horror! How could it exist. But it did.

The osprey lifted off the tarmac and rose into the sky. Whatever Hana's fate was, she'd soon meet it. Haley asked from the cockpit entrance, "Hey, Tanaka. Do you want some airsickness tablets?"

Hana shut her eyes and groaned.

Chapter Five

"Every successful conspiracy remains secret after completion. There is only the desired effect which will always be attributed to reasonable, plausible but false causes." – Cornelius Crane

* * *

Romania, The town of Border, September 13th, 19:32

The sun vanished beneath the horizon.

At Crane's behest, Chloe Armitage leaped from the command shadowstar drone. The canopy dropped back into position, securing Crane's privacy. Her lord, in little more than name only, was attempting to view the future again. He'd tried to keep his precognitive powers secret but she'd inferred them from the fact he always knew more than he had any right to know. She couldn't attribute all of Crane's knowledge to nearly a thousand years of study and a latent genius ability, ergo he had a precognitive power. Let Crane believe she didn't know, whatever power he had he still couldn't read her mind. While her body remained trapped in his service, her soul was inviolate.

She flipped open her smartphone and checked her messages. When she'd retired to the command shadowstar drone to sleep the day away, James and the chameleons had been searching for Hana Tanaka in Tokyo, and Chloe expected an updated report. There was a single message from James, it read, 'Hana Tanaka secured without loss. Departed Tokyo at 07:30 NYC time. En route to Anchorage and then to Fort Dix. J.'

Chloe voice dialed James' phone, lifted her own to her ear, and walked casually away from the drone into the empty town square. While Crane was busy with his precognitive vision, she could find out if James' mission to Tokyo had been successful.

James answered on the second ring, "Chloe?"

"Yes, James. I've read your text. Tell me what happened," Chloe said with quiet urgency. Her future rose or fell upon Hana Tanaka.

"We breached Tanaka's apartment. Shadowstone Japan had secured the site but I spoofed their surveillance systems, and the chameleons picked up her scent from the unwashed clothes in her laundry. From that point on, finding Tanaka was like watching hounds track down a rabbit. Gullette led us to an old military surplus warehouse that looked like no one had touched it since the cold war. A pair of vampire guards confronted me within the warehouse. After some negotiations and promises, I got them to agree to take me to their leader. They feared concealed weapons, and I had to strip naked to reach their inner sanctum. The chameleons kept themselves camouflaged and followed me inside. Their big boss was an 'old world,' sort of guy, probably more Chinese than Japanese I think, who had clearly been around a long time. I'm sure they saw me as nothing more than fresh meat for their table. They had no idea Gullette and Kavanne were in the chamber with them. Once I identified Hana Tanaka, the chameleons attacked with the advantage of surprise. Caught the vampires unawares and ripped most of them apart. Gullette and Kavanne—"

"Wait! Most of them apart? Some of them escaped?"

"Yes, Sakura grabbed her sister as soon as it started to go down. She threatened to kill Hana unless we allowed her to leave. I said, 'sure,' to keep Hana alive and they backed out through a bolt hole. Sakura tried to kill Hana at the end, but Fumio caught Sakura's wrist and pushed Hana toward us, and locked a steel door behind them. Once we had Hana Tanaka secured, we left – after all, Fumio and Sakura Tanaka weren't the mission."

"Correct. Then what happened?"

"As I was saying, Gullette and Kavanne are bona fide killing machines. Dangerous enough by themselves and out of this world when paired in a tight space."

"Wait a moment. What was Shemina doing?"

"She was back in the osprey."

"Why?"

"No, special reason."

There was a subtle shift of tone in James' voice. Clearly, he couldn't speak about the chameleons with them within earshot. Which, frankly, was probably anywhere within a mile of them. There was something James needed to share but it would have to wait until they were alone together. Chloe leaned her head forward slightly and said, "Okay. Noted. What happened next?"

"I used a few rags gleaned from the vampires to clean the blood splatter off Tanaka and myself, returned upstairs to the warehouse, got dressed and returned to the airport. We left Tokyo as soon as we could. As for Tanaka, I've got the chameleons watching her. Tokyo airport is missing three of their ground crew staff. Tanaka was watching as the chameleons fed. She's quiet and compliant now, if a bit pale and queasy – I gave her some air-sickness pills. I've also removed all potential weapons from her reach. I don't want her getting any ideas about noble suicide as a form of escape."

Chloe nodded, her blood thrilling through her veins. Hana Tanaka was the real prize captured in Japan "Excellent work, James. Keep her safe. Forget about Fort Dix and divert to my penthouse in Manhattan. You can land the osprey on the helipad above my hangar, and bring Ms. Tanaka down to the penthouse. I'll send you the security codes after this call. What Crane and I are doing in Romania will be complete soon. I'll probably be home before you arrive. In any event, send me a text once you reach my penthouse rooftop."

"Yes, Chloe. Will do."

"Two more things," she noted.

"Yes, Chloe?"

"One, Crane's movements. Are you still in position to track his command drone?"

"Yes. The Shadowstone trackers default back to the military satellite network if the Panopticon is offline. The Panopticon is online intermittently, about every fifteen minutes for a ten second burst. It's infuriating, we can see it's being used but can't easily identify precisely where, but it looks like Arizona, Nevada, New Mexico, or Texas are all good candidates—"

"And?"

"Yes, Chloe. I'll send the data through immediately. You'll get a series of date-stamped tracks."

"Very good, James. Keep me appraised if anything changes."

"Yes, Chloe, and two?"

"What happened to the cure for vampirism?"

"I had to trade it to Sakura for Hana. She escaped with her brother Fumio."

Chloe pursed her lips. James had regrettably lost the cure for vampirism. The cure was a loose end until she created the opportunity to end it once and for all. There would be no place for a cure for vampirism in the world she would create. She said, "You have your instructions, James."

"Yes, Chloe. I'm on it."

She closed the line and returned her smartphone to its armor protected sleeve on her left arm. She scanned the village with her vampire senses. It was an automatic check, a hunter's vigilance which never left her. Nothing had changed, the population was tense and quiet. The inner cordon of praetorians was slipping into place from their ospreys. The two freshly-refueled shadowstar drones were rising again into the twilight sky on jets of cobalt fire. Somewhere, the mekrarian vampire, Akimitsu would be stirring with the night, no doubt ready to put into play whatever plan Mekra and himself had composed to bedevil Crane with.

She allowed herself to hope. A rare indulgence; she normally didn't trade in hope or despair, she either did or did not do. But for a brief moment she hoped for a new life without the chains of Crane's traps upon her mind and body. Hana Tanaka would prove to be the agent of her release from Crane's silver-charged implant and that would open the door to once more engage Anton Slayne upon the path to assassinate her king.

Chloe took a long breath and sighed, releasing her hope to the quiet pools of the past where it belonged. Her hand fell to the handle of the Red

Dragon belted at her waist. A breeze whipped up and tugged at her dark hair, sending black wisps across her smooth forehead. She swept them aside with the palm of her hand, and unclipped her tactical helmet from her hip. She lifted her helmet and pulled it down over her head. The heads-up display fired up, giving her a tactical overlay of the village slaved off the sensors on the two shadowstar drones flying high overhead. With the Panopticon out of the loop, there was minimal intelligence added to the feed. However, she could see the locations of all the warm bodies and the praetorians. Not surprisingly, there was no sign of Akimitsu. The Vampire Dominion didn't have effective technology to identify a mekrarian vampire, at least not yet.

Her phone vibrated and Crane's recent movements appeared on her visor's display. The tracks covered half the world and back again. From Queens, New York, to the forests of Japan, and then back to Queens. Then to her own penthouse to pick her up for the current mission. What had he been doing in Japan and what was happening in Queens? James had identified a research station in Queens; one Clayton Maze had taken the loremaster corpses to after the battle in Minneapolis. Crane kept returning to the same research station in the last couple of days. Chloe suspected it had something to do with the Order of Thoth loremaster technology, but she had little more than her own suspicions to go on. Crane's recent movements remained a mystery she had no time to solve and comprehension would have to wait. Her left hand caressed the handle of her katana and she waited for the night to grow fully dark.

Chloe smiled quietly to herself, then whispered a voice command, sending her penthouse's front door security code to James. He deserved a reward, and her trust served a second purpose of anchoring his loyalty. It was his nature to respond to trust with loyalty. A useful, if somewhat inexplicable trait.

She took a breath and let it out.

Her strategy was almost back on track.

* * *

Mekra's astral form floated a foot above the cold concrete floor.

The underground bunker dwelled in near darkness except for the fading twilight ghosting down a long stairwell. In the main chamber at the bottom of the stairs, Akimitsu, Whispering Death and the three former Red Empire fighters stood arrayed in a semi-circle before her. They gazed upon Mekra's near naked floating form with unfocused eyes, their minds enraptured by her presence. She bent her will and flattened theirs. It was a simple thing. An act she could do without thinking about it, controlling them was as natural as breathing. Her voice sang in their minds. "Hearken unto me."

How could they do otherwise. She asked a rhetorical question with a wave of her hand at Akimitsu, "You have the key?"

He lifted a dark-blue crowbar, a hexagonal shaft of metal spanning more than six feet, acquired within Azuga before the previous dawn. It would fulfill the need for a key to her prison.

She asked, "Is it possible for Crane to count all the humans in this town and track their life signs?"

"No one knows," Whispering Death said. "But it is likely."

Mekra nodded, the Red Empire officer was a wealth of information on the capabilities of Crane's forces. She said in sage tones, "War does not lend itself to certainty. We will have to allow for the possibility. We will disguise our numbers and prepare in stealth while our numbers grow."

The men looked at her expectantly, awaiting her instructions. She spelled out her plan, beginning by indicating the lesser three with a casual wave of her left hand. "You will proceed north to the town of Border. You will pass through the outer cordon of Crane's human allies and begin converting the town to our kind. Sup lightly on each new member of our tribe, and move quickly and silently from conquest to conquest. Begin with two to replace Akimitsu and Whispering Death, and then proceed to five more and then ten, and so on." She paused for a moment. "As our numbers swell with each doubling, we will become a tide. We will overwhelm Crane's forces. He is too few to hold us once we have become many. His armored men will fall before us as a child's scratchings in the sand are dissolved by a flood." She waved her hand at the three ex-members of the Red Empire again and thrust it toward the exit at the top of the stairs. "Fly, fly my brave warriors, and take the town for your queen."

The three vampires vanished up the stairs.

Mekra turned her attention to the remaining two men, and said, "Mark your way with stealth, and find your way to the door of my prison. Await my command, then clear the boulders and fit the key as I have instructed you. If one falls to the wayside, the other shall complete the task."

She said no more. Her mind filled their minds with exact visuals of what she needed done. After all, she'd watched Crane perform the very same task in the recent past and she remembered what he'd done perfectly. She nodded once, and her last two men turned and raced up the stairs into the darkening night.

Mekra rose through the ceiling of the bunker, passing through concrete and rock until she emerged into the cool night air. She rose high above Azuga, drifting to the north to access a vantage point mid-way between her prison and the town of Border. She paused and waited; soon her attempt to distract Crane with the conversion of more than two thousand humans to mekrarian vampires would begin. She would raise an army against Crane while two of her number opened her prison and freed her. She stared with hard, black eyes at the town square in the middle of Border.

What would Crane do next?

* * *

Cornelius' eyes flicked open.

The loremaster vision receded reluctantly from his mind. It's tendrils gripping with nightmarish power upon his soul. He absently rubbed his right forearm where the loremaster implant cooled within his flesh. It was certain; Mekra had a telepathic connection with her blood offspring. It was the only way to make sense of Akimitsu's unerring path toward Mekra's donjon. The elite Obsidian Claw ninja had recruited four members of a Red Empire fist team in the Chinese city of Hami. They'd arrived in a fast Red Empire scout helicopter, quickly ditched by its crew before its destruction by a pair of air-to-air missiles from his high-flying drones. Of the mekrarian crew there was no physical sign, however they were close, the near future was ripe with threat from them. His efforts to keep Mekra contained within her donjon, while ridding the world of her hellish spawn, rested upon a knife edge.

Catastrophe awaited the merest misstep. He couldn't allow Mekra to detect his hidden dagger poised to strike at her plans. The trap he was laying had to work. There was only one thing he could bait the trap with that would hold Mekra's focus – himself.

Cornelius frowned, his eyes flashing with determination. It'd become necessary to become bait. He snorted dismissively, and flicked a switch on the command drone's console. The canopy lifted up and back, and he leaped out into the fresh night air. He landed on the pale concrete of the town square. It was time to live up to his part in the deadly theater playing out this night. He scanned the town with his vampire senses; it reeked with terrified people holding themselves under house arrest. The fictional outbreak of airborne Ebola had done its work, generating a compliant and vulnerable population. An expendable town which would soon die, but not in vain. Their lives would buy the destruction of Mekra's spawn and ensure the secret of her existence remained hidden from all but Armitage and himself.

They were heroes in their own way, they just didn't know it. It was the destiny of some to die for causes of which they were ignorant, so others may live and prosper. The necessary and imminent sacrifice of their lives shielded from their awareness by a pervasive network of merciful deception.

Lie laid upon lie; such was the way of power.

Cornelius' eyes tightened, and he loosened his great bastard sword within its scabbard. His forces stood poised for action, and he was ready to play his role. All he had to do now was wait for Mekra's next move.

* * *

The night-lit fairyland forest arched overhead.

Akimitsu glided beneath the huge trees. He remained in the deepest shadows, pressing himself against the thick boles as he flashed from forest giant to forest giant. Whispering Death followed ten yards behind his left shoulder. They blurred from trunk to trunk until the long-sought rock wall and narrow trail rose before them.

Akimitsu gazed at the pile of rocks in front of the secret prison entrance. His queen was inside. He hefted the blued-steel crowbar with his pale hands. Its hexagonal shape and length would neatly fit the requirements of the lock to Mekra's prison. All they needed to do was clear the boulders, and they would be quickly inside.

He leaned flat against the wide bole of a mature oak tree forty yards short of the trail. His nostrils widened, taking in the heavy, smoky aromas of the oaks, the rank fetid carpet of autumn leaves underfoot, even the rock face had a faint earthy scent. His gaze rose up into the night sky, thick branches and leaf canopy mostly obscured the view, but here and there the deep night of the vast universe lay revealed in all her eternal glory.

Akimitsu stared into the infinite depths of space, reveling in his awesome life as a vampire, his old life reduced to a stale memory that had occurred to someone else. His heart beat like a drum, blood thrilled through his veins. Vigorous life and urgent desires filled him to overflowing. Unknowable possibilities littered a blessed future like rubies and emeralds scattered upon an infinite shore.

He regarded the stones heaped against his queen's prison door. Upon her signal he would move, and with Whispering Death at his shoulder the way would soon be clear. All he had to do was wait for his queen's command.

Akimitsu smiled quietly in the gathering dark; soon, the waiting would end.

* * *

The human population of Border dropped by two.

The shadowstar sensor arrays monitored the local inhabitants with exquisite sensitivity. Two humans were cooling well below their normal healthy body temperature. They moved and vanished, falling past the programmed categories of the shadowstar's advanced equipment. Clearly, they had become mekrarians. Cornelius leaned against the hull of his command shadowstar drone, parked in the middle of the town square. Armitage waited a few yards away, scanning the surrounding buildings for threats.

Cornelius lifted his gaze toward the southern flank of the town. The incursion was growing. His lip curled; he could swat these new vampires like flies with a well-placed aerial bombardment. But he needed to wait and allow events to progress as he'd foreseen – it was the best chance he had to grasp victory against Mekra's spawn.

A handful of quiet minutes fled into the past. Another five humans cooled into mekrarian vampires and vanished from the sensors. First two, and then five, three of the raider II crew had invaded the town, leaving two mekrarians unaccounted for. They had attempted to hide the fact they had split their force by converting two humans first to replace the other two. If he was correct, the next five minutes would raise the total to ten. His mind raced forward; unchecked, Mekra's transformation of the town would run out of warm bodies in less than an hour.

And Cornelius had to let it happen. He had a single chance to draw the whole of the mekrarian spawn to the one location – and destroy them all. He had to draw the other two mekrarian vampires into the open; and without doubt they would appear in front of Mekra's door. Quite possibly as her newly converted army attacked his praetorian forces in an attempt to draw his attention away from the entrance to her donjon. He activated a silent command via his tactical link to the two shadowstars flying top cover. A pair of weapon bay doors dropped open. A hypersonic missile carrying a five-hundred-pound warhead flicked from standby to armed. Its designated target – the front door of Mekra's donjon.

When Mekra's two 'saviors,' arrived outside her donjon, they'd receive a hot reception. He scanned the sensor array reports. The clock had ticked over another five minutes and the number of vanished inhabitants of the town increased to ten. Events were proceeding in accordance with his plan. Cornelius had previously primed his troops with a small set of simple aliased commands. He broadcast across the tactical link. "Initiate Alpha." It meant, 'Prepare for imminent contact with the enemy,' and if Mekra had a convert within earshot, she wouldn't be able to use a telepathic link to understand the meaning of his orders. As for his men, they would be checking their weapons and lifting their vigilance, but he'd already impressed upon them the necessity of maintaining the appearance of a relaxed posture.

It was essential Mekra believed she had the upper hand until Cornelius could strike decisively. Once he'd eliminated the two missing mekrarians, he would sanitize the town of Border and the surrounding terrain. Mekra would remain imprisoned in her donjon to continue to serve in her role as the fountain of life for vampires. A fountain dedicated to his exclusive use.

In less than five minutes, the ten mekrarians would recruit another ten, and then twenty, forty, eighty, a hundred and sixty, followed by more than three hundred. The mekrarian army was growing before his eyes.

He regarded the silent town with a glacial stare and whispered, "And so it begins."

* * *

Mekra writhed in a blood drenched delirium.

The experience of the feasting of her minions upon the town concentrated into a sublime ecstasy within her soul. She'd dropped back into her physical body, deep within her prison, unable to sustain the concentration necessary to maintain her astral form.

Her panting quieted. Her mind stilled. Now the blood had run out, all the warm humans were gone, there were only Crane, Armitage and the praetorians left. She viewed a gestalt image of the town from nearly two and a half thousand sets of eyes. Crane's forces appeared alert, but oblivious to the true threat. They stood arrayed in three loose groups with their flying craft in the center of town.

There were too many children of her blood to manage individually, all she could do with so many was to ignite their souls with an overwhelming lust to kill her enemies. She broadcast a single word to her followers with a cold whisper, "Attack!"

Mekra turned her attention to two souls standing silently in the nearby forest. She'd excluded them alone from her broadcast command. She had to wait, it would be mere seconds for her army to engage Crane and draw his attention away from her prison. Then she would give her next command. She turned her mind to her swarming minions, immersing herself in their rampant experience.

The streets whipped past. Bare feet flew over ancient cobblestones. Exultant screams split the air. Fresh blood left a coppery tang upon her tongue. Crane stood before her surrounded by a thin line of his soldiers. He lifted his great sword above his head, reflecting a gray, dusky gleam beneath the street lights, and shouted a desperate command.

Mekra surged forward within thousands of her children.

She was one; she was many.

* * *

The first of the mekrarian vampires emerged from an alleyway leading into the town square.

Cornelius lifted his bastard sword and shouted, "To Me! To Me!"

The three ospreys located around the edges of the square rose on thundering engines into the evening sky. The praetorians raced toward the center of the square where Cornelius and Armitage stood next to his shadowstar drone. He touched a stud on the base of his helmet and the command drone's engines fired up; the canopy lifting up and back. There was no point staying a second longer than they had to.

More mekrarians howled from the opposite side of the wide square. Cornelius whirled around. The streets leading into the town square swarmed with dark figures. There was nothing left in Border except for vampires. Four thousand and thirty-four humans had vanished, replaced by two to three thousand mekrarian vampires. His men fell back to a tight square around his position. Their newly deployed mini guns held with steady hands. Gloved fingers pressed studs, igniting the under-barrel thermal units. Tongues of blue fire leaped into life hanging three inches in front of the mini gun's nested barrels.

General Dieter Franz, blurred through his men's line and joined Cornelius and Armitage next to the command shadowstar drone. He nodded once at Cornelius and ignored Armitage. He drew his gleaming long sword and faced the mob.

Cornelius shouted to his troops, "Hold!"

The dark-eyed vampires swarmed forward from every direction.

He shouted again, "Hold!"

The three ospreys took up position facing outward in a triangle twenty feet above his men, their rear ramps lowered for quick evacuation. On each aircraft, a newly installed 20mm nose cannon slewed around, lining up on the surging crowd.

The first mekrarian vampire reached thirty yards short of Cornelius's praetorian lines; he commanded his troops with a shout, "Fire!"

Forty arcs of liquid fire splashed across the front ranks of the shrieking horde. The flames stuck like glue. Flesh shriveled and sloughed, screams of triumph turning to howls of agony. The airborne cannons thundered into fiery life, tearing long lines through the surging crowd, sending separated limbs, torsos, and heads flying in gouts of blood. Forty mini guns spun into action, lines of bright tracers chasing hollow point 7.62mm rounds into the crowd, cutting through flesh and bone like chainsaws.

The mekrarian vampires leaped, dodged, spun aside, and came on, clambering over the sizzling dying dismembered dead and spreading pools of gore.

The swarm closed to just less than twenty feet from the staunch praetorian line. Cornelius glanced at the sensor feed trained on Mekra's donjon. Nothing had changed, the boulders concealing the door to Mekra's donjon remained in place. He stared back at the swarm, dying in a curtain of blood and fire but still they inched forward like an approaching tide of sudden death. Had he miscalculated Mekra's strategy?

He might not live to find out.

* * *

The forest crowded around him, reaching oppressive limbs over his head.

Akimitsu ached to act but he remained still, awaiting the command of his beloved queen.

"Free me! Free me now," Mekra called to her devoted servants.

Akimitsu and Whispering Death responded as one, leaping forward to the pathway before Mekra's prison door. Their hands blurred, and the rocks exploded out of their way. They worked furiously and with perfect precision, within seconds the great stone slab stood before them. The inch and a half wide keyhole revealed six-feet off the ground. Akimitsu lifted the steel crowbar and pressed the tip to the entrance of the keyhole.

Honoring a deeply ingrained battle instinct, Whispering Death lifted his gaze past Akimitsu's shoulder, staring up into the night sky. His eyes widened, and he shouted, "RUN!" while blurring away into the forest.

Akimitsu whirled; his gaze tracking where Whispering Death had stared. A hypersonic cruise missile streaked down toward him. He made his choice in an instant; thrusting the bar home and shouting, "For my Qu—"

His world vanished within the center of an exploding five-hundred-pound warhead.

* * *

Chloe's blade dripped vampire blood upon the cold concrete.

The closest mekrarians were leaping over the praetorian wall. Many died en route, torn apart by streams of mini gun fire, or they landed aflame, a living torch writhing in agony upon the pale flagstones. The rest fell to the three blades of the Vampire Dominion elite. It was a brute force attack. The mekrarians were whip fast, strong and tough, but an hour ago these vampires had been unskilled civilians devoid of combat experience. The crowd swarmed and pressed forward into the hail of iron and fire. Relentless, uncaring and nigh on unstoppable.

Children emerged from the swarm, and rushed the praetorians. Jets of liquid fire reached out, smothering them in sheets of flame. Some ran howling, others stood and shrieked, living candles three or four feet tall, screeching in torment before they fell spasming to the ground.

This is obscene! Chloe thought. The whole population of Border had fallen to Mekra's blood. A toddler wailed; black eyes wide with blood lust. It leaped, only for mini gun fire to cut it in half. Beyond its twitching body parts, a greybeard blurred forward for a dozen steps before falling apart under the hammer blows of sustained cannon fire. Chloe stared and shook her head.

A praetorian called out, "I'm dry." He stepped back from the line and drew his long blade. As if it was a signal, the line began to falter as more voices called out the same words. The mekrarians surged as the defense weakened.

"Retreat!" Crane commanded. His face set in grim lines, his stern voice cutting through the cacophony of cannon fire, turbines, and wailing screams, but his eyes shone with triumph. The praetorians who had run out of ammunition were the first to move, leaping into the open holds of the hovering ospreys.

"Now, Chloe," Crane called as he rushed into the command drone's open cabin. The shadowstar lifted six feet off the town square.

A pair of mekrarians, landed before her. Chloe had been holding back on her supreme ramp, now she unleashed it. Her blade blurred through a flat arc. Their heads rolled away on ropes of blood as their bodies slumped to the concrete. The command drone had risen to twenty feet. With her supreme ramp in full flower, she bent her knees, and launched herself upward. She flipped once, landing upright with her boots upon her seat within the cabin.

The ospreys roared and leaped away. The command drone surged vertically into the sky. Chloe slid into her padded seat. She risked a glance over the side as the shadowstar slammed upward through the air on screaming jets of blue fire. Beneath her the surviving mekrarians crashed into the space vacated by Crane's forces. The milled about for a moment and then fled. She turned to Crane; her eyes wide. "They're running – they'll escape. Half of them remain alive "

"I expected as much," Crane uttered, his voice filled with absolute finality, "they will be dealt with."

Chloe took a breath and nodded once.

There was no doubt, Crane was right.

* * *

The door to Mekra's prison stood shrouded in falling rock dust.

Whispering Death moved like dark lightning through the haze. Akimitsu had succeeded before Crane's missile vaporized him; the door was open. A crescent moon shaped opening lay revealed on the left edge of the doorway, high and wide enough for a large man to pass through with ease. He slipped through the opening in a flash. He blurred to his right and pulled down a black-iron lever in the wall. He dashed back outside into the gray-rock mist, whipped out the steaming crow bar with a grimace of pain as the hot metal seared his flesh, and dashed back in. He slammed the black-iron lever back up. Counterweights grumbled and groaned within the rock face. The circular boulder rotated a quarter turn back to its closed position. He pushed the crowbar into the inner key hole, and let it rest short of contact with the locking mechanism. From the outside, the prison remained closed and locked. From the inside, with the key in place, he could reopen it.

Had Crane seen him. He must have been watching the door, expecting just such an attempt to free his divine captive. Hence the nearly instantaneous missile strike once Akimitsu and Whispering Death had stepped away from their concealment within the nearby forest. Perhaps he'd been fast enough for Crane not to notice his entrance into the prison. Was his progress obscured by the falling rock dust generated by the explosion? Could Crane be deceived this time?

He called out, "I am here, mistress."

Her voice resonated within the corridor. "Come below, free my body. Crane readies a counter attack – it is his way."

Whispering Death rushed in near silence down the dark corridor toward the final cell of his queen. Only the pervasive darkness witnessed his actions. He was thankful for it. The deep shadows were comfortable, reassuring, a source of stealth and strength, and soon his queen would walk at his side within them. He reached the bottom chamber, brought down and threw open Mekra's sarcophagus. He gasped, her divine beauty stealing his breath away.

"My manacles," Mekra said, raising her iron-bound left-hand half a dozen inches. "Together we can defeat these chains."

Whispering Death wrapped his hands around the heavy links and clambered over the sarcophagus to bring his powerful legs into play. He thrust upward. Mekra strained with him. One of the links screeched and fell apart. Her left hand came free.

Mekra's eyes shone within the gloom. She smiled, delirious with anticipation. "Now the rest."

One by one, they snapped her bonds. Whispering Death leaped aside and Mekra stepped free of her silver prison. She raised her hands above her head, the manacles surrounding her wrists dangling one or two clinking links. Her breasts lifted with a long breath, her mouth opened wide and she laughed a single sharp, "Ha!"

She dropped her hands and stared around the walls of her prison for a brief moment until her gaze rested upon the corridor to the exit. Her eyes grew unfocused as if she was viewing a far place, and she uttered a whisper of dreadful certainty, "I have come to murder the light."

Whispering Death fell to his knees and bowed low before her awesome presence.

A slim hand appeared beneath his chin and raised him to his feet.

"For freeing me, I shall exalt you as first amongst my people."

Whispering Death looked into her glistening black orbs, and his heart burst with joy.

He'd found his destiny in service to a goddess.

* * *

The pale light of the drone's console illuminated the cabin.

Cornelius dialed up the head of Shadowstone Europe and asked, "Kohler, is the outer cordon secure?"

The reply came across the tactical link. "Everyone is still in place. The cordons remain tight. All Shadowstone staff and Romanian paramilitaries are accounted for."

"Good, man. Hold your position and await further orders," Crane commanded, and cut the link.

A heads-up display covered the front of the command drone's canopy. The three ospreys packed with general Dieter Franz and his praetorian forces were accelerating away from the town. Crane glanced at his fleeing praetorians for a second and spoke into his tactical link to the pilotless shadowstars flying top cover, "Issue command four-one-delta-foxtrot-echo, on my mark." He glanced down at the altimeter, the command drone was already two miles above the town and accelerating from supersonic to hypersonic. He spoke again, slowly, carefully enunciating each word of the voice command, "Four … three … two … one … mark!"

Four hypersonic cruise missiles streaked down toward the town of Border, targeting the corners of a square three miles on a side with the town at the center. The canopy of the command shadowstar drone darkened in programmed anticipation of this specific directive.

The drone rose higher, accelerating past three miles above the town.

The four cruise missiles simultaneously reached fifty yards above the ground. Each missile collaborated with the other three to ensure a synchronized strike. Nuclear triggers fired as one. Four miniature suns flared into existence. The night sky lit up with a white flash beneath the command drone. Flanked by its sister craft, Cornelius' shadowstar fled at hypersonic speed above the rising blast waves.

He scanned his instruments and sensors. Beneath them, massive waves of heat and pressure converged at six-hundred miles per hour, obliterating the towns of Border and Azuga. The atomic explosions swept through the surrounding forest, reaping all life and lifting the ash up into towering mushroom clouds glittering with fell lights. Ten miles to the north, the silhouette of the city of Braşov rose starkly against the night, its towers gleaming briefly in a false day.

General Franz and his praetorians vanished from Cornelius' sensors. The three ospreys coming apart in balls of tumbling fire. The Shadowstone and Romanian military and paramilitary positions vanished into clouds of dust and super-heated gas.

Beside him, Armitage watched him with quiet eyes and a silent tongue. Her opinion no longer mattered to him. He had to eliminate the mekrarian menace root and branch – and now there was no one left alive to report upon a missile strike on a remote cliff face or reveal the illusion of an outbreak of airborne Ebola. His surgical strike excised the mekrarian abominations like a rogue cancer from the body of the world, and kept his deepest secrets protected. The only other person who knew the full truth sat beside him, doubly bound to protect his life. It was the best possible outcome from a precarious and dangerous situation. In time, he could rebuild the praetorians and Shadowstone, or replace them with a brand-new organization built around the Day Guard.

Cornelius checked his tactical helmet feed on the entrance to Mekra's donjon. The first of the flanking shadowstars continued to maintain a camera on the donjon door.

"Damn!" he uttered through gritted teeth. A haze of rock dust and smoke from the forest fire almost completely obscured the entrance. The boulders had vanished, but the door appeared closed. The forest surrounding the donjon was aflame. Fire was everywhere, great tongues of flame licking high into the night. Clouds of dark, hot smoke rose over the desolation and further obscured the donjon in an impenetrable haze. He could wait a few minutes for the environment to cool and stabilize, then he would drop down through the thick smoke and dust, and confirm Mekra remained safely imprisoned. His eyes narrowed. A little smoke and fire meant nothing, surely, Mekra remained trapped and all her vile spawn were dead.

His lips curled in triumphant anticipation.

* * *

Boiling clouds of smoke and flame covered the sky.

Mekra stepped through the open doorway of her prison. The forest was aflame as far as the eye could see. Titanic trees burned like giant candles, shooting fountains of sparks into the clouds of ash and turning the night into a hellish version of the day.

Whispering Death said behind her left shoulder, "Mistress, we can find transport in the nearby city to our north. We must hurry before Crane returns to check your prison. We can use the chaos caused by Crane's strike to cover our escape."

Mekra stepped aside with a brief smile, and directed him with a nod. "Then guide me to safety and transport, and once we have found it, we will embark upon a journey."

"Mistress?"

"To your former home," she said, tilting her head forward and watching him closely, "Matahat al Diydan."

Whispering Death's eyes widened. "Mistress, that is the most dangerous place for us."

Mekra stared at him and pressed gently upon his soul. "I require an army capable of defeating Crane and his forces. The Red Empire shall become one with my people and you will assist me with their conversion to our cause."

Whispering Death nodded and smiled broadly, his long fangs prominent over his bottom lip. "Of course, my Mistress. Your will be done."

Mekra indicated the world with a casual wave of her right hand and ordered, "Lead on. I will follow you to our goal."

Whispering Death nodded once, then frowned. He took a deep breath, looked around at the fires, then up at the clouds. "First we must hide for a time." He still held the steel bar, and the door rolled close behind them. He turned and blurred between the flaming trees, heading toward the ruins of Azuga.

Mekra followed after him.

* * *

Cornelius' command shadowstar drone pulled to a halt, hovering six feet above the mountain path.

His triumph had unaccountably fled, replaced by a pervasive sense of foreboding. He needed to check Mekra's donjon. He needed to witness she remained secured within her silver sarcophagus. The four mushroom clouds were still rising across the valley, and would do so for another five to ten minutes. He ignored their haunting rise, grabbed the six-foot hexagonal bar he used as a key, and leaped from the hovering drone to the stone ledge before Mekra's donjon door. He slammed the key home, and clenched his fists twice as he waited for the door to roll to the right. As soon as the gap was wide enough, he withdrew the key, and slipped through. He hit the safe lever to stop the door rolling back and raced down the corridor to the holding chamber.

Mekra's donjon was eerily silent. He couldn't hear her suppressed heartbeat. He pulled to a halt at the bottom of the corridor. Even in the pitch dark, his vampire senses allowed him to see in shades of gray. Mekra's sarcophagus lay open and empty. Snapped chain links littered the floor. His jaw dropped open, he howled in rage and flung the steel bar at the nearest wall where it crashed into the stone with a resounding clang.

Cornelius whirled, blurring back up the corridor. He'd reached the top before gravity dropped the bar from the wall to the stone floor. He flashed through the entrance to the donjon and leaped into the command shadowstar drone.

Armitage took one look at his face and remarked, "Not good news?"

"Damn you," Cornelius shouted. "She's gone!" He launched the drone in a vertical climb at maximum power. His last two nuclear weapons rested in his drone's weapons bays. He could use them now to cover a larger territory, but he'd be without nuclear options for several days. He made a snap decision. He would use one. The shadowstar rocketed upward, pressing him back into his seat. The hypersonic drone pulled fifteen gees. Enough acceleration to render a human unconscious, but a vampire could withstand such forces. The drone leveled off at three miles above the donjon. Cornelius armed the missile, targeted the donjon for an air burst and dialed up the yield of the warhead to its maximum one hundred and fifty kilotons. He pressed a button on his console. The missile dropped from its bay beneath the drone and speared toward the ground. He slammed the drone into a maximum angular climb away from the blast.

The seconds stretched, the shadowstar shuddering with maximum acceleration, Armitage and himself pinned back against their seats by the trenchant forces driving the aircraft up and away from the empty donjon.

An intense flash lit up the smoke clouds beneath them. The drone went hypersonic, arcing high into the atmosphere, the curvature of the world sliding away on both sides. Cornelius called general Haras Mosule over a secured, private link, "Haras, get your force off the ground. Scour the blast territory, covering Azuga and Border out to a circle ten miles across. Ensure nothing reaches the city of Braşov alive."

"Yes, Sir," Haras replied.

Cornelius declared in deadly tones, "Kill everything. Human, vampire, I don't care. Nothing shall survive tonight."

"Yes, Cornelius. I will see it done."

"Good," Cornelius remarked and closed the link.

He set a course back to Manhattan. He needed to prepare for the possibility Mekra had survived and would mobilize against him. His mouth set into a grim line, a shiver stealing over his shoulders. The worst possible outcome had manifested. He was entering a field of direst need. He lifted his head and breathed deeply.

There were still options – after all – he still held the Key of Ahknaton.

Only one question remained: how much risk would he take on to win?

Chapter Six

World Saved from Airborne Ebola Outbreak

Romanian authorities have confirmed the outbreak of a novel form of airborne Ebola within the towns of Border and Azuga, south of the regional city of Braşov has been sanitized with a nuclear strike at 8:27 pm on Wednesday evening.

In a statement from Bucharest, the country's president declared a state of emergency with immediate effect, restricting all travel into the affected area until medical authorities confirmed the region was safe for human occupation.

– News articles on the Internet.

"There was a fifth explosion four minutes after the first lot went off. What are they not telling us?"

– Blog comment from a Braşov resident on the Internet.

* * *

Arizona, Phoenix, B-Double Rig, September 13th, 10:28

Four mushroom clouds rose like flaming demons into the night sky.

Jon Thunder-Axe pulled his palms down his face. For a moment he stared in disbelief at the high-definition monitor. A low-Earth orbit night-synchronous military satellite using an ultra-optics camera trained on the town of Border in Romania provided the feed. Jon had used the Panopticon access codes to keep a monitor dedicated for more than a day on the Vampire Dominion operation in Eastern Europe.

An alarm beeped. Jon looked away from the horrific destruction scourging Romania and studied the readout on a second monitor. The Panopticon had taken a day to narrow a search for Arthur Slayne. He was in a holding cell in a Shadowstone safe house back in Phoenix. A nuclear strike in Europe and finding Arthur, everything was happening at once. Jon flipped a switch on the console in front of him and opened an intercom into the rig's cabin. "Dwayne. I found Arthur. He's back in Phoenix. Can you get us back there as soon as possible?"

"Sure. I can get us straight down route sixty and into the western outskirts of Sun City in thirty minutes."

Jon glanced at a third monitor displaying a detailed map and the rig's location. He flicked a key on his keyboard and the map displayed the location of the Shadowstone safe house holding Arthur with a red pin icon. He half-snorted with wry amusement, in a rare stroke of good luck they were on the same side of Phoenix as the safe house.

He executed a series of commands on the keyboard and whirled around in his chair to face the opposite side of the trailer. The schematics of the safe house broke apart and exploded into a three-dimensional image on a large fourth screen. How could he help Arthur to escape? The Panopticon highlighted the systems open to manipulation, prime amongst them the locks on Arthur's cell.

Jon tapped his forefinger against the console beneath the fourth monitor. Metadata appeared at his touch. Four men guarded Arthur. They didn't have official Shadowstone designations and the Panopticon listed them as auxiliaries. They could be anyone, but the only people who could have captured him at the Nevada airport were associated with Crane and the rest of the vampires. Therefore, these guards may be vampires or worse, rogue Ramp masters and able to operate during daylight. They would have to be someone special to guard Arthur Slayne. If Jon had been at full strength, he could have used his sorcerer's mist to disable the opposition, walk in and free Arthur himself. But it was still too soon after the battle at the conclave in Minneapolis; he couldn't even Ramp. No, they'd need a distraction if they were going to free Arthur.

He glanced at his wristwatch, it was half past ten and heading toward lunchtime. He looked back over his shoulder at the map displaying the location of the safe house. It was in a suburban street with houses to either side. An idea sparked; he hit the intercom, and said, "Dwayne, I'll shoot through the address for the Shadowstone safe house in a minute, but I want you to find a pizza shop on the way there."

"You hungry?"

"No. But were going to get into the pizza delivery business."

"Sure. Sure."

Jon typed a string of characters and said, "I've sent the address."

"Got it. ... OK. I've got a pizza shop open about a mile short of the safe house."

"That'll do."

"We'll be there in thirty to thirty-five minutes."

"Cool, ring ahead and order three large pizzas to go, and we want the delivery bags too – to keep them hot."

"Got it. Any specific types?"

"I don't care, whatever takes your fancy ... unless it's pineapple. I can't abide pineapple on a pizza."

"No problem."

Jon rested his eyes for a minute. The nuclear strikes were outside his control. He could do nothing about them and had to let the shock go. He breathed slow and deep, once, twice, three times. He opened his eyes and reassessed the situation. When the time came, he'd unlock Arthur's cell. Arthur would have to do the rest. He could only hope their distraction would work and give Arthur enough time to seize the initiative and escape.

No doubt, his guards would be competent and well equipped. They'd only get one chance to help Arthur. They'd have to make it count. They wouldn't get another. The opposition was too powerful to allow them a second chance at freeing Arthur Slayne.

That was for sure.

* * *

The doorbell rang. A ditsy ding-dong-ding-dong sound.

Dwayne kept his cap low, shielding his eyes from the bright Arizona mid-day sunshine. He held the thick pizza delivery bag balanced on his left hand and tapped the front doorbell a second time. He called out, "Hey, did someone order pizza?"

He wondered if Jon's plan would work. Jon had briefed him. The four guards looked like Red Empire fighters. Jon had picked up their voices via the Panopticon using cameras and microphones within the safe house. They mostly spoke in Arabic, sometimes in Russian or English. Jon instructed that they were all located in the main lounge room on the ground floor, apparently watching the news feed of the nuclear devastation in Romania, and they had seemed to be as surprised as anyone else that it had happened.

Dwayne wasn't wearing a communications earbud. He needed to look the part of a simple food delivery man. There were plenty of free lancers operating food delivery businesses from their own cars without livery. It was an easy disguise to adopt on short notice, although the B-Double rig remained beyond line of sight around the nearest street corner – after all, no one used B-Double rigs to deliver pizza.

He lifted his hand to hit the doorbell for a third time. The door pulled back; a heavy-set man dressed in gray robes with a red sash loomed within the doorway. He stared at Dwayne with dark eyes over a beak of a nose and a thick bushy black beard, and snapped, "What do you want?"

"Hi, buddy. Did you order pizza?"

"No!"

Dwayne glanced to the left and right as if looking for a house number. "Is this number nine?"

The man's lip curled derisively. "No. That's next door."

Dwayne pulled a surprised, non-plussed face, and double checked the number seven displayed prominently to the left of the door. "Geez, my bad. Sorry for wasting your time."

The man frowned at him for half a second, then his eyes flattened and he thrust the door wide open. The emotional temperature on the porch dropped below freezing. Dwayne turned to run, the pizza delivery bag falling toward the floor. The man's hands flashed to his shoulder and hip, and dragged him irresistibly into the entrance hallway. An alarm blared deeper within the house. A backhander appeared from nowhere and smashed across Dwayne's face, sending him flying through an archway into another room on his left.

Starry lights blazed for an instant before his world fell into darkness.

* * *

The lock on the cell door clicked open.

An alarm blared somewhere above the ceiling. Arthur rose out of the depths of his meditation and opened his eyes. A multitude of shadows fell reluctantly away from the chambers of his mind. He lurched up from the floor, his bare feet slapping across the cold stone. He hitched up his simple white canvas pants at their elasticized waist, frowned and gathered himself. This was the real world, not a dream, not an illusion caused by his own fractured mind. The alarm was real. He pushed tentatively on the door and it slid free to the left. A moment later, he was through the doorway and into the hall.

Three of his guards blurred down the stairwell and halted at the bottom of the stairs. Their leader appeared behind them and shouted, "Take him alive!"

Arthur snorted. "Not likely." There was no way he'd allow them to put him back into a cage. The fist team blurred forward, racing as one down the fifty-yard corridor in a flash. A lust for freedom welled within Arthur's soul, and he rode it to the heights of the wild Ramp.

His opponents wore their casual gray robes. They were unarmored, but wore their swords belted at their waists with red sashes. Arthur was bare chested, wearing only a pair of loose trousers. His wild Ramp flowered as the men swarmed him in the confined space of the corridor. Reality snapped into razor-sharp clarity. Cobalt fire coruscated along nerve and muscle fibers conditioned by decades of action. Time slowed as his senses accelerated, his foes resolving in flight. The first slid toward his ankles, seeking to sweep his feet from beneath him. The next two ran the walls to the left and right, attacking his torso at hip and shoulder. The last stood back, guarding the stairs. His eyes glinting beneath the strip lights, and his hands resting on the handles of his swords.

Arthur leaped to the right, foiling the slider attempting to take out his feet. The move put him directly in the path of the right-side wall runner and he feinted with a right arm block. The Red Empire fighter's left arm snaked around the outside of Arthur's block, encompassing Arthur's shoulder. Arthur slapped with his left hand, catching the fighter's right wrist, and sending it wide. His slid his right-hand knuckles down across the fighter's torso, reaching for what he needed most of all. The left-side wall-runner launched himself low toward Arthur's hips in a second near-simultaneous tackle. The right-side fighter slammed into his shoulder, but without purchase with both hands, his right hand slid over the back of Arthur's neck as Arthur went with the impact as the fighter flew past. Arthur cartwheeled mid-air, the second wall-runner from the left flying underneath him. Arthur landed on his feet, one of the right-side wall-runner fighter's blades in the grip of his right hand.

Arthur stood between his foes, three rising from the floor on the left, and their leader thirty yards away on the right at the foot of the stairs. The fist team leader's eyes flashed with anger and he shouted, "Kill him."

So much for taking me alive, Arthur considered for a moment, then his foes were upon him.

The fighter with a single blade was the first to reach Arthur, striking down with an overhead blow. Arthur reached deep into his wild Ramp, activating his speed talent. He flicked his stolen blade like a spear into his foe's unguarded chest before slapping his palms together above his forehead, catching the descending sword. In the same movement, he launched himself backward, kicking the stricken man away while ripping the newly captured blade from the mortally wounded fighter's grip. The man fell backward – his face frozen in shock – the blood-splashed hilt of his own weapon jutting out of his breastbone.

Arthur flipped backward, avoiding the flashing strikes of the other two fighters, and landing in a loose crouch. The fist team leader blurred in close from the stairwell, his gleaming swords slashing from left and right. Arthur leaned backward into a deep arch beneath the leader's blades, his right hand brushing the floor while the other ripped his stolen blade down across the leader's inner thigh. Cloth, skin and flesh parted, a ribbon of bright blood trailing the arc of the blade, painting the floor with a line of gore. He pressed with his right-hand fingers, twisting violently to the left, gathering his feet beneath him and rising from the floor in a single fluid motion.

The leader staggered backward, bright arterial blood spraying from the deep slash beneath his groin. Arthur blurred forward to his left, diving between the other two fighters, his sole blade flashing left and right, blocking reflexive attacks by the two men. He landed next to the first man, dying upon the floor, his eyes gazing with a fading stare into emptiness. Arthur grasped the hilt of the sword embedded in the man's heart and ripped it out of his sternum. He whirled, standing astride the fallen man.

The other two fighters had already turned and were almost upon him. Arthur snapped his two blades into a classic Red Empire high and low position, painting ribbons of blood across the corridor's stone walls. He allowed his opponents to reach attacking distance. At the last moment, he moved the blades slightly off line, inviting both men to reach for a first strike with their nearest weapons. Nerves schooled by years of Red Empire discipline responded to the narrowest of opportunities and they both reached with their swords to take Arthur's life away. He shifted again, beating past their weapons, deflecting their attacks high. He ran his stolen two-foot-long blades through their chests. He blurred forward, ripping the razor-sharp steel through their ribcages with his forward momentum. Blood sheeted to his left and right; one man grunted behind him, the other gurgled. Arthur didn't look back, neither human nor vampire could survive such wounds.

The leader staggered back to the stairs. His pale face shining with perspiration, his trousers red with blood, a long wide trail of gore staining the corridor. He stared at Arthur with dark eyes and said between gasps, "Who ... are you ... really?"

Arthur halted a yard short of the man. His hands snapped left and right, his blades scissoring through the man's neck in a sudden blur. The fist team leader's head rolled to the left; his body slumped to the right – blood gouting over the stairs.

Arthur glanced back along the gore-splattered corridor. Four devout men lay dead. He knelt on one knee next to the beheaded leader's corpse, bowed his head and prayed in solemn tones, "I have taken their lives. They have fought with faith and courage. They have died good deaths with blades in hand. Let them take their sacred honor with them into the next life."

For a moment, he closed his eyes in respect for the valiantly deceased.

A muted thrumming rose over the silence. Arthur glanced at the stairwell, there was an aircraft roaming over the house. He blurred up the stairs toward the upper level.

Only the vampires and their lackeys had air-power in the United States.

* * *

The osprey II drone loomed in the monitor.

Shadowstone had found them. Jon launched upward from his chair in the first trailer of the B-Double rig. There was a red button on the wall. Arthur had built a self-defense system into the trailer. He reached the button and slammed it. A light flicked from red to green above the red button. The B-Double's defensive system activated. Above his head, hydraulics kicked into action, a door over the roof of the trailer slid aside and a 7.62mm minigun with a drum of specialized high-explosive armor-piercing ammunition rose up, twisting to track the incoming osprey drone.

Jon's mind raced. He could run. As a seasoned Ramp master, he could match Olympic times even without the Ramp. But he couldn't move fast enough to dodge bullets. All he could do was pray Arthur's system would kill the drone before it killed him. He stared at the monitor. A wicked long barrel hung beneath the nose of the osprey. A 20mm cannon staring directly into the camera feeding the hi-def display.

He shook his head. Why hadn't the Panopticon warned him earlier? His eyes narrowed, because it was in limited mode. Running on a single processor had disabled predictive threat assessment. Now he would pay the price.

Jon inhaled. As soon as some bastard had dragged Dwayne into the house, the mission to free Arthur had gone south. But there was nothing more he could do. He'd unlocked Arthur's cell. Arthur would have to do the rest. He prayed Dwayne was still alive.

The minigun began firing. A deep reassuring thrum reverberating through the trailer.

Jon stared at the monitor, unable to drag his gaze away. The osprey's 20mm cannon burst into life, pale fire leaping from its barrel. Light, sparks and fire ripped through the body of the trailer. Jon threw himself flat to the floor. The 20mm cannon rounds slashed through the air above him, hellish thunder tearing the racked equipment of the trailer apart. The Panopticon's iridescent blue heart winked out behind him. The cannon fire slewed toward the back of the trailer.

Counterpointing the osprey's cannon, the minigun continued to fire; its system running on multiple redundant power sources. Something exploded outside and away from the trailer. The 20mm cannon thundered, but no more rounds slashed through the trailer.

The fuel cell in the second—

Light so hard it was a wave of white noise ripped Jon's life away.

* * *

A massive headache thudded through Dwayne's skull.

His ears rang. Dust coated his nose and mouth. Blood dribbled past his lips. He half rose from the floor, hacking and coughing, blinking furiously, tears streaming down his cheeks. A familiar voice rang out behind him, "Dwayne," and strong hands gripped and supported his shoulders. Nausea seized him with a rush, and he crunched forward, vomiting breakfast over a dust covered rug.

Arthur patted his back and said, "Can you get up? We have to get out of here."

Dwayne panted and nodded once.

"Good man," Arthur said, lifting him to his feet, and carrying him forward.

Dwayne staggered, only Arthur's strong right arm stopping him from falling over. The front door hung open, barely attached to its hinges. Smoke billowed through the doorway and they stumbled through it together. They stepped into the front yard, Arthur taking him around to the side of the house.

"Jon?" Dwayne asked, looking back over his shoulder toward the parked B-Double rig. There was a thick plume of black smoke rising from that direction and a second plume about a hundred yards beyond it. There were people screaming and crying, dazed figures walking in the street. In the distance, sirens began to wail.

"He's gone," Arthur remarked grimly, his voice tight with barely checked heartbreak. "I swear this damn war will kill us all."

Dwayne rubbed his hand down his face, he could barely breathe. Jon had been a close friend for the three decades he'd worked with Arthur. They staggered around the corner of the house, a wide garage on the far side had escaped most of the blasts.

Arthur eyed the shut roller door and glanced at Dwayne. "Are you okay to stand?"

"Yeah, sure," Dwayne answered softly. He'd gone numb, not able to really believe Jon was dead.

Arthur let him go, and moved to the roller door. He squatted in front of it, eased his fingers underneath it. Took a good grip and stood up. Metal brackets snapped to the left and right and the door sailed up with a crunch. Arthur strode into the garage and Dwayne followed him. There was a sleek white SUV with Arizona number plates facing the driveway. A thick cable snaked from the vehicle to a charger on the wall. Arthur lifted a key ring with a General Motors logo and thumbed a button on it. The lights on the SUV flashed and the doors unlocked. He shrugged as he pulled the cable out, dangled the car keys, and remarked, "They left this on the kitchen bench and I picked it up on the way through."

Dwayne went to the right-hand side of the car and got into the front passenger seat. Arthur got in beside him, started the vehicle and drove it discretely and carefully down the driveway and into the street. The sirens were already getting closer. The last thing they needed was the police to detain them for questioning. They passed stunned and stricken people on the sidewalks, accelerated, and left the smoke, fire and clamor behind them.

Arthur broke the silence. "I'm hitting the I-10 west toward LA. I've got clothes and equipment at the international airport." He glanced at various instruments on the console display. "Range isn't a problem. We'll get there in about six hours. I need you to fill me in. I lost a day from early on the eleventh of September."

Dwayne looked at him. "What happened?"

"A sleeper dart."

"Ah, geez. You don't know anything."

Arthur handed him a bottle of water from a side pocket and said, "What did I miss out on?"

"You went into the Panopticon fortress with the Mirovar force team, and came out with the Panopticon in a P-Case. You handed it off to me at the Black Rock roadhouse and I took it to Jon's. We fired it up in the B-Double rig and found you. We also identified a full list of the vampires and sent it to the Red Empire."

"Anything else?"

"Francis is dead, he died in the fortress."

"Crap. He was good man."

"The Blake force team is all but gone. Only Justin survived."

"What? Were they involved at the fortress?"

"No," Dwayne said. The sleeper dart had hit Arthur hard. How much had he forgotten? "They died at your airport in Nevada."

Arthur shook his head and sighed. "I don't remember what happened, or what was supposed to happen that day. ... What of Crane and Armitage?"

"By all accounts, still alive, Justin said. Anton saved his life at your airport in Nevada instead of taking a shot on Crane's command shadowstar drone."

Arthur shook his head again and lifted his hands from the steering wheel to spread them wide. "I don't know Anton. I haven't spoken with him ... not that I can remember." He pressed his lips together, then relaxed and said, "Well, at least he's looking after his team mates – that's a good thing for a young fellow to do." He glanced at Dwayne. "Nevada airport, huh? I figure we would have been attempting to exfil out of the country."

"You were carrying a replica of the Panopticon P-Case."

Arthur pulled a disbelieving face. "What?"

"You had a copy that you took with you from the Black Rock roadhouse."

"Are you sure?"

"I was there. I saw the swap. At the time, only you and I knew about it and the two cases were identical. They were even wrapped with Faraday tape in exactly the same way." Dwayne looked at Arthur and asked, "How come you don't remember your own plans?"

Arthur flicked the SUV into self-driving mode. He leaned back in his seat and rubbed both hands down his face. He took a breath and asked, "Have you ever heard of Davit Assadourian?"

Dwayne shook his head.

"He was an interesting guy, lived in the ninth century in what is now Armenia and Azerbaijan. He devised a technique for partitioning the mind, creating a hierarchy of selves. Mirror personalities if you will, where memory and agency can hide and come forth based on preset events. A way to give yourself compulsions that could never be detected or even revealed until the compulsions had played out in full."

"And you did this to yourself?"

"Yes. It was necessary to hide my intent from Crane. He's got a precognitive power. I'm sure of it, and I'm sure it feeds off intent. I mean what else could precognition work off?"

Dwayne frowned. He had no idea how to answer Arthur's seemingly rhetorical question. The key point was simple. "So, what next? Do you get to reintegrate these mirror personalities?"

Arthur pursed his lips and shook his head slowly. "Assadourian was a little vague about that. It's supposed to happen once all the compulsions have been expressed, but if all the triggering conditions are not met, then that will never happen."

"You're stuck like this?"

"Most likely. Especially, given I have no idea what the unfired triggers are or how many remain."

Dwayne looked down the road, they were approaching the ramp onto the freeway. "You'll have to live with it."

"I already am." Arthur half-snorted dismissively. "I'm used to it now. Call it a price paid for a strategic advantage and be done with it." He took a deep breath and asked, "What's the news on Anton and the rest of the Mirovar force team?"

"According to Justin, apart from Francis, they were all alive after the battle at the airport. I don't know any more than that. They've all gone to ground."

Arthur nodded slowly. He gazed into the distance and said decisively, "I have to go to Matahat al Diydan."

"Right. Do you need me to come with you?"

"No. I have another job for you. But we have to reach LAX first. I have a private jet I can use to get to Dagestan."

"Another job?"

"Yes, I need you to go to Boston for me. I'll brief you later, first I need you to go over all the details of everything you know about the last two days, and I mean everything."

"Of course, ... I haven't mentioned the nukes?"

"The nukes?"

"In Romania."

Arthur lifted his hands from the steering wheel again, and patted the air in front of his bare chest. "Yes. Like details. Like those sorts of details. Now please start from the beginning."

Dwayne opened the water bottle and took a sip from it and then a longer slug. He shook his head, almost overwhelmed by events. Half of what he knew about the last couple of days, he'd heard from Jon. It was surreal, how could Jon be dead? He'd been talking with him less than an hour ago. He set the water bottle aside and rubbed both his hands down his face. He'd grieve later, he was sure of it – for now, he had to hold it together. He looked through the windshield at the road rolling past them, and launched into a full recounting of events. It was a good thing they had at least another five hours in the car. He'd probably need every minute to bring Arthur up to speed on what had happened.

It was time for Arthur to get back into the game.

Chapter Seven

"Certainty of the path precedes the first misstep." – The Way of the Faithful, a book of Red Empire lore.

* * *

New York City, Cornelius Crane's Citadel, The Hangar, September 13th, 16:30

Cornelius' eyes snapped open.

The damnable child, Anton Slayne, had returned to the top of his list of threats. Even worse, his grandfather shadowed him, while Mekra composed another vector of deadly risk beside the Slaynes. Mekra was still alive, Haras and his forces had come up empty handed. His foes had multiplied, and a new death cusp beckoned within the ancient ruins of the Temple of Thoth.

He drew a pale hand across his brow, wiping away a sheen of perspiration. The loremaster implant cooled within his right forearm. The cabin of his command shadowstar closed in around him, he panted for a moment. He slowed his breathing and flicked a switch on the console. The canopy lifted and retracted backward over the hull. He leaped out of the drone and strode over the cold concrete of the deserted hangar.

Thoughts buzzed through him like crazed bees. There were long shadows over his enemies, others stood ready to take their place should they fall. The loremaster implant had provided fresh insight. A new figure flanked Mekra, an officer of the Red Empire named, Whispering Death.

Cornelius' face paled to chalk, a horrific idea freezing his soul. Mekrarians were immune to silver. Mekra had a Red Empire operative at her beck and call. He could show her the way to Dagestan. He could lead her through the secret entrance into the fortress of Matahat al Diydan.

His mind cast back briefly to his general, Haras Mosule, the famous Tanin al Layl, 'the Night Dragon' of the Red Empire and his conversion into a vampire. Haras had informed him the same night of the exact location and nature of the secret defenses of Matahat. A fortress carved from the roots of a mountain over the richest vein of silver in the world. A fortress whose very walls reeked with a metal toxic to vampires.

An impregnable redoubt his kind could never breach. Even with the advent of nuclear and chemical weapons, it remained untouchable, buried beneath a mountain of ancient granite, and despite the best efforts of his vampire scientists, a bio-weapon targeting the Ramp masters was still to be perfected. Of course – perfection of such weapons was necessary – it wouldn't do to wipe out the food source along with the Ramp masters.

But with the help of a rogue officer of the Red Empire, Mekra and her silver-resistant spawn could invade it. What if they took it over? What if a new threat of mekrarian Red Empire warriors swarmed forth from the depths of Matahat?

Cornelius had to know. He withdrew his smartphone, voice dialed Haras, and declared, "New Orders."

"Yes, Sir?"

"Mekra lives. She has escaped her donjon in Transylvania and may be proceeding to Matahat with at least one of her spawn, perhaps more. Take your full force and cover the approaches to Matahat but remain hidden from the Red Empire. If you find her, kill her on sight. All weapons are sanctioned for use."

Haras paused for a long moment. "Mekra's alive?"

"Yes, Haras. She was my prisoner."

There was another long pause, then in decisive tones, Haras replied, "Your will, my king."

"Good man. Now good hunting." Cornelius put his phone away in a pouch on his left sleeve.

He rubbed his face. He couldn't see beyond the imminent death cusp. Perhaps this is how it would end, one death cusp after another until he failed to survive … a single note pinged like a tolling bell. He took his hands from his face and stared at the elevator doors.

They slid open, revealing the slim, blonde form of his executive assistant, Ursula Zielinkski. She walked briskly forward, holding a written report before her, and said, "Sir. The Panopticon has been destroyed, but additional video footage has revealed Arthur Slayne is still alive."

"I know he's alive, but where is he?"

"Last seen in Phoenix at one of our safe houses."

"Wait! What? How long ago?"

"Two hours."

Cornelius took a deep breath and let it out slowly. "What took so long?"

Ursula looked at him with steady eyes. "We are seriously understaffed, Sir. Without the Panopticon, our few remaining vampire staff are forced to review video feeds by hand. The only reason we examined these specific feeds is because we tracked the Panopticon to a B-Double rig in close vicinity of the safe house. The team of day guards and Shadowstone operatives we sent in with an osprey drone have all died. Our drone and the tractor trailer housing the Panopticon destroyed each other. Our final footage is of Slayne leaving in one of our cars from the safe house's garage, accompanied by a Mr. 'Dwayne Washington,' a maintenance chief from the Panopticon fortress."

"What was Slayne doing at one of our safe houses?"

"He was a prisoner. He escaped at twenty past eleven in the morning local time; killing four Ramp masters who appear to be Red Empire assassins."

Cornelius strode toward her. She held out the report and he stripped it from her fingers in a blur of motion. "What the hell was the Red Empire doing in one of our safe houses? Did Armitage have ownership of this safe house?"

"Yes, Sir. Flight logs indicate Armitage's aide-de-camp, James Haley, flew there after the battle in Nevada. Slayne was put into a cell five minutes after Haley arrived, apparently, he'd been drugged with a sleeper dart. As for the assassins," she shook her head, "I don't know."

"Indeed," Cornelius stated coldly, his eyes lit with a glacial fire. He stood, statue like, his gaze unfocused for a long moment. Ursula waited patiently. He looked down at her and declared in tones of cold steel, "Complete the evacuation of this citadel immediately. Shift all operations to the East Coast Hub and join my personal effects on the Odysseus. I need a last line of defense on that yacht and you're the only person of proven loyalty I can trust with the role."

She nodded and said emphatically, "Yes, Sir!"

"While you're here. What of Wesson's mission to Brazil? Was she successful?"

"Yes, the serum doses were retrieved. She's now at Fort Dix and rebuilding the Day Guard as we speak."

"Excellent. You may go."

Ursula stepped back, turned and left for the elevator. A moment later, she was gone. The hangar falling into abject silence behind her.

Cornelius rubbed his chin. Armitage had captured Slayne at the airport, but how had she done it? She was with him the whole time. Who else had the capability to snatch an operative as wily and capable as the elder Slayne? It couldn't have been Haley; he was little more than a messenger boy helping Armitage with daylight operations. It couldn't have been the Red Empire operatives Slayne had just dispatched. She must be in league with another force. He frowned. Whomever she'd aligned herself with could not be a threat that exceeded the approaching death cusp. She'd not sent her allies against him. No unknown figure had appeared in his most recent vision, and Armitage had no motivation to kill him unless she'd become suicidal – an option, Cornelius discarded without further consideration.

The time for grand strategy had passed. The death cusp would arise within the next one ... perhaps two days at most. His enemies would converge upon the ruins of the Temple of Thoth intent upon his death.

He studied the command shadowstar drone resting like a black-carapaced insect in the center of the hangar. It retained a single nuclear armed hypersonic cruise missile. A weapon, that if used at the right time could vaporize all of his opponents at once. His vision begged an obvious question; what would draw his opponents to the ruins?

Cornelius closed his eyes for a long moment, he would once again be bait, dangling the threat of the use of the Key of Ahknaton to draw his foes in. Little did his opponents know he feared to use it. Ahknaton had believed he'd resurrect his beloved, instead he'd birthed a vampire. What could anyone ask for that wouldn't result in a different unexpected outcome? Use of the Key was the most dangerous path available, and he'd only walk that path in the utmost of direst need. However, while Mekra and her spawn still lived – his most desperate hour was nigh well upon him. He was beginning to seriously contemplate using the key despite the absence of the Interpretive CODEX. He could still attempt the task of reshaping reality to his will based upon his extensive research of Metaframe lore.

And yet, if he could bring his opponents to 'a field of battle of his choosing,' he could turn the war in his favor with a single decisive nuclear strike. That still appeared to be the less risky of the two options in front of him. Victory remained possible, and after victory, there would be reconstruction, but this time with new technologies and new wisdom born of experience. He would reset the world, a great and grand rebirth; once again with vampires hidden from their prey – as it should always be.

Cornelius pressed his lips together and reflected for a brief moment. What of the other precognitives? What of, Li Wu; would she come to the same conclusion as himself or would she see different things? The loss of the Panopticon had devolved the loremaster implant to lesser systems but still it had worked for him. It would still work for Li Wu. He frowned in frustration. Li Wu's choices could not be known. It had become clear that when precognitives of near or equal power competed with each other they become invisible to each other.

He sighed and dismissed such unknowable unknowns as idle thoughts.

As of this moment, one thing seemed certain. If he went to the Temple of Thoth, Anton Slayne with his grandfather would meet him there, followed by Mekra and her followers. He no longer needed to rely on Armitage and Haley to search for the younger Slayne. All he had to do was wait in the right location, and Slayne would soon come to him.

Cornelius' eyes hardened. It would be best to lay a trap and be rid of the Slaynes, Mekra and anyone who attended them once and for all. The approaching death cusp would be the biggest snare of all time.

He voice-dialed general Shen Zhen. Force-Asia must reposition to Aswan. Their arrival, would without doubt, be visible to those who opposed him. It was time to bring his many enemies to the Temple of Thoth.

The end game was about to begin.

* * *

Rows of floodlights illuminated a broad swathe of tarmac swarming with men and machines.

Louise Wesson supervised the arrival of a dozen brand new osprey II drones into the Shadowstone hangars at Fort Dix. These were the latest Block II versions with a 20mm cannon slung beneath the craft's nose. The fleet would enable her to transport her Day Guard force anywhere upon the planet within twenty-four hours.

She looked to her left. "Major Hunter."

The newly promoted day guard officer glanced up from a digital note board, signaled with a wave of his hand for a squad of troopers to continue unloading equipment from a nearby truck, and said, "Ma'am?"

"What's the ETA for the phase fours from the UK?"

"Fifteen minutes, Ma'am. They're coming in on an A400 transport seconded from the RAF."

Louise glanced at her wristwatch. It'd be quarter past eight when they arrived. "Get them billeted, showered, fed and ready to interview. We have a long night in front of us."

"Yes, Ma'am."

"And the additional stocks of smart-rifles and ammunition?"

"Nearly all squared away."

Her stomach grumbled. She ignored it for now. She'd taken her dose of the Day Guard serum over thirty hours earlier in the flight home from the ruined Amazonian research facility. As soon as she was strong enough, she'd asked Hunter to hit her with the pressure-point sequence demonstrated by Jay Creeley. She was still eating every two hours and was nearly always hungry, but her physical powers were exploding along with her mass. She'd gained twenty pounds over the last day, but not an inch around her waistline.

She nodded at Hunter and said, "Excellent. Take charge here. I've got to hit the mess again. I'll be in the main hall ready to give the first briefing and begin the interviews. Meet me there with the phase fours at twenty-two hundred hours."

Hunter saluted. "Yes, Ma'am," and turned away to help his men clear the last of the weapons boxes off the tarmac.

Louise strode away, heading for the mess hall. If the phase IVs mostly came on board with the mission, and with their 'chemical,' preparation, they could have a much higher survival rate with the serum, resulting in a final force approaching three hundred troops.

She'd organized them into an order of battle, based on platoons and companies reporting to Major Hunter, and Hunter to herself. The lab was running twenty-four-seven producing new Day Guards. Everyone knew the score. Everyone knew the risks. Everyone knew who the real enemy were – vampires.

Everyone was a volunteer.

She would never lead men into battle who weren't crystal clear about what they were risking their lives for. If she couldn't keep them alive, then at least they'd die knowing what they'd sacrificed themselves for. She demanded nothing less for herself. She couldn't demand anything less for her men.

There'd been too many lies.

* * *

Chloe studied the descending night.

The metropolis of New York city glittered beneath the deep twilight. Her eyes watched but her mind was elsewhere. James' arrival with Hana Tanaka was imminent. Soon, if it was at all possible, she'd be free of Crane's diabolical implant. A dull rumble impinged upon her hearing and she concentrated upon the source. An osprey II drone was landing on the roof of her building. If she tuned her senses just right, the thick reinforced concrete, steel, and nanoceramic armor above her head was not impervious to her vampiric hearing.

Her smartphone pinged with a message and she gazed down at the screen. 'Arrived. I'll be down in 2 minutes. J.'

Chloe glided away from the window and took a position facing the entry hall. Her left hand rose to her mouth; and she drew her thumb and forefinger together across her lips, finishing by tapping her lips with her forefinger. She stopped, dropping her hand to her side. She frowned, and smiled slightly. Yes, she could acknowledge her own nervousness. It wasn't often she truly needed something from someone else. One thing was certain, she'd never forgive Ms. Tanaka for being this important to her.

She pulled her favorite dragon-embossed black silk bathrobe fully closed and tied the sash in a knot.

The door code sang as James entered the necessary digits on the external control pad. A moment later, the heavy door swung aside with a faint hum of hydraulic rams. Hana Tanaka stepped into the entrance way, James' left hand propelling her forward. She was little more than a slim slip of a girl, not more than five feet four inches tall, wearing blue jeans, sneakers, a white t-shirt and a simple non-descript gray jacket. James gave her another nudge and she walked forward, coming to a rest ten feet short of Chloe. James veered to Chloe's left and placed the scabbarded Black Dragon upon the kitchen island bench along with a small data stick. She noted the delivery of Arthur Slayne's famous sword with a nod in his direction, and returned her attention to the implant scientist. The young woman stood before her, panting quietly with an elevated heart rate.

Chloe looked directly at her and said, "Ms. Hana Tanaka. I expect you already know who I am."

The woman nodded. Her eyes darted toward the window. Her pupils dilated; her heart rate accelerated.

She followed Tanaka's gaze and gestured with her right hand toward the tall windows. "See the night, Ms. Tanaka. Please, consider it carefully. The night is my realm. There is nowhere you can go. I can follow you anywhere." Chloe stared at Tanaka with hard eyes; her voice heavy with finality. "There can be no escape."

Tanaka panted, trembling faintly, her feet frozen to the floor. She stared at Chloe with wide eyes.

"I can save you or destroy you, is that clear?"

"Yes," she replied, her voice flat and dull, her shoulders slumping.

Chloe waited for a long moment, watching the young scientist with all her attention. She smiled slightly, and lifted her gaze. She waved her right hand. "I propose to save you," she declared, her voice ringing with conviction. "Help me now, willingly and without reservation, and I will gift you a new identity in South America. You will receive a generous monthly stipend, enough to live a more than comfortable life with iron clad security. I guarantee you will be both anonymous and safe."

Tanaka's eyes brightened slightly and she stood a little taller.

Chloe smiled dryly. "I recommend you leave your career as an implant scientist behind you and find a new life purpose. One that is not tied to your past, but fulfilling; perhaps charity, working with the poor, or operating a school for orphaned children in Uruguay or Argentina."

The young woman frowned; her eyes filled with disbelief.

Chloe arched her right eyebrow. "This is a one-time offer, and I promise you the alternative will plumb depths of horror beyond anything you could possibly imagine. But that option will cost me time and effort I'm disinclined to spend." She paused for a long moment. "You really have a choice between two paths, one that returns you to the world safe and sound, and the other that ends in your utter torment and destruction." Chloe adopted an open generous expression on her face. "The power is in your hands, what do you choose to do with it?"

Tanaka stared at Chloe, the disbelief draining from her in waves. She blurted out, "The implants are programmable." She paused for a moment as if organizing her thoughts, then proceeded with a semblance of calm. "I devised a dedicated interface. A secret back door that only I knew about. There is only a single instance of the software available and its on my smartphone. I can use that to disable the implant. Once disabled, you can safely remove the implant. However, you must keep it warm as it maintains alignment with its paired implant via quantum entanglement. If it loses power, and more than fifteen seconds out of contact with a warm body will do that, Crane's implant will alert him. He will know something has gone wrong."

Tanaka's heart rate tempered, losing its panic. Fresh blood suffused the capillaries beneath her skin, bringing a healthy blush to her cheeks. Her terror and despair morphing into hope before Chloe's eyes.

Chloe nodded, glanced at James, and asked, "Have you got any tape?"

"Sure, Chloe. I'll be back in a couple of minutes," he answered, turning and leaving the room. The external door opening and closing behind him with a soft thud.

Chloe indicated her kitchen with a wave of her right hand; followed with a casual gesture toward a small drinks cabinet on the opposite wall. "Would you like a drink, Hana."

"Water will be fine."

"Wise choice," Chloe said, moving behind the island bench and filling a pristine glass with cold filtered water from the tap. She placed the glass on the bench in front of Tanaka. The scientist picked it up and drank half of it before putting it down again. "I have to apologize for James and the chameleons," Chloe said. "You shouldn't have had to witness them feeding. I'll make sure that never happens again."

Tanaka paused for a handful of seconds, her face blanching. She nodded her head. "Thank you."

The door opened again, and James returned, holding a thick roll of gray gaffer tape.

Chloe leaned across the island bench and said casually, "Show me how your phone app works."

Tanaka pulled her phone from her pocket. It was a modern slim flexible model. She opened it quickly and logged into her specialized application. She pressed several commands with her nimble fingers before turning her phone's screen to face Chloe. "The application has already found your implant. Its pair is nearby, within Manhattan."

James frowned. "GPS?"

"No," Tanaka answered. "It's quantum entanglement. On a basic level, the paired implants are essentially one object. If you know where one is, the other can always be found."

James' lip curled, but he didn't say anything else.

Chloe arched an eyebrow and asked, "Two questions. One, how do you fire this implant, and two, how do you disarm it?"

"There are two armed modes: Armed/Safe, and Armed/Active. Your implant is currently Armed/Safe," Tanaka lifted the phone to show Chloe the status. There was a symbol on the phone of an oval implant outlined in a green envelop with a single diagonal red line running through it. "It will fire if the other implant signals it to do so, or if it is tampered with. For example, trying to remove it. But, it won't accidentally fire or respond to any other commands apart from the mode setting function. If," Tanaka waved her hands in a flat arc, "and only if, I set the mode to Armed/Active, then it can be fired by a command from this phone." Her gaze flicked for a moment toward James and the .45 automatic holstered beneath his left shoulder.

"Wonderful," Chloe remarked sardonically. "I presume there is a disarmed mode."

"Yes, that is correct."

"Show me," Chloe said, indicating with a wave of her hand for Tanaka to place the phone between them where she could watch precisely what Tanaka was doing. Tanaka nodded and followed suit, pushing the phone over the surface of the polished stone benchtop and operating it upside down. Chloe accelerated her senses. Time slowed. To all outward appearance she was simply paying attention, but around her, everyone slowed to a snail's pace. If Tanaka made a false move, Chloe would tear her hand off. She needed her alive, but she could easily sacrifice one of her limbs if she proved false.

There was also a small chance Tanaka had already reversed the commands for this very scenario. Where setting Disarm would activate the Armed/Active mode, followed by Tanaka punching the kill switch. Tanaka could have reprogrammed the simple act of setting the mode to fire the implant sitting beneath Chloe's skull, sending a lethal dose of powdered silver into her brain stem.

For an instant Chloe's hand trembled. She quelled the impulse to destroy the phone instantly. She needed to follow through on the disarming process. She would have to wear the risk of Tanaka lying to her despite the fact it turned her stomach to do so. It was so much easier to face an opponent in a fight than to sit opposite someone and bet on their compliance.

Against the risk of deception, Tanaka could have fired the implant at any time since its insertion – but she hadn't done so. No, she feared retribution, immediately from James or at some point in the future, and she needed a bargaining chip. A chip she was playing this very moment. Chloe stared at her and gambled Tanaka was playing her bargaining chip for both their lives.

One way or another, right or wrong, she'd find out in the next few seconds. Tanaka's slender fingers moved over the surface of the phone in slow motion. The display evolved, the sheath around the implant symbol shifting from green with a diagonal red bar to wholly red. A message appeared above the symbol in bold white letters, 'DISARMED.'

Tanaka put down the phone and stepped back. She regarded Chloe with a steady gaze and waved at the phone. "It is done. The implant can be safely removed."

Chloe looked across at James and asked, "Could you please pass me your combat knife and the gaffer tape."

James nodded. He walked over and placed the roll of gray gaffer tape on the bench top, and pulled a modern Ka-Bar fighting knife from a sheath at his belt. He flipped the weapon end for end and handed the knife to Chloe handle first.

Chloe took the knife and regarded it. "Nice. This will do perfectly." She nodded to a corridor leading away from the kitchen and said, "James, go down the hall. There's a bathroom on the left. Please be a dear and fetch me a towel."

"Yes, Chloe," James said and left, quickly vanishing down the hall. He returned moments later, carrying a thick black towel.

Chloe pushed the top of her silk bathrobe down over her arms, exposing her upper body while leaving the bathrobe sashed at her waist. James' eyes widened for a moment, flashing with a sudden heat, before he glanced respectfully away. She took the towel, wrapped it over her shoulders and knotted it into place beneath her chin. The red-dragon-embossed black silk bathrobe really was her favorite and she didn't want to get blood on it.

She picked up the gaffer tape, and cut a pair of two-foot-long lengths before hanging the strips from the edge of the bench. She took a step back from the island bench and dove into a supreme Ramp. She had to have maximum control and speed. Her left hand flew to the nape of her neck and brushed upward lifting her dark hair out of the way. With her right she pressed the tip of the blade in next to the implant, guiding it by feel past her spine. She rotated her hand a quarter circle capturing the far end of the implant against the point of the blade. She pulled the knife handle in a tight circle toward the right around her skull, levering the implant out. The blood slicked device slipped out of the cut beneath her skull and dropped into her left hand.

For a moment, blood sluiced down the back of her neck, soaking into the folds of the black towel. Chloe brought her left hand down and opened it in front of her chest. The gore-streaked implant gleamed beneath the kitchen lights; half bathed in a slick pool of her blood. She looked at it for a long moment, a wave of relief flooding through her.

She drew the hem of her bathrobe aside, and quickly taped the implant with the first strip of gaffer tape to the inside of her lower right leg. She took care to ensure the weaponized end was pointing down past her ankle and was just outside the first strip of tape. She applied the second strip of tape immediately below the first, guarding her flesh from the inevitable blast of silver. The whole ensemble would sit above the combat boot on her right foot. The end result: Crane would soon die and his precious control device would fire harmlessly.

Chloe dropped her hem, wiped the remaining blood on the back of her neck away with the towel, and refitted her black silk bathrobe over her pale shoulders and arms. She looked at Tanaka and smiled. "You have done well, and ... you will be rewarded. However, you mentioned we can use this phone to track Crane's implant?"

"Yes," she answered.

"Show me, and while you're at it. Reset the passwords to null."

Tanaka's eyes widened. "If I do that you won't need me?"

"Absolutely, and for the best too. You cannot go incognito while holding onto this phone. My enemies will use it to track you down, and you don't want that to happen, do you?"

Tanaka shook her head once.

"No, the phone must stay with me where I can ensure our mutual safety. Agreed?"

Tanaka hesitated for a second, then said, "Yes." She reached for the phone, reversing it again so Chloe could watch. She reset the passwords to null and followed with opening the tracking function. Crane's implant appeared on a popular mapping application; the address displayed in fine print at the bottom of the display.

Crane was at his citadel in Manhattan. Crane's master implant carried no silver. She couldn't use it as a weapon, even if she could get around Jean Philippe Allemande's curse. At the very least, she'd always know where he was.

Chloe looked up from the phone and addressed Tanaka directly. "Excellent. Ms. Tanaka. You have done very well indeed." She picked up the phone, looked across at James, and commanded, "Please escort Ms. Tanaka back to the drone and give her to the chameleons."

Tanaka blanched, gasped, and stammered, "W ... what? No! Wait! You promised—"

Chloe cut her off, her eyes glittering like diamonds. "I have no room for loose ends."

James strode into position behind Tanaka, his big hands clamping down on her shoulders.

"Make me a vampire. I can help you," Tanaka implored. She pointed to the data stick next to the Black Dragon. "All the implant science and engineering data are on that stick. I know it intimately. I can guide you on everything in there. I can save you valuable time. If you replace Crane, you'll need to be able to control—"

"Enough!" Chloe snapped, then continued in hard, tight tones. "Unfortunately for you Ms. Tanaka, I intend to make your control implant technology obsolete." She stared hard at the quailing young woman, then nodded at James. He lifted the young scientist bodily off the floor, carrying her away, her arms and legs flailing helplessly, her protestations becoming louder and louder. Before he reached the door, Chloe called after him, "No evidence, James."

James shouted, "Yes, Chloe," his voice almost lost amongst the girl's incoherent shrieks. He slapped a heavy right hand over the scientist's mouth, while tucking her beneath his left arm. Moments later, the front door opened and closed behind them.

Hana Tanaka knew Chloe was subverting Crane's control. She knew far too much. Chloe pressed her lips together for a moment before whispering to the empty room, "There will be no loose ends."

Especially not this close to the end game.

* * *

James emerged from the stairwell into the early Autumn night air.

Tanaka continued to struggle. He held her jaw shut, muffling her screams and ensuring she couldn't bite his hand. Perhaps he should plug her with a .45 round before giving her to the lizards. It'd be a mercy, but Chloe had been adamant there would be no evidence of her death left behind. He carried her toward the osprey II drone. It squatted over the center of the helipad in the middle of the building's roof.

James strode across the concrete. This deed was one best done quickly. Harming a woman never sat well with him. Some would call him a chauvinist; they could call him whatever they liked. The bottom line was Chloe needed Tanaka dead and disappeared. The chameleons would do a wonderful job of getting rid of the evidence. He closed the distance to the bottom of the osprey's ramp. He scanned the hold, it appeared empty. He assumed the chameleons were still inside the drone, waiting patiently for the trip back to the warehouse south of Brooklyn. He hoped they hadn't decided tonight was the night to part ways with Chloe. He called out, "Gullette, Kavanne, Shemina – I have a snack for you."

He threw Tanaka into the hold. She didn't land; her sudden shriek ending mid-breath, her body vanishing mid-air in a spray of blood and entrails as the chameleons tore her apart. They ghosted into view; each holding an arm, leg or most of the torso. Their great jaws crunched down, stripping flesh greedily from the young woman's bones. James pressed his lips into a thin line and turned away. He'd seen enough to report back to Chloe. He didn't need to witness the final denouement of the lizard's feast. He hurried across the roof top, and descended down the stairs to Chloe's penthouse.

He'd hose out the osprey's hold once he'd taken the drone and the lizards back to the small warehouse south of Brooklyn.

That would complete the disappearance of Hana Tanaka.

* * *

Chloe raised a crystal flute of Krug champagne and clinked it against its twin held by James.

She toasted to the future. "Here's to being free of Crane."

"Amen," James said.

She smiled at her assistant. He'd proven to be diligent, capable and well prepared. He was someone she could trust to get difficult tasks done. He'd just related the fact the chameleons appeared to be entering one of their exceedingly rare breeding cycles. It never rains but it pours. No doubt, the chameleons could become volatile at any moment. Still, she was no stranger to chaos.

Chloe sipped her champagne, regarding James speculatively. It was too early to transform him into a vampire. She wasn't ready for such a step. There was still the problem of daylight. Until she fulfilled her plans, she needed a watcher.

And her plans required Crane to die. With the implant removed, her original strategy to use Anton Slayne against Crane was back on the table. Assisting the process was Crane's belief she would protect him from all threats. When the time came, she could simply step aside and allow Anton's Slayne's hatred to take its natural course.

There was an energy gathering in the course of events. She could feel it in her bones. Like a rising crescendo in a grand symphony reaching for a hidden climax. It was a whirlwind; one she must ride, or it would sweep her away. It was imperative she reacquire the younger Slayne, and the last contact she had was with Arthur Slayne upon his escape from the safe house six hours earlier. Would Arthur Slayne lead them to his grandson?

"James," she inquired, looking past her glass of champagne at him. "Do you have a situation report on Arthur Slayne?"

He put down his glass on the island bench and pulled out his smart phone. He studied it for a long moment, flicking from screen to screen. He looked up from the display and smiled. "Given Slayne's escape from the safe house, I've been actively tracking private flights out of the CONUS. A long-bodied Spike 512 flew out of LAX five minutes ago, bound for Mezhdunarodnyy Aeroport Makhachkala, aka Uytash airport in Dagestan. The timeframe aligns perfectly with a car trip from Phoenix to Los Angeles international airport. I think its highly likely it's Slayne. He should arrive in approx. six and a half hours from now at oh three hundred our time, or ten in the morning local time in Dagestan."

Chloe nodded. "I concur." She raised a quizzical eyebrow. "It begs a question ..."

"What's in Dagestan?"

Chloe smiled knowingly and responded coyly. "Now, that's a very good question. One I'm sure we will answer imminently. But first we have other business to attend to." She tilted her head forward, her gaze filling with intensity. She ran her right forefinger down the front of James' shirt and said, "You have brought me many gifts, Hana Tanaka, the Black Dragon, the management of the chameleons, and the tracking of my chief adversaries." Her right hand reached James' belt and she clenched her fist around it, drawing him to her.

James responded, his hands sliding around behind her back.

Chloe leaned up, kissing him hard upon the lips. Her hand slipped off the belt and reached lower; he was already hard. It was time to celebrate a victory against Crane. He'd never understand she'd slipped his leash until it was too late. James had proven his worth and deserved his reward – as much as she did. She wasn't above using a man for mutual pleasure.

She allowed James to lift her bodily onto the polished stone benchtop. Her black silk bathrobe slipped away and she wrapped her powerful thighs around him. She covered his face with hot kisses as he tore his belt open. His pants and underwear dropped away. She ripped his shirt open and he shrugged the remnants off. She restrained herself carefully, she'd have to be gentle with him, after all – he was still human.

But not for much longer.

Chapter Eight

"Real acceptance is forged like fine steel. If you have not confronted true horrors, understood evil, suffered hopelessness and despair, found faith, and made yourself completely accountable for your own choices, actions and outcomes, then I can guarantee that any acceptance you pretend to have will be as brittle and temporary as a snowball in the middle of summer." – (Translated from the original 9th Century Armenian) by Arthur Slayne

– From, 'An interpretation of the collected works on "The Way of the Faithful," by 9th century Red Empire mystic, Davit Assadourian of the Tatev Monastery,' by Arthur Slayne (3rd Rank Candidate Thesis) – Original manuscript kept in the main library at Matahat al Diydan.

* * *

Republic of Dagestan, the road to Matahat al Diydan, September 14th, 20:34

Two marble gravestones stood at attention over freshly turned soil.

Li raised her left hand to her mouth, a chill freezing her soul. Her vision after the dreadful battles with the vampire swarms had left her with the belief that two members of their small team would soon lose their lives. She stared at gold letters gleaming coldly beneath a bright dawn, and whispered, "Chiara Morte and Anton Slayne."

But was this fate, or was this a warning of an avoidable future?

Li dwelled within her vision. The sun warmed the bare skin on her arms. Clouds floated serenely across an azure sky. A gentle breeze laced with the scents of the surrounding forest graced the glade holding her friend's graves. On the edges of her sight small birds flitted and dove, and something warm and furry lifted a wet nose beyond the edge of the undergrowth before retreating back within the forest. A bird called nearby, a musical inquiry without answer.

What if Chiara and Anton did not die, what then?

She searched with her mind, plumbing the depths of her loremaster arts. The soft breeze stilled. The sky darkened to a deeper blue. A twig snapped behind her. She whirled around but there was no one there. In the distance the sky trembled as if shaken by a god.

The temperature plummeted, her breath misting before her.

Dark clouds congealed from nothing, massing and swirling before her.

The forest glade melted away. The sun flew across the sky taking up a new position behind Li's left shoulder, setting the storm clouds in stark contrast to the azure sky. She stood upon a sun-drenched hilltop overlooking vast arrays of soldiers armed with futuristic weapons. She glanced left and right; she was on the forward edge of a mobile command center. She turned around; a cold shiver raced up her spine. There was Anton, and his father William Slayne, Peter and Chiara, and others she hadn't met before, but their names flooded through her an instant later. Their body armor gleamed darkly in the sunlight and above them hung a great flag of a Red Dragon on a black field.

The assembled officers moved to the sides and Chloe Armitage strode from their midst, a look of dreadful ferocity on her face, her eyes blazing with conviction. She lifted the Red Dragon sword above her head, its blade wreathed in golden fire and shouted, "Our enemy is upon us! To war! To war!"

The wind strengthened, whipping the great Dragon banner back and forth. Li whirled to face the approaching storm. A towering figure of solid darkness emerged from the clouds, dropping to the plain below. Lightning sheeted across the sky as thunder cracked overhead. A swarm of dark others, smaller than the first and monstrously shaped in more ways than she could follow, trailed in its wake.

The towering shadow strode toward them, its voice boomed across the sky, "We must embrace what we can't defeat."

Li didn't hesitate, the Green Dragon appeared in her hand, wreathed in the same golden flame that flowered around all their weapons. Her fangs descended into attack position and she followed her queen's call to battle.

Her perspective shifted again and the scenes of imminent battle faded. Li returned to the forest glade and her humble humanity. The two tombstones remained untouched, immaculate reminders of an obvious conclusion. To avoid the horrors of a vampire army, invasion, and war, Anton and Chiara must die.

Li's stomach sank. She cursed her power. How could she make such a decision? And what did it really mean? Did she need to kill Chiara and Anton herself, or simply stand by and allow them to die at another's hand? What if she shared the vision with the rest of the team? Would that make a difference? Would foreknowledge doom the team to one fate or the other? Was there a third way? Could she navigate a path between both options, and find a better fate for all?

Li stared at the gravestones, her mouth an open 'O.' A chill shiver rose up her spine. She was not alone. She whirled, her father stood ten feet away, a soft smile curling the edges of his mouth. His skin glowing with the healthy vibrancy of life. He stared into her eyes with an avid hunger, his dark-brown eyes fading to a tawny color with vertical slit pupils, and he snapped with a voice dredged from beyond the grave, "Save your friends!"

Li stepped forward, her eyes flashing with tightly controlled outrage. Her hand slapped around the handle of the Green Dragon at her waist. The creature wearing her father's form before her faded. Her blade swept free of its scabbard with a hiss. The creature vanished silently. She stood for a moment, her heart beating in her ears, facing the dawn.

A shadow flitted across the solar disc. A great black and white bird flying toward her, diving, swooping with mighty pinions outstretched. It passed closely overhead, the wash from its flight buffeting her, sending her hair flying. She turned to follow its flight. It pulled to a halt, hovered for a moment on beating wings, before twisting and turning to land upon the tombstones. It was enormous, as tall as a man with a long dark beak. It turned its head slightly and regarded her with speculative obsidian eyes. The scimitar beak yawned open and it croaked in an inhuman voice, "Choose!"

"What? Choose what?" Li implored.

"The fate of all," the bird uttered in heavy tones. It faded for a moment, and then vanished.

The vision evaporated. The hired Toyota Landcruiser jostled over a pothole. Li opened her eyes and sucked in a deep breath. The others hadn't noticed her brief lapse of concentration. She returned her attention to her loremaster laptop, she was attempting to haze any watching devices. The content of her vision weighed like cold lead within her soul.

She would have to make a choice, but what was the right choice? What was obvious could be deceptive but one thing was crystal clear. Li steeled herself and whispered, "I'm no one's plaything. Not even a god's."

Omens be damned; she'd find another path.

* * *

Anton leaned against the passenger side door of the battered Toyota Landcruiser they'd hired at Uytash airport an hour earlier.

The slim bitumen road, and the sheer gray rock wall to his right, rolled continuously into view of the car's headlights and then slid past into the night behind them. He reflected upon what he'd learned from his missing grandfather. He closed his eyes for a long moment, still emotionally floored by the revelation Armitage had targeted him for manipulation to her own ends. In all honesty, it was probably the primary reason he was still alive. She'd let him live during those moments when she could have killed him. His lip curled and he promised himself to make sure she regretted those choices. To that end, he'd spent every spare moment while traveling from Nevada to Dagestan practicing accessing the wild ramp without sparking a berserk state. The normal Ramp required a calm state of mind, the wild ramp was the opposite, riding on an emotional wave. The wild ramp changed based on the emotions used. The positive emotions: love, kindness, and joy, allowed more control. The negative emotions: rage, hatred, and shocked grief, led inevitably to a total loss of control. If he allowed his darker emotions to dominate, his life would become a brutally short nightmare of berserk possession.

He hadn't mastered the wild ramp – not yet. Every time he wild ramped, he flirted with catastrophe. Every one of his wild ramps could lead to berserk rage, and a killing spree until he burned out and died from heat exhaustion.

But if he could learn to be at peace with his emotions, if he could master the wild ramp, then he was stronger, faster and literally harder than a normal Ramp master could ever expect to be. In one test, Peter had held him while he'd wild ramped from joy, and while he'd not been able to break Peter's grip, it had been a near thing. They'd tested his punch against a steel panel. He'd hit it while wild ramped and left a fist size imprint without damaging his hand. The test reminded him of the first training session back in the barn in Maine, when he'd caught Jay's fist and broken the bones in Jay's hand. It had been a fateful foretelling of what had come to pass.

He wondered for a moment what had become of Jay. He didn't harbor ill will toward the man, but if they met again, he'd take care around him. Anton knew all too well what resentment and vengeance could do to someone's soul. He'd indulged those emotions from the night he'd first met Armitage and lost his mother and father to death and imprisonment. His devotion to personal vengeance had held him back. He could see that now, as clearly as he could see Armitage's plan for him.

Armitage had wanted him to drown in a lust for revenge. He reflected upon the night at Armitage manor, her ancient family home overlooking the town of Whitby in northern England. Statues of cranes had dominated the gardens and grounds. Crane's banner and portraits had hung proudly upon the walls. The sword used to cut off his mother's head had lain on plush velvet within a glass cabinet, like a treasured family heirloom.

Armitage had staged her manor to inflame his hatred for Crane.

His grandfather had wondered about Armitage's goal during the ride to the caves beneath the Panopticon fortress. Anton believed he'd answered Arthur's question. Armitage was cultivating him to be a weapon against the king of the vampires. For some unknown reason, she couldn't kill Crane herself, and needed someone else to do it for her.

As his first warning vision at the homeless shelter in Boston had illustrated – Armitage was fucking with his mind – literally. Well, he wouldn't continue to fall for her cat and mouse game. He understood her strategy, and while the need to bring Crane and Armitage to justice would never wane, he'd put Li, Peter, and Chiara first. They were his family now.

He'd lost everyone else. He wouldn't allow anyone to take them away – saving Justin Blake at Arthur's airport had taught him that. The team was more important to him than personal retribution. He loved them all, each in their own way. Something welled from deep inside, seizing his heart with an implacable grip. He would protect them all or die trying.

There was no other way.

Li's voice came from behind him in the SUV's cabin, cutting through his thoughts, "We've been made by a drone. I can't haze it."

Anton twisted partially around and glanced over his left shoulder at her. Li's lips pressed into a flat frustrated line; her eyes scanning her laptop's display. He turned back to the front and leaned forward, attempting to spot the flier through the front windscreen. He sighed; it was a hopeless task. He couldn't see anything against the night sky while blinded by the twin cones of illumination leading the car.

Chiara remarked calmly from the seat directly behind him, "It'll be a Red Empire drone. They know we're coming. They've probably known since we landed at the airport."

Li said, "I'm sure they'll recognize you, Chiara, but would they know the rest of us?"

Chiara nodded in the shadows of the cabin. "They know us all. They have a dossier on everyone in the Order."

"Well, yes," Li remarked dryly. "I can imagine they do. Especially, given your reports back to the Red Empire."

Chiara frowned and sighed quietly. "I believed differently back then. I can't change the past but I can choose a new path now."

Li nodded once. "I hope so."

Chiara reached across the cabin and grasped Li's knee. "You can trust me. I won't put you, or any of us, in danger."

Li paused for a second, then replied, "Well, we'll soon find out."

A road sign written in Russian rose out of the night and whipped past. Peter remarked from the driver's seat, "Another five clicks and we'll arrive in Gimry."

Chiara said, "Matahat's less than a mile out of town. There is no easy access via a ground vehicle."

"We can park in town and walk the rest of the way," Peter suggested.

"Let's do it," Li agreed.

Chiara's purpose remained unspoken. The team had spent the last two and a half days of travel discussing her plan to depose and replace her father as the Red Ghost. Anton had surprised everyone, including himself, by siding with Li and Peter and proposing caution. There were too many unknowns in Chiara's plan.

In his heart of hearts, her plan was a risk Chiara didn't need to take, and was uncertain of success and without sure benefits. What if she killed her father only to discover the wrath of the Red Empire instead of their unwavering allegiance? If it failed, there was no way back from Chiara's plan. There were no second chances, and no escape routes.

He frowned as the lights of Gimry emerged from the darkness. They were about to entrust their lives to the Red Empire, and for better or worse, they'd soon find out their fates.

The Toyota Landcruiser jolted up and down over a large pothole.

Anton wondered briefly if it was an omen of what was to come.

* * *

Three Red Empire guards dressed for combat watched them approach.

Chiara led Anton, Peter, and Li, to the top of a narrow stone stairway that zig zagged back and forth halfway up the mountain face. The main entrance of Matahat al Diydan loomed before them. A simple stone archway, a dozen feet wide at the base and fifteen feet high, overlooking a broad guard platform. The ubiquitous silver impregnated candles burned in sconces around the platform and back down along the stairway. Harmless to humans, the fumes from the candles would paralyze an approaching vampire.

Peter whispered dryly behind her, "I kinda expected more."

No one else spoke, and Peter returned to silence. The nearest guard lifted his right hand and said in a stern voice, "Chiara Morte, the Red Ghost expects you, but who are these others you have brought with you?"

"They are supplicants seeking the mercy of the Red Empire," she called out in formal tones.

A second guard, older than the others with a hint of gray in his well-groomed beard stepped forward, and said, "On your honor as a prince of the Red Empire, will you give surety for their actions within our sacred domain?"

"I do," Chiara affirmed.

He turned to the other guards and asked, "Do you stand witness to Chiara Morte's oath?"

They chorused, "We do."

He stared back at her with hard, dark-brown eyes. "Your oath is struck. They shall enter under your protection. You shall endure whatever punishment any of them earn." He flicked his head once to the right, toward the youngest guard and said, "Go with Keen-As-A-Knife. He will escort you to the chamber of the high council. The Red Ghost is expecting you."

Chiara nodded. She glanced around the team once to check they were actually following her in, then strode forward confidently after the young guard. The other two guards stepped aside, watching the team pass between them into Matahat al Diydan – the fabled Maze of Worms, ancestral seat and fortress inviolate of the Red Empire. Unknown to the outer world for more than two millennia. Chiara's birthplace, her childhood home, and by her status as a prince of the Red Empire – her right to rule.

Keen-As-A-Knife led her forward into the ancient fortress. The dark-gray stone of the mountain's heart underfoot. Minute flecks of silver glinting faintly from every surface. The cool air wafting past her. Her resonate footsteps on the edge of echoing along the corridors. She'd come home.

Fine silver writing gleamed upon the walls. 'The Neophyte's Guidance,' immortalized in silver letters embedded in the gray stone. She knew them all by heart, memorized by her seventh birthday. One of the precepts caught her eye. Instruction 104: "The master instructs, 'Certainty leads to rigidity. Rigidity leads to vulnerability. Vulnerability leads to failure.'

The neophyte asks, 'Why doesn't vulnerability lead to death?'

The master answers, 'Because failure is worse than death.'"

On the wall opposite was Instruction 186: "The master instructs, 'Resolve is the foundation of courage.'

The neophyte asks, 'Where does resolve come from?'

The master answers, 'Resolve comes from accepting our fate.'"

The two precepts from The Way of the Faithful rang like bells within her soul. Was she resolved? Did she fear failure more than death? Hard memories of her childhood flooded through her. Her father had spared no effort or agony to make a weapon of her, and now she was coming back to confront him. A confrontation that was long overdue.

Would he welcome his only child with loving arms? Only if he misunderstood the crimes he'd committed against the Way of the Faithful. She nodded once to herself. She would bring her father to justice. She would see it done. Surely, there was nothing that could stand in the way of her righteous wrath.

Not even her friends.

Not even the love of her life – Anton Slayne.

* * *

Dalien Morte flicked a red-laser pointer over a frozen image of the fifth nuclear explosion in Romania.

A coordinated nuclear strike had obliterated the town of Border, and the surrounding villages and countryside. Crane had detonated another weapon less than a handful of minutes later.

The final atomic blast had been the largest of the five and begged the following question: what was Crane trying to kill with his fifth strike? The praetorians of the Vampire Dominion had combed the rubble throughout the remainder of the night looking for someone or something. Were the vampires successful, or had their prey escaped them?

He turned to the right and faced the nearly full membership of the high council, the ruling body of the Red Empire. There were twenty men dressed in the red cloaks of war arrayed around a terraced theater of dark stone facing the high-definition screen. Their faces hidden beneath cowls; their weapons close to hand. They were the top elite of the Red Empire. The least of their number had earned his second rank five years ago, and all but one had proven their courage, wisdom, and loyalty on many occasions.

Dalien paused for a moment and glanced warily toward the left-hand-side of the theater. Arthur Slayne had arrived nine hours earlier. He was a ranking prince of the Red Empire, and before the high council, he could issue a challenge for the title of Red Ghost. He was no longer carrying the Black Dragon and was therefore less of a threat. However, he had a speed talent, was a master of the Wild ramp, and was a noted survivor. If he challenged for the rule of the Red Empire, Dalien would first choose a champion to defeat or at least wound the elder Slayne before facing him himself. But had Slayne come to contest the rulership of the Red Empire or some other purpose? As was usual with the Slaynes, such questions went unanswered until after events had revealed their intent. It was better to assume he was a threat and prepare for the inevitable attack.

His eyes tightened. His daughter was on her way to the chamber; led by a junior gate guard and accompanied by Li Wu, Peter Lamb, and Arthur Slayne's grandson, Anton Slayne. She had been out of touch for three weeks since the explosive events in England. He would debrief Chiara personally, and close the gap in her reports. But more important than three weeks of reports, it was time for her to come home. Time to welcome her back into the bonds of faith, family and tradition. As for her companions, he would be pleased to welcome them into the sole surviving force fighting the vampire menace – if they proved worthy. He frowned for a moment. One of her companions was a Slayne … would he survive the necessary test?

Dalien's lips pressed briefly into a grim smile – not if he could help it. He turned his mind back to the business at hand and asked the assembly, "What is Crane's strategy? Who is he seeking? And has he found them?"

Slayne leaned forward slightly and said, "I think we need to consider the possibility that Mekra is alive. That Crane has been keeping her prisoner for nearly five centuries in Transylvania. That she has escaped her prison and spawned a new type of vampire. Everyone has seen the footage from the Panopticon of the fight in Border broadcast by Jon Thunder-Axe before his death. Those new vampires were a swarm. They behaved like a hive mind. I think the power behind the hive is Mekra. I think Mekra is back and pursuing her own agenda."

The chamber fell into silence.

A voice called out derisively from the side opposite Slayne, "Preposterous. If Mekra was in Romania all this time, how did she spawn a new type of vampire in Japan?"

"She must have had help," Arthur said.

There were several other murmurs and mutters before a gray-bearded elder sitting opposite the screen interjected with a calm but penetrating voice, "It would be prudent to prepare for the possibility. If false, we have lost nothing but a short amount of time and effort. If true, we have positioned the Red Empire to survive the coming storm." His words cut the mutters and murmurs down to nothing.

Slayne broke the silence and directed a question at Dalien. "What preparations have been mounted?"

"We have six petrels armed with your new quad-mounted air to air missiles ready to fly at a moment's notice," he answered.

"Twenty-four shots would be decisive against Crane's remaining shadowstars."

"According to your specifications, perhaps?"

"Proven in battle three nights past," Slayne said confidently. "Four missiles per Shadowstar is more than we need."

"If they don't shoot us down first from long range."

Arthur Slayne nodded once, conceding the point that his prototype hypersonic missiles were only effective at short range. "Regardless, we must occupy the Temple of Thoth and prevent Crane accessing it. He has the Key of Ahknaton. Mekra's freedom and these new vampires will force his hand. In desperation to maintain his supremacy, he will go to the temple, descend to the chamber of the Metaframe and use the Key in an effort to secure his rule – and in the process bring about a catastrophe."

"He doesn't have the CODEX. Would he risk the Key?" a cowled figure to Dalien's right asked.

Slayne gestured toward the theater screen with a wave of his right hand – day old footage of a towering mushroom cloud rising before everyone's eyes. "You've all seen the video of the battle of Border. The fake pandemic. The swarm. The reckless devastation. The nuclear strikes. The sacrifice of his own praetorians." Slayne stood up and waved his hand across the breadth of the high council, and then clenched it into a fist. "We have one chance to avoid utter disaster. Crane will go to the temple. He must go to the temple. I'd stake my life on it. This battle will come whether we wish it or not. Crane has the key. Mekra is roaming the world. Crane's fear will drive him to use it. He will go to the Temple of Thoth. He will go to the chamber of the Metaframe, and he will use the key to reshape reality to his liking and unimaginable horrors will result."

"He doesn't know how to use the Key?" asserted another member of the high council.

"It doesn't matter if he knows how to use it or not, the outcomes are uncertain either way," Slayne declared. "If he uses the key the world will be far worse for it."

Dalien took a step forward. Most of the high council did not believe Slayne's fanciful notion of the return of Mekra. Let Slayne hoist himself upon his own petard. He asked a leading question to allow Slayne to dig himself into a deeper hole, "What do you propose?"

Slayne's mouth grinned beneath the cowl. "I'm glad you asked. As everyone here knows, the petrels and raiders are fully armed and fueled. We can use the petrels to position a hundred and fifty fighters on the ground at the Temple of Thoth in three hours, and then reinforce that position with a dozen raiders and another thirty fighters three hours later."

Dalien frowned. "You would leave this fortress not just undefended but deserted?"

"For now, the temple is more important."

Voices called out around the chamber, "Ridiculous," "Bizarre," "A crazed heretic," and "This citadel will never be surrendered."

Dalien took a step forward, patting down upon the air with both hands, and the chamber returned to silence. He fixed Slayne with a hard stare and nodded for him to sit down. Slayne returned to his seat, his shoulders set and his jawline firm. He slouched forward without any sign of genuine obedience to the Red Ghost.

Princes, they had substantial leeway within the Way of the Faithful. Slayne often stretched those boundaries. One day, the boundaries would snap back and Slayne would find himself outside the protection of the Way of the Faithful.

Dalien said derisively, directing his words at Slayne and any within the council who might provide safe harbor for his views, "You've spent too long studying the techniques of Assadourian. Your sanity has fled along with your strategic skills."

Slayne's lips pressed together into a thin line but he remained silent.

Dalien glanced at Slayne's weapon, a beautifully wrought katana but not the Black Dragon. He remarked, as if it was a legitimate order of business before the high council, "Tell me, prince Arthur, what happened to the Black Dragon?"

"Lost to Armitage on the night of the eleventh."

"A pity. She appears to have your measure."

"At least I've been willing to enter combat with her."

Dalien's lip curled. He stared hard at Slayne, a rising hatred gripping his soul, and remarked, "For the benefit of everyone here, it must be noted that the vampire general, Chloe Armitage has seen the CODEX."

"What?!" Slayne uttered in dismay.

"Yes," Dalien snapped. "Of course, in your long absences from this council you did not know. I allowed a viewing of the CODEX in trade to the great advantage of the Red Empire. We know where Crane's citadel rests in New York City."

"She has seen the Papyrus of Hakron the Scribe! We must assume she has understood both documents in full," Slayne declared.

"How? She had no recording device," Dalien replied.

"Her mind is a thing of utmost cunning," Slayne asserted, chopping his right hand into his left palm with a slap. "She will have recorded it somehow. Even if it was memorization at a glance. There is no way she would have asked for a viewing of the CODEX without a means to take it away with her." The elder Slayne looked at Dalien with deep disappointment in his eyes and said quietly but distinctly, "It is a shame your predecessor's term in office was as short as it was. Your father was the better man."

Dalien's eyes widened and his heart beat with barely suppressed fury. He snapped through gritted teeth, "Easy for a prince to say who is unwilling to wear the responsibility of the Red Ghost's mantle."

Slayne stared hard at him with a level and unwavering gaze. "I've never sought to rule the Red Empire."

"So, you claim," Dalien snapped. His lip curled derisively. "My father should never have allowed your candidacy," he shook his head, "and at the third rank too."

"Your father was a far-sighted man. He could see what you're oblivious to – the real strategic picture."

Dalien ground his teeth.

Slayne said in level tones, "If I wanted to rule the Red Empire, I'd be ruling it now. You know as well as I do that no one here could survive single combat with me."

"An idle boast," Dalien declared. "Of course, my father never really trusted you. He never granted you access to the CODEX."

Slayne raised an eyebrow. "A single caveat, and understandable given my access to the Papyrus. He didn't want to concentrate such power into my hands. I would have taken the same prudent action in his place. And, you may notice – I didn't bring the Papyrus to the Red Empire."

"An oversight I would not have allowed."

"Well, fortunately, you weren't the Red Ghost, and your father's contract remains binding or have you lost all honor such that you would disavow your father's promise too?"

"Honor? You speak of honor?"

"Yes, I do. After all, only one of us has cut a deal with the vampires."

Dalien gasped, his face flushed. The chamber was silent for a long moment.

Footsteps resounded from the entrance hall to Dalien's left. He snapped his head around to look into the corridor. His daughter regarded him with her mother's eyes. It was like a spear through his heart, he'd not seen Chiara for a decade. Oh, how she'd grown into the power of her name. He was torn between the desire to strike Slayne down despite the repercussions, and striding across the chamber to embrace his daughter, but no – neither action before the high council. He held tight to his feelings. He ruled the Red Empire, he had to demonstrate self-discipline. He would let her come to him and the elder Slayne could wait until the right opportunity presented itself. He nodded toward Chiara and gestured with an embracive wave at the assembly of the high council. "My fellow esteemed members of the high council of the Red Empire, I offer you my daughter, Chiara Morte, prince of the Red Empire. Here to take her place within our ruling body."

His daughter strode into the chamber followed by three members of the Order of Thoth. Her eyes gleamed with determination, steely, resolved to do famous deeds as befit a child of the great and noble Morte family name.

On the corner of Dalien's eye, Arthur Slayne saw his grandson and sat upright; his attention one hundred percent focused upon Anton Slayne. There was more than one family reunion in play. Dalien smiled grimly, it was time for the Morte's to see victory over the Slaynes.

A victory that had waited through more than two thousand years of bitter conflict.

* * *

Her father welcomed Chiara with open arms.

He hugged her tight.

Not yet! Not Yet! flooded her mind. She had to wait for the right moment to challenge him to a fight to the death. She had to wait to extract justice from his blood-soaked corpse. She had to wait to assume her rule over the Red Empire as her father's rightful replacement.

He let her go, and retreated to the far side of the stage. Her gaze flashed around the high council chamber. There were more than twelve men present. There was a quorum of the high council, a challenge could be issued by a prince and it would have to be honored by everyone there. She looked at her father, a thousand memories clamoring with discordant voices within her. Whips, chains, drugs, violence, and trenchant instruction, had filled the days and nights of her childhood for year upon year. She could not remember when it had started. It had only stopped when her father inserted her into the Mirovar force team as a nine-year-old runaway, and in the following years she'd learned a different way from Juliette and Francis Mirovar.

Not even the Way of the Faithful advocated her father's methods. No, her father had experimented upon her in an effort to achieve a nigh-impossible goal – the co-option of the Order of Thoth to the rule of the Red Empire. A mission that had failed; now there was no Order to co-opt and only a living weapon who'd outlived her original mission.

She stared at her father; breathing steadily, hesitating because her friends did not believe as she believed. She had to bring them with her. She couldn't leave them behind, especially Anton. He was the other half of her soul. But now she was here, she faltered. She dropped her gaze for a moment, took a step backward and looked back at her father. Perhaps her friends were right. Now was the time to wait until the path forward became clear. Her father was a dangerous creature. He had strayed far from the Way. His honor lost – irredeemable, but here he stood – before the high council with no one calling him out. Could she still rely on the Red Empire to honor the Way? Had she brought her friends into a deadly trap? Had she brought Anton to his death?

Her father ignored her momentarily, his gaze swept avidly over her friends, a slight but humorless smile curling the edges of his mouth. "Of course, my daughter's friends are welcome here. But you must realize, that no one leaves this citadel alive as anything except a member of the Red Empire."

Li asked, "And what do you need from us?"

"To prove yourself worthy."

"How?" Peter asked.

"What are you doing?" she asked her father.

Her father ignored her question and stepped away from the center of the stage. He signaled one of his functionaries. Hidden counterweights shifted. The stage floor separated and began folding back in on itself. Each stone flagstone twisting and turning on its center axis before snapping away, revealing a square opening ten feet wide on a side.

Chiara's friends stepped forward to peer into the darkness. Chiara joined them. A set of ancient gas lamps installed more than a century earlier flickered into operation. A pale-yellow light illuminated a narrow spiral staircase descending down for hundreds of feet.

She looked hard at her father; her eyes wide, did he dare such a thing?

He nodded once toward her and declared, "The test of the Olgoi Khorkhoi."

"They are under my protection!" Chiara said in a half-shout.

"Then you shall share their fate if they refuse."

She took a step toward her father, waved back at her friends, and snapped, "They have no training. No instruction. They are unprepared."

The edge of her father's mouth lifted in a derisive grin. He gazed at her friends and declared, "You are all children of the Order of Thoth. If you best a single worm we will grant you provisional membership sufficient to save your life and allow you to join us in our war against the vampires."

"And if we refuse?" Anton asked.

Her father's smile broadened at the implied offer of refusal. "Then every hand in the Red Empire will be turned against you."

Anton stared back, his eyes tightening. He said with a voice filled with resolve, "Let's do it."

Dalien lifted his hand and declared in loud formal tones, "So shall it be. If you survive the test, you will be reborn as members of our sacred congregation. The Red Empire will give you new names and you will forget your old lives. You will know the truth and you shall have honor to sustain you in our noble war against the scourge of the vampires. For this is our way."

Dalien pointed at Peter and said, "You shall be first," his finger waved through the air toward Li, "you second," and then his gaze fell upon Anton, "and you, young Slayne, shall be last." His gaze swept the three candidates. "Let us see if you are worthy of a Red Empire name."

It remained unspoken that they would win their new names or die. He looked at Chiara and said, "You know the way. To you falls the honor of leading us down to the domain of the Olgoi Khorkhoi. To the viewing platforms and the final descent to the sands of the maze of worms."

Chiara flicked her gaze over Li, Peter, and finally Anton, and they moved closer to her. She stepped down onto the first steps of the spiral staircase, and they followed behind her. Her father and the rest of the high council followed after them. In almost silent tones she whispered advice over her shoulders. A typical Red Empire candidate of the first rank completed years of training, study and instruction before facing a single worm in the maze. Li, Peter, and Anton would receive less than a handful of minutes of ad-hoc instruction before they reached the bottom of the stairs.

Her heart beat wildly in her chest.

She could only trust that her brief words would be enough.

The gods help them all if they weren't.

* * *

Dalien descended the stairs.

His daughter whispered hurried instructions over her shoulders to her friends. She tried to hide her concern, but she kept glancing at Anton Slayne.

The way my daughter looks at the younger Slayne – she's in love with him, he thought with a frown. Of course, he could never allow such a match. However, he could turn her feelings to his advantage. There were no bonds stronger than love. Especially love tragically lost – an event he had long and intimate knowledge of. He touched his earbud with his right hand and whispered a command to the Olgoi Khorkhoi handlers. The third candidate would face the 'mother of all tests.'

Dalien couldn't help but allow his lips to curl into a half-smile. He could regain full control over his wayward daughter by consoling her grief while removing a sure ally of Arthur Slayne. He stared hard at Anton Slayne's back. The young man had no future in the Red Empire.

He would see to that.

* * *

Overhead gas lamps left few shadows on the viewing platform.

Anton scanned the nearest portion of the maze. A narrow set of stairs zigged-zagged back and forth from the front edge of the viewing platform to the pale-yellow sands more than one hundred feet below. Additional gas lamps sat another three hundred feet opposite the platform above four round cave entrances leading back into the mountain. There was nothing to set one cave mouth apart from the other three – there were no hints of where survival lay or where doom was waiting.

Dalien Morte interrupted Anton's study of the maze entrance with a sharp order. "Candidates! Stand before us and hold out your left hands, palm down!"

Peter, Li, and Anton responded as one, and an attendant passed in front of them. He daubed the back of each outstretched hand with a dash of colored dye: red, blue and white respectively. Morte continued his instructions. "There are flags positioned in plain view within the maze. Find the flag matching the color on your hand and return back to this platform with it."

"And if we don't find our flag?" Anton asked.

Morte looked into his eyes and remarked coldly, "In the long and storied history of the Red Empire, no one has left the maze without their flag. You either return with your flag or remain in the maze forever." He paused for a moment, his right hand rising to an earbud in his ear. He said, "The first worm is ready." He nodded at Peter and gestured to the top of the stairs into the maze. "Take your position at the edge of the platform."

Peter had divested himself of his weapons, his leather combat vest and his axes resting twenty yards back against the rear of the platform, along with the Green and Blue Dragons. The maze was a test without weapons of any sort. Evasion of the deadly worms was the only relevant skill. He moved to the edge of the platform, rotating his thick arms in a full circle and taking a couple of big breaths. He was feeling nervous. He had every right to feel concerned – this was an unforeseen threat and they were all unprepared for it.

Dalien glanced at the timekeeper standing in front of the assembled members of the high council, and raised his right hand. A moment later his hand swooped down like a descending hawk and he snapped, "Go!"

Peter descended the stairs in a blur, crossed the arena and vanished into the cave on the right side of the rock wall. Anton glanced at the timekeeper. He held an old silver stopwatch, its longest hand ticking the seconds away. How long did a maze run normally last? When would they know if Peter was in trouble and what could he do about it without incurring the wrath of nearly two hundred Red Empire fighters on their home territory?

Anton rubbed his forehead with his right hand. There was little choice but to pray to the gods for Peter's safety and hope his native abilities would be sufficient against a largely unknown threat. Chiara had tried to explain the best tactics, but there were too many options to be clear about what would or would not work.

His gaze snapped down to the open space before the caves. A creature out of legend emerged from the left most cave mouth. It slivered over the sand, paused, lifted its head toward the platform and swayed left and right. A thin rust-colored cowl flared open around its gaping maw. The creature's throat widened, the inward pointing teeth, like razor-sharp daggers, gleamed wetly beneath the pale gas lights. It emerged fully from the cave, its body measuring more than twenty feet from maw to cruelly barbed tail. The tail flicked and lashed, then the creature blurred across the sand, vanishing into the same cave Peter had traveled down.

The seconds ticked by, ten, twenty, thirty … the creature was fast, as fast as a vampire or a Ramp master. This was its home territory. Had it caught Peter or not. There was a faint yell from deep within the maze, "Frack!" that seemed to issue from all the cave mouths at once.

The silence returned like a pall of smoke, obscuring everything. The seconds dragged past, forty, fifty … why was it taking so long?

Peter burst out of the cave mouth opposite the stairs, his boots kicking a spray of sand behind him as he blurred across the open space. He took the stairs in great bounding leaps and landed on the platform. His eyes were wide. His face pale and covered in a sheen of perspiration. His chest heaved with heroic breaths. He lifted his left hand and held up a slim foot long pole crowned with a triangle of red fabric. His gaze focused on Dalien Morte's face and he declared, "Done!"

Morte stood before Peter and placed his hands on Peter's massive shoulders and said, "You have been found worthy." He flicked his head to the left toward Peter's weapons vest and guided him away from the edge of the platform.

Peter nudged Anton as he passed and whispered, "Don't worry, you'll ace it."

Anton lifted an eyebrow. "At least you've got your weapons back."

Morte turned to him and remarked, "Young Slayne, anyone who has passed the test of the Olgoi Khorkhoi is entitled to carry their own weapons until their death. Such is the law of the Red Empire."

Anton nodded. "Good to know."

Morte looked at Li and summoned her with a 'come to me,' flick of the fingers of his right hand. She approached Morte and stood on the edge of the platform facing down into the maze. He reached his right hand in front of her and said, "Wait. Each candidate has a fresh worm. The handlers are calling the last worm back to the pits." His lips curled into a sardonic grin. "Don't worry, you won't have to wait long."

Just over a minute passed. Morte responded to an unseen signal and raised his right hand. Li stood upon the edge of the platform, poised, calm, resolute. Morte dropped his right hand and commanded, "Go!"

Li flashed down the stairs and across the open space into the left most cave entrance.

A voice murmured behind Anton, "Ahh! She has gone into 'The Neck.'"

Anton whirled, the man who'd spoken, an elderly member of the high council, regarded him with dark eyes and said quietly, "I'm not allowed to offer advice, so do not ask me for help." He indicated with a nod of his head that Anton should return his attention to the maze. Anton took a deep breath, glanced longingly at the Blue Dragon resting against the back wall and wondered for the briefest of moments, *This is all bullshit*, before returning to face the front of the viewing platform.

Again, time seemed to both drag and rush past. What the hell was happening? Anton glanced at Peter. He'd donned his vest and fitted his battle-axes into their holsters. He was ready to fight – if need be – but here in the heart of the Red Empire there was no hope for survival, even if they stood together. They were at the mercy of others and Anton hated it, but he had to wear it. The current circumstance was better than the alternative of facing the Vampire Dominion alone. Anton gripped the cold steel rails to the left of the entrance to the maze and stared down at the cave mouths. Where was Li? He couldn't afford to lose her. He couldn't afford to lose anyone else he loved.

It would break him.

He uttered a silent prayer to any gods who might be listening to save Li from death, to return her safely to the platform.

The seconds ticked by, forty, fifty, a minute, a minute ten. Where was she? She was taking longer than Peter had. Where in fucking hell was the worm? Anton glanced over his shoulder at the Green and Blue Dragons, with both in hand he'd be hard to beat. Perhaps he could win their escape from this mess. Motion caught the edge of his eye. Li burst from the second cave mouth from the left and blurred across the sand; a small strip of blue fabric fluttering in her left hand. Behind her a great worm raced. Its rust-colored cowl open. Its great maw stretched wide, dagger-teeth arching – it closed the gap in a spray of sand.

She hit the stairs.

The worm flexed, leaping through the air – sailing in a cloud of grit on a collision course with Li.

She pulled to a halt, the worm slamming into the stone wall mere feet in front of her. She leaped high, somersaulting forward.

The worm crashed back from the wall and rolled away beneath her.

She landed upon the first landing where the stairs zagged back up the rock face. She spun and blurred up and up.

The worm descended to the pale-yellow sands of the maze floor, hissing loudly in frustration.

Li reached the viewing platform and came to an abrupt halt. She looked at Dalien Morte, raised the blue flag toward him and remarked dryly, "Interesting."

He grinned at her, stepped forward, received the blue flag and placed his hands upon her shoulders. He declared forthrightly, "You have been found worthy, now retrieve your weapon. I'm sure you will become a great child of the Red Empire."

Anton agreed. Li was a phenomenal asset for anyone. No wonder Morte wanted her in the Red Empire. Morte turned to face him and said, "Anton Slayne, child of the Order of Thoth, come forward to the entrance to the maze of worms, come forward to the test of your worth to join the mighty Red Empire."

Okay, why do I get the extra formality? he asked himself as he obeyed.

Again, Morte extended his right arm and guarded Anton from entering the maze early. He remarked to Anton, "We await a fresh worm."

Anton grinned lopsidedly and said, "I'm not actually a member of the Order of Thoth. Does that change anything?"

Morte's eyes flattened and he said, "No. It does not change anything."

"Any last-minute advice?" Anton asked insouciantly.

"Avoid dying," Morte said with a slight shrug, a faint smile ghosting across his face. He raised his right hand. He looked at Anton as if seeing him for the last time and said quietly, "The worms are ready."

Worms?

Morte's right hand fell like the judgment of doom and he shouted, "Go!"

Anton blurred down the stairs into the maze.

* * *

"What did you just say?" Chiara snapped at her father.

He turned to her as Anton vanished into the far-right-hand-side cave mouth. The same cave mouth Peter had used, and the one closest to the Olgoi Khorkhoi pits where the handlers stabled the creatures. Her father looked at her with a perplexed expression and said, "Whatever do you mean?"

"Worms. I swear, I heard you say worms."

Morte tilted his head and remarked knowingly, "The Red Ghost has discretion over the scale of each test."

"How many did you send in?"

"Three."

Chiara gasped. "He has no instruction."

"He is a Slayne. That should be enough."

A pair of great worms blurred into the open space beneath the viewing platform. They raised their heads toward the platform, their cowls flared wide, a vivid purple beneath the gas lamps."

Chiara's mouth dropped open; her eyes widened in shock. She whispered hoarsely, "Mothers." A murmur swept through the assembly behind her. She shouted, "You sent in mothers!"

Dalien's mouth twitched, his lips curling into a slow grin. "Yes. Mothers."

"How could you? It's unforgiveable."

Her father stared at her in silence.

A cowled figure separated from the high council, and moved to the right side of the viewing platform. He clasped his hands behind his back and stared intently into the maze. The rest of the high council joined him. Would the high council of the Red Empire soon have a new member or would Anton die?

Chiara ran to the entrance of the maze and gripped the rail with white knuckles. Not Anton, no, not Anton, he had to survive. She loved him. She couldn't lose him. But mothers? No one used mothers for a test. Pregnant worms had an uplift in intelligence and co-operated with each other for mutual defense and attack.

To enter a test against mothers was suicide.

"Anton," she whispered. A figure stepped to the rail to her left. He held a stopwatch in his hand. The seconds were already ticking away the final moments of Anton's life.

"No," she murmured and gripped the black rail tighter. "No, no, no."

She stared at the dark caves that had swallowed her love. Would he ever return? She closed her eyes and prayed. The gods were Anton's only hope.

For no one could intervene in a test of the Olgoi Khorkhoi. To do so was to dishonor the whole of the Red Empire; every sword would be set against them.

She could do nothing but wait.

* * *

Anton blurred along the corridor.

The caves looked natural, but were smooth and circular, worn down over millennia of use and no small amount of modification. Gas lamps hung from a single pipe running along the cave ceiling, covering the intersections of the maze. Their buttery yellow glow left long patches of gloom between each turn of the maze. A shadowy darkness that could easily hide a ravenous beast.

Chiara had been specific about the layout, but there was little advice she could give regarding the worms. She had confided to Anton a day previously that she had benefited from her size and lightness when the Red Empire tested her at nine years of age. Anton, with his six feet one inch frame and more than two-hundred and fifty pounds of hard-packed muscle and bone couldn't rely on having light feet over the sands.

He had only one viable strategy and that was speed. He had to find his flag fast and get the hell back to the platform before the worm found him. Chiara had been adamant. The slightest touch of a worm killed in seconds of agonizing torment. The tail venom was even deadlier, delivering instant death. Their maws were wide enough to engulf a man whole. Their inward curving fangs allowed no escape. Less intelligent than a chameleon, the Olgoi Khorkhoi were just as fast, and deemed to be more dangerous.

The tunnels whipped past. Anton had always been an excellent runner. The Ramp vastly enhanced his speed. He remained calm, operating within the classic Ramp. He couldn't afford to risk going berserk against a worm without weapons – that would be insane. The classic Ramp would have to be enough for now, with the wild Ramp kept in reserve in case all appeared lost.

Chiara had whispered a hurried description of the maze while descending the stairs from the council chamber. There were two main rings around the central arena. The outer ring held seven cul-de-sacs. The inner ring held one cul-de-sac known as 'The Neck.' The handlers placed flags into individual cul-de-sacs for each test, and upon her father's signal, they released the worms into the inner ring.

She had advised that the quickest way through the maze was to find his flag in 'The Neck,' before the worm reached him. Of course, the handlers only ever placed one in eight flags in 'The Neck.' If the flag wasn't there, the worm released into the inner ring would find him before he returned to the arena and the safety of the viewing platform. But if he avoided The Neck, then he must search the outer ring with far more intersections and a greater distance to cover to find his flag in any one of seven locations.

Anton hit the first intersection. Directly ahead was a great portcullis, down and locked. Beyond the steel bars, two handlers holding long poles mounted with what appeared to be an adaption of cattle prods, watched him, their faces hidden in the shadows of their pale-gray hoods. One pressed a stud on his pole and bright blue sparks flared and crackled between the prongs. The second drew his thumb left to right across his throat and grinned with malice.

Charming, Anton thought to himself and ran on. The tunnel branched hard left into the inner ring. Anton took the corner, kicking up sand in his wake, and ran into the gloom. A distant lamp shone upon the next intersection; reaching it alive was his first goal.

The worm was already in the maze and hunting him – assuming there was only one worm. Morte senior had mentioned, 'The worms are ready,' just before Anton descended. Had Morte got it wrong, or was he facing more than one worm? He couldn't know for sure until more than one worm showed themselves. As for the worm or worms – where were they? There was no sign of anything livelier than a spider in a web or a beetle scuttling across the sand.

He hit the next intersection and broke right, ran forward and broke right again into the first cul-de-sac. There was a single gas lamp sitting in the middle of the ceiling. The space was sixty feet across with a low stone bench against the far wall. Anton rushed to it, scanning the surface – there was no flag. He whirled and blurred from the empty chamber.

The cul-de-sacs were death traps with a single entrance. According to Chiara, if a worm caught a candidate in a cul-de-sac, it was a quick form of suicide. He raced along the outer ring, checking the cul-de-sacs: the second, third, fourth, fifth and sixth. They were all empty – not a flag in any of them – or a worm.

Anton pulled to a halt. Something was dreadfully wrong. His flag was in one of two remaining locations: The Neck, or The Deeps. He was somewhere between them. The Deeps was at the very end of the outer ring. It was one long cul-de-sac from where he stood. He could run back along the way he'd just come, but cut right at the next intersection, then cut directly into The Neck, from there it was a short distance to the arena. But if the flag wasn't there, he'd have to double back all the way to where he stood and then beyond to The Deeps. No, he had to go to The Deeps first.

He listened hard. The maze could have been a tomb. Anton stilled his breathing and concentrated … the only thing he could hear was the beat of his own heart and the rushing of blood through his ears. He blurred away, the tunnel a long stretch of gas lit pools separated by long shrouds of gloom before him. An itch clawed at the middle of his back. Where was the worm? Surely, he should had seen some sign of it by now. Was it waiting somewhere in front of him? Was that the reason for the deathly silence of the maze?

The tunnel sloped gently downward and opened up into the final chamber. Anton slid to a stop before the back wall, reached down to a low platform and picked up a foot long polished stick with a triangle of white cloth hanging off the top end. He turned and stared for a moment back down the tunnel. There was nothing there. He pressed his lips together in a thin line. Karmic shit was accumulating and when it finally hit the fan – all hell would break loose – he could feel it like an approaching storm.

He blurred back up the rise into the outer ring proper. The first right hand tunnel cut through to The Neck. He rushed down it, the patches of gas light and gloom strobing over him. He emerged into the long open space of The Neck to his right. On the far-left corner, another tunnel mouth beckoned – it was a direct path into the central arena. The floor was thick with pale-yellow sand. Gas lights illuminated the open chamber and an empty viewing platform lorded it over The Neck – and still, no worm was in sight.

Anton rushed forward.

The sand geysered directly in his path, a massive worm erupting from beneath the surface. Its vivid purple cowl rippled around its open maw; black dagger teeth gleaming beneath the gas light. It took his breath away. His heart clenched in atavistic terror and he kicked hard right. Unarmed – he had to find a way around it.

The worm reared higher, its eyeless maw swaying a dozen feet off the sand at the top of a sinuous 'S.' Its cowl flared again and it shrieked. Its dreadful call echoing off the rock walls. Anton dug deep, ramped hard, pushed vertically up the stone wall a dozen or more feet and launched himself high over the creature's head.

The creature lunged; its maw snapping shut with a wet slap.

Anton flew above it, landed and tumbled toward the exit tunnel. He rose to his feet. His hands were empty. A single thought raced through his mind. *Where's the fucking flag?*

The worm recovered and pivoted toward him, hissing with fury, its tail lashed to its right, shivering, poised to strike.

A scrap of white cloth poked out of the sand half a dozen feet in front of the rising column of the worm.

Anton launched himself toward the flag.

The worm shrieked, its wicked barb lancing forward like a missile.

Anton flung his right hand wide.

The barb speared into the sand in front of his face, throwing grit into his eyes.

Blinking wildly, he rolled to the left.

The barb stabbed like an out-of-control jackhammer across the sand. Pale gobs of poisonous ichor splashing through the air, sizzling and steaming wherever they landed.

He pushed hard off the sand rising into the air, the barb rising and falling beneath him.

The worm snapped toward him. Its great maw agape. Its purple cowl quivering, great dagger fangs gleaming like polished obsidian beneath the gas lights.

Anton hit the sand and blurred forward on all fours, snatching up the white flag and rolling forward, the great worm smashing into the sand behind him. Once again, the worm was between him and the relative safety of the arena. He dug deep and blurred forward, reaching the wall, veered hard left, wall-running around a quarter of 'The Neck,' before returning to the sandy floor.

The worm twisted through a hundred and eighty degrees. Its sinuous body snaking around, its maw tracking his movement.

He blurred past it, veering left then right.

The creature's barb lanced toward him, stabbing down into the sand.

Anton kicked away in a spray of grit.

Behind him the worm shrieked again.

Anton's stomach clenched – the creature would be upon his unprotected back in moments. He burst from the tunnel into the arena. Two more worms lay upon the pale-yellow sands before the platform, forming a blocking line in front of the stairs.

He frowned. He had three worms. Dalien Morte was trying to kill him. Well, Dalien Morte could fucking well get in line.

The sands rustled within the cave behind him. He risked a glance over his shoulder. The third worm ghosted from the gloom into the gas lit arena almost on his heels. Its purple cowl flaring, its great maw gaping. A guttural hissing coming from deep within it.

He blurred across the sands to the center of the arena and came to a sudden halt in a spray of sand. Above the stairs, intense voices muttered from the platform. He ignored them; no help could come from there. The worms surrounded him. There was nowhere to go. The creatures paused, lifted their maws and hissed in unison, a shrill thrum hammering the air around him. He shook his head once; they were working together – so much for rumors of their limitations. They had simply waited for him to come back to herd him into a kill box.

Despite his better judgment Anton risked a single glance upward. An unbidden thought raced through him, *For we who are about to die*— ... he caught Chiara's gaze. Her face was pale, her eyes wide, a pair of tears trembled at the edges of her eyes. A rare terror coursed across her face and pierced Anton's heart like a knife. He drew upon the powerful emotional flow and wild ramped to the max.

The worms flexed, rearing up and back as one, then launched themselves at him.

There was no time to think. A thin sliver of space beckoned just to the right of the worm slashing in from the front right-quarter. Anton took the offered escape and blurred into the gap. The worm reacted, ripping its barbed tail forward and the path to safety vanished – replaced with deadly threat.

Worms were smart – who knew?

The wild Ramp flowered in full on a wave of realized love and urgent need to survive. He planted his right boot hard through the shallow sand to the bedrock below. He pivoted to the left, the full force of his wild Ramp rushing up the line of his body from anchored right foot through his right fist, pale-blue Ramp fire coursing along every nerve, sinew and bone. Every ounce of power was behind the blow, delivered with his utmost speed. His fist connected with the skin of the worm and plunged in; the creature's skin stretching around his iron-like hand. Ancient nerve toxins invaded the pores of his skin, extinguishing the Ramp fire and replacing it with flooding shadows. His fist went deeper, colliding with cartilaginous plates that absorbed and distributed the impact force in a wave around the creature's vital organs.

The worm shuddered and buckled around his fist. The blow thrusting the creature half-a-dozen feet to his left. A gap opened between the worm's body and its barbed tail. The fatal weapon, glistening venom oozing along its length, lashed wildly to his right. He blurred forward between the worm's body and its flailing barb.

Anton broke past the creature, a terrible fire crippling his right hand, tendrils of agony racing up his arm. He dashed for the stairs, sand kicking aside with every step. Shrill screeches echoed across the maze as the three worms collided with massive thuds in a writhing tower behind him.

He rose up the stairs, reached the top, and lifted the white flag in his left hand. His mouth gaped open to speak, but rising shadows from his right arm claimed his world in a storm of torment. A moment later, he hit the stone floor of the platform.

And everything went dark.

* * *

"He's still breathing," Chiara said, lifting her cheek from above Anton's face.

"He shouldn't be," her father declared. The surprise in his voice alloyed with disappointment. "No one touches an Olgoi Khorkhoi with their bare skin and lives to tell the tale."

"Wait, he's starting to wake up," Li said, kneeling on one knee on the other side of Anton, her hand on his shoulder.

Peter stated with a wide grin, "He's going to make it."

"It must be the wild Ramp," a hooded figure from behind Chiara suggested. "It's the only viable explanation. It must have burnt off most of the poison before it could kill him."

Chiara stared at Anton's face. Whoever had just spoken was right. Anton was someone special. There was no one like him. The speaker's voice sounded familiar. She began to turn her head to look more closely.

Anton raised his right hand and fumbled at her left arm, then gently grasped her wrist. Chiara's head snapped back to face him. He raised his head off the floor and opened his eyes, blinking at the lights. He groaned, then said, "How long have I been out?"

"About five minutes," she answered.

"You should be dead," Li said to Anton. "Apparently, the wild Ramp is the answer. It blunted the poison. Knocking you out instead of killing you."

"We'll go with that for now," Anton said wearily, crunching forward into a sitting position. "You'll have to excuse me if I don't offer to test the theory again, I've got a throbbing headache." He pushed back against the floor and rose to his feet. He took a couple of deep breaths and flexed his fingers.

"Are you alright?" Chiara asked.

"I think so."

Peter slapped him on the back. "Awesome effort against three worms."

"Doesn't that make him a prince?" Li asked the Red Ghost.

"Not yet it doesn't," Chiara's father declared. He moved in front of Anton, clasped his shoulders and said in formal tones with a hint of regret. "You have been found worthy." He nodded toward the Blue Dragon. "You may retrieve your weapon."

Anton nodded and went to the rear wall to pick up his katana, a moment later he returned.

Chiara looked at Li, Peter and Anton for a long moment. In a surprise move, her father submitted them to the test of the Olgoi Khorkhoi and they had passed. While their membership in the Red Empire was provisional, it was now irrevocable. Her friends had the protection of the Way of the Faithful. They were as safe as they could be if her next step failed. Her gaze tightened. Her resolve rested on adamantine foundations – she would not fail. She glanced around the viewing platform. It was a flat stone circle sixty feet across with all the current members of the high council upon it. A quorum was present, enough for binding decisions that all would honor. Her father had already turned to ascend the stairs to the high council chamber. She called out, "Red Ghost!" he turned and she addressed him directly in clear powerful tones. "Before the high council," his eyes flattened and his mouth clenched tight, "as a prince of the Red Empire, I assert my right to challenge you for the title of Red Ghost."

Her formal challenge before the high council created an absolute obligation. Her father had to respond. He glanced around the assembly for a moment, then arrested his gaze upon his daughter's face. "As you wish," he said quietly, then raised his voice and declared in ringing tones, "By my right as the Red Ghost, I choose a champion to fight my challenger to the death. If my champion wins, then we will mourn the honored dead. If my champion loses then I will fight my challenger to the death."

The high council members, stepped back to form a circle. They drew their weapons, lifted them high, and called out in unison, "There shall be only one."

Chiara loosened her katana. A death match would occur in a circle not more than thirty feet wide. The naked blades of the members of the high council would mark its boundary. They would ensure the Way of the Faithful was honored in full. Only one combatant would leave the sacred circle alive.

The assembled circle parted and her father walked toward her. Who would he choose? There was no one next to her he could choose. Her father veered at the last moment to place his left hand on Anton's right shoulder, he looked into Anton's frozen face and said, "I choose you, Anton Slayne, to be my champion. You shall fight for my right to rule. You shall kill my challenger."

"What?!" Anton exclaimed, a bewildered look seizing his face. He stared hard at Chiara. "How?"

Chiara uttered, "You can't choose—"

"Yes, I can," her father declared. "Have you forgotten your lessons? Perhaps I did not instruct you as well as I thought."

A cold well opened within her soul. Her father could pick a champion from anyone who'd passed the test of the Olgoi Khorkhoi. She'd always seen this moment occurring without the possibility of the Red Ghost choosing one of her friends – but the last few minutes had moved so quickly. *Anton had almost died...* She stared back at Anton. Abject horror reached with long clammy fingers from the depths of her soul and froze her heart.

Anton drew back from her father's hand as if scalded. He shouted, "I will not fight—"

"NO!" a hooded figure thundered from the back of the assembled circle of councilors. He hustled his way to the front, threw back his cowl and declared, "Anton! You cannot refuse to fight. It's suicide."

Anton stared at his grandfather, his mouth dropped open, and he said, "Arthur? Arthur, you're alive!"

Chiara's heart burst, she could neither kill Anton, nor allow him to withdraw from the challenge. If he refused to fight, then every member of the Red Empire would be honor bound to kill him immediately – even with all his skills and the wild Ramp he would inevitably fall beneath their blades. Her father had chosen well. He'd won. The frigid agony within her soul congealed into bitter defeat. There was only one option left, she uttered loudly ensuring everyone on the platform heard, "I concede." She dropped to her knees, swayed forward, and laid her naked blade upon the cold stone. She pressed her forehead to the hard flagstones before her father's feet, and declared loudly, "I throw myself upon the Red Ghost's mercy."

The assembly fell to silence.

"Take her to the dungeons," her father commanded in stern implacable tones.

Strong hands grasped her arms and lifted her to her feet. She didn't resist. Resistance was hopeless at this point. She'd failed, her fate rested in her father's hands. She looked at Anton, he was frowning, a storm brewing behind his blue eyes, but he held his emotions in check and asked her father, "I'm going with her."

"As you will," her father responded with a telling glance at her.

The Red Empire would not tolerate any attempt to escape justice. She walked between the two guards. Anton called out behind her, "Arthur ... we'll catch up later." Then he was at her shoulder and asked, "How can I help?"

"Don't interfere Anton. Allow the Way to take its course."

Anton hesitated a second, eying the guards knowingly, and said, "Sure. Whatever. I'm not going anywhere without you."

Chiara closed her eyes for a moment, the bitterness in her heart for her father balanced on a knife edge against her love for Anton. She reached back with her left hand and Anton squeezed it. The knife slipped away and the bitterness receded. Now she'd lost, there was nothing left to do against her father. She smiled, hesitantly at first and then fully – she still had Anton.

And that was more than enough.

* * *

Dalien Morte surveyed his command center at the heart of the Matahat fortress, his mind elsewhere.

He remained dumbfounded by his daughter's ambition. He'd not expected her to challenge him for rule of the Red Empire. Fortunately, she'd laid herself open with her attachment to the younger Slayne. Of course, if Anton Slayne had not survived the mothers in the maze, he could have selected the elder Slayne as his champion, but then his daughter would almost certainly be dead – an outcome far from his heart's desire.

The original plan for Chiara was for her to rise to the top of the Order of Thoth and then fold the whole organization into the Red Empire. He would unite the Ramp masters under one banner and Chiara would return in triumph to serve at his right hand as his loyal, obedient and devoted daughter. Instead of the original plan, the Order was all but destroyed, and Chiara hated him with a dark passion. Now, she languished in his dungeons while her future waited upon his judgment. A judgment that rested in uncertainty. Could the devoted and obedient daughter he'd sent to conquer the Order of Thoth from the inside return to her home at his side?

He did not know the answer.

"Shabbah al Ahmar," Khufu called out. Stealing his attention away from the subject of his wayward daughter. "Our forces are in position."

Dalien returned his attention to the main screen. It displayed the disposition of all the Red Empire fist teams arrayed against the vampires previously revealed by the stolen Panopticon. With the destruction of the Panopticon by Shadowstone forces just over twenty-four hours earlier, the data was already becoming stale. The opportunity to strike decisively against the vampires was slipping away. Already the praetorians were out of reach. In any event, even the Red Empire could not muster enough fighters around the world to kill eight-hundred plus vampires at the same time. However, most of the civilian vampires remained vulnerable. They were by far the majority of vampires, and his fist teams were in place against them. He looked into Khufu's eyes and snapped orders, "Initiate the strike. Kill them all."

"Your will, Shabbah al Ahmar," Khufu replied and turned away. He issued a set of orders in rapid succession to his staff and the command center set to work.

The main screen displayed a fresh map of the world covered in hundreds of white stars, each one a verified location of a civilian vampire. His fist teams stood out as named red circles. The red circles rested over clusters of white stars – vampire covens ripe for destruction. The night of long knives had begun. Nothing would interfere with the mass slaughter of the vampires. Despite the strange setbacks of his daughter's challenge and Anton Slayne's survival in the maze. Tonight, would be a night of triumph for the Red Empire over the Vampire Dominion.

History would remember this triumph forever.

A flashing red light and a sharp buzz stole his attention away from the glory writ large upon the main display. He looked at a secondary screen to the left. An older prop-driven osprey I had landed without permission twenty kilometers short of Matahat. He flicked his gaze at his operations chief and snapped a quick question, "Khufu! What is happening?"

The operations chief consulted his computers for a moment, then turned to Dalien and said, "Shabbah al Ahmar, it is a scheduled shipment of premium food supplies from our base at Raukhivka in Ukraine. The pilot is a Red Empire helper who has made the trip many times. He claims a technical fault has temporarily grounded his aircraft."

"Send a team to investigate," Dalien directed.

"Yes, Shabbah al Ahmar," Khufu replied. He tapped his earbud and issued a command to a waiting team in the hangar. He turned back to Dalien. "A raider is on its way."

Dalien nodded.

Arthur Slayne approached him and stood upon his left. He asked quietly, "Have you got any cameras on the airport in Raukhivka?"

Dalien lifted a quizzical eyebrow. The rest of the command center was busy coordinating the massive attack on the civilian vampire population. He regarded Li Wu. She sat at a console with her loremaster laptop sitting in front of her, logged into the main Red Empire servers and exploring the use of her netmaster/loremaster abilities. Peter Lamb sat near her, watching her and the rest of the operations center with interest, but otherwise at a loose end. "Let us see how useful Miss. Wu can be."

Li looked up upon hearing her name. "Sir?"

"Miss. Wu, find the Raukhivka airport feeds and present them upon screen number three."

She nodded and set to work. Within a handful of seconds, the requested feeds appeared 'picture in picture,' within a six-foot-wide screen to the right of the main screen. She was fast, very fast. Li Wu would make an excellent addition to the Red Empire command center operations team.

Dalien studied the views. Raukhivka lay within a dark shroud, deserted, and without any signs of life.

"Seems a little quiet," Slayne remarked beside him.

"There should at least be a site guard on duty," Dalien said.

"The cameras were running a continuous loop from oh four forty-five to nineteen ten," Li noted, causing Khufu to look up from his console and turn to the Red Ghost. "From before sunrise to sunset, there was no real coverage? Someone has spoofed our cameras."

Dalien frowned, surely vampires had not attacked the secret site. Perhaps someone else was working against the interests of the Red Empire.

Slayne steepled his fingers and observed with a wry tone. "Vampires?" He brushed Dalien's left wrist and asked with mocking eyes, "So, who was really on that osprey I?"

Dalien flicked a glance at Khufu, who replied, "The pilot has identified himself as a Red Empire helper with all the correct identification codes. As I reported earlier, he was due to deliver a shipment of food supplies."

"He could have been turned," Slayne said.

"Why would a vampire come here?" Dalien asked. "It would be suicide."

"Crane's attempt to sanitize the town of Border didn't work. Whatever he was trying to kill – it has escaped. Perhaps it's coming here."

"No one but you believe Mekra has returned."

"No one believed Cassandra either."

Dalien snorted. "Be that as it may. The raider team will find out the truth."

Slayne looked at him and said, "Let's hope they do so in time."

Dalien frowned. On the night of the greatest triumph of the Red Empire over the vampires, Arthur Slayne managed to find a way to dampen the mood. Surely, Slayne was wrong. Mekra was long dead. Dust beneath the sun. Yes, there was some strange vampire that had emerged out of Japan and crossed northern China to Romania. A thing detested by Crane, that had spawned a small army in the town of Border. Crane had mustered and thrown his forces against the vampire swarm, and undoubtedly destroyed them all with nuclear weapons.

Dalien lifted his chin and stared down his nose at Slayne.

There was no way he would listen to a Slayne.

Not now, not ever.

* * *

The night air caressed Mekra's skin.

In her long life, Mekra had never physically ranged into Dagestan. The threat of the Red Empire and their silver laden fortress at Matahat al Diydan had been too great an obstacle to overcome. But now, silver was no longer the threat it once was, Crane had seen to that. Constant exposure to silver had transformed her into a new form of vampire – one immune to silver – and the trait passed on to her thralls with her blood.

She strode down the osprey's ramp onto the rough stone of the mountain clearing. The pilot had brought the flying craft down next to a narrow path that wound its way around the hills and mountains of Dagestan to the village of Gimry. A small town, whose obscurity helped mask the ancient citadel of the Red Empire from the human world. The vampires had known of Matahat for millennia. The famous redoubt of the Red Empire, the fortress inviolate – proof against vampires due to the rich veins of silver threaded throughout its many halls and chambers.

But with her coming, it would be inviolate no longer. She looked up at the night sky, luxuriating in the infinite darkness. The world was sharp, detailed, achingly beautiful – a fairy wonderland to her senses. She drew in a deep breath and lifted her arms up into a wide 'V,' her manacles removed long ago at Raukhivka. Her heart thrilled to the beat of her newly won freedom.

Whispering Death said behind her left shoulder, "My queen, the Red Empire will undoubtedly investigate our landing. They will send a scout helicopter. Matahat al Diydan is but twenty kilometers away. My former comrades are a handful of minutes away from here."

Mekra let her hands fall, turned and smiled at him. "Then we must make haste. We have to gift the Red Empire with our majesty. Lead our small band to their secret entrance and disable their wards."

The former Red Empire officer nodded and blurred away. Mekra bent her will upon the other three. The pilot and two mechanics from Raukhivka lacked the talents of Whispering Death being mere helpers of the Red Empire, but their new blood had come from her own veins. They would serve well in the conversion of the Red Empire fortress to her will. She sent them on after Whispering Death, and then followed after them. It was best to see those she'd taken into her fold; it eased the means of control.

She blurred after them to Matahat al Diydan. Whispering Death thought of the distance in a measure called kilometers. An invention that had occurred after her imprisonment by Crane. She had absorbed Whispering Death's mind, his knowledge, his experience. She knew everything he knew and knew it in intimate detail. The same was true for Akimitsu, and every other human who'd fallen under her thrall. The town of Border in Romania had included some gems. She'd picked up history, mathematics, the sciences, and she spoke more than half a dozen new languages fluently. What would she know once she'd consumed the Red Empire? Hunger flared within her soul just thinking about it.

For beyond the Red Empire lay the Vampire Dominion, and beyond them lay the world.

Could her desires ever be satisfied?

She was willing to find out.

* * *

Tamsah al Ramil regarded the secret entrance into the Olgoi Khorkhoi pits.

His heart wavered with indecision. He had not been able to devise a defense against the abundant silver within Matahat al Diydan. He'd hoped to conceive of a solution as he pursued the truth speaker and her friends from Nevada to Dagestan. A vain hope, now shattered upon the hard rocks of reality. He'd watched from afar as the four young Ramp masters entered Matahat al Diydan through the main entrance.

Tamsah had relocated to the ancient secret entrance on the other side of the mountain. The entrance was close to the Olgoi Khorkhoi pits. He was pleased to discover that the words of their handlers were faintly audible to his vampire ears. They had rapidly tested three new candidates and found them worthy. The truth speaker was alive and safe for the moment.

One question remained: what to do next?

Tamsah pressed his lips together and prepared to depart. There was nothing he could do to assist the truth speaker at this time. A distant movement caught his eye, something unexpected against the background hum of life. A low tree branch moved slightly for the second time eighty yards distant from his hiding spot. A lithe figure emerged from the brush thirty feet opposite the cave mouth to the pits, a control device held aloft in their right hand. It was Whispering Death, but changed, his eyes were black orbs and long slim fangs hung over his bottom lip.

What horror is this? Tamsah asked himself silently. Whispering Death had become a vampire, a strange vampire of a new type. Three more male vampires followed Whispering Death. There was no clangor, no siren, no alarms, Whispering Death had disabled the digital wards with his handheld device.

A near-naked creature of arresting beauty stepped from the brush, strode across the short clearing, and joined the other four at the entrance to the cave. Tamsah's heart froze, a cold shiver rippling over his skin. It could only be Mekra; she was alive, transformed, and had come to Matahat al Diydan.

Tamsah stilled his heart and breathing, his body froze in place.

Whispering Death, Mekra and the other three strange vampires vanished through the secret entrance. They showed no fatigue, rigidity, or fear – they must be immune to silver.

Tamsah resumed the beat of his heart and took a breath. He steeled his resolve. Despite his shameful status and physical vulnerability to silver, he must warn the Red Empire of the incursion of vampires. Vampires who held no fear of silver. He turned and rushed toward the main entrance.

He had to save the truth speaker.

Chapter Nine

"Faith, humility, fanaticism, and arrogance walk the same path. Faith and humility seek to understand the way, fanaticism and arrogance assume they know the way." – The Way of the Faithful, a book of Red Empire lore.

* * *

Republic of Dagestan, Matahat al Diydan, The Olgoi Khorkhoi Pits, September 14th, 22:04

Pale lanterns mounted on ancient-iron poles illuminated great shadowed rectangles carved into the bedrock of the mountain.

Within the gloomy pits, Olgoi Khorkhoi rustled and breathed, or lay quiescent as if asleep. Whispering Death ignored the worms, and led his queen and the other mekrarian vampires into the great chamber of the Olgoi Khorkhoi pits. He had used all his knowledge to mute the alarms, disable the wards, bypass the traps, and spoof the sensors from the secret entrance. He had led his queen, along the hidden path through a set of narrow winding caves and into the lowest part of Matahat al Diydan. At the last, he'd quietly closed and locked the great doors of the secret entrance behind them. No one would escape this way from the conversion of the Red Empire to Mekra's will. He glanced back over his shoulder at his lovely queen. What did she require next?

His queen searched the massive chamber with an intent gaze, paused for a moment, and said quietly, "Wait."

Her eyelids closed and her posture stiffened. Whispering Death waited quietly. He'd seen this before, most recently within the cellars of the Red Empire base at Raukhivka. His queen was astral traveling ... and ... her eyelids, like dark rose petals, opened. She had already returned. She regarded him with her glistening black orbs, and placed a blissful hand lightly upon his shoulder. Her gentle touch rocked him to the core. Truly, only the blessed lived within her service.

She instructed him with honeyed words of wisdom. "There are five handlers wearing gray robes of the hearth, sitting at ease within their chamber next to the pits. They are drinking coffee and smoking cigarettes before they attempt the task of recovering three mothers from the maze. We shall take them all, silently and with dispatch." She tightened her grip slightly and commanded with resolute authority, "Go now, fulfill our destiny."

The need to obey flooded Whispering Death's soul. He turned and blurred along the stone walkways above the pits, veering this way and that toward the left wall of the massive chamber. He tapped his speed talent and rushed through the open archway into the handlers' midst. Five faces looked at him blankly, then began to register shock and surprise. His blades flashed, to wound and to disable, not to kill. The other helpers and his queen came in behind him and they all set to work: cutting, bleeding, silencing, while supping lightly to replace the divine blood they were giving to the Olgoi Khorkhoi handlers. In a handful of minutes, their numbers would double from five to ten.

The conquest of Matahat al Diydan had begun.

* * *

Tamsah al Ramil wheezed and rubbed crimson tears from his eyes with the back of his hand.

Sliver laced candles burned in sconces along the stairway and lit the guard platform before the main entrance of Matahat al Diydan. The stench of silver clawed at his nose. His lips had gone numb and he could no longer feel his fingers properly. His muscles were sluggish, his nerves dull, his senses washed out. All symptoms of slow silver poisoning. A good sharp dose of silver would lay a vampire out flat, paralyzed and helpless without any of these symptoms. Exposure to tiny amounts of silver created a number of distressing effects until a vampire weakened to the point of falling down. Without intervention, paralysis would set in. For the moment he could still move, and so he advanced up the final stone steps to the main entrance of Matahat al Diydan.

The three gate guards regarded him warily.

Tamsah lifted a weary hand and flicked his hood back.

Flashes of recognition flew across the guard's faces. The senior guard's eyes narrowed with doubt and a touch of suspicion. He lifted his right hand, palm forward in warning, and stated, "Tamsah al Ramil. You were declared dead two weeks ago."

The second guard looked askance. "Candles were lit in your honor, Sand Crocodile. We held sacred vigils for your everlasting soul."

Tamsah staggered and fell to one knee. He propped himself up with a hand on his thigh and lifted his face, heaving in a desperate breath.

The youngest guard took a hesitant step toward Tamsah and asked, "Is he wounded?"

"Or drunk?" asked the second guard, his face seized by a frown.

"No!" snapped the senior guard decisively. "The silver of Matahat is sickening him! He's a vampire!"

"This is true," Tamsah admitted with a tired wince, "but you must alarm. Matahat is under assault from a new breed of vampire led by Mekra herself."

"What nonsense is this?" uttered the second guard.

"Isn't he supposed to walk into the sunlight?" asked the youngest guard.

The senior guard shook his finger at Tamsah and accused, "Why aren't you dead by your own hand? Have you no honor?"

Tamsah swept the three guards with a tired gaze and declared, "There's no time for these questions. You have to alarm."

The senior guard puffed out his chest and slapped it with the palm of his hand. "We are the Red Empire. We don't take orders from vampires."

"May I have the honor of killing him?" asked the youngest guard. "He would be my first."

"If the Red Ghost so wills it, Keen-As-A-Knife. But first, he will be interrogated."

"Call the damn alarm." Tamsah shouted, then rolled to the side and fell onto his back with a groan of agony.

The guards regarded him silently for a moment.

"What if I 'accidentally,' killed him now?" asked Keen-As-A-Knife.

The other two guards smiled and slapped the young guard's shoulders, and the second guard remarked, "The unblooded warrior is ever eager for his first kill."

The senior guard tapped his headset and spoke into the microphone next to his mouth, "Command, we have a vampire captured at the main entrance. It is Tamsah al Ramil. What are your orders?" He paused for a quarter of a minute. "Yes, Sir." He took a couple of steps closer to Tamsah and peered into his face. "The Red Ghost is coming to deal with you personally. He will be here in five minutes."

Tamsah sighed. He could barely move, and speaking was almost more of an effort than he could make. "Five minutes," he whispered into the night. If Mekra and her vampires were like regular vampires, they could double their numbers in five minutes. How long would it take to get these obstinate bastards to listen? He pressed his lips together. He knew them all too well. It would take too long.

He'd failed to protect the truth speaker.

* * *

Anton leaned against the steel-banded hardwood of the cell door.

There was a foot square black-iron grill set at head height in the heavily-reinforced door. Chiara was on the other side, trapped within the cell on her father's orders. Anton glanced to his left and right along the wide corridor. The left dropped and curved away to the Olgoi Khorkhoi pits and the right ran a short distance to the guard station, the doorway back to the viewing platform and a second doorway into the main body of the citadel.

A grizzled one-armed veteran ran the dungeon aided by a young offsider who was little more than a child. Both wore gray robes: the elder with a red sash, the younger with a white one. Neither carried a weapon.

Anton rubbed his chin, hardly anyone carried a weapon within Matahat al Diydan. They obviously felt safe in their silver impregnated citadel.

He studied the dungeon's main chamber. The keys to the cells rested on a hook behind the guard station's wooden counter. The dungeon was nearly silent, and the other cells rested with their doors open. Chiara was the only prisoner. The Red Empire was clearly a law-abiding community with no offenders to speak of.

Anton had memorized the path from the maze to the dungeons. The two locations seemed to be on the same level of the citadel. He'd noted any salient features for future reference. The Red Empire was a strange mix of the ancient and the modern. Gas lights on the ceiling ran alongside fiber-optic cables, and faintly-humming-circular fans. The dungeon's small cramped cells looked carved from ancient stone but the doors were reminiscent of the twentieth century. A modern laptop computer sat open on an antique desk behind the counter along with an old rotary-dial phone handset. The door they'd entered the dungeons through was an up-to-date reinforced matte-steel barrier with an electronic swipe-key lock. Its twin stood within the wall opposite the station and clearly led into the main body of the citadel.

One thing Anton had learned deep in his soul over the last few months: have two escape paths. It was essential to understand the security features of any location the team was in. He asked Chiara quietly, "How come there are no cameras?"

There was a brief pause, and Chiara replied, "We are the Red Empire. Matahat al Diydan is the fortress inviolate. Vampires cannot enter here. The Order would not dare to come, and regular humans are ignorant of our existence and unable to pose a threat. We monitor and guard the boundaries of our domain but of the interior – we are not slaves, we do not need to be watched, our honor guards us all."

"Does anyone wear a camera, perhaps on a tactical communications rig?"

"There are no internal cameras. There are armed guards at the main entrance, and four fully-armed fist teams ready for instant deployment within the hangar. There are the CODEX guards, and my father's personal guard are armed. The members of the high council wear their weapons when the council sits. But there is no reason to worry. Our armor and weapons are always close at hand and we can mobilize the whole fortress in minutes."

An uneasy knot sat at the pit of Anton's stomach. Too much hellish shit had gone down in his life over the last few months and he didn't trust

Dalien Morte at all. Chiara's father had sent three worms against him instead of one. The Red Ghost had tried to kill him; and what's more, his grandfather hadn't intervened upon his behalf and remained hidden during the test. Once the test was over and Chiara had challenged her father, then Arthur had revealed his presence and warned Anton about refusing to fight Chiara to the death.

A warning he would've ignored. He'd rather die than kill Chiara. He looked down at the smooth stone floor of the corridor without really seeing it. With his obsession for vengeance cut down to size, something else had flowered within his heart. He was in love with Chiara. Li and Peter were still vital to him, and he still hungered to bring Crane and Armitage to justice for their crimes against his family and the world, but Chiara stood before them all.

He had to get her out of this cell before something worse than imprisonment happened.

Chiara's voice came quietly through the grill, "Why do you ask, Anton? Are you planning a jail break?"

Anton turned and looked through the grill. A single candle burned on a low stone bench behind her, throwing her face into shadow. His eyes tightened and he stated, "You shouldn't be in there."

"It is the Way, Anton. It must be allowed to take its course."

Anton opened his mouth to answer when something moved on the edge of his vision. He glanced to his left. The old dungeon keeper patted his young apprentice lightly on the head and remarked, "The pits are overly quiet. Go check them for me."

"Yes, grandfather," the boy replied, and trotted down the hall toward Anton.

Anton turned his back to the cell door and waited for the boy to reach him. He put his left hand up and asked, "What's the matter?"

The boy halted and turned his face up to Anton and said solemnly, "The pits are too quiet. The handlers sent mothers in against you." The boy paused for a moment, eying Anton with obvious wonder. "And you survived."

Anton inclined his head, then glanced to the left and the silent corridor leading down to the Olgoi Khorkhoi pits. "Is there something wrong?"

"There has been no song sung by the handlers. There has been no screech from the mothers," the boy said. He glanced back at the old man behind the counter and then looked at Anton. "I have to go."

Anton nodded and the boy jogged down the corridor and vanished to the left around the curve. He turned his head and asked over his shoulder, "You heard that? What do you make of it?"

"Probably nothing," Chiara replied, but there was an edge of concern in her voice.

Anton frowned and loosened the Blue Dragon in its scabbard across his back. He took a breath and pulled the Ramp into a hair-trigger presence within. People could believe what they want. He wasn't taking chances. He looked down the corridor to the left. What would the boy find? He pressed his lips into a thin line. Something was wrong. He could feel it. The boy was going to find trouble.

Lots of trouble.

* * *

Whispering Death snatched the boy up, his powerful hand wrapped around the boy's mouth to stop him shouting out.

He opened his mouth wide and bent the boy's head back – exposing his throat.

"Wait," his queen whispered sternly behind him.

Whispering Death whirled around. His queen, three former Red Empire helpers, and five former Olgoi Khorkhoi handlers stood before him. His queen's eyes flicked avidly over the boy's pale throat and back to Whispering Death. She'd recently fed but was tense with hunger. The five handlers were slavering, freshly turned and half-mad with blood lust, their gazes locked upon the boy. Perhaps his queen felt their needs within her own heart. Her nose twitched, her eyes widened and she ordered, "No. Keep him fresh for now."

She looked past him, and he glanced back over his shoulder along the empty corridor. The hall rose slowly in a curving arc to their right. The dungeons were close by, and beyond the dungeons the citadel lay oblivious to their presence. He asked quietly, "What is your will, my queen?"

His queen indicated the osprey I pilot with a casual wave of her right hand and whispered, "Pass the boy, and free your weapons."

Whispering Death handed the struggling boy to the pilot. A muffled whimper escaped from the lad as the pilot adjusted his grip around the boy's mouth. Mekra regarded the pilot for a moment and he staggered backward as if slapped with a sledgehammer.

She lifted her hand and addressed her devotees in barely audible tones. "There are three of them. We take the old man with us as he has the key to the citadel." She faced Whispering Death and commanded, "Kill the warrior, turn the prisoner, and follow us to the living quarters."

Whispering Death nodded. He drew his swords and rushed toward the dungeons, the rest of his queen's small force on his heels.

He prepared to tap his speed talent; it was time to fight.

* * *

"What—" Anton uttered.

There was no time to speak. A lithe warrior was upon him, his pair of blades flashing in deadly arcs high and low. Anton ramped hard, the Blue Dragon appeared in his hands, flicking left and right as he dodged backward. He retreated too slowly, the tip of the warrior's left blade slashing through the front of his right thigh, sending a ribbon of blood splashing across the stone wall.

The warrior was fast, extraordinarily so. He had a speed talent, long fangs and completely black eyes. What the hell was he? A new type of vampire? Anton went full defensive. Every move dedicated to staying alive against the onslaught of razor-sharp blades smashing in against him. A posse of new vampires rushed through the corridor toward the guard station and the old warrior manning it. They carried the boy with them, his fists striking the vampire carrying him without effect. The group of vampires swept past Anton and the warrior, ignoring the fight in front of Chiara's cell.

The old man shouted a startled oath behind him.

Anton drew on his need to protect Chiara. He rode his adamant desire to save her to the heights of the wild Ramp. His senses accelerated and everything slowed around him. He stepped forward, beating back the lithe warrior with a flurry of strokes – bright sparks flickering away from his opponent's blades.

The black-eyed warrior leaped backward, set his blades low to the left and right and said, "You're a Slayne. It matters not. You cannot stand against the might of our queen."

There was a grunt behind Anton, and the second doorway into the main body of the citadel opened with a crash of metal against stone. Anton stared at the warrior and grinned with grim intent. "Let's put that to the test."

The two men launched themselves at each other at the same moment. Anton drew the Blue Dragon down in a diagonal arc from right to left. The warrior raised his blades, the left to block the descending katana, the right driving forward toward Anton's chest.

Anton pivoted left, narrowing the target of his chest. The Blue Dragon smashed through the raised blade in a shower of sparks, slashing through the warrior's left arm just below the shoulder, cutting deep into the vampire's chest as Anton twisted away out of range of the attack on his left.

The warrior fell back to the wall. The left side of his chest a gaping wound gushing blood, his left arm lost to the floor. He slid down the wall leaving a gore-soaked slick against the gray stone. He came to rest on the stone floor in a spreading crimson pool. He looked up at Anton with glistening eyes the color of night, and remarked almost casually, "Ahhh… a dragon blade." His eyes lost focus and he receded into final stillness.

"Anton!" Chiara called from her cell.

He barely heard her; the wild Ramp was in full flower. He stared left and right looking for foes, searching for his next kill. The other vampires, the grizzled old warrior, and the boy had vanished through the open doorway.

Now louder, she called again, "Anton, Look at me."

He paused, snorted, and spat upon the cold stone of the floor. His eyes wide, he turned to Chiara's cell.

"Anton, come to me! Remember who you are!" she implored; her face pressed against the narrow bars.

He took a deep, heaving breath and let it out. He looked hard at the iron grate on her door. Chiara stood on the other side, a shivering potent presence. He had to get her free. Anton whirled to face the guard station and the corridors leading away from the dungeon back into the citadel. The second great polished metal door slammed shut – the barest hint of a dark hand behind it. Automatic locks clicked back into place.

They were alone in the dungeons. Anton rushed to the hook behind the guard station and lifted the keys. The laptop lay in fragments. The phone torn from the desk and crushed into plastic shards upon the floor. He blurred back to Chiara's cell and opened the door with the third key he tried. She rushed into his arms and he held her close and tight, smothering her neck with kisses. This was real, this was true, he crushed her against him and her arms reached around him and held him tight. For a moment, they were each other's world.

He stepped back and said, "Vampires."

"How?" Chiara asked.

"A new type. Hard to kill and immune to silver."

She glanced past his shoulders. "Both doors are locked."

"And communications are down. We can't go that way or call for help."

She glanced back down the corridor. "Then, we go to the pits, and out the secret entrance. We skirt the mountain and come back through the main entrance. We can warn the Red Empire before these vampires gain a foothold."

"Done," Anton agreed. It was as good a plan as any he could have thought of on the spur of the moment.

Chiara glanced down at his bloody thigh, her eyes widened, and she said, "Anton! You're bleeding!" She knelt down before him and spread the cut cloth apart. "Nasty. Quickly, tear off your shirtsleeves."

Anton tore his sleeves off one after the other and handed them to Chiara.

She quickly tied them into a makeshift tourniquet over the wound. "That's the best we can do for now. She rose and blurred to the guard station. She rummaged beneath the counter and emerged with a pair of two-foot blades in hand. She twirled them a couple of times and thrust them out hard. "These will do if we meet any more vampires."

Anton lifted an eyebrow and grinned. "Sorted then."

They looked down the corridor together and blurred away into the gloom.

It was time to warn the Red Empire.

If they could.

* * *

Tamsah al Ramil lay propped against the mountain side twenty feet short of the main entrance.

Silver was seeping slowly through every pore of his skin. He could barely move, breathe or talk. If he struggled mightily, he could make the edge of the platform and topple off over the side. He might survive the fall or not, but it was his only chance to escape the pervasive silver present at the entrance into Matahat al Diydan.

Dalien Morte and his four personal guards emerged from the doorway and strode toward him. Morte came to a stop at his feet, glowered at him and accused, "Why are you here? Why have you not ended your shame?"

Tamsah drew in a breath and said slowly, "I have ... a greater ... purpose."

"Purpose! What purpose could a vampire have?"

Tamsah shook his head once. "Not important now ... you ... under attack."

Morte's eyes narrowed to a hard stare and he snapped, "What the hell do you mean?"

"Mekra—"

"Mekra! What is it with this rumor of her return?"

"She ... is ... here."

"Here! How could she be here?"

"Changed ... immune ... silver ... secret entrance ... must alarm."

Morte paused; his face seized by a question. He whispered, more to himself than anyone else, "Crane's Romanian ruse." A dreadful realization flashed across his face. He tapped his earbud. "Khufu, what's the status on the secret entrance to the pits?" He waited, staring down at Tamsah. His eyes widened and his face paled. "Time locked! And the team sent to investigate the osprey that landed short of Matahat? ... Abandoned! Get them back to the hangar and send two teams down to the pits and report back immediately. Move the citadel to yellow alert. Wake everyone up."

Tamsah closed his eyes for a moment, summoning his final strength. He stared hard at his former master's face, lifted his trembling right hand, pointed his forefinger at Morte and said in deliberate tones, "You ... sold us ... out!"

Morte sneered, his eyes filling with hatred. His guards and the gate guards glanced at each other, seemingly perplexed by Tamsah's allegation.

"To ... the ... vamp—"

Morte's gleaming katana flashed beneath the gas lights and silver candles, slashing through Tamsah's neck. His head rolled forward off his shoulders and down his chest, coming to rest on the cold stone next to his hips. His vampire vitality ebbed away as blood splashed in freshets around him.

Above his feet, Morte uttered, "No one can trust a vampire."

A single word filled his world with a final shining light. He rose into—

Honor.

* * *

Mekra's followers had knocked the old man and the boy unconscious.

Silence and speed were of the essence. The corridor out of the dungeons had led to a rising stairwell that repeatedly zigged and zagged upward. They had blurred up the flights of stairs, carrying their burdens until they reached the first landing. A wide corridor led off it, past a great pair of open fire doors and onto another stairwell leading up into the citadel. She blurred to the fire doors. They led through to the sacred hearth of the Red Empire. Here were all the off-duty members of the Red Empire citadel, their wives and children – most were already asleep in the early to bed and early to rise discipline of the Way of the Faithful.

The living quarters were Mekra's primary target. She'd scouted Matahat al Diydan earlier in the day while hiding within the dark spaces of Raukhivka airport in Ukraine. It had been a simple thing to roam the corridors and chambers of the Red Empire citadel. The directions of her astral investigations rested upon the memories of Whispering Death, absorbed from his mind in the moments of his conversion, and then put to valuable use. When she'd finished with the people here, most would belong to her, and the rest would be dead to slake the thirst of the newly turned vampires.

She bent her will tightly upon her devotees and they blurred silently through the complex of corridors, rooms and suites, striking everyone they found to render them unconscious. Men, women and children, all would fall to the sublime majesty of her rule.

Mekra remained behind and closed the great fire doors. She spun the locking wheel home, and a dozen steel bolts rammed deep into the bedrock. She punched a code lifted from Whispering Death's memories into a keypad on the door and a '10:00,' minute counter flashed up on a display above the keypad. It immediately dropped to 09:59, then 09:58 ... ten minutes would allow two cycles of conversion. By knocking people unconscious first, they could convert in batches, rather than one at a time. There were more than three hundred beating hearts within the hearth and within the next ten minutes she would claim most of them.

"Time locks," she murmured to herself. Another invention of the modern world she could turn against those who would oppose her.

She would not miss Whispering Death. In a very real sense, his memories lived on within her expanding mind. While his body would soon be dust, his essence remained alive within her memory, an immortality she offered to all the offspring of her blood.

She was one; she was many.

Mekra left the locked doors behind her and ran forward into the hotel complex of the Red Empire citadel. Already screams were erupting and in one location blades crashed trenchantly into the flesh of her extended body. From another place near the back of the complex of rooms an alarm erupted in strident ululation. The Red Empire were fighting back. Her devotees would need her help if they were to get as many as they could.

It was time for the Red Empire to belong to her divine self. She blurred along the corridors, an ever-growing set of eyes feeding her vision of the world. She lived her minion's experiences: the biting, the cutting, the bleeding, the killing, and the dying. Her presence swelled within the interconnected chambers as more and more souls fell to the power of her blood. Mekra reeled; steadying herself with a hand against the nearest wall. The ecstasy of blood conversion of so many momentarily overwhelming her senses.

Sometimes it was too much to be a goddess.

* * *

A pair of great doors loomed before Anton and Chiara.

"These are normally open for airflow," Chiara said, as she examined the keypad on the left wall next to the heavily-reinforced doors leading to the secret exit.

"Can they be opened?" Anton asked.

"No," Chiara said, shaking her head. "They've been time-locked for an hour and still have fifty-one minutes to run. We can't escape that way."

"Don't tell me, the only way back into the citadel is through the maze?"

"It's the only way."

Anton shook his head and said, "I told you not to tell me that."

Chiara raised an eyebrow. "We can equip ourselves with handler's prods. They have trained the worms to avoid them. It will greatly cut the risk of being hunted by them."

"Let's do it."

Chiara led Anton back to an equipment room next to the entrance to the pits. She pulled two nine-foot poles from a rack on the wall and gave one to Anton. Anton quickly examined his pole. There was a black switch a quarter of the way above the base. Anton flicked the switch on and a bright-blue electric spark erupted between two silvery prongs at the top of the pole. He looked at Chiara and remarked dryly, "Kinda like an oversized cattle prod," and flicked the switch off.

"Worm prods, my love, the worms detest electricity. But mothers are," and she shook her head, "unpredictable." She stooped and examined the quick tourniquet she'd applied to his right thigh. It was holding up for now, but soaked with blood. He needed sutures and perhaps surgery, but there'd been no time to stop for proper treatment. She asked, "Can you keep running?"

"I think so. The blade scored a deep slash, but mostly muscle, no arteries or tendons ... I think."

Chiara pressed her lips into a thin line. "There's nothing more to be done."

"What's the problem?"

"You know how sharks go into a feeding frenzy when there's blood in the water."

"Yes."

"Worms are the same."

Anton blinked. "So be it. Let's do it fast." He remembered his test. One of the entrances to the central arena led back to the pits. They could cut straight into the middle of the maze in a relatively short distance from the pits. Perhaps there would be no worms. "By the way," he said, "this time we're armed. Are we breaking any 'sudden death,' laws if we kill one?"

Chiara nodded. "No one is going to have a problem if we kill a worm tonight. Not with vampires taking over Matahat."

Anton moved past Chiara. A single corridor led from the pits toward the maze. Someone with a dark sense of humor had carved, 'Abandon all hope ye who enter here,' into the rock over the entrance. They glanced at each other, flicked on their handler's worm prods, and blurred forward.

Their best hope lay in speed.

* * *

Khufu's voice resounded through Dalien Morte's earbud, "Vampires are attacking the hearth. The doors are locked."

Dalien pulled to a sudden halt. His four guards fanning out around him, scanning the killing halls running back from the main entrance for threats. There were none, at least not yet. His gaze washed over the 7.62mm miniguns armed with silver and hollow-point rounds facing past him toward

223

the main entrance. Those sentry weapons were useless against a threat rising from the pits. He tapped his earbud and said, "Report in full! What is happening?"

"I sent two fist teams down from the hangar. They are at the entrance to the hearth. Someone has closed and locked the doors from the inside. I have voice reports of multiple vampires within the hearth. I have raised the alert level to red."

Dalien nodded. "Arm all warriors."

"Already happening."

Khufu was a good man, able and effective. Dalien looked to his left, he was opposite the main stairwell up to the hangar and down to the hearth. He closed his eyes for a brief moment, a cold chill seizing his heart. The hearth was an ancient complex of rooms, mess halls, and living quarters, where half his fighters were currently resting, along with all the wives and children of the Red Empire – over three hundred souls in total. Whoever had locked the door did not consider more than seventy fighters a threat.

A chill wind blew through his soul. Not a threat but an opportunity for the attackers now they had eliminated both escape and interference. He signaled his squad with a wave of his hand and made for the stairwell. As he descended toward the hearth he ordered, "Khufu, send an explosives team down from the hangar with two dozen shaped charges. We need to take the fire doors down immediately. I'm going there now. Send all available forces to reinforce my position as soon as they mobilize."

"Your will, Shabbah al Ahmar."

Dalien stared into the gloom of the stairwell. The time for talk was over. He blurred back and forth down the steps, his personal guards at his heels. He reached the next landing in seconds, and spilled out into a wide corridor that ran past the entrance to the hearth before reaching a second stairwell down to the dungeons and the pits.

Nine fully armed fighters stood helplessly before the locked doors of the hearth. They looked to him as one. He strode up to his men, picked one man out, and commanded, "Sacred Blade, go to the dungeons and report back what you find." The indicated fighter, turned and blurred away. Chiara was still down there. Whatever occupied the hearth had entered through the secret entrance on the far side of the Olgoi Khorkhoi pits. His daughter's fate was unknown. She could be alive, dead or turned into one of the damned. He tapped his earbud and demanded, "Khufu! Status on the explosives team."

"En route, Shabbah al Ahmar. They will arrive within a minute."

Dalien pressed his lips into a thin line and studied the great fire doors. The gods only knew what was happening in there. A sick ball of dread congealed in the pit of his stomach. His people would never shut and lock this door. No, someone else must have done so; and no one within was in a position to reopen the doors or it would have happened. Were they trapped, helpless, or already dead?

Or even worse? Dalien left the final dreadful question unanswered.

Another voice came through his earbud, "Red Ghost, the dungeons are empty, but Whispering Death's corpse is here. Dead from a great sword blow and he was a vampire. A vampire of a new sort."

"Good work, Sacred Blade. Return immediately."

Dalien frowned, and put the pieces of the puzzle together. Whispering Death had led the new vampires into the heart of Matahat al Diydan. As a trusted officer, he'd easily made his way past more than a dozen wards, traps and locks guarding the secret entrance. His betrayal of all honor would live in infamy forever. As for Chiara and the younger Slayne, they were missing and presumably still alive, or captured and turned by the vampiric forces occupying the hearth. He ground his teeth. If his daughter and the young Slayne had fallen to the vampires, there was nothing more he could do. Chiara would share her mother's fate. If still alive and beneath them in the pits, then the only escape was back through the maze and the mothers were still hunting. His daughter trod a path fraught with much danger, but no more or less than standing before the locked fire doors of the hearth of the Red Empire with an unknown number of vampires rampaging upon the other side.

He uttered in helpless frustration, "Where the hell are the explosives team?"

No one answered. Grim faces met his gaze in every direction. He took a long breath and loosened his katana in its scabbard. Matahat al Diydan was descending into hell. Could he save the Red Empire's ancient home from these new vampires? He lifted his chin and stared hard at the doors, as if the sheer power of his will could penetrate stone, hardwood and steel. There were so many things he'd striven for in life. Such ambitions as would challenge the gods, but now he stood with a fraction of his warriors and found himself wishing to only see his beloved Tania again, and to have Chiara at his side with a smile upon her face.

"Come men," he called to his fighters. "Stir your blood for battle, for battle is upon us." He drew his sword and lifted the blade high. "For the Red Empire!"

The men raised their weapons and chorused as one, "For the Red Empire!"

Steps resounded upon the stairwell. The explosives team and the first of the reinforcements were arriving. The enemy had entered the hearth of the Red Empire and he would see them expunged from the Red Empire's most holy space.

Even if it was the last thing, he ever did.

* * *

Mekra's swarm multiplied within the hearth.

The newly converted rose, blurred and struck the survivors of the first wave. A pair of doors crashed open, leading deeper into the recesses of the complex of halls and chambers. Her swarm followed into the new spaces. She went with them, soon she would be everywhere.

Sirens blared. Men shouted desperate orders. Blades smashed against each other in trenchant combat, but only a few would find final death. Mekra's thralls pounced upon the wounded, dragging them away and restoring them to her blood. Mekra strode the halls, her hunger swelling with the new souls flooding her mind. She could not keep their rampant bloodlust walled off entirely, some of it inevitable seeped through and became her own.

Rulership was ever thus: a symbiosis of the ruler with the ruled.

Two of her new minions tore a wooden door to splinters and surged into the chamber beyond. Mekra peered into the room, her gaze drawn by the throbbing beat of a child's heart. She drew closer to the open doorway. A young woman clutched her offspring close to her chest, and backed away from her two thralls.

The mother and child were so fresh, so tempting.

She had to have them.

* * *

The alarm ululated throughout the hearth.

The young mother clutched her two-year-old son to her chest and backed into a corner of her bedroom. Two vampires stalked her, advancing on her left and right. Minutes before, they had been members of the Red Empire, trusted friends and colleagues of long standing. She'd known them most of her young life. Now they were damned creatures of darkness, watching her every move with avid eyes and slavering mouths.

A slim, voluptuous creature glided through the open door. Her flawless skin hid the nightmare within. The other two vampires shrank away in obeisance, and she announced in soft, clear tones of fateful inevitability, "These two are mine."

Their gazes locked, wide brown eyes against orbs of midnight darkness.

She quailed within, a shrill scream tore through her mind, but long hard discipline clamped her mouth shut. She drew a razor-sharp dagger from a sheath at her side. Along with all full members of the Red Empire, she had trained in the Ramp. Once the yellow alert sounded, she'd armed herself.

Two more vampires appeared behind their hell-born queen, their teeth champing and grinding, leering at her with naked blood lust.

She blinked; was there anywhere she could take her son to safety? Five pairs of staring black orbs reflected the dreadful truth of her position.

She summoned the Ramp, her eyes wide, her heart shattering in pieces. She swallowed a sob and shouted, "We'll never belong to you." In a sudden movement, she shoved her blade into the base of her son's skull, robbing him of his life in an instant.

The vampires blurred forward. Pale hands reaching for her, fingers outstretched to catch and grip in bonds like iron.

Her knife flashed for a second time, driving up and in until the hilt slammed hard against the top of her throat.

All horror vanished with her life.

* * *

Anton and Chiara burst into the arena at the center of the maze.

Chiara led Anton by a dozen steps. His right thigh had taken more damage than he'd been willing to admit. He could still run, but his top speed was slower than his normal Ramp. At least there were no worms in sight and the sand of the arena was too shallow for a worm to hide in. Chiara reached the middle of the arena, the stairs to the viewing platform were another one hundred and fifty feet past her.

Anton swiveled his head left and right. He waved his worm prod back and forth in front of him, blue sparks sizzling between the prongs. Movement to the right caught his eye. A mother worm blurred into the arena from one of the middle cave mouths on an intercept course with him. Chiara reached the stairs, leaped up to the first landing and pivoted to face back into the arena. Her face paled and she called out, "Anton!" She lifted her worm prod above her head and blurred back down the stairs.

He lifted his pace to the limits of his injured thigh, but the worm beat him to the bottom of the stairs. It turned and reared its head, shrieking a dreadful challenge over the arena. No doubt the other two worms were coming. They were about to catch him again.

Chiara raised her worm prod, its tip sparking furiously, and drove it forward into the rear of the worm.

The mother worm uttered a screech that resounded off the walls of the arena and lashed its barbed tail, fending off Chiara's strikes. Anton raised his worm prod, bright blue sparks leaping between the prongs. He thrust the tip at the mother worm's head. It lunged forward, its maw closing around the end of the prod. A pale light flickered within its purple cowl. There was a dreadful crunch. It reared back leaving Anton holding the lower seven feet of the worm prod. It turned aside and spat. The top of the prod flew onto the sand covered in a phlegmy goo. The mother turned back toward him and reared up, its cowl flared wide, a vivid purple ring around its gaping maw and row after row of razor-sharp black dagger teeth. It screeched again, a piercing howl of rage and hunger.

Anton dropped the beheaded worm prod and drew the Blue Dragon clear. He shouted, "Fuck it."

Chiara shouted, "Move! Move!" and drove her worm prod into the rear of the worm again and again.

The enraged mother worm struck forward, her maw a purple ringed blur.

Anton dove deep into the wild Ramp and blurred to his right. He pivoted left and brought the Blue Dragon down in a great slashing strike. The gleaming blade sliced into the worm coming to a halt against cross-matted cartilaginous plates. The worm reared back, dragging itself off Anton's blade. He rushed in, striking again and again, while crying out, "I," the worm's skin split wider, "haven't," clear gobs of ichor splashed, "any," cartilaginous plates split apart, "fucking," foul-smelling brown ichor spurted in ropy streams, "time left!"

The worm split in two. The head segment dropped to his left and lay still upon the sands, surrounded by gooey brown ichor the consistency of diarrhea. The rest of the body lurched and shuddered spraying more brown ichor over the sands in half a dozen ropy streams. Anton staggered past it, gritting his teeth against the pain in his right thigh and wrinkling his nose at the stench of the worm's liquid guts.

Chiara beckoned him forward with a wave of her hand. "Come on, Anton, we must hurry."

Anton heaved a breath. The other two mother worms blurred into the arena. A sudden reckless impulse to turn and continue the killing seized him with trenchant fingers. He stopped for a moment, torn between safety and death.

"Anton!" Chiara called desperately from the viewing platform.

He blinked, turned and ran half-limping up the stairs. The need to kill ebbing like an outgoing tide. Perhaps he was beginning to master the wild Ramp. His thigh thudded like a beating drum and he absently brushed it with his right hand. His hand came away smeared with fresh blood.

Anton reached the viewing platform and Chiara said, "Anton, your thigh is bleeding again. We have to get to the command center. They have medical kits there." She moved in close, supporting him on his right side. "We have to keep your weight off it for now. ... Are you ready?"

"Yes," Anton said, noticing the blood dripping like a faulty faucet from his right boot onto the cold stone floor.

"Good. The command center is only a short distance past the high council chambers." Chiara noted. "We'll just have to climb up three-hundred feet of stairs first."

"Bonus!" Anton said with a lopsided grin, and they blurred up the stairwell together.

Perhaps they could make it after all.

* * *

Twenty-four shaped charges clung to the hinges, locks and wall-bolts of the great doors to the sacred hearth of the Red Empire.

"Fire," Dalien shouted from the end of the wide corridor and cupped his hands over his ears.

The commander of the explosives team pressed a stud on a hand-held device. White light flashed, thunder roared, debris smashed against the walls, and gray smoke bloomed into the center of the hallway. The two great doors shuddered and fell inward, a thunderous pair of booms echoing through the citadel.

"All teams advance," Dalien shouted, striding before his men into the clouds of billowing smoke. Six fist teams went with him, aided by the four second-rank warriors of his elite personal guard. Thirty-five skilled Ramp masters, fully armed, armored, and wearing the red cloak of war strode to battle.

He reached the threshold of the hearth. The fire doors lay flat upon the floor, fragments of stone and metal adhered to the walls like unwanted memory. Wild screams and tortured yells rang from the interior halls and chambers of the sacred hearth. Piercing the settling smoke as easily as they pierced his heart.

The triumph of the past day burned to bitter ashes within his soul.

Dalien peered through the smoke and debris, and stared into the bowels of hell. A wave of armed vampires, all former fighters, stormed down the first hall toward his force. He strode forward, his face stiff, his katana held high above his head. His men came with him, razor-sharp weapons glowing with a pale nimbus beneath the gas lights.

He charged the vampire ranks while shouting to his men, "For the Red Empire!"

"The Red Empire!" they shouted back with grim determination at his side.

Battle erupted twenty feet within the entrance hall of the sacred hearth of Matahat al Diydan. Dalien ramped hard, drawing on decades of practice and war. His blade fell through a deadly arc, carving through the upper torso of the vampire facing him, blood splashing in a sheet following his katana. The man on his right side took a blade in the face and staggered away. One of Dalien's personal guards instantly replaced him. There was no time to think. It was a crushing melee of Ramp masters versus vampires in a hall twenty feet across and a hundred more long.

Only the best would survive.

* * *

Anton limped into the command center, leaning on Chiara's shoulder.

Chiara pulled over an office chair and Anton sat down in it. She rushed away to the other side of the room. He looked around the command center. A dozen or so staff sat at command consoles and another dozen fighters stood fitting armor and checking sub-machine guns near the chamber's main doors. His grandfather strode over to him, clapped him on the left shoulder, and stated the obvious with cheerful relief, "You made it."

"What's happening?" Anton glanced around the room. The main screens all showed the outer world. There was no view of what was occurring within the citadel. The Red Empire had no capacity to look within. "There's new vampires everywhere."

"We know, Mekra is here. She escaped her prison in Romania yesterday."

"Mekra? The real Mekra?"

Peter and Li, both armed with their usual weapons strode up and stood to Arthur's right facing Anton.

"Yes, it's her." Li nodded once.

Anton lifted his hand to forestall further comment and addressed Arthur. "You know what we all need to do?"

Arthur nodded once; his eyes fixed on Anton's face.

"Then how can I help?"

Arthur glanced to his left, where Chiara rushed over, holding an open medical kit before her, and said, "Right now? By holding still."

"No time for anesthetic," Peter said, stepping behind him and slapping his heavy hands on Anton's shoulders to help him hold still.

Chiara was already cutting his trouser away, revealing a deep gash in the front of his right thigh. Blood oozed from the wound trickling to both sides of his thigh before splatting on the polished-stone floor. She didn't wait for permission, her hands blurring with a needle and thick, heavy black thread.

Li said, "The sutures are the latest tech. They'll hold under Ramp conditions. That's why the Red Empire use them. We should have had this back in the Order too."

Anton winced, riding above the pain. He looked back at Arthur. He trusted him. He always seemed to have the answers, and he had their backs. He asked, "Now what?"

Arthur frowned and looked around the room. Anton followed his gaze, breathing in the atmosphere. The place was on the verge of panic, forestalled only by grim determination and ingrained discipline. The twelve fighters were marshaling at the door. There was a bald fellow giving orders and staff rushed to obey. His grandfather leaned forward and said quietly, "Be ready to run. This place is done."

"Where will we run to?"

"The hangar."

The twelve soldiers blurred away, to some battle or another. Anton had no idea what was really going on.

Anton, Li, and Peter, looked at Arthur with wide eyes. Chiara pressed her lips together and slapped a healing balm impregnated gauze over the sutured wound and began strapping it with a sticking bandage. Her eyes narrowed and she declared, "Matahat will never fall." But there was a cold shard of doubt in her voice.

Anton looked around his friends. Could they escape the fall of the Red Empire or would they all die?

Or worse, would they become vampires?

* * *

Dalien's thrust into the hearth had reached its limit.

They were too few to take the sacred living chambers from the vampires. They'd fallen back to the hearth's entrance, leaving a trail of dead and wounded. To his horror, vampires fell upon the men who were too wounded to escape and instead of killing them, they poured their own blood into his men's gaping wounds. Moments later, the poor wights added their agonized screams to the cacophony within the hall.

Dalien dispatched another vampire, a man recruited the previous year, and pulled back from the front line. His personal bodyguards filled the vacated space, their weapons flashing and grinding against the blades of their former comrades. He tapped his earbud and snapped, "Khufu, send every last man who can carry a blade to my position, and evacuate the rest."

"Your—"

"And initiate the immolation protocol. Burn the drives. Go to the hangar and save what's left of the Red Empire."

"Your will, Shabbah al Ahmar."

The clash of battle fell to silence. Dalien strode to the front of his men. The vampires had fallen back, dragging the screaming wounded with them. The fallen but not yet dead clutched at the air and writhed in torment as they vanished behind the wall of vampires. The mass of vampires stilled, then parted like the Red Sea for Moses. A vision of dark beauty walked calmly between them and into the gas light.

It was Mekra, in the flesh, wearing nothing but a wisp of gray silk wrapped around her nubile hips. She walked carefully on bare feet between the fallen and halted half-a-dozen feet in front of her ranks. She smiled at Dalien, her long fangs gleaming ivory against her dark skin. She regarded him with eyes of solid, shining darkness and said, "There is no need for further slaughter. The time of the Ramp masters has come to a close. A new regime has arrived. Join us in immortality and rule as my champion."

Dalien paused, staring hard past the vampires into the depths of the halls and chambers beyond. Nothing stirred, nor was there a whisper of sound. Not a single soul survived within the hearth. There were only vampires before him.

Dalien's eyes tightened with absolute determination. He lifted his gore-soaked blade and shouted, "HONOR!"

He rushed the vampire bitch, his surviving men blurring beside him. He would not dishonor his oaths.

Not anymore.

Chapter Ten

"Those who are fearful will find courage.
Those who are fearless will not know courage.
Those who are doubtful will find faith.
Those who are certain will not know faith.
Those who are shameful will find honor.
Those who are shameless will not know honor."

– On Courage, Faith, and Honor – The Way of the Faithful, a book of Red Empire lore.

* * *

Republic of Dagestan, Matahat al Diydan, The Command Center, September 14th, 22:21

Red lights strobed; alarms wailed.

The immolation protocol for Matahat al Diydan had begun. Arthur Slayne waved Anton and his friends toward the doors leading to the killing halls. He reached the doors first and threw them open. Khufu marshaled the rest of the command center staff, sending them upon Anton, Li, Peter, and Chiara's heels and following after as the last to leave. Racks of computers and networking equipment sparked and sputtered against the stone walls. Blue flames flickered and gray smoke plumed upward. The immolation protocol only affected the command center, after all – Matahat al Diydan was the fortress inviolate.

Arthur led them all into the killing halls; the defensive zone between the command center, the main entrance and the high and low stairwells that provided access to the hangar above and the hearth, dungeons and pits below.

Arthur raced through the killing halls. Turning left and right to follow the shortest path to the stairwells. He bypassed traps, weapon emplacements, and gossamer shields, all designed to foil any frontal assault through the main entrance. He frowned at the silent sentry weapons. Wicked multi-barrels facing down corridor kill zones, drums of high-velocity ammunition mounted upon them. The citadel was falling and they hadn't fired a shot. He shook his head as he passed them, a useless Maginot line facing the wrong way. He burst into an open area facing onto the landing for the main stairwell of the citadel. The clang of weapons, and shouts of fury and agony, warred with each other in the depths of Matahat. A chaotic symphony rising up the stairs.

Anton gripped his shoulder with a strong hand. Arthur turned to face his grandson. Anton declared, his eyes blazing, "We must help them."

"No." Arthur shook his head. "We can't make a difference down there."

Chiara pressed forward. "What of the families?"

"It's too late. They've been turned."

Chiara's eyes widened and her face paled.

The command center staff pulled to a halt behind their small group. None made an attempt to go below. Khufu bustled through them and asked, "What are you waiting for? The Red Ghost's orders were explicit. We must evacuate and save who we can. There are many fighters beyond these walls. Half the Red Empire's people are still alive out in the world."

Arthur sighed and pressed his lips together. The fall of Matahat had come to pass. A shiver rippled up his back; where would Mekra turn her attention to next? He addressed Khufu and said, "One moment, please." He gripped Anton's shoulder, stared into his grandson's eyes for a moment and then flicked his gaze around Peter, Li and Chiara. "We have no time. Don't waste the sacrifice of the men below." He put an edge of command into his voice. "We all leave now."

Khufu glanced down the stairwell, and then locked gazes with Arthur. "My family?"

Arthur shook his head.

Khufu closed his eyes for a moment, his face frozen with grief.

Arthur clapped a strong hand on his shoulder and squeezed. He faced the group and called out, "Everyone, follow me."

Anton pressed his lips together as if preparing to object, but he obeyed. They ran to the stairwell and rose as one toward the hanger.

It was time to escape hell.

* * *

Dalien crashed his katana with all his strength against two upraised blades, sweeping them aside to the left.

He pivoted in a blur, his return stroke sweeping through a horizontal arc to the right, cutting his foe in half. The vampire fell away, joining the gory tumult writhing upon the stone floor.

A figure rushed into the vacated space in front of him. Dalien was at peak Ramp, and yet her movements blurred. Mekra appeared before him. Up close, her left hand shot out and grabbed his right wrist in an iron grip.

He let go of the handle of his sword with his left hand, and swept his fist forward. Aiming the knife-edge of his gauntlet at Mekra's face.

She leaned back. His strike passed in front of her face. Her right hand flashed up, grasped his left wrist and pushed it further to the left. She pushed forward with her body, spread-eagling his arms to the left and right.

Dalien ducked his chin, minimizing the exposure of his throat. Fighting with every trick he knew to remain – human.

Mekra thrust herself upon him with a leap, her thighs wrapping around his hips in an unbreakable hold. Her hands flashed forward from Dalien's wrists to his head. She tilted her head to the right and pushed his head back, exposing his throat. She lunged forward, bright fangs tearing into flesh, muscle, and his carotid artery. No blood splashed. She fitted her mouth perfectly over the gaping wound, blood rushing out of his body and down her throat.

Dalien staggered backward, then fell to his knees. Around him, the swarm overwhelmed his personal guards. He pushed back against Mekra but to no avail. The vampire queen found purchase upon the stone floor, pressing him inexorably backward. His legs slid around beneath him and he fell flat upon his back.

The pressure lessened. A dulcet voice spoke above him, "This one will be first born."

His vision cleared. Mekra kneeled astride his chest, her knees upon his arms. She flashed her hand past her face, tearing her wrist open with her fangs. A moment later, she pressed her punctured wrist against the wound in his throat. He tried to move, but other vampires had arrived, holding his wrists and ankles still with iron grips. Her blood rushed into his veins. A brutal fire tearing away his mortality.

"Tania, Chiara," he whispered once.

Mekra's blood claimed him a moment later.

* * *

Dalien Morte writhed at her feet.

Mekra regarded him with keen interest. The torment of his rebirth would be over in moments, but his memories were already flooding her mind with new knowledge. She riffled through the content of Morte's soul; his daughter held recent prominence. She was the last thing he'd thought of as he'd fallen beneath her fangs. A last desperate wish for her safety. Chiara Morte had managed to avoid joining her growing divine soul. She remained trapped within her mortality, and on the run with the youngest member of the Slaynes.

The Mortes and the Slaynes, two noble family lines that had been present in Hakron's efforts against her from the very beginning, and now they were here at the end. She stepped over Morte's trembling body and proceeded into the corridor. The sounds of battle had stilled, replaced with wails of terror and screams of agony as every human within reach came to her rule.

Mekra swayed. So many, so quickly, her mind thrilled and grew with each new vampire, but each new convert brought with them a drunken blood lust that threatened to unmoor her mind, and send it fluttering away like a leaf on the wind. She growled and asserted her will, flooding all of her swarm with a single thought, *Find your loved ones.*

Sleek forms blurred past her, leaving the chambers behind her a silent tomb for the dead and drained. The newly birthed rose from the polished stone and sped away – Dalien Morte within their number. In moments, Mekra stood alone, but she was never alone, she was many. More than two hundred and thirty pairs of eyes searched the citadel for the remaining fresh humans. Her swarm flooded through the tunnels and chambers beneath the mountain. A multitude of searching tentacles extending her reach, finding fresh humans and bringing them to her expanding soul. The remains of the Red Empire within Matahat al Diydan would soon come to her eternal life. The Red Empire's final hesitation before their wives and children would be her strength.

For no one could stand before those they loved.

* * *

"My love, embrace me."

The sultry words came from behind Keen-As-A-Knife. He whirled around to face the main entrance; his weapons raised in tight fists. Only the senior guard, Lion Heart, remained with him. Scorpion Tail, had left minutes ago upon the summons of Khufu to fight the growing swarm.

Lion Heart stood closer to the entrance; his blades shook within his hands. His wife, her lustrous blonde hair hanging free down to the small of her back, emerged from the main corridor.

"Kendra?" Lion Heart whispered hoarsely, his back rigid, his feet rooted upon the cold stone.

She lifted her gaze, her eyes wholly black orbs gleaming in the gas light, long slim fangs hanging past her sensual bottom lip. She took another step forward, her hips swaying invitingly. She raised her hands slowly up her torso, arching her back as they curved over her generous breasts. She pouted, and smiled. "Do you still desire this body?"

"Not this," her husband whispered in barely audible tones. His hands faltered, his twin swords dropping lower.

"Daddy! Daddy!" piped childish voices, a pair of children ghosting into view beside their mother.

Keen-As-A-Knife's mouth dropped open and he took a pair of involuntary steps backward. The trembling tips of his blades swapping from Kendra to the pale faces of her two young children.

The children blurred forward, passing Lion Heart's frozen blades and embracing his thighs. He fell backwards, dropping down to the polished stone, his blades falling to clatter and skid across the stone platform. The children arched backward, teeth champing. They lunged down as one, their mouths agape.

Kendra advanced, a dagger in her right hand, her eyes locked on her husband's face. She slashed the dagger across her left wrist and dark blood splashed upon the stone. She uttered in tones of dreadful inevitability, "You will join us now."

Lion Heart cried out. A single scream of utter despair echoed across the surrounding valley.

The children raised their heads, the smaller of the two twisted her five-year-old face around to leer at Keen-As-A-Knife. They hissed like serpents through blood drenched mouths, then fell to their gluttonous feasting.

It couldn't be, but it was. Keen-As-A-Knife turned and ran down the stairs. His heart filled with horror; hot bitter tears of shame and defeat rolling down his face.

The Red Empire had fallen.

* * *

A siren ululated throughout the hangar like a lost demon.

Arthur Slayne emerged out of the rising stairwell and onto the hangar floor. He scanned the barely organized chaos across the enormous chamber. Flashing red lights contrasted with the electric lamps overhead, casting crimson shadows over half a dozen petrels lined up against the far wall. The aircraft were an ultra-modern Russian knockoff of the osprey II and just as capable. He'd armed these craft with quad mounts of his stinger III anti-air hypersonic missile prototypes. Weapons effective against shadowstars – if they got close enough.

On the near side of the hangar, rows of raider II scout helicopters rested on trolleys. There were at least twenty in the hangar, and another one hovered like an angry wasp a hundred feet past the massive rectangular entrance stretching across the left wall of the immense chamber. Men ran to and fro. A pair of EV weapons trucks trundling from craft to craft at the rear of the raider lines. All the aircraft were ready to fly – but who would fly them? It wouldn't do to leave any for Mekra to claim.

Peter, Li, Anton and Chiara stepped up beside him. Behind them, Khufu came at the head of the command center staff. They were all Ramp masters; they could fight, but they weren't specialized fighters. There were damn few of those left. All the ready forces in the hangar had been committed. The remainder were technical and support specialists; essential to the operation of Matahat al Diydan and the Red Empire, but, and Arthur pressed his lips together and raised an eyebrow, most likely looking for a new job if they survived the night.

He glanced to his left, and addressed Anton and his friends. "Take a raider from the front of the line and get ready to take off. We have to get back to Uytash airport."

They nodded assent without back chat, and blurred away toward the front of the hangar. It was a small relief; they realized he had the best handle on events and were following his lead. The citadel was falling. It was an utter disaster. Mekra had emerged in a new vampire form, one resistant to silver. Even he had never considered the possibility, however, out of every disaster opportunity flowed like a river for those with the ability to seize it.

He prepared to follow Anton and the rest, when purposeful movement caught the edge of his right eye. He flicked his head right. A tight knit group of fighters strode through the chaos toward him. The foremost bearing a silver scroll case.

The scroll bearer addressed Arthur. "Shabbah al Ahmar is dead." He handed the silver scroll case to Arthur and declared in formal tones, "As the ranking prince, you are the new ruler of the Red Empire."

Arthur lifted the scroll case by its silvery chain, and regarded it for a brief moment.

The CODEX guards chorused as one, "Long live Shabbah al Ahmar!" Their leader regarded Arthur with wary and determined eyes, and inquired, "What is your will, Shabbah al Ahmar?"

Only fighters of the second rank could join the elite ranks of the CODEX guards. They were all equivalent to senior fist team leaders and were the combat elite of the Red Empire. Arthur pointed toward the front rank of the raider IIs and commanded, "Take one of the raiders and wait outside the citadel for me to join you."

"Your will, Shabbah al Ahmar," the scroll bearer stated. He led his team away, blurring toward the scout helicopter beside Anton's.

Arthur slipped the chain over his head and tucked the scroll case inside his shirt. He'd already memorized the Papyrus of Hakron the Scribe many years in the past. Soon, he'd know all the secrets of the Metaframe.

Khufu rose from the stairwell and said to Arthur, "Strictly speaking, Dalien Morte is not dead. However," he shrugged his shoulders, "no vampire can hold the mantle of the Red Ghost. What is your will, Shabbah—"

A dreadful howl rose from the depths of the stairwell. Stamping feet echoed from the stairs. Mekra's swarm had arrived.

The command center staff spilled out of the stairwell before the leading edge of the vampires. There was no thought of fighting back, there was only escape and immediate survival. Arthur and Khufu remained, twin rocks around which the others flowed. Khufu whirled to face the threat, his twin blades snapping into guard position in front of him.

The front rank of vampires came into view.

Khufu's face froze with horror. He hesitated, his twin blades hanging limply within his hands. His children and his wife swarmed over him, taking him down to the cold stone. Bared fangs blurred, biting down hard at any available flesh. Bright blood splashed though the air, splattering in streamers upon the walls and stairs. The vampire children had no finesse when feeding.

Arthur tapped his speed talent, and blurred away after his grandson before the rising swarm of vampires overtook him.

It was time to leave.

* * *

A string of orange warning lights began rotating and flashing above the wide mouth of the hangar.

A low rumble resounded beneath the high-pitched wails of the swarm and the whine of spooling jet engines. The top lip of the hangar shuddered then began descending with a low rumble of heavy machinery.

"They're locking us in!" Chiara shouted, waiting just outside the helicopter door.

Peter clambered into the pilot's seat, began flicking switches, and said, "I've got this."

Mekrarian vampires swarmed into the massive chamber spreading out in a wave, claiming the mechanics and support staff nearest the stairs. Those beyond the edge of the vampires ran for their lives.

Li leaned out of the cabin, threw multiple-grenade launchers to Chiara and Anton, and shouted, "Slow 'em down." She disappeared back into the cabin.

Anton turned from the open door, and stared down the gap between two rows of scout helicopters. He ramped hard, time slowing down, the hangar snapping into sharp detail. Arthur was half-way to the raider, sprinting toward them like an Olympic champion. Behind him, twenty, thirty – there were too many to count – vampires rushed after him. The swarming mob caught and dragged down anyone slower than Arthur. Wails, shrieks and yells rent the air as turbines thundered and aircraft prepared to take off.

Like army ants. Like giant army ants, Anton thought, and pulled the trigger on his MGL, sending grenade after grenade looping into the approaching wave. Chiara's shots joined his in the same moment. Submachine fire burst into life above his left shoulder, Li undoubtedly joining the fray from the cabin doorway. The grenades cracked, flamed and smoked. One of the parked raiders exploded in a ball of flame sending debris slashing through the crowded vampires.

Arthur reached him, pulled to a jarring halt just in front of him, and yelled in his face, "Inside, now!"

Chiara leaped through the cabin doorway. Anton followed behind her. Arthur leaped up and slammed the door shut behind him. Their escape craft was already a yard off the stone floor and moving forward with gathering speed.

A bright stream of fire on their right lanced into the vampires spreading across the hangar floor between the lines of raiders and petrels, sending bodies tumbling in clouds of pink mist. A raider hovered outside the hangar, its side-mounted 7.62mm minigun spitting fire into the mass of vampires surging over the hangar floor. A third raider sped through the narrowing exit to join it.

Their raider's nose dipped slightly and it accelerated forward toward the shrinking gap. Anton stared through the windscreen, gritted his teeth, held his breath, and braced for impact.

Peter swore, "Frack it!"

Another raider raced past them, its rotors shattering against the lowering stone, the body of the craft flying out through the shrinking gap and vanishing from sight as it dropped helplessly away.

Their scout helicopter dipped lower, scraping its belly along the stone floor in a shower of sparks, its rotors avoiding the descending stone wall by the slimmest of margins.

Their craft leaped into the open air and Anton exhaled a deep breath.

"Take out the petrels," Arthur commanded Peter, "and get me a dedicated link with those other two raiders."

Peter pivoted his scout helicopter, bringing its missiles and guns to bear upon the interior of the hangar. The great stone door was closing, sliding into place, a short sliver of space remained to shoot through. He thumbed the firing stud, and all four hellfire III missiles streaked away, vanishing through the gap into the space beyond. Flames shot from beneath the colossal door for a moment and then vanished as the enormous stone door slammed shut. He flicked a switch and declared, "Got a tight link on the other two raiders ... damn it! It wasn't a clear shot. The gods only know what we hit in there."

Arthur tapped an earbud in his right ear and called out, "Uytash ... Yes, Uytash airport. Follow me."

Anton stared at Arthur and asked, "How come you've got a tactical headset?"

"I'm a member of the high council," Arthur answered. "Not that it matters now."

The raider veered away to the east, the other two scout helicopters falling like geese into a 'V' formation behind it.

"Where are we going after Uytash?" Li asked from one of the back seats.

"To Aswan in Egypt," Arthur replied. "From there it's a short ride to the ruins of the Temple of Thoth."

"The Temple of Thoth?" Anton asked.

"Yes, Anton. The Temple of Thoth."

"Why?"

Arthur tapped the side of his nose and said, "I have a hunch."

"What the hell does that mean?"

"Crane's going there and we have to stop him."

"Didn't we play this game a couple of nights ago?"

"Yes, Anton, but now we'll win."

"I like this plan," Peter remarked dryly from the front. "It has a certain … simplicity."

Arthur raised an eyebrow, turned his head to face Peter's back and said with a half-smile, "Wait and see, young man, wait and see."

Anton frowned and fell into silence. With his grandfather there was no telling what he might have up his sleeve. His right thigh was throbbing, and his headache had returned. He closed his eyes for a moment and leaned back into his chair. How long would it take a fast flier like a raider to get to Uytash airport? Ten, fifteen minutes at most. Also … how long had Arthur been a senior member of the Red Empire? And what would they find at the Temple of Thoth? He had a lot of questions, but they could wait. He was grateful they were all still alive. It could so easily have gone the other way. He opened his eyes, reached over and took Chiara's hand. She squeezed back, looking at him with a brittle half-smile on her face. She glanced back toward the mountain receding into the darkness behind them; her face became an inscrutable mask but her eyes filled with emotions too complex to read.

He squeezed her hand again and pulled gently. She rose, crossed the narrow aisle between their seats and sat down in his lap. She buried her head into his shoulder and he held her tight. She sobbed against his chest, and he brushed the tears from her cheek with his left hand.

Chiara's sobs cut through him like a knife.

* * *

Mekra had brought the Red Empire to its knees.

She surveyed the empty screens and smoking ruins of the command center. Recently gained memories of new converts filled in the gaps left by the broken systems. The slaughter of the civilian vampires of Crane's dominion by the remaining far-flung forces of the Red Empire continued apace. There was no place for the lesser vampires in her world. She could neither convert nor drive their submission to her will. It was time for her to sweep away all signs of Crane's world.

She uttered quietly, "The world will fall to my rule as leaves fly before a gale."

The last human soul within Matahat al Diydan succumbed to her blood. She let go her restraints of will, and fell to the floor, her mind dissolving into restful darkness. There had been so much blood, rivers of it from Romania to Dagestan, she was drowning in it. She needed time to digest the new minds and grow into her knowledge. She broadcast a last trenchant command to carry her thralls until she awoke.

Protect me. Protect me, Dalien Morte.

* * *

Dalien's queen rested upon the cold stone floor.

She was quiescent. None dared touch her. The only reason to move her would be if she was in imminent danger. Dalien regarded her for a moment with eyes of solid, glossy black and murmured with abject wonder, "Why did I resist?"

He was a vampire. His former life a fleeting memory. There was only his queen, and obedience to her divine will. He shook his head slowly, astonished by his foolishness. Fortunately, an immortal eternity stretched before him to make good his lapse of judgment.

Other vampires crowded around, peering with shining black eyes at their queen, then flicking their gaze toward him. They expected him to direct them in her absence. They had all heard her final commands and he was the only one she had spoken of by name.

He thrilled to serve. There could be nothing more glorious than to advance his blessed queen's cause. He addressed the crowd surrounding him. "We must protect our queen." The other vampires stared at him in avid silence. "We must set this citadel to rights and repair the damage that has been done." They nodded in unison. "Pick up your former tools. Quell the fires. Salvage our aircraft and weapons. Restore our command center. Now go to work."

The vampires flashed away.

Dalien reflected upon the immediate needs of his queen's dominion. There were two hundred and thirty-two vampires within Matahat al Diydan. Within two days they would need to kill the same number of humans to slake their thirst. The town of Gimry was nearby. It had a population of nearly five thousand. The town would last about five weeks.

Then they'd need more.

Chapter Eleven

"The art of goalless preparation relies on constantly placing obstacles and hindrances in the path of your enemy, while secretly locating all manner of beneficial assets in the vicinity of your enemy's positions. In this way, you are always within reach of a weapon or a shield, becoming infinitely adaptable to changing circumstance." – Arthur Slayne

* * *

Republic of Dagestan, Uytash Airport, Private Hangar, September 14th, 22:40

The three raiders came in hot and fast.

The scout helicopters filed through the enormous doorway, coming to land in Arthur Slayne's privately owned hangar. Anton was first out the raider's door, wincing as he landed on the pale concrete of the hangar floor. Ramp epigenetics conferred higher pain tolerance than normal. A Ramp master could still think, Ramp and operate through pain that would knock a normal person flat, but Anton's leg was far from its best. Chiara had stitched his thigh well and the wound was stable, but the cut was deep.

He walked gingerly away from the scout helicopter, turned and looked back for the others. Chiara, Li, Arthur and Peter exited from both sides of the raider. Beyond them, four CODEX guards and another four-man Red Empire fist team dropped to the concrete from the other two raiders. He twisted around and surveyed the hangar. There was a single craft in it. A long sleek white dart, whose very lines spoke of one thing – speed.

Arthur's hand landed on Anton's left shoulder and he said, "Isn't she a beauty. She's a custom built long-bodied Spike 512."

Peter gave a low whistle behind him. His grandfather approached the sleek aircraft, opened a panel in the skin with a touch and placed his right palm on a reader. An amber light began flashing on the upper-left corner of the reader, and his fingers flew over a keypad beneath the glass plate. A moment later the light turned to a solid green. There was a slight hiss and a rectangular seam opened up in the side of the hull. A door opened, and swung down until its leading edge rested an inch above the concrete floor. On the inside of the door a narrow set of stairs rose into the main cabin.

Arthur squeezed Anton's left shoulder, and said, "Let's go inside." He turned his head and called out over his shoulder to the rest, "Follow me. We have to move quickly. It's imperative we get to the Temple of Thoth before the vampires, and we have to stop at Aswan first and pick up the rest of the team."

"Who's meeting us in Aswan?" Anton asked, following Arthur up the stairs into the long narrow cabin.

"Take this," Arthur said, handing Anton a liter of water and a high-protein food pack from a bin opposite the door, "and grab a seat. I'll fill everyone in at the same time."

Chiara took a bottle of water and a food pack from Arthur as she passed, and took the seat across the aisle from Anton. Peter followed next, and Arthur steered him forward to the cockpit. Peter took up a position sideways, hulking in the narrow space leading into the cockpit. Li was next and sat behind Anton. A mix of CODEX guards and Red Empire fighters followed Li into the cabin and took seats as they could find them. With two seats in the cockpit and twelve in the cabin, they were close to maxing the aircraft's capacity out.

Anton took a good swig from his water bottle, caught his grandfather's eye and raised a quizzical eyebrow. His grandfather nodded once at Anton, then addressed everyone in the cabin. "We're leaving in five minutes. We will be flying to Aswan where we will link up with Ahmad Bakhoum, Order of Thoth force leader for Egypt."

One of the CODEX guards spoke up, "Ahh... 'The Eagle,' we know of him and his team. Good operators, even if infidels."

"Yes," Arthur said dryly. "In addition, Justin Blake has rounded up all his cousins in New Zealand and everyone from Australia who could attend." His eyes flicked over the group. "It looks like we'll have a force of twenty-six Ramp masters to hold the Temple of Thoth."

"Hold it?" Li asked. "How long can we hold out for?"

"We only need to hold it until dawn."

Li frowned for a moment. "Aswan is west of here. The vampires will have another hour of night to do their work."

"So, we'll have to last an extra hour," Anton stated.

"Yes, Li. It will be a long night," Arthur confirmed with a nod.

"What's your thinking, Arthur?" Anton asked. "What are you planning for?"

"Anything and everything, as usual," Arthur said, he pursed his lips for a moment then spread his hands wide. "Okay. This is what I really think."

"As opposed to what you don't really think," Li interjected.

"I see Utah and Nevada are still raw."

"We lost a lot of good people."

"No doubt. But take a step back and consider the big picture. Crane is losing control. The Vampire Dominion is on its knees. Its future rests upon a knife edge. A little push in the right direction will destroy it."

Li didn't reply. Anton looked around the cabin. Arthur's optimistic passion was infectious. The Red Empire fighters were looking intently at Arthur. One of them whispered enthusiastically, "Shabbah al Ahmar."

Arthur slammed his right fist into his left palm. "This is our moment. Mekra hates Crane with a passion built from centuries of imprisonment. There will be enough surviving equipment at Matahat and the rest of the Red Empire for her to track what Crane is doing. Crane is desperate. The fall of Matahat will push him over the edge. He will go to the temple with the Key of Ahknaton and attempt to use it to secure his rule. Mekra will see Crane coming to the temple, she will fear his use of the Key. Her hate and fear will drive her to commit her whole force against Crane at the temple. We will be waiting and we will be prepared. Crane has the fastest transports and his forces are closer to Egypt than Mekra and her vampires. He'll arrive first and come up hard against the anvil we will prepare. Mekra will become the hammer. We'll crush Crane between us and Mekra, seize the Key and use it to destroy all the remaining vampires forever."

Anton glanced at Li, expecting her to interject. Surely, she had an opinion to offer. Li remained silent, her lips pressed together slightly, her brow creased faintly with a light frown. She lifted a hand to her chin and rubbed it thoughtfully.

Peter said behind Arthur, "So you're planning to position us against two competing vampire armies." He paused for a moment. "I admire your audacity, but how the hell are we going to survive?"

Arthur glanced behind him, lifted his fist before his chest and shook it. "We only have to hold them until sunrise. We'll have all the equipment we need from Ahmad and his team. Sentry guns, claymores, tactical links, weapons, everything we could possibly use to hold the vampires back." He turned and looked directly at Li. "The only thing we lack now is a loremaster vision to show us what we're missing. Li, can you help us now? Can you help us defeat Crane and the Vampire Dominion?"

Li arched an eyebrow and opened her loremaster laptop. "I'll see what I can do." A moment later, Li's eyes closed, her face paled, and her eyelids fluttered like she was dreaming.

Anton held his breath.

* * *

A golden tongue of flame captured Li Wu's visionary gaze.

The legacy of Juliette Mirovar infused her soul. She rested in silence, centered deep within herself. Her mind ranging far and wide had come to this place, drawn to it by a poignant sense of loss, dread and mystery. Ancient desert-bound ruins, overlayed with a ghostly outline of an ancient pristine architecture, told a story more than five millennia old. The Temple of Thoth lay before her, and over its ancient ruins, darkly armored vampires strode beneath a glowering storm-swept sky. Their tall ruler lifted his mailed fist high, a dark glow within it.

The golden flame rose briefly, a mere arm's length away, then vanished as if exhausted. The shadows on the periphery of her vision deepened, drawing energy into themselves, congealing, solidifying – something wreathed in terror was coming. Li had seen enough and withdrew from the vision before Set could reveal himself. While she'd bested him in their last encounter in the roadhouse in Nevada, it was poor strategy to allow him to keep taking shots at her. He only had to win once, whereas she had to win time and time again. Sooner or later, her luck would run out.

She opened her eyes, adjusted her position in her seat and regarded the elder Slayne with steady eyes.

"What did you see?" he asked.

Everyone in the aircraft looked at her. They were hanging on her every word. They all believed she knew everything. They trusted what she would tell them. The reality was different. She could only see what was likely, not what was certain; and while she would always relate any tactical or strategically important information, she'd not revealed that Anton and Chiara, were soon for the grave or worse.

At least as far as she understood her visions.

She took a breath and sighed. "There's a place, ruins in a desert. Crane is there with his praetorians."

"How many vampires?" Arthur asked.

"Sixty plus," Li replied. "All of his remaining praetorians. His generals and Armitage are with him. I think there are three or five shadowstars as well."

"What happens?"

"Crane has the Key of Ahknaton. He lifts it up to the sky while a great storm rages overhead."

"As I expected, he's going to the temple. Mekra's too much of a threat. He will attempt to use the Key. We can intercept him and capture the Key. With the Key we can reset this whole mess and undo vampires."

"What?" Anton interjected.

"Yes," Arthur said, glancing at Anton before returning his attention to Li. "We can reset the Metaframe back to the world prior to the existence of Mekra as a vampire. Ahknaton moved us to a world where vampires are possible. Moving us back should eliminate them."

"What happens then?" Peter asked from behind Arthur. "Would they vanish into thin air? Die? Become human?"

"Any of the above," Arthur replied. "We know for a fact that everything we had five thousand years ago allowed us to live without vampires."

Chiara frowned. "Surely, you're not talking about reversing time."

Arthur tilted his head slightly to the right and regarded her with keen eyes. "Exactly. No time travel involved. We reset the framework of reality at this time going forward," and he air-quoted with his fingers, "'to not include vampires,' and they will have to change to something else – presumably back to humans."

"Presumably?" Li asked sardonically.

"Yes, I know. Presumably – it's not certain – but Mekra was human before she became the first vampire. The most likely shift is back to human. It's our best bet."

Anton nodded. "Makes sense to me."

Chiara stated boldly, "Of course, we should do this."

Peter gazed at Anton; his eyebrows raised. "Not the best recommendation going around," he glanced at Arthur, "but I'll buy it."

Li looked around the cabin. The CODEX guards and the other Red Empire fighters looked to Arthur. He was their Red Ghost now. They would follow his lead, even if it led into hell itself. She tilted her head for a brief quizzical moment. She had no better strategy. She brought her head back up and nodded once. "Agreed. This is our best course."

Arthur nodded decisively and turned toward Peter. "Okay, let's get you authorized to fly this beast." The pair disappeared into the cockpit. Li looked around without focusing on anyone in particular. A single thought hammered through her mind.

Our best course? Even if we all die tonight?

It had come to this.

* * *

James Haley's osprey II thundered into land.

The jet's wash blew up gales of sandy grit around the drone. James reflected upon Chloe's orders. She'd been explicit, 'Use the secret entrance a mile south of the ruins to enter the Tomb of Ahknaton. Set up for my arrival with the Key. Find a place to observe in secret and keep me appraised of the situation.'

James had asked her how she knew what to do?

She'd answered, 'For my whole life as a vampire, I've studied Crane in intimate detail. He is desperate. He will go to the Temple of Thoth and attempt to use the Key of Ahknaton. Your job with the chameleons is to ensure that no other than Crane or myself uses the Key. While Crane is alive, I can't touch the Key, nor can I attack him to stop him using the Key. Ideally, it will be me with the Key and Crane will be dead, but if he reaches the tomb alive, I'll have to reset my strategy.'

James had asked about using the chameleon's capture ability. Chloe had paused for a moment and then said, 'It seemed like an option at the time I trained them, but events have not played out in ways that allow us to use it.'

He returned to the task at hand and focused on the GPS coordinates displayed on the osprey's main screen. Chloe had given him the exact location of the secret entrance. As to how she knew about this entrance or precisely where it would be beneath the shifting sands of the Egyptian desert, she'd not mentioned.

He flicked a switch, and floodlights around the drone's wings and body lit up the desert in a wide circle. A forest of boulders rose out of the sand, like a giant's marble game lost on an endless beach. The entrance was beneath the nearest great stone. He hit another button, releasing the locks on the rear ramp, and made his way to the hold. The three chameleons were invisible. They'd do that sometimes, and he was sure it was just to piss him off.

James walked into the middle of the hold, and said in conversational tones, "Gullette?"

Massive taloned hands ghosted onto James' shoulders, and he flinched before he could stop himself. He pressed his lips tightly together and forced himself to stillness while every nerve shrieked an ancient command, 'RUN!' Gullette's head moved in over his right shoulder, his breath huffing out in clouds redolent with fresh blood and meat. They'd hunted and fed at Aswan airport as he refueled the osprey after the long flight from New York City via Casablanca. Aswan airport was missing a pair of baggage handlers. He didn't try to move, and waited for Gullette to speak. They'd played this game before.

"Meat-that-talks," Gullette remarked derisively, "vermin's slave monkey, you short life!"

James frowned and turned his head slowly to the right. The corners of Gullette's mouth turned upward in a lizard's grin. His rows of serrated teeth, so reminiscent of a shark's, gleamed beneath the hold's lights. James' gaze locked on the baleful yellow lamps of Gullette's eyes, and he said quietly, "So, you keep reminding me, and yet, I'm still breathing."

Gullette's grin widened and he croaked, like a single barked laugh. Kavanne and Shemina ghosted into view on James' left and right at the corners of a triangle around him. Gullette lifted his hands and let James go – for now.

He turned and looked up at the towering lizard and declared, "We have a mission. You have a bargain with Chloe. We have kept our side of the bargain and our business will be done tonight."

"Done? ... Done tonight! ... Yes!"

The lizards suddenly froze.

Shemina's tail jerked erect. She bobbed her head forward, hissing avidly at James. Kavanne lifted his hands wide and back, his talons elongating, spines erupting along his arms and back. He lifted his massive gray head and roared at Gullette. James' guts froze as he slapped his hands over his ears. Gullette snapped his head left and right, issuing an ululating call.

The sound went on and on, cutting through James' head like a buzzsaw.

Kavanne and Shemina froze for a long moment, then settled back into relaxed postures. A moment later Gullette stopped his call and hissed quietly through his teeth. He said to James in tones of utter finality, "Must finish, all mission business, before dawn."

James exhaled deeply and nodded. Gullette had just averted something dreadful with his strange sound. Shemina had been about to attack him, and Kavanne looked ready to go into a killing frenzy. Gullette's weird ululating call had relaxed both of them. The female chameleon was coming into a breeding cycle. James was sure of it. Kavanne was ready to try and kill Gullette for the breeding rights, but Gullette had a way to slow things down, or put Kavanne and Shemina at ease. How long could Gullette keep control? If they survived the night, it was probably a moot point. Chloe always had a plan and James trusted her with his life.

"Okay, let's get this job done," James said, slapping the controls of the ramp. It folded down to the sands. Selecting a tactical flashlight from a wall rack near the ramp doorway, he led the chameleons out into the desert. They circled around the drone and approached the boulders sitting atop the sand.

Gullette uncurled a long finger at the nearest boulder, his eyes half lidded, and said, "Hidden space. Sands keep long secrets. Best way down."

James eyed the rock. It stood starkly massive beneath the osprey's floodlights. It must've been at least ten feet in diameter, and probably weighed as much as a small tank. "Can you move it?"

Gullette nodded. He croaked at Kavanne and they moved to the far side of the boulder. James moved around to get a better view of what was happening, holding his flashlight above his right shoulder. The cone of light bathed the two chameleons as they moved into the boulder's shadow. They planted their feet into the sand and leaned onto the stone. Their muscles bulged, rippling beneath gray-pebbled white-streaked skin. They coughed and croaked. Their nostrils flared as one, and between a snarl and a grunt, the boulder shifted, then rolled forward a dozen feet. The lizards snorted, arched their necks, and drew in great gulps of air.

"Where's the door?" James asked. He strode forward, kicking at the sand with his boots. Where was the freaking entrance? Had Chloe made a mistake?

Gullette leaned forward and swiped his open hand through the sand, revealing a flat, ocher stone. James kicked the rest of the sand aside revealing a square of stone a yard on each side. There were a pair of deep grooves on one side. James grasped them and pulled, but was unable to budge the stone.

Gullette snorted derisively and James stepped back, shining his flashlight upon the sand-edged door. The chameleon moved into position over the flat stone. He slotted the fingers of his right hand into the right-side groove, and braced himself with his left hand against the side of the boulder. He pulled back with his right hand and the stone door lifted up. He pulled it upright and let it go with a crash.

James stepped forward and played his flashlight down into the space beneath the door. There was a six-foot drop to a landing and then stairs moving down at a forty-five-degree angle. He glanced at the two chameleons; a third shadow stretched over the sand past the boulder. Shemina appeared a moment later and croaked at the other two. They both looked at her avidly and then took a step backward.

James frowned. Shemina almost never spoke to the others, at least in his presence. What was she on about now? He pressed his lips together. Unless he could learn lizard-speak in the next couple of hours, he'd probably never know. Chloe wouldn't keep the chameleons alive any longer than she needed to. He was sure of that.

Gullette turned his head toward James, uncurled his right hand at the descending stairs and endless darkness below, and said, "You go first, we promise no eat, Meat-that-talks."

James looked at him for a long moment and then leaped down to the platform. He landed in a crouch, his feet stirring up little swirls of ancient dust. He descended the stairs down to a second platform that opened up into a long tunnel heading toward the temple ruins. It looked like a straight line to Ahknaton's tomb beneath the Temple of Thoth. He advanced at a run, following the powerful cone of light from his flashlight. He didn't want to spend another second longer with the chameleons then he had too. A mile to the tomb, he'd get there in six to seven minutes. Get the lizards all set. Install a listener-watcher device and get back out in fifteen minutes tops. He carried a high-power Glock .45, loaded with specialized high-explosive ammunition holstered beneath his left shoulder. If he drew it on the chameleons, they'd kill him before he could fire it. He was beyond trusting Gullette to keep his word. He'd invested his life into Chloe's plans. He would either survive this night or die trying.

It was the mission he'd chosen.

* * *

General Haras Mosule regarded the open hangar on the mountain face.

He looked upon Matahat al Diydan with an unnamable feeling seeping through his soul. Was it loss ... longing ... regret? He couldn't quite put his finger on it. He'd been a prince of the Red Empire, second in command to the Red Ghost in the middle of the nineteenth century. If things had turned out differently, he could have ruled the Red Empire. If things had turned out differently, he'd also be long dead from old-age or combat. He lifted his eyebrows, his lips quirking slightly. In the end it was the blood that had kept him living in the darkness. Once he'd imbibed the nectar of the gods, there was no looking back. Nothing equaled the delicious sensuality of feeding upon fresh, warm blood. Nothing came close. The night he'd found service within the highest ranks of the Vampire Dominion was the night his true life had begun.

Haras scanned the mountain, searching with all the power of his vampire senses. Matahat al Diydan, the maze of worms, the fortress inviolate … but was it still unconquered? Haras had followed Mekra's trail from Romania to Dagestan. Had she conquered where the Vampire Dominion had failed? On the night of his conversion into a vampire by Cornelius, he'd brought detailed knowledge of the citadel's layout and defenses to his new king. Information that had grown stale as the years passed. Given the pervasive silver within the fortress, a frontal assault by vampires was out of the question. Crane had forbidden the use of atomic weapons for fear of destroying the CODEX. The Red Empire could defend against chemical weapons with multiple methods, most recently with the innovation of Gossamer – a technology the Vampire Dominion had so far failed to duplicate. The path most likely to succeed was a bio-weapon to kill the Ramp masters, after which loyal vaccinated humans could retrieve the CODEX.

Cornelius had intimated as much when discussing the recent progress with the Day Guard. Cornelius probably had a secret research lab developing such a weapon. Not that he'd shared such information with his most loyal general. Haras frowned; it troubled him that Cornelius kept so many secrets from him, but still – his fate was far better than burning to ashes in a Red Empire funeral pyre.

Haras nodded decisively to himself. The vampires must compartmentalize their secrets to avoid aiding their many enemies. It was the best way to win the war.

Movement at the lip of the hangar entrance caught Haras' eye. The wrecked nose of a Russian-made petrel I aircraft emerged from the interior. The main body and half a wing followed, muscled forward by a dozen vampires. They pushed the wreck out. It toppled down the mountain side before vanishing with a rolling crash into a ravine. Haras focused hard, the vampires on the edge of the hangar resolved into sharp detail. Their eyes were wholly black orbs, and long-thin fangs hung over their bottom lips.

The spawn of Mekra. Matahat had fallen!

Haras waited until the vampires vanished back into the hangar. He turned and fled back to his waiting shadowstar. His pod door was open and he clambered inside, taking his position before the controls. The door closed with a faint hiss as he initiated a call through to his king.

Cornelius' face appeared on the screen, behind him was an empty and opulent boardroom Haras didn't recognize. Cornelius asked, "What news of Matahat?"

Haras replied, "It has been overrun by the spawn of Mekra."

"Did any escape? Were any CODEX guards seen?"

"None were witnessed by us."

"Does she have an army?"

"I believe so."

Cornelius lifted his head and looked down his nose. "She will move upon the Temple of Thoth."

"Why will she go there?"

Cornelius' mouth twitched with a hint of a sardonic grin. "To stop me."

"To stop you! From doing what?"

Cornelius arched an eyebrow. "Aren't you making a report?"

"Of course, my king. Yes, Mekra has conquered Matahat. She has converted numerous members of the Red Empire. There will be hundreds of abominations under her command."

"Indeed," Cornelius replied, "and her capacity to move them en masse?"

"They have Russian built petrel Is. They are equivalent to the osprey II for performance. She could pack a lot of vampires into an individual aircraft. If she has enough aircraft, she could conceivably move her whole force to the temple at the same time."

Cornelius pursed his lips for a moment. "She may have enough aircraft … petrels … she could reach the Temple of Thoth in three hours, but we can detect her approach and destroy her in the air. Let her come – it will be to her own destruction." He leaned forward, his face filling the screen. "Take your shadowstars to the Temple of Thoth and secure the site. Send your praetorians to Aswan to stage with Force-Asia."

"My shadowstars and ospreys are low on fuel, we must land at Uytash airport and refuel before we can travel to Egypt."

"So be it. Now go, and make sure no one gets to the Temple of Thoth before you do."

Haras nodded. "Your will, my king."

Cornelius smiled without mirth and said, "Good hunting."

The video conference closed a moment later. The display filled with a news feed from the newly established East Coast Hub. There were reports coming in, 'For General's Eyes Only,' from the small team of vampires operating at the fledgling citadel. Haras read the lead report and did a double take; teams of Red Empire operatives were slaughtering civilian vampires all over the world. It was a simultaneous and very well coordinated attack. The loss of the Panopticon was having real effects on the Vampire Dominion. If the civilian vampires lost faith in the protection of the praetorians – they'd go rogue and chaos would result.

Haras hit the controls and his shadowstar lifted into the air, rising to join his second shadowstar circling five miles above. A pair of ospreys half-filled with the remaining praetorians of Force-Africa kept a similar track a mile beneath them. After the necessary refueling, the ospreys would land at Aswan airport in nearly three and a half hours. His shadowstars would arrive at the temple much earlier, close to midnight local Aswan time.

He shook his head. Within the last few days, they'd both routed the Order of Thoth and lost the Panopticon. Now, Matahat had fallen, and roving bands of Red Empire killers were murdering the civilian vampires.

To top it all off, his king was marshaling all his military might at Aswan and the Temple of Thoth, where vampires had begun five thousand years earlier, to conduct a strategy that was not entirely clear.

Haras stared at the news feed again and whispered to himself, "What a bitch of a night this is."

* * *

Early autumn rain fell gently against his study's windows.

Gabriel Toussaint ignored the patter and examined the three-dimensional model of a modified SARS virus on his computer's display. He'd dedicated the last forty years of his immortal life to genetic research for the Vampire Dominion. His was a one-man virological enterprise.

His ground floor Parisian apartment expressed his exquisite and refined tastes. He'd decorated it in the style of an eighteenth-century prince. It was situated within a private enclave with armed guards to keep out the common ruffians. Behind his expansive book and journal lined study rested a refrigerated room housing an up-to-date mini-supercomputer crunching the genetic variations he was aiming to instill into the virus.

Beneath his apartment, another four levels held a secret biosafety level four laboratory where the actual viruses he worked on resided. The challenge was a deep one; create a bioweapon that was harmless to most of humanity, but deadly to the Ramp masters. He couldn't target the gene clusters underpinning the Ramp. They were widespread throughout the human population and Cornelius Crane had been horrifically explicit about his fate if he accidentally released a dangerous virus upon the human herd.

He shuddered at the thought of Crane's promised punishment. Of course, such an eventuality would never happen. He was too clever and too careful. He was a scientific and technical genius chosen and blessed with immortality by Crane. All he had to do was deliver a weapon Crane could use against the Ramp masters. He was currently examining using the Ramp itself to trigger his modified version of SARS into action. Ramp masters had a notoriously enhanced metabolism. He could use such a metabolism to kick start the modified virus into action. After which it would take effect over the next two to five days, long enough for a carrier to infect everyone around them before they showed symptoms and died.

It was a work in progress, but soon, within a year or two at most, the virus would be perfected. Then dens of Ramp masters such as the fabled fortress of Matahat al Diydan would be easy prey to the results of his scientific genius. Crane would be delighted. He would lift Gabriel high within the glorious ranks of the Vampire Dominion. He would become a favorite of the king. A trusted adviser. He would live in the lap of luxury, surrounded by fresh blood, and protected against all foes by the invincible Chloe Armitage and the king's praetorians for the rest of his immortal life.

He smiled briefly, indulging his dream of the future for a long moment. But such dreams required hard work if they were to ever come to fruition. He turned to a second computer display on his left and searched the online journals for new research. There were amazing things happening in China at labs in Beijing, Wuhan and Shenzhen. Even after the COVID epidemic of 2020-23, humanity persisted in their reckless gain-of-function research. There was no shortage of international funding for enhancing commonplace viruses such as influenza, SARS, or MERS to attack human beings. He sometimes wondered just how self-destructive humans could be. Their scientists and leaders were so hubristic and arrogant; didn't they know that they should leave such work to their betters? With someone who actually cared for the future of the human race. He shook his head with a moment of disbelief. It wouldn't do vampires any good if humanity accidentally wiped themselves out with a lab accident. That would be catastrophic, perhaps Crane had a plan to combat such an event.

Gabriel's ears twitched. Was that a sound outside his window? Something unexpected? A scratching or a shuffling? His head flicked up from his display.

The glass on the window exploded inward in a fury of metal, fire and light. He shrieked and blurred backward, his chair tumbling away; a wave of heat ravaged his face, evaporating his marvelous blond coiffure. Powerfully muscled men garbed in red cloaks and wielding bright short swords, blurred single file into his study.

"The Red Empire," Gabriel said, naked disgust snarling through his blackened lips. He wasn't a fighter but he was still a night-born killer. He lunged at his nearest foe.

Gleaming blades slashed through the air. Razor-sharp metal cutting through flesh, blood and bone. His head flew from his shoulders, a bright spray of blood painting a pair of crimson ribbons across his ornate plaster ceiling. His head landed on his exquisite Persian rug and rolled beneath a beautiful eighteenth century chair made of gilded wood. He peered back into his study. A line of agony clawed at the base of his throat. His vampire vitality dooming him to a final few seconds of vivid life.

Booted feet stamped across his gorgeous rug. One man ordered in stern tones, "Mine the lab. Crush the foundations. We're taking this whole poisonous site down!"

"Death to the vampires!" shouted another.

"For the Red Empire," declared two more in unison.

The killers unceremoniously dumped black duffel bags upon his perfect parquetry flooring and glorious Persian rug. The men pulled satchels of C4 explosives from them and vanished down the basement stairs toward his lab. Clearly, his long-hidden laboratory was no longer a secret.

Gabriel's vision clouded, and darkness swept his world away.

* * *

James Haley clambered his way out of the secret entrance.

He rose to his feet, regarded the slab of stone that served as a door and the massive boulder next to it that had hidden the entrance. He went to the far edge of the stone door, braced himself, squatted, and dug his fingers in beneath the edge of the lip. If he could close the door and kick some sand over it, then no one else could easily find the secret entrance to Ahknaton's tomb. He was six feet four in his socks and two-hundred and thirty pounds. Fighting fit and ready for anything. He took a deep breath and heaved. Nothing happened. The stone door must've weighed north of six-hundred pounds. There was no way to put it back.

James stepped backward from the shadowed square of darkness in the desert floor. He couldn't hide the entrance. He looked around at the forest of boulders. Still … it wasn't exactly obvious. He ran back to the rear of the osprey and mounted the ramp. He smacked a red button on the wall of the hull and the ramp rose up and closed with a clang. The hold felt empty without the chameleons in it. A 'normal,' emptiness and much welcomed after their nearly constant threats to eat him.

He strode forward into the cockpit and sat down in the pilot's chair. He slapped a small flat box the size of a smartphone onto the console and plugged it into a universal port with a black cable. The device linked back to a listener-watcher glued onto a wall in Ahknaton's tomb. A paired camera-microphone he could use to keep an eye on what was happening with the chameleons. It was pitch black within the tomb. Conditions, the chameleons were comfortable with. The camera saw deep into the infra-red, ultra-violet and operated with highly effective light intensifier technology. The three chameleons were waiting around in full view, the camouflage ability inactive. They were in place and everything was ready to go.

James went to work on his keyboard, composing a brief, yet full report of the current status of his mission. He sent it to Chloe a moment later. He fired up the engines and lifted the drone off the sands. He'd spotted an outcropping of stone on a nearby hill while coming in. It might be suitable for use as an observation site over the secret entrance and the temple. But before he left, he directed the drone to hover closely over the disturbed sands, and the moved boulder. The backwash of the jets erased all signs of tracks in a cloud of ocher grit. It would make finding the secret entrance harder for anyone else. He lifted his head and stared into the distance at his proposed hidden lookout. A moment later, the craft dipped its nose and accelerated toward the designated hill.

He settled back into the pilot's chair and relaxed – an avid croaking erupted over the communications link. James frowned and stared at the green-tinged window filled with writhing forms on the drone's main screen. What the hell were the lizards up to now? He stared harder, his eyes widening with recognition.

James whispered, "What the fuck?!"

* * *

James' text evaporated from Chloe's smartphone's screen.

He had done well. The chameleons were in place within Ahknaton's tomb waiting for her or Crane to arrive with the Key. As for the entrance being open. It was a yard wide and a mile south of the temple. The chances of anyone noticing that one boulder amongst the many near it, had moved, were vanishingly small. In any event, James could keep an eye on both the temple and the secret entrance, and keep her up to date with any changes. She would adapt her strategy as the game unfolded; it was her way. As for James, while he continued to prove his usefulness, she'd keep him around – just like Marcus.

She glanced at the clock on her penthouse hangar wall. It read, '16:45.' While it was late afternoon in New York City, the night was bleeding away in Dagestan and Egypt. She was waiting for Crane to call her. She consulted Hana Tanaka's phone. According to the implant tracking app, Crane's arrival was imminent. He would come in his command shadowstar and they would fly to Egypt with the Key of Ahknaton. Mekra was an all but unstoppable threat. The only recourse Crane had was to use the Key against her. His need to destroy Mekra would force him to overreach and bring about his undoing.

Chloe leaned back in her chair, and swung her right leg over her left, her armored plates sliding across each other with a soft hiss. She was ready for war. Her auto-pistols sat in their holsters at her hips. She wore a bandolier of spare magazines over her chest, and the Red Dragon rested in its scabbard across her lap. Her smartphone lay upon the right armrest next to Hana Tanaka's mobile phone, and her uprated tactical helmet sat to the left of her foot.

The smartphone buzzed – it was Crane. She answered, "Sir?"

"Chloe, prepare yourself for war. I'm descending to your penthouse now. ETA in five minutes."

"Yes, Sir. I will be ready. I'll have the hangar doors open for your arrival."

"Good," Crane replied and closed the call.

Chloe opened an app on her phone and commanded the hangar doors to open. She remained in her seat as the engines whirred and the great doors dropped by a foot and receded to the left and right. She sat in the shadows; safe from the growing rectangle of trenchant afternoon sunlight slashing into the chamber. The minutes ticked by. The sound of the approaching drone grew in her ears, then Crane's command shadowstar appeared, descending on pale jets of blue fire. The craft came to a halt upon the hangar floor, and Chloe sent the command for the overhead doors to close.

A minute later, the sunlight vanished, and the drone's canopy lifted and pushed backward. Crane beckoned her to the cabin with a wave of his right hand. She strode to the craft and leaped into her seat. He glanced at her and smiled grimly. "Good. I'm glad you brought your auto-pistols. We'll need every weapon we can muster."

She lifted an eyebrow. Crane wore his armor, and his great Damascene bastard sword rested on a rack behind his seat. He'd strapped a scroll case at his waist, and of the Key, only a few links of titanium gleamed at his throat. She commanded the hangar doors to open, and asked, "What is the status of your forces?"

"We are marshaling Force-Asia and Force-Africa at Aswan before we strike the Temple of Thoth."

"Strike? Is it already defended?"

"Haras is on his way from Dagestan with shadowstars five and six. He'll arrive at the temple around midnight. It is unknown if he will arrive first, or be preceded by Arthur Slayne and his remaining scraps of the Order of Thoth and the Red Empire."

"Scraps? Does Matahat still stand?"

"It has fallen. Mekra has converted the Red Empire at Matahat to her spawn. She has an army, and Russian built petrels to move them where she will."

Chloe tilted her head and said in level tones, "Mekra is a formidable opponent."

"Indeed … for us both."

Chloe nodded. Once free of Crane, she'd have to deal with Mekra too. She raised a quizzical eyebrow and asked, "Our operations are unmasked. We must assume Mekra and Slayne will see your forces marshaling in

Aswan, mere miles from the Temple of Thoth. They will assume the Key of Ahknaton is in play and act accordingly."

Crane snorted. "Indeed! I'm planning on it."

"And?"

"We will crush the Slayne's, then escape in this drone. Mekra will arrive to confront a sacrifice force we will leave at the temple. We'll then take her and all her spawn out with a one-hundred and fifty kiloton nuclear blast. It will be … as the young people now say it … game over!"

Chloe tilted her head and remained silent. She might need that nuke too – for exactly the same purpose.

Crane tapped his chest and stared at her. "You will be my bodyguard in all this. I'll know if the implant ceases to function. So don't even consider the possibility of treachery."

"Of course, Cornelius."

He harrumphed, glanced up at the open doors and said, "There is no more time to waste. Let us be on our way." He set the controls and the drone rose smoothly into the air.

New York City gleamed in the afternoon sunlight. The transparent armor of the canopy was proof against the deadly rays of the sun. Chloe drank in the sight as the shadowstar ascended into the azure sky. She closed her eyes for a moment. Crane was taking the Key of Ahknaton to the Temple of Thoth. His many enemies stood arrayed against him. He trusted Chloe's implant was still functioning while she'd strapped it harmlessly above her right ankle. All she needed to do was step aside at the right moment and allow someone else to kill him. She'd bypass Jean Philippe Allemande's curse. Crane would die and she would be freed.

But she would need to be careful. From the moment of acquiring the Key of Ahknaton to using it, she would be vulnerable. His praetorians may seek revenge – they held no love for 'the Enforcer,' within their ranks. She must see their numbers diminished before Crane died, to minimize the risk of their intervention. The coming battle would serve that purpose. Let Crane's loyal soldiers bleed upon the battlefield until the moment was ripe to end her long servitude and seize her liberty.

Crane's voice snapped through her reverie, "Fuck it! Not thirteen too!" He glanced across at Chloe and said, "Yes. As you well know, I have many research stations investigating things of interest to me. All important. All essential. And I seem to be losing an inordinate number of them tonight to roving gangs of Red Empire assassins."

A news feed from the newly installed vampire team at the East Coast Hub streamed down the drone's main screen. Chief amongst the reports were lists of attacks on the civilian vampire population. The Panopticon was gone. The new Panopticon was not yet up and running and wouldn't be for another month. The vampires at the fledgling command center were using whatever systems they could access. Chloe lifted an eyebrow. They were doing a reasonable job despite the lack of the Panopticon. Perhaps she'd keep them alive once Crane was gone. He started pontificating about his losses, going on and on about it. She kept a straight face and smiled on the inside. The smallest push would end Crane's dominion forever.

And allow for the rise of her own.

* * *

Mekra opened her eyes.

A crowd of her thralls surrounded her, staring at her with wide eyes filled with abject devotion. Chief amongst them stood Dalien Morte. She rose to her feet and asked him, "How long have I slept?"

Morte answered with an avid stare, "An hour and twenty minutes, my queen. I have counted every moment."

"And what of our defenses?"

"The wreckage in the hanger has been cleared. We retain four operational petrels, and a dozen raiders. The citadel is secured."

"And what of Crane and his vampires?"

Morte glanced around the chamber his eyes narrowing as he surveyed the destruction wrought by the immolation protocol.

Mekra followed his gaze. The immolation protocol had destroyed the advanced IT systems, except for a single large display. Detailed information about the room leaped into her mind. She knew the room intimately. Some of her thralls had installed and operated the systems, and she owned all their memories and knowledge.

Morte touched his tactical headset and ordered, "Khufu, share your feed to the main screen."

"You have the command petrel aloft. Good." Mekra reached with her mind, linking instantly with Khufu and three others within the aircraft. The aircraft was loitering in a wide circle two miles above Matahat. She looked through their eyes, and witnessed what they saw. She pulled her full attention back to the command center a moment later. A detailed geographical map covered the main screen; with Matahat at the center and Uytash airport on the periphery.

It was easier to ask, than plumb for new memories. Mekra said, "What have you seen while I slept?"

"Shadowstars and ospreys have landed at Uytash, refueled and departed on track to Aswan in Egypt. All his forces have relocated from western China to Aswan."

"Crane knows we are here," she said. "He is marshaling his forces at the Temple of Thoth. He has the Key and the Papyrus. Where is the CODEX?"

"Taken by Slayne. Records show a long-bodied Spike 512 left Uytash fifty minutes ago with a flight plan to Aswan."

"Slayne has gone to the temple too. It matters not, Slayne has little chance to get the Key from Crane. Crane will attempt to use the Key to destroy us all. Crane is the threat that we must destroy. When can we leave? We must all go to the Temple of Thoth and overwhelm Crane, Armitage and their praetorians."

"My queen, I would advise—"

Mekra pushed her will upon Morte. She knew vastly more than he could ever know. She'd consumed thousands of minds within the last two days. Minds she'd integrated within the last hour and a half. There was nothing Morte could advise her upon. She stated in low tones, "You will obey."

Morte froze for an instant and then remarked in a voice filled with adoration. "Yes, my queen. We can all be onboard and away within ten minutes."

"Bring the command petrel down. That will be my craft. We will only take the petrels. Arm everyone for war and pack them in tight. Select your sixty best fighters and embark them upon the command petrel. The raiders cannot keep up, so leave them behind. Speed is of the essence."

Morte bowed and said, "Your will, my queen."

Ten minutes later, the Olgoi Khorkhoi inherited the empty halls of Matahat al Diydan.

* * *

"Come on, Anton, meet my friends," Arthur said, leading Anton down the stairs.

"We'll have to make this quick. We haven't got much time." His grandfather emphasized as he strode forward. Anton followed him out onto the pale concrete of the Aswan airport hangar. Presumably, another asset owned by Arthur Slayne Inc. His grandfather seemed to have a near infinite supply of resources, helpers, and assets at hand. It was a mystery to Anton how he'd built his empire while fighting the vampires. Perhaps, one day, Arthur would show him how it all worked. Waiting to greet them were a few familiar faces, Justin Blake and Anita Chang amongst them. Anton remembered Anita from the battle at the Order conclave held in Minneapolis. It had been a disaster for the Order, but in a silver lining, Li had discovered where the Panopticon was located from a captured tactical helmet.

As for Justin … he engulfed Anton in a bear-hug, lifting him off his feet. He said, "How's it hanging, little brother."

"Good! Yeah, all good, Justin," Anton said, his boots returned to the concrete with a thump. "Great to see you up and around."

Justin smiled, and clapped him on the shoulder. "Fighting fit, thanks to you." He turned to another six men, all tall, brown, wide, and covered in fearsome tattoos. They all bore a striking family resemblance to Justin and he called out to them, "Cousins, meet Anton Slayne. He saved my life. He's one of us now."

Anton stood his ground as half a dozen New Zealand Maori warriors swamped him with friendly slaps and buffets that would have knocked a regular person over. He escaped the mauling with a minimum necessity of good grace, and caught up with his grandfather.

Arthur promptly put his arm around his shoulders and directed him to another group of five men wearing gear strongly reminiscent of the Red Empire, except the cowls and cloaks were pale gray. His grandfather waved at the five men, and said, "Anton, meet Ahmad Bakhoum, Omar El-Masri, Ali Abusir, Mostafa Minya, and Youssef Shenouda. They all belong to an ancient clan that has been eliminating vampires in Egypt and watching over the Temple of Thoth for thousands of years. The Order of Thoth is lucky to count them within its numbers."

One of the men arched a bushy eyebrow and said, "This is true, Arthur." He took a step forward and stared at Anton with hard, dark eyes. "So, this is your grandson." He nodded his head slightly. "We are honored to fight alongside any Slayne."

Anton put out his hand and said, "I'm sure the honor is all mine."

The man smiled, shook Anton's hand, and said, "Call me Ahmad, all my friends do."

"Sure, will do," Anton replied with a respectful nod.

Arthur put a hand on Anton's shoulder and said, "Ahmad, we need to move quickly." He glanced past the men at a row of four medium trucks bearing short shipping containers, and six high-end SUVs. "I see that everything is prepared."

"As per your specifications," Ahmad answered. He glanced back over his shoulder at the heavy vehicles. "Our helpers will drive the trucks. The SUVs are armored to the current standard."

"Did the new stinger IIIs arrive in time?" Arthur asked.

Ahmad gestured to a set of four military boxes resting next to the SUVs. "Last night. Now ready to distribute to the team."

Arthur pressed his lips into a tight line. "It's a personal nightmare of mine that Crane will get a couple of shadowstars to the temple before we get there."

Ahmad nodded, and his men murmured beside him.

Arthur glanced at the four shipping containers. "You were able to get four containers packed. I only asked for three."

"It was a package deal," Ahmad said. He shrugged his shoulders. "My cousin works for the local ministry of defense. I could get eight sentry guns for the price of six."

"All to the good," Arthur said. "Now, I have a special mission for you."

"Yes?"

"Take your team in one of the SUVs and go to these coordinates." Arthur withdrew a printed sheet from his coat and handed it to Ahmad. "There's a secret entrance into the Temple of Thoth under a boulder. It leads to the Tomb of Ahknaton. We need to check it out and see if anyone else has accessed it."

"A secret entrance?"

"Yes. It's spelled out in the Papyrus of Hakron the Scribe."

"But you'd need—"

"The CODEX. Got it. Read it on the flight here. I memorized the Papyrus a long time ago. Now it all makes sense. I really need you to check that secret entrance."

"Consider it done."

"Thanks Ahmad. I knew I could rely on you and your team," Arthur said. He turned and faced the rest of the Ramp masters in the middle of the hangar, and called out, "Okay everyone, listen up." He waited for a long moment for everyone's voices to fall to silence. "We need to be on our way to the Temple of Thoth within five minutes. Ahmad has provided new Order nightglasses, and tactical headsets in each of the SUVs. All the vehicles are mobile WIFI stations with satellite links for encrypted communications."

Arthur paused for effect. "I won't sugar-coat the dangers. Crane is going to throw everything he has at the Temple of Thoth in the next few hours, and we are the only force in position with a hope of stopping him. And after Crane, we'll face Mekra."

Anton surveyed the grim faces. No one was backing out. They were all committed to the fight. Determination filled the air. A will to win through, regardless of the odds stacked against them.

His grandfather gestured toward Li. "Thanks to Li Wu's loremaster abilities," and then turned back to the group, "we know that Crane will be coming to the temple tonight. He will bring the Key of Ahknaton with him. I have read both the Papyrus of Hakron the Scribe, and the CODEX. We have one strategy left: kill Crane, seize the Key of Ahknaton, and use it to reset the Metaframe back to the configuration prior to Ahknaton. This should eliminate vampires, including Mekra's new version. There is one other player who has read the Papyrus and the CODEX: Chloe Armitage. The Papyrus describes a secret entrance a mile south of the temple. An entrance that leads directly to Ahknaton's tomb and hence, for anyone with the Key of Ahknaton, the Chamber of the Divine Engine of Thoth. We must assume that Armitage is aware of the secret entrance. Has she told Crane about the secret entrance? I don't know, but," and his lips curled into a lopsided grin, "I suspect she hasn't shared that little advantage with her king."

Arthur swept his gaze across the group. "I know that everyone," and he looked at Li, "thinks I keep too many secrets. That I play my cards too close to my chest, and don't enable informed decisions. Well, tonight I'm placing every card I've got on the table for everyone to see. We're up against Crane, his generals and praetorians. Mekra and her converts from the Red Empire with all their equipment, and Chloe Armitage with whatever secret allies she has in place. Our only advantage, is time and position. The longer we can hold the temple, the more desperate Crane will become. He can't afford to fight a two-front battle against Mekra and us. His desperation will force errors that we can take advantage of. The wild card is Armitage. We can't know her true plan, but we can expect her to support Crane until she can move decisively against him; and when she does move – she'll be the most dangerous opponent we face."

Arthur paused and frowned, every line on his face tightening. He said, "If I was a betting man, I wouldn't give us even money to survive tonight. If anyone wants to back out, now is the time to do it. There is no shame or dishonor in withdrawal. Leave, create families, carry what you know forward to the next generation. If we fail tonight, this burden will fall to you. If, on the other hand, you wish to stay, then know this," he slapped his right fist into the palm of his left hand; then waved his forefinger around the group. "This is the final battle. All the players will be there. Whoever wins will win it all. This night will decide the future of the world. A future ruled by vampires or a future ruled by humanity." He clenched and shook his right fist. "If you stay, you will help make that decision in favor of everything and everyone we love."

Anton's grandfather paused again, then asked, "Does anyone want to leave?"

No one moved, then Justin declared, "Let's kill 'em all!"

Shouts rang out through the hangar, echoing Justin's proposal. As they subsided, Arthur called out, "By teams then: pick up two stingers and get to your vehicles."

The group split up streaming across the concrete floor to the military boxes and the waiting SUVs. The truck's big diesels fired up. Arthur grabbed Anton on the shoulder and pulled him close. "Come with me," he said, leading Anton toward where Peter, Li, and Chiara were waiting for them near the stinger missiles. Arthur addressed Anton and his friends. "If all this goes to shit, get Li to safety and go back to Anton's home in Boston."

They all looked at Arthur for a long moment.

"It's a plan 'Z.' I sent Dwayne to Boston to set everything up." Arthur looked around the small group. "Succeed or fail tonight, I want to keep you alive." He tapped Peter on the chest. "You've got the codes to my Spike 512. Use it to escape with anyone who survives. She's got the legs to get back to the States. There are new identities for all of you on the plane. Make use of them. Crane has a Panopticon replacement in the wings. Once it comes online, life will get a lot tougher for all of you." He put his hands on Anton and Peter's shoulders and said, "Keep Li safe. She's the only one who can keep you all safe."

Peter shrugged and said, "We would have done that anyway."

Li elbowed Peter in the ribs and insisted indignantly. "I'm not some precious snowflake who can't fight."

Arthur looked at her and said, "Everyone will fight tonight. Many will not survive." He raised his eyebrows and sighed. "I've done all I can for now. Let's get this show on the road." He led them to the stingers, picked two up, gave one to Peter and kept the other one in hand. The rest of the teams were nearly all in their SUVs, engines firing up all along the line of vehicles.

Anton freed the strap holding the Blue Dragon across his shoulders, and took it in hand. He whispered to himself, "'Once more unto the breach.'" He tilted his head. It seemed his high-school English literature classes hadn't been a total waste of time. He followed the rest and clambered into the back seat of the SUV. He found himself wedged between Chiara on the right and Li on the left, with Arthur riding shotgun while Peter took the driver's seat, his missile launcher stowed beside him.

Anton leaned back in his seat and closed his good eye.

The good soldier rested while he could.

* * *

General Haras Mosule scanned his scopes.

A convoy of vehicles streamed at high speed over the sands. They began pulling to a halt as they approached the Temple of Thoth. Three SUVs were leading, followed by four large trucks, and another pair of SUVs. A sixth SUV was tracking over the dunes a mile south of the temple. He broadcast a command to his second shadowstar flying a quarter mile off his shoulder, "Slave your combat system to my drone and tighten up."

"Yes, Sir," the praetorian squad leader answered.

Each shadowstar carried four hypersonic cruise missiles armed with five-hundred-pound warheads. He selected a vehicle-by-vehicle attack upon the convoy below. With eight missiles and nine vehicles, he skipped the middle truck, and ignored the lone SUV off to the south. He would follow the missiles by leading a strafing run with his 30mm cannon to finish off the final vehicle and all it carried. They could mop up the remaining SUV with a second pass. A green light flicked on. The missile system reported its ready status. Haras hit the fire button on his console. His shadowstar shuddered slightly as the four missiles streaked away. Another four missiles speared down toward the convoy from the second shadowstar loitering two-hundred yards off his left-hand side.

There was only one group of people who would be arriving at the Temple of Thoth at this time: Arthur Slayne and his cohorts. They would all be dead in seconds. It would be a great victory for the Vampire Dominion.

Haras banked his craft into a steep dive, following his missiles toward the desert floor. A pair of bay doors opened beneath his craft, his 30mm Gatling cannon dropping down into firing position. His wingman followed off his left shoulder with his weapons hot.

It was time to end all things related to Arthur Slayne.

* * *

The ruins of the Temple of Thoth rose like jagged teeth out of the night.

Peter pulled the lead SUV to a halt, its tires crunching over the sand. The other vehicles pulling to a stop in a line behind him.

"SHADOWSTARS!" Li called out across the tactical link, "RUN!"

Arthur threw open the SUV's right door. Carrying his stinger III with one hand, he blurred out into the desert, Anton and Chiara on his heels. Peter and Li vanished in the opposite direction toward the ruins with another stinger missile within the cradle of Peter's arms. On the edge of Arthur's vision, others were fleeing the doomed convoy. Justin Blake with Anita Chang at his side blurred forward thirty yards on Arthur's right. Three of Justin's Maori cousins were another hundred feet away in a horizontal line flowing away from the line of vehicles. In the distance, a mixed band of CODEX guards and Red Empire fighters sprinted for their lives from the rear SUVs. Order helpers shouted in helpless terror from the trucks, leaping to the desert floor, and running away as fast as they could.

Spurred by a sixth sense conditioned by decades of combat, Arthur shouted across the tactical link, "Dive." He hit the sand a moment later, the stinger missile held tightly by his right hand beneath his body. The night turned to day behind him. A wave of super-heated air rolled over top of him like a steamroller and then vanished.

Arthur leaped to his feet and whirled to face the devastation. Thanks to Li's warning, the Ramp masters all had a chance of reaching safety – the helpers remained within reach of the dreadful conflagration. Only a single truck remained intact, its container blackened, a rear tire on fire. Burning debris rained down; gouts of orange flame and black smoke rising into the night sky – the missiles had obliterated the convoy. He called out over the tactical link, "Stingers!"

The shadowstars would be swooping down like fell birds of prey drawn to feast upon the last truck and the survivors on the ground. He turned around, snapping the rocket launcher to his shoulder. He opened himself to the heights of the wild Ramp. Time slowed precipitously. His vision snapped into razor sharp clarity ... there it was, a shadow occulting the stars, a growing pale blue glow circling the craft's rear. A shadowstar was heading straight for him.

He adjusted the position of the launcher. The missile lock alert cut through the desert air. He pressed the firing stud. The stinger III speared away, almost simultaneously another seven missiles raced away from a pair of ragged lines running parallel with the flaming wreckage.

The missiles converged on two spots in the sky.

He threw the spent launcher aside, and whirled around. *Where's Anton?* he shouted silently. Whispering voices beyond the walls of his soul pounced like vengeful banshees upon his concern for his beloved grandson. Their voices cut through his mind like cold steel. Fell ghosts clamoring for their long-denied release. He slapped the side of his head with his left hand and blinked repeatedly, peering owlishly through his nightglasses.

Where was his grandson?

* * *

The missile warner screamed its alarm.

Four hypersonic surface-to-air missiles were closing upon Haras' shadowstar. Automatic countermeasures bloomed in colorful rosettes across the night sky. Directed infra-red lasers from both shadowstars sliced the air with crimson strings of pure energy. Silvery chaff plumed to the left and right in glittering clouds. The four incoming tracks on his threat display dropped to three, then to two as the incoming missiles failed against his craft's defenses.

His second shadowstar evaporated in a hellish glare of white light and streaming fingers of white-hot metal; a squad of his praetorians vanishing with it. The threat display dropped to a single track aimed at his drone. The shadowstar bucked like a wild thing, accelerating with dizzying forces that would have laid a human out flat. The missile warner continued to shriek – the final missile was upon them.

Haras' fist hit the console, activating the ejection sequence. All four life pods blew away from the main body of the shadowstar. It exploded a moment later, his life pod shuddering from the blast wave, turning, twisting, falling toward the desert two miles below. His display flickered with multiple red status alarms, then switched to a video conference with Cornelius Crane.

Cornelius demanded, "Report. My command drone has lost connection to drones five and six. What's your current status?"

"Both down, Sir."

"You're in your life pod, aren't you?"

"Yes, Sir. Currently falling, Sir."

"You were shot down by Slayne?"

Haras nodded toward Cornelius' face on the screen.

"I'm sure your chute will deploy in time," Cornelius observed matter-of-factly. "Once you're upon the ground, find your praetorians and take a position where you can observe the temple. I'll be there with Force-Asia in two hours' time. We can link up with Force-Africa in Aswan and retake the temple from Slayne as a combined force."

"Yes, Sir."

The life pod jerked, its parachute activating. The video conference ended and the screen displayed a 'last position,' map. He was coming down to rest five miles north of the temple. His three personal guards dropped to the dunes within a quarter mile of his position. They'd be able to hook up and head toward the temple.

Haras sighed. It was not an auspicious start to the battle. Still, the cruise missiles would have done a lot of damage to Slayne and his followers.

The enemy would be far worse off.

* * *

"Casualties? Report!" Arthur's voice came through Anton's tactical headset with a tinny squeak.

He shook his head, and spat bloody sand out of his mouth. He coughed, and coughed again, his lungs raw, his throat scoured by sand and fire. His leg had slowed him down and he'd caught more of the blast than any of the others near him.

"Anton?" Chiara called out.

He looked up. She was striding toward him, her face glistening in the light of the fires behind him. His grandfather reached him first. His strong hands patting at his back. Anton jerked upward slapping his shoulders down with both hands. Was he on fire?

"You're okay," Arthur said, his eyes flicked away from Anton and he stared past Anton's right shoulder. He frowned and whispered harshly, "All our helpers are dead, and we lost three more. Flying debris killed one of Blake's cousins, a CODEX guard, and one of the Red Empire fighters."

Anton's heart sank. They hadn't even started to defend the temple, and already they were losing people. His eyes narrowed and he shook his head.

Why was the world so hard? He stared at the fires engulfing the shattered vehicles. Flecks of gray ash were falling like snow, collecting in a fine layer on the hairs on his forearms. He brushed them off with a sick feeling in his stomach. Some of the ash was previously human. Why would anyone volunteer to be a helper of the Order or the Red Empire? All it led to was a nameless grave.

He'd seen a lot of death recently, but this was worse somehow. Tonight, it was cutting through him like a knife. What did it all mean?

Arthur looked into his eyes and squeezed his shoulder. "We'll have to make do with what we have." He flicked his gaze toward the lone surviving truck. "Let's get that rear tire quenched before the fire gets away from us. We can salvage the gear in that truck."

Chiara appeared at his side, her hand finding Anton's. She gave it a squeeze. She looked at him with wide brown eyes. "We made it through this. We'll make it the rest of the way."

Anton nodded. His grandfather and Chiara were right. They had to keep fighting regardless of the odds against them. Giving up was not an option. He steeled himself, reset his Order nightglasses, earbud and tactical headset, and smiled grimly at them. "Okay, let's get this done."

They ran to the sole remaining truck, followed by the other survivors. Only the gods knew how much time they had left before the vampires arrived in force.

They would have to be ready by then.

* * *

The SUV ground to a halt.

The vehicle's headlights illuminated a forest of boulders. Ahmad 'The Eagle,' Bakhoum, force leader of the only surviving force team of the Order of Thoth called to his team, "Out."

All four car doors opened, and his men stepped out onto the sands. Everyone wore Order nightglasses, rendering the desert into a half-lit twilight realm. Omar and Ali lifted electrobinoculars to their faces and scanned the surrounding desert horizon for threats. Mostafa and Youssef stood ready with H&K 417 assault rifles to meet any adversary. A long moment later, Omar and Ali chorused one after the other, "All clear."

Ahmad studied the fires to the north and stroked his bushy beard. His eyes narrowed and he turned and spat upon the sands. The vampires had drawn first blood. He turned away from the destruction, flicked on a tactical flashlight and advanced on the boulders. He swept the cone of light across the sand behind the first boulder. Arthur Slayne's intelligence was good. There was a secret entrance. His right hand held the flashlight steady and he tapped his earbud, activating communications across the nightglasses' tactical link. "Arthur, are you seeing this?"

"Got it. Yes, that's the entrance. Someone got here before us." Arthur paused for a long moment, then said, "Mekra's still at Dagestan, or on her way. The only other player who could know about the secret entrance is Chloe Armitage. Someone allied with her is down there. Perhaps the same force that snatched me from my airport in Nevada. Ahmad, we can't afford to be caught out in the open here or caught between two forces allied against us. We will have to find out who's down there, even if it's a case of make contact and withdraw. We need to know what we are dealing with. The secret entrance is also a potential escape path, but we can't use it, if it's blocked by someone, we can't fight our way through."

"You can trust my team, Arthur. We've got this. We shouldn't be more than five or ten minutes."

"Thanks, Ahmad. Get in and get back out as quick as you can. If there's anything down there, withdraw to the surface and we'll work out what to do about it. Don't take any risks you don't have too."

"You know me, Arthur. I'm a careful man," Ahmad replied and closed the call. He cocked his H&K MP5 submachine gun and called to his team. "Follow me, we're going in." With his submachine gun at the ready, he directed his flashlight down the secret entrance, and followed it into the shadows.

It was time to find out who or what was hiding in the Tomb of Ahknaton.

* * *

The five cowled figures vanished into the secret entrance.

James Haley shook his head. No matter how many times he witnessed Ramp masters move, it always sent an uncanny shiver up his spine. One moment they were standing around the hole, the next, they were gone. But for all their powers they hadn't seen him. The desert camouflage tarp he'd dragged over his osprey II had blocked any external detection while allowing for the full deployment of his craft's high-end sensor array.

A mile to the north, all hell had broken loose at the Temple of Thoth. A thin line of shattered vehicles burned vigorously near the ruins, lighting up the night sky for miles around. Five miles north of the temple ruins, a pair of shadowstars lay smeared across the dunes. Crane's forces had made contact with Slayne's and it looked like everyone had lost. A result that strengthened Chloe's hand in this high-stakes game.

His fingers flew over his keyboard. He prepared a report for Chloe and watched the tomb monitor like a hawk. It wouldn't take long for a team of Ramp masters to traverse the stairs and underground tunnel to Ahknaton's tomb. As to what would happen when they encountered the chameleons – his money was on the lizards. But he'd wait until he was sure of the result before finalizing and sending his report.

Before his eyes, the chameleon's vanished into hidden silence.

They knew the Order was coming.

Chapter Twelve

"A doubtful mind is a thinking mind." – The Way of the Faithful, a book of Red Empire lore.

$* * *$

Egypt, The Temple of Thoth, The Tomb of Ahknaton, September 15th, 00:15

Shemina cocked her head, listening intently.

An ancient instinct flared within her soul. She flicked her head toward the secret tunnel leading to the surface. Prey were moving along it at great speed. However, these ones could not be eaten, having undergone the change that spoiled the flesh and made them almost dangerous. She could send Gullette and Kavanne to kill them, but not this time. She coughed a quick command, leaped and twisted mid-air. She landed on the ceiling, spreading her hands and feet into wide pads, glossy black talons driving into the hard rock. She flattened herself and matched the ocher stone with tingling skin. Gullette and Kavanne joined her a moment later. They could stay immobilized in such positions for hours without discomfort.

Shemina waited, breathing quietly. Why reveal their presence by killing these few men? It was best to remain hidden, and wait until the vermin brought the Key of Ahknaton to the tomb. At the last possible moment, they would seize the Key and use it to restore the primacy of The People. The vermin would be no more, the changed prey animals would be no more. She would return the world to its natural order with The People at the apex of all life.

She'd completed the act of mating mere minutes before. After the event, she'd asserted her call; as a fertile and pregnant female, she could govern males at will. She had allowed both to mate with her. Neither would know who the father of her child was. Both would fight or die to protect her. It was for the best. Her ancestors would have driven the successful male off, or killed them to preserve their hunting territory. With so few of The People and so many prey in the world, such responses were no longer necessary.

A light appeared, washing over the floor of the chamber. A changed animal followed it. He stepped carefully into the room; a gun held high near his chest. He moved to the left, a second changed animal entered and moved to the right. Three more followed them, their weapons held high to cover the others, portable lights illuminating the chamber like a new day. They scanned the chamber, covering the floor, walls and ceiling with their hand-held lights. One stared straight at her, his face filled with searching interest, but not a scrap of recognition.

"There's no one here," one of the animals muttered.

Another animal, who seemed to lead the rest, turned his back to the device glued to the wall by Meat-that-talks, and made a slight gesture to one of the others. That one, walked casually past him as if examining another part of the wall. With his actions covered by the leader's body, he glued a similar device against the same wall facing the entrance into the depths beneath the temple. Now, there were two remote watchers in the chamber.

After a short time of examining the corners of the chamber, the central stone plinth, and a short distance into the depths of the temple, the animals left in silence, returning back up the tunnel to the secret entrance.

Shemina regarded the two devices attached to the wall and smiled; it wouldn't matter. It never mattered who was watching. It only mattered what was being done. All she had to do was wait, and whoever amongst the vermin or changed animals won the battle above, they would bring the Key to her. And when the time was right, when she was sure how to use the Key, then she would strike. Gullette's strategy had its merits. His only flaw was misunderstanding who amongst The People had the more powerful call.

A flaw now corrected.

* * *

The ancient ruins reached with stark pillars of stone into the night sky.

Three bodies lay beneath gray blankets before the temple: two members of the Red Empire, and one of Justin Blake's New Zealand cousins. Justin and his extended family stood in a semi-circle with their heads bowed in silent respect for their fallen relative, while the Red Empire fighters sang a soft song of lament and honor opposite them.

The fighter's notes carried on the night air, cutting through Justin's heart. His grief rising in a wave from deep within. His whole force team had died less than a week before. He'd lost so many; the wounds to his soul were still raw and bleeding, and now he counted his cousin Akira amongst the fallen. Justin pressed his lips together, his vision blurring. He took his nightglasses off and swept a big hand across his eyes, tears rolling down his cheeks.

Guilt knotted his guts. He'd invited Akira to this fight, and the young warrior had leaped at the chance to prove himself in battle. Perhaps he should never have asked him to come. Akira had followed Justin to his death, the boy had barely lived before he'd lost his life on a battleground far from home. Justin closed his eyes. The burden was almost too much to bear.

The Red Empire fighter's song came to a close. The most senior member of the CODEX guards, a man he'd met for the first time in the hangar at Aswan, approached and said quietly, "You shed tears for the fallen?"

"He was family," Justin replied, "and too young to die."

"He has died with honor, and joins the honored dead. He is beyond all suffering now."

Justin's lips curled into a mirthless grin for a moment. He was about to say something derisive that came from the pain within, but he steadied himself, took a heaving breath and said, "Thanks, Batbayar."

Batbayar gestured to the three bodies draped with blankets. "He walks with a new family now. He will never be alone nor unloved."

Justin paused, digesting Batbayar's words. He replaced his nightglasses and scanned the desert horizon. The two shadowstars that attacked their convoy had crashed to the north. Their enemy was out there somewhere. He took another breath and let it out. True grieving would have to wait. There was too much at stake, and letting his own pain get in the way of what he must do was not an option. He remarked, "The vampires are not far away."

"And we will fight them together," Batbayar said, his eyes filled with purpose, "as brothers in arms."

"Yes," Justin replied. He reached out his hand, and Batbayar grasped his wrist. Justin took the CODEX captain's wrist and stared into his dark eyes. "Brothers in arms."

"For honor," Batbayar declared.

Justin answered, "For victory."

"For honor. For victory," rolled around the diverse group of Maori, Order, and Red Empire Ramp masters.

Justin let go of Batbayar and they looked toward Arthur Slayne at the same time. Arthur was supervising the unloading of the one surviving truck thirty yards away. Ahmad and his team were returning within their SUV; the car's headlights resolving into a pair of white points across the sand dunes. Justin asked, "Shall we go."

Batbayar replied, "Yes."

It was time to discuss strategy with Arthur Slayne.

* * *

Justin and Batbayar's boots slid across the sand as they came down the short rise from the temple ruins.

The whisper of their boots mingled with the whispering voices behind the walls of his mind. Arthur glanced over at the approaching Ramp masters, and then stepped away from the growing piles of equipment salvaged from the shipping container. He faced Justin and Batbayar; their teams followed after them, forming a loose line ten to fifteen feet behind their leaders. To his left, Ahmad's SUV approached and pulled to a halt. The car's doors swung open and the Egyptian force team stepped out onto the sands. Ahmad strode forward, his four men a yard behind. They'd already provided their report over the tactical link. The Tomb of Ahknaton was as quiet ... as a tomb. Only a Shadowstone device was present to monitor what happened within the chamber. It had to be Armitage's work. Crane was both too direct for such an approach, and most likely lacked knowledge of the secret entrance.

Arthur looked across the dunes to the south, toward a row of hills arising out of the desert. Somewhere amongst the rising stone rested one or more agents of Armitage. Let them watch. He knew they were somewhere there, but did they know that Arthur knew? He thought not.

He called out to the crew unloading the container, "Peter, Li, Chiara, and Anton. Time for a quick meeting. We have to get this defense organized." Anton and his friends took up positions behind Arthur, seated upon the military lock-boxes piled upon the sand.

Arthur addressed Ahmad. "Ahmad, tell everyone what you found within the secret entrance."

Ahmad stepped forward, looked around the group and said, "The entrance was open when we got to it. We made our way down to the Tomb of Ahknaton, and there was no one there. We identified a Shadowstone listener-watcher glued to the wall facing into the base of the complex beneath the temple, and we placed a device of our own next to it. As we left, we counted three repeater stations leading back to the surface. Shadowstone are already here." He looked at Arthur and raised an eyebrow.

Arthur waved his hands apart. "Yes. Armitage beat us here, with one, or at most a handful of operatives."

"How can you know that?" asked Li behind him.

"If Crane had Shadowstone forces nearby, he would've used them to secure the site. That really only leaves Armitage, and she's the only one near Crane who knows about the secret entrance. Armitage is hiding her awareness of a second pathway into the Tomb of Ahknaton from Crane. She plays her own game against her king. Secrecy in positioning is a signature of her strategy."

Arthur turned to face Li and addressed her directly. "When Armitage forms an attack, you will not know which direction she will come from. It is a key strength of her technique."

He turned back to the group, and looked at Ahmad, Justin and Batbayar, the senior lieutenants within the remaining Ramp masters, and then gestured to the equipment piled behind him. "We need to get this setup and distributed correctly. I assume everyone is familiar with a layered defense, so I won't go into too much detail. I'd originally planned for a sequence of four redoubts at the first and second landings, at the far end of the Halls of the Gods, and lastly, at the third landing prior to the Chamber of Worlds. Given we were only able to salvage a quarter of our equipment, we have to adapt. We have two 7.62 minigun sentry weapons with one thousand rounds each. The ammo is high-explosive, armor-piercing, with every tenth-round pure silver. A good ammo load versus praetorians. We'll place one at the first landing and make that our first line of defense, and the second gun at the second landing." He looked at Batbayar and ordered, "Batbayar, you're on the sentry weapons."

"Got it," Batbayar answered.

Arthur pointed at a set of dark-green military boxes. "Claymores, and lots of 'em. They can be fired remotely, or by low-infra-red contact beams, and are loaded with standard ball bearings. No silver but they'll still make a mess of a vampire caught in front of one. Batbayar, they are for you too. I'm sure you can find ways to align them with our defensive positions."

Batbayar nodded his head and grinned.

Arthur looked around the group and tapped his nightglasses. "The SUV and the truck, are still operating as hubs and maintaining satellite links for our encrypted tactical network." He gestured toward a pallet loaded with shoe-box sized cardboard boxes, and glanced at the Red Empire fist team leader. "Bone Shredder, I need your team setting up a distributed network throughout the underground complex. I have fifty encrypted WIFI repeaters. Their batteries will run all night. As long as one is operational, our tactical communications network will be operational. You good to go with that?"

Bone Shredder nodded. "Your will, Shabbah al Ahmar."

Arthur pursed his lips for a moment. With battle against the vampires imminent, and the mantle of the Red Ghost upon his shoulders, the CODEX guards and the Red Empire fist team had quickly aligned with his leadership. He liked their attitude, even if it was a bit fixed in stone. He said, "Good man."

He glanced around the group. "While our nightglasses can work in thermal-imaging mode in total darkness, vampires can still see better than us. To take away their advantage, we'll place twenty-four-hour battery-powered lamps throughout the complex." He turned and gestured to Peter and Anton, and pointed at another pallet loaded with shiny black boxes. "You two. That's your job. Take the lights down and run them all the way to the Tomb of Ahknaton. I want this place lit up like a Christmas tree."

Anton nodded, and Peter said, "Right boss."

Justin raised a quizzical eyebrow.

Arthur looked at him, and said, "Justin, you and your cousins will build the redoubts. I have trolleys, empty sandbags and shovels. I haven't gone with portable armor because if we lose the first redoubt, the vampires could lift the armor, and advance behind it."

"Understood," Justin said.

"Or throw sandbags at us," one of Justin's cousins remarked sardonically.

"Let's hope they're reduced to sandbags as weapons," Arthur said, his eyes flashing. "Moving on." He addressed Ahmad with a pointed forefinger. "Ahmad, I need your team to set up a security perimeter." He glanced over his shoulder at Li and Chiara. "Li, set up for netmaster slash loremaster overwatch in Ahmad's SUV. Chiara you're Li's bodyguard. I want you near her and ready to fight at any time. If need be, use the SUV to withdraw to another more defensible position. Your number one goal tonight is to keep Li alive. Grab one of the SAWs, they have the same ammo load I used at the airport in Nevada." Arthur paused for a second, struck by the jarring oddness of knowing the equipment fit out of the Nevada airport trap, without being able to remember a single thing about what had happened that night due to a Shadowstone sleeper dart. He turned and looked directly at Li. "Li, please broadcast your findings over our tactical network. Watch our perimeter and keep us up to date."

Ahmad, Li, and Chiara all nodded their assent.

Arthur looked around the assembled Ramp masters and asked, "Any questions? Is everyone clear?"

The extended team responded with a chorus of shaking heads on the questions and affirmations on the clarity.

"Good. Keep the chatter up, and the coordination high. One last thing, no one goes into the Halls of the Gods without me. It's a maze of deadly traps, but since I've read the CODEX and the Papyrus, I know the way through. Is that crystal clear?"

More nods greeted his words.

"Oh, and one more last thing ... assume we're being watched. Keep the equipment in the boxes until you're underground. The less Armitage knows the better." He paused for a moment. "Okay, let's get to work."

Everyone moved with a purpose and Arthur rubbed his hand back through his salt and pepper hair. Everyone had a job and knew what they had to do. He picked up a satchel of shaped charges and a large-bladed shovel. He strode toward the entrance to the lower levels of the Temple of Thoth. It was open but only led into the first descending hall to the first landing. Someone had placed a false wall there generations earlier to hide the true depths of the Temple of Thoth. He had to take the wall down so everyone else could get to work.

The shaped charges should be enough to open the passage way into the depths of the Temple of Thoth. He walked through the broader team. The final conflict was upon them. It had come down to these men and women, at this place, on this night. They would defeat the vampires or humanity would lose forever.

This was humanity's last chance for independence.

* * *

Anton waved his flashlight into the Tomb of Ahknaton.

It was empty of all life. The air was as still as the inside of a grave. He consulted the hand-drawn A4 map provided by his grandfather. Yes, this was the end of the line. Soft footsteps brushed along the curving hall behind him. He glanced over his right shoulder. Peter approached him holding a nearly empty sack. Anton asked him, "How many lights have we got left?"

Peter lifted his sack, as if weighing it. "Half a dozen."

Anton folded the paper map and stuffed it into a shirt pocket. He flashed the light into all four corners of the room, and swept it across the ceiling. There was nothing there, and yet … something deep within him said otherwise.

He stepped warily into the room. Ancient Egyptian hieroglyphs covered the walls and told a tale of eternal life. A great rectangular plinth, four feet high and wide, and eight feet long dominated the chamber. The ceiling arched overhead. The architecture, like everything about the Temple of Thoth was vastly ahead of its time. Opposite the plinth was an open doorway, leading to a stairwell. He said over his shoulder at Peter, "I'm checking out the stairs."

"I'll start setting up lights," Peter said.

Anton passed around the far side of the plinth, ignoring the two listener-watchers attached barely a yard apart on the far wall. Armitage and Shadowstone would know they'd set up these lights. That didn't matter; if the fighting got this far down into the temple, the Order … no, not the Order anymore, the Ramp masters would be in deep shit, and would need every advantage they could muster.

He reached the stairs and mounted them. They didn't rise far, perhaps twenty feet at most. A long ten-feet wide corridor with an arched ceiling vanished into the darkness at the limits of his flashlight. Ahmad and his team were telling the truth and that was good to know. He pressed his lips together and frowned at his growing wariness. He took a breath and sighed. If Arthur trusted them, then they were trustworthy.

Anton flicked his flashlight over the ocher stone walls. Here was an escape pathway that popped out a mile south of the temple ruins. If he could get the surviving SUV, or even the truck near that entrance it would provide an escape route back to Aswan and from there to the world. All be it, an escape path watched by Armitage. He was damned if he'd enter a battle without an escape route for Chiara, Li, Peter and himself at a bare minimum. He frowned; he should take up escape paths with Arthur at the earliest opportunity. Fighting in a noble last stand where all the good guys died bravely while losing wasn't something he was willing to sign up for.

He turned on his heel, and made his way back down the stairs and into the tomb. The chamber was well lit, Peter had already emptied his sack and positioned the battery-powered lamps. Each unit was the size of a fist and had a base that would stick to anything after ten seconds of pressure. Peter had covered the corners, the entrance to the tomb, and the middle of the plinth. He looked at Anton and stated, "All done."

Anton nodded, and Peter turned away and vanished into the curving hallway back into the temple complex. Anton moved to follow his friend, and a shiver crawled up his spine. There it was again – the feeling that something wasn't quite right. He took a deep breath and exhaled, settling his nerves. Surely it was just the anticipation of battle. But something ... he reached for understanding ... there was something on the edge of his awareness ... tenuous ... like plunging his hand into endless shadow and groping for a thing unknown. He ramped hard. The room snapped into sharp clarity, ocher dust motes floating within the newly installed illumination. There was a whisper of a hint of something dreadful within the tomb.

It was undeniable, someone or something was watching him, and yet – there was no one there. Anton's eyes flashed to the high-tech devices glued to the wall. Was it just that? No. A camera and a microphone couldn't spark the visceral shiver crawling up his spine. The tomb was alive with something that creeped him out.

He started forward, suddenly wanting to be as far from this cursed chamber as he could be. He murmured, "Peter?"

"Anton?" Peter called from the hallway. He appeared a moment later, filling the doorway with his broad shoulders. "Are you okay?"

"On my way!" he replied breathlessly.

Peter clamped a big hand upon his shoulder and said, "Seriously, are you okay?"

Anton shook his head and said, "It's nothing. This place gives me the shivers."

"It's just stone."

"Yeah," Anton said, easing his way past his friend. "Let's get back to the others."

"Sure," Peter said.

Anton strode forward, leaving the strange tomb behind him. With an ounce of luck, he'd never pass that way again. He lifted his pace to a jog ascending the curving hall in front of Peter. Whatever he'd left behind in the Tomb of Ahknaton, it gave him the shivers. Was he jumping at shadows? Was their one escape route out of the temple already compromised?

He couldn't be sure one way or the other.

* * *

Arthur adjusted Anton's nightglasses and handed them back to him.

He instructed his grandson. "You should be able to pick up feeds from our cameras located throughout the temple complex. They're all numbered and you can rotate through them like flipping through a rolodex."

"Thanks," Anton said, fitting the glasses onto his face. He looked at his grandfather and asked, "… what's a rolodex, old man?"

Arthur's fist lanced forward in a surprise blow, hitting him hard enough in the left shoulder to hurt.

Anton winced, rolling his shoulder while looking at his grandfather ruefully, and said, "Okay, okay. Not too old then."

"Right. Now we've got that clarified – pay attention. Pick up cameras one and two."

Anton tapped the side of his nightglasses. He was only using the right side of the frame. A black 'pirate,' patch continued to shield his slowly healing left eye. He'd lost the organ in battle to the vampire, Marcus Drake, at Armitage's manor in Yorkshire, England. He focused on the first camera feeds with his remaining eye; the nightglasses responding automatically to his eye movements. The feed expanded in high definition revealing a view along the barrels of a 7.62mm minigun. The sentry weapon sat in the middle of the first landing, its barrels facing up the first descending hall from the main entrance. It was the first defense the vampires would encounter.

"Check cameras three and four." Arthur instructed.

Anton rolled his nightglasses forward to the third camera. A forest of claymore mines faced up the second descending hall toward the first landing. They were the second line of defense. He checked the fourth camera. It showed the same view, but further back toward the second landing.

"Camera five."

The second sentry weapon, identical to the first but located in the middle of the second landing and guarding the second descending hall.

"The next four cameras."

Anton cycled through the views. The second landing opened onto a spiral stone staircase down to the Halls of the Gods. The four cameras covered a sequence of angles on the stairs. The stairwell was undefended, except for a pair of mini-claymores secreted just within the entrance from the base of the stairwell into the Halls of the Gods.

"Camera ten."

Anton cycled to the next camera. It faced onto an open space just within the entrance of the Halls of the Gods.

"Crane will stage at the entrance to the halls before he sends his forces through," Arthur said. He shook his head. "We won't be able to stop them noticing the middle hall is the one we used to pass through the maze of traps."

"We left a heat trail, didn't we?" Anton said. "There will be enough of a difference in heat between the halls for the vampires to detect our passage. But hang on a second, we can mask that." He called out to his friend, "Hey, Peter, have we got any flares?"

Peter looked up from where he was loading a multi-grenade launcher with silver flechette rounds. He put the weapon down on the stone floor and rummaged within a satchel near his feet. He pulled out a plastic packet of six handheld flares and lifted them up with a grin. "I picked these up in Arthur's plane. I figured we might need a backup light source in an emergency, but they burn hot enough to be dangerous if you don't know how to use them. We could use these to mask a heat trail."

Arthur raised an eyebrow and said, "Outstanding! Peter, take them back through the maze and use them to mask which entrance we used into the Halls." He lifted his right forefinger. "Take care with the pressure plates in the other halls. The first trap on the left is a crushing wall; on the right its a caustic pit that opens beneath your feet."

"Got it," Peter said, rising to his feet.

"... Ahh ..." Arthur said. "That's facing into the maze, not from this direction."

"Got it twice," Peter said with a glance back over his shoulder as he hurdled the line of sandbags and vanished.

Arthur caught Anton's gaze and said, "Let's continue, check cameras eleven and twelve."

"Got it. That's here, covering the approach from the maze to our first redoubt."

"Camera thirteen."

Anton flicked to the next camera. It hung above a set of sand bags in a square chamber, facing a rising hallway. He remarked, "It covers the third descending hall down to the third landing and our second redoubt."

"Can you see weapons in the third descending hall?"

"No. There are more claymores, but they're hidden."

"Correct. Cameras fourteen and fifteen."

"Views of the spiral staircase beneath the secret door in the third landing floor. No weapons there, except a mini-claymore on a low-infrared beam just before the entrance into the Chamber of Worlds."

"Hopefully a surprise for Crane. The last person through has to arm it."

"Will they push us back that far?"

"Assume the worst, Anton, and then work back from there. My starting assumption is that Crane kills us all, reaches the Chamber of the Metaframe with the Key of Ahknaton and changes the world to empower himself and defeat Mekra. My strategy is always to assume the worst and mitigate the risks of that occurring. Basically, eliminate the possibility of failure until success is the only option left. So, Anton, what weapons do we have in the Chamber of Worlds?"

"Only what we bring with us. If we're pushed back to there, it'll be a hand-to-hand melee."

Arthur nodded once. "And, our final seven cameras?"

"One of them is Ahmad's, positioned in the Tomb of Ahknaton facing the exit to the Curving Hall. There is another at the base of The Chamber of Worlds facing into the Curving Hall from the bottom of the Chamber. That will give us warning if someone is coming up from the Tomb to the Chamber of Worlds. Camera eighteen is facing down into the long passage to the secret entrance a mile south of the temple. Then there are another four attached to the truck covering the above ground approaches to the temple ruins."

"Good, Anton. You've got it all laid out." He paused for a moment, as if considering something. "Are you still getting odd feelings?"

His grandfather had spared ten minutes to return to the Tomb of Ahknaton and check out Anton's uncanny feeling about the place. Arthur had poked around the chamber, then they'd left without any firm conclusions. His second visit had left him cold; no shivers, nothing out of the ordinary. He put the whole thing down to pre-battle nerves and his grandfather had agreed. Anton answered, "No. I'm cool."

"Remember to fight from joy. Combat is a release. The wild Ramp is best when it comes from joy, and protecting those you love. Keep that foremost and you'll be okay."

Anton nodded. "You really do understand how to fight this war don't you?"

Arthur frowned slightly, clapped Anton on the right shoulder with his left hand and remarked ruefully, "I'm a shadow of my former self."

Anton made to reply, but Arthur squeezed his shoulder and said, "Okay, now make sure everyone else is up to speed on the cameras, weapons and our final evacuation path through the secret entrance."

Anton stilled his next question and said, "Yes, Arthur." He pushed up from the wall of sandbags and began moving through the group, checking everyone's nightglasses to ensure they were operational, and they were fully across the camera network, weapon emplacements, and their sole escape path. He looked back once over his right shoulder. His grandfather was watching him, a warm smile gracing his lips.

Warmth flooded Anton's heart. His grandfather really cared about him. He cared about them all. He was doing his best to make sure they could not only survive but win this fight.

It was inspiring.

* * *

Three shadowstars and five osprey IIs thundered down to the dunes.

Cornelius sat within the cockpit of his command shadowstar drone and stared at the stony fingers rising from the sand. He'd been to the temple ruins multiple times over the last millennia. He'd built the fake wall with his own hands to hide the main part of the underground complex. He'd made certain researchers and treasure hunters of ancient Egypt artifacts had uniformly avoided this site as a 'non-place,' unworthy of investigation.

His agents had ensured that no one launched, funded or staffed an expedition to examine the 'innocuous,' ruins thirty miles west of Aswan. He had kept the Temple of Thoth secret from the world. A place overlooked by everyone in favor of more fruitful locations of historical and archaeological interest.

The wreckage of Arthur Slayne's convoy glowed a dim red nearby, vague wisps of gray smoke rising from the shattered vehicles. A single truck bearing an empty shipping container and a late-model SUV remained intact – but deserted. Anyone who'd survived Haras' cruise missile attacks had gone underground.

He fully expected Slayne had demolished his ancient wall within the last two hours and the Ramp masters had occupied the lower complex like a nest of rats within a sewer.

He would eradicate Arthur Slayne and his followers like the vermin they were. Unfortunately, the pressure of time had not allowed for the acquisition and deployment of nerve agents that would have made this a quick and decisive battle. But still, he had many weapons on hand to crush Slayne and his accomplices.

His strategy was simple: break Slayne and his forces as quickly as possible. Then draw Mekra and all her spawn to the temple and destroy them with the nuke. Losses didn't matter, he could replace everyone in time. If necessary, he could rebuild the Vampire Dominion from the ground up. As for the Key of Ahknaton, it remained in reserve on a titanium chain around his neck, but to play the ultimate trump card, he had to secure possession of the underground temple complex.

He glanced at Armitage seated beside him. She arched a quizzical eyebrow at his studied regard. His chief enforcer was a weapon par excellence. She was his greatest asset and his best defense. With Haras

Mosule, Shen Zhen, and the combined forces of Africa and Asia, he'd marshaled sixty praetorians in addition to his generals and himself.

This night, the elite of the Vampire Dominion would go to war. He broadcast a command across his tactical network, "Prepare for battle. We will begin our engagement of the enemy in ten minutes time." He flipped a switch. The command drone's canopy lifted up and glided backward. He regarded Armitage again. She nodded and leaped from the drone to the sands below. Crane lifted his great bastard sword from the rack behind his head and followed her a moment later.

It was time to end Slayne once and for all.

* * *

Praetorians rushed over the sand.

Chloe Armitage watched their endeavors carefully. She couldn't afford for Crane's most loyal soldiers to be too successful. They had to bleed and bleed some more, to create an opportunity for Crane to die. If Crane defeated Slayne and his forces within the temple complex, then she'd lose her immediate opportunity to rid herself of him.

She strode forward over the dunes, entering the above-ground ruins of the Temple of Thoth. A broken archway reached for the night sky with crooked fingers carved from stone. Just beyond its base was the floor of an ancient antechamber, its walls and ceiling now vanished. Slayne's forces had swept the sands away, revealing a rectangular opening ten-feet wide and thirty-feet long. She walked around to the far end of the rectangle, stepping past shards of wood ripped from the opening in the floor.

With every sense on a hair-thin trigger, Chloe dared a glance within. She'd read the detailed and precise instructions of the Papyrus of Hakron the Scribe, but Hakron hadn't fully described such mundane features as the first descending hall. From where she stood, Chloe couldn't see the first landing. The curve of the ceiling occluded the far end of the hall. Someone would have to go down the hall and find out what waited at the first landing. She smirked. That would be an excellent job for a squad or two of Crane's soldiers. Let them find out what Arthur Slayne had prepared for them. After all, she was protecting the King's life. It wasn't her job to be the sharp end of the spear tonight. She edged to the left and walked back to where Crane was supervising his forces.

Haras Mosule and Shen Zhen stood in front of Crane. The former had showed up as Crane's forces landed. Emerging out of the night, no worse for wear given the loss of his two shadowstars, and flanked by his three personal praetorian guards. All the generals had their personal guards, except for Chloe, she'd never needed anyone else to protect her. It was another way in which she was different from the rest of the Vampire Dominion leadership.

A praetorian lifted his gaze from a ruggedized laptop and called out to Crane, "Sir. They're running a tactical network through hubs in the surviving vehicles. They can reach the satellite networks."

Crane gestured toward the truck and the SUV. "Kill those satellite links. Destroy the hubs."

Praetorians rushed to obey. Tearing away antennas and ripping out electronic kit from the two surviving vehicles. That would cut Li Wu off from wider network resources. It should harm her ability to function. Should being the operative word. Chloe had her doubts.

Crane gestured to the north-east and shouted, "Mekra's in the air and will arrive in less than half an hour!" Crane issued more commands. The other two shadowstars rose into the night sky. They would provide top cover versus Mekra's approaching force. His high-flying drones carried stinger II missiles and their 30mm Gatling cannons for air-to-air combat. Did Mekra inherit any special equipment from the Red Empire? They would soon find out.

A squad of praetorians opened two military lock boxes. One loaded with hunter-killer drones, identical to the ones used in the Minneapolis sewers by Shadowstone. The other carried four larger drones about the size of a basketball, fitted with sensors. Once activated, the hunter-killers would kill anything human they found in their vicinity. The hunter-killers rose like a swarm of oversized insects and flew off to the temple's entrance. Each one carried a miniature shaped charge sufficient to cut a deep hole through a human skull. The four sensor drones followed in their wake. Even if the hunter-killers didn't eliminate any of the Ramp masters, the sensor drones would reveal whatever was waiting for them. Slayne would struggle to keep his secrets.

Chloe frowned; the temperature was dropping precipitously. She looked skyward, the stars had vanished, replaced by towering thunderheads.

Crane noticed her skyward gaze and lifted his face to the heavens. He looked back at her and asked, "What's with this unseasonal storm?"

Crane had come too late to southern Germany in 1945 to witness the rise and fall of the eldritch storm over the Phoenix citadel. Chloe stared up at the writhing clouds. Was history about to repeat itself? Surely not, the inverted pyramid above the Chamber of the Metaframe was not the same pyramid built and operated by Siegfried von Frankenstein. There would be no interdimensional portals tonight. No monstrous human-skins occupied by living darkness. She closed her eyes for a moment – no child adepts of the Metaframe saving the world. No, tonight would be simpler. She replied, "Probably nothing."

A great fat drop of rain appeared out of the darkness and splashed over her left cheek. She reached up with her right hand and brushed the water away. Hakron had mentioned a storm in his papyrus. The storm had preceded the appearance of the Metaframe. The same had happened over Germany in 1945, and now, more than eighty years later it was happening again. The use of the Metaframe was imminent.

Maybe not nothing?

She glanced across at Crane. He was still staring into the sky, a hint of titanium chain at his throat. He had the Key of Ahknaton resting just above his heart. While he possessed it, he was first in line to use it. And time was running out for anyone else to push him aside. If she was ever going to take the Key, Crane would have to die first. Jean Philippe Allemande's curse also forbade her to touch the Key of Ahknaton.

Chloe looked toward the entrance down into the temple complex beneath the ruins. The last mini-flier vanished from sight. She took a breath and sighed, and gave a silent prayer to whatever gods might be listening, for something she'd never prayed for before.

For Arthur Slayne to win.

Chapter Thirteen

"Where you believe your defenses are most certain, from that direction your nemesis will strike." – The Way of the Faithful, a book of Red Empire lore.

* * *

Egypt, The Temple of Thoth, The Halls of the Gods, September 15th, 02:10

A cloud of hunter-killer micro-drones filled Anton's nightglasses.

"Shit!" Anton remarked to no-one in particular. Everyone crouched behind a waist-high wall of sandbags at the rear of the Halls of the Gods. The drones were flying down the first descending hall toward the first landing. They flashed past the camera mounted on the first sentry weapon. The 7.62mm mini-gun system remained silent. The sentry system couldn't recognize a flier that could fit into Anton's palm as a target.

"Li!" Arthur called out from behind Anton.

"Already on it!" Li replied calmly. She sat on Anton's immediate right, her back to the sandbags, slightly hunched over the loremaster laptop resting on her thighs. Her eyes staring behind her nightglasses, and whatever she was doing was beyond anything Anton could grasp.

The swarm of fliers advanced. Anton tapped his nightglasses, flipping through the cameras along the flier's route to the first redoubt. The drones had already flown down the second descending hall, and were flitting past the second sentry gun like a swarm of metallic insects.

Arthur called out, "They'll go for your head. You can cut them down mid-air. Ready your blades."

Anton drew the Blue Dragon from its scabbard across his shoulders, the magnificent blade gleaming beneath the lights Peter and himself had installed throughout the underground temple complex. He was ready for whatever might come at them. He glanced down to his right, Li was like someone frozen, ramping to accelerate her mind across the tactical network. Bone Shredder's Red Empire fist team had laced the underground temple complex with WIFI repeaters to extend Li's reach over the tactical network. Could she kill these fliers before they arrived? If she couldn't – how many would die?

Twenty-one other fighters drew weapons behind the wall of sandbags. Anton stared at the three open archways of the Halls of the Gods facing onto the redoubt. The three separate arched shadows were a mere sixty feet away from the sandbags. The middle opening was directly in front of him.

"Ten seconds," Arthur called out.

The swarm raced down the first spiral staircase, reached the entrance to the Halls of the Gods, and split up into three groups, each mini-swarm hurtling into one of the available paths. The hall's ancient traps provided no defense against such an attack. The first flier zipped out of the middle exit with a whirring hum, heading directly for Anton.

Anton lifted the Blue Dragon above his head, poised to strike. More drones than he could count emerged from the three archways, and rushed the sandbagged redoubt.

Li called out, "Got 'em!"

The humming drones faltered, dipped and fell to the floor. Their rotors flickering left and right like spasming limbs, collecting like flotsam washed ashore on the far-side of the wall of sandbags.

There was a collective sigh of relief within the group of Ramp masters.

Arthur pointed over the wall at a larger drone, and said firmly, "Those drones had cameras. Crane knows exactly where we are."

Anton looked over his shoulder at his grandfather. "What can we do about that?"

Arthur clapped a hand on Anton's shoulder and said, "We hold this position. He still has to come to us." He leaned forward and clapped a hand on Li's shoulder. "Great work, Li. You saved us again."

She looked up and said, "Just doing my part."

Arthur regarded her steadily and said, "You're the only one who can do what you do." He glanced around the nearest team members, Anton, Peter and Chiara, and stated, "It's essential you keep Li safe."

Li put her laptop aside, rose to her feet, slapped her hand on the handle of the Green Dragon scabbarded at her waist, and declared forthrightly, "I can fight too."

"I know you can, but," Arthur waved his hand across the assembled fighters, "so can everyone else, but only one of us is a loremaster."

Li paused and tilted her head slightly. Her lips pressed into a thin line, but she didn't dispute Arthur's claim.

Arthur nodded and flicked his gaze across Anton, Peter and Chiara's faces. "Are we clear?"

Peter answered, "Crystal."

"Got it," Anton said.

Chiara nodded silently, placing a hand on Li's shoulder and giving it a squeeze.

Everyone had their mission. Some more than one when the vampires came. Anton looked around the circle of Li, Chiara, Peter, and Arthur. He cared about the rest of the broader team. He didn't want any of them to die, but these four before him – they were his family now. He would do his best to keep all of them alive.

And right now, that was all that truly mattered to him.

* * *

The black tarpaulin flapped beneath the growing storm.

Cornelius stared at the ruggedized laptop resting on a hastily erected portable table. Suddenly, the screen turned to a gray haze of flickering static. The praetorian operating the drone swarm looked up from his laptop and said, "Sir, the drones are lost."

"I can see that!" Cornelius snapped.

"Someone hacked our drones." His soldier explained quickly.

Armitage remarked sagely on his left, "That would be Li Wu. Despite the loss of global network resources, she cracked our drone's encryption. She is quite the genius. Really, Cornelius, you should consider capturing and turning her. She'd be a real asset."

Cornelius stared at his enforcer for a moment. "Li Wu is not the mission here. Eliminating the Ramp Masters before Mekra arrives is." He strode away from the portable table hosting the laptop, and advanced upon his two remaining generals. "Haras, Shen. Are your men ready to fight?"

Haras slapped his right hand against his burnished breastplate. "Of course, my king."

"We are hungry for blood, my lord," Shen Zhen remarked in the polished tones of an Oxford don. He'd spent a dozen years in England during the 1860s shortly after his conversion before taking the mantle of Cornelius' agent in the far east. He waved a casual hand at two ranks of waiting soldiers. "My men are ready."

"Excellent," Cornelius said. He'd watched the drone swarm progress carefully. There were a pair of sentry weapons backed by claymores within the upper parts of the temple complex. Whomever went down first would die. He paused for a fraction of a second. He could send in Armitage. She'd be the only one with the capability to get past the deadly machines, but if she failed, he'd lose his most powerful defense. No, it was best to send others, take losses, and progress to final victory with Armitage at his side.

Cornelius addressed his two generals. "Do we have any long chains?"

General Shen Zhen remarked, "Sir, we have long chains for securing loads in both our ospreys."

"Fetch them and bring them here."

Shen signaled two of his personal guards to the task and they blurred away. Twenty seconds later, they returned bearing four spools of stout gray-metal chains.

Cornelius surveyed Shen's two lines of soldiers and requested, "I need four good brave men."

Shen turned to his troops and shouted, "Let the Crimson Dragons step forth."

Four praetorians marched forward from the front rank and strode over to Cornelius and the two generals. They saluted Shen and bowed to Cornelius. As one, they declared, "We are ready to serve."

Cornelius considered silently; *I hope you're ready to die.* He lifted his face, and stared sternly down his nose at the four soldiers. "Tonight, we shall eradicate the last of the Ramp masters and make the world forever safe for all vampires. For those of you who survive tonight's battle, I shall bestow on you broad estates, where you shall hunt at leisure and live the lives of immortal gods. Are you ready to win such eternal gifts?"

The men nodded vigorously and replied with various assents.

"Then stiffen your sinews, harden your faces, bare your fangs, and prepare for blood."

The praetorians growled, flexed their fingers, bared their fangs, snarled, and hissed with violent anticipation.

Cornelius lifted his left eyebrow and indicated General Shen Zhen with a wave of his hand. "Your men are to be connected to these chains so that we can pull them to safety, and allow their vampire vitality to heal their bodies if they are wounded."

Shen Zhen nodded and gave the orders. The four spools were set up on frames so they could run out whilst the near end remained locked above ground. He gave a final order, and the squad of four praetorians blurred forward and vanished through the temple entrance into the first descending hall.

A moment later, harsh thunder erupted from under the sands. Yellow-silvery light flashed and strobed, creating a pulsating glow around the entrance. The first chain stopped moving, while the other three chains unreeled at speed. More gunfire erupted from the first hall, silvery-yellow light flashing from the entrance. Two of the chains stopped suddenly, leaving only the fourth slithering over the sands; the spool unraveling like a crazed fisherman's reel. There was another brief round of minigun fire, strobing silvery-golden light emanating from the entrance, then the fourth chain came to a sudden halt.

Cornelius stared at the entrance for a brief moment. He turned to Shen Zhen and remarked, "Pull back the chains. Retrieve the bodies." His gaze swung between his two remaining generals. "Now we have four shields. Take the first sentry weapon down, and get us inside the temple."

"Yes, Sir," the two men chorused.

He stepped back, and glanced over his left shoulder toward the north-east. The storm clouds blocked out all the stars. Still, there were no incoming aircraft to see. Despite the fact his tactical helmet provided live feeds from the two remaining shadowstars executing lazy circles three miles above the temple, he couldn't help himself – he had to check with his own eyes.

He couldn't allow Mekra to wedge him into a two-front battle against Slayne and herself – that would be suicide. There was a very real risk that Mekra wouldn't take the bait of his forces at the temple. She might hold back. She might leave members of her swarm back at Matahat al Diydan. Perhaps his single nuclear warhead wouldn't be enough to wipe her and her abominable progeny out of existence.

He lifted his gaze to the heavens. Fat drops of rain splashed off his helmet and face. The storm was uncanny, sending an inexplicable shiver up his spine.

Upon arrival at the Temple of Thoth, he'd vowed to preserve the Vampire Dominion. But something beyond his understanding had changed. The balance of risk had shifted.

Cornelius took a deep breath and exhaled, staring up at the gathering thunderheads. A great bolt of lightning slashed across the sky, thunder crashing in its wake. He had to use the Key of Ahknaton to save his life. No matter the losses amongst his generals and praetorians; he had to break Slayne's defense and access the Chamber of the Divine Engine of Thoth. Once there, he could use the Key to reshape reality in his favor. Even if he was the only one left standing with the Key before Mekra arrived, he could still win.

His shadowstars sent an automated report, appearing on his helmet's heads-up display. Mekra's aircraft were already on the way. His high-flying shadowstars had managed to pick them up on long range radar despite the eldritch storm. They were two hundred miles away and approaching at speed.

Mekra would arrive within another twenty minutes.

* * *

"Contact," Peter half-shouted to Anton's right.

Li placed her loremaster laptop atop the sandbags and Anton watched from above her left shoulder. The sentry weapon at the first landing whirred into action. Golden fire bloomed from the spinning barrels. A steam of fiery-silvery light appeared as a string hanging on an invisible point in the distance. The gun swung left and right, sparks flickering off stone and metal within the hall. Black-armored human forms blurred, spun, and veered in every direction, desperate to avoid contact with the deadly stream.

One fell, then two more, and finally the last fell backwards in a pink mist to land upon the ocher stone of the first hall's floor. A counter in the bottom right-hand corner of the screen registered the remaining ammunition in the first sentry weapon's magazine, '785 of 1000.'

"Four down," Peter remarked with an insouciant grin. "What ... fifty odd to go?"

"At least, but not much more than that," Anton agreed. There'd been much discussion amongst the group as to Crane's forces. There'd been a short window of opportunity before the vampires had discovered and destroyed the cameras and external satellite links on the surviving truck and Ahmad's SUV. But, before they'd gone down, it seemed they were facing three shadowstars, five ospreys, and approximately sixty praetorians. Arthur had remarked that all of Crane's generals were in play. Crane was throwing everything he had left at them. He was desperate, but would he make a fatal mistake?

"Look," Li said, gesturing at the screen. "They're dragging back the bodies."

"It won't be due to a sudden attack of compassion on the part of Crane," Arthur opined behind Anton's right shoulder. "He has a use for the corpses."

Li looked over her left shoulder at Arthur. "Like what?"

"A big bag of toughened meat covered in two layers of nano-ceramic armor. My guess is the next squad will be coming down the first hall with," and he air quoted with his fingers, "'vampire shields.'"

"Vampire shields!" Justin remarked sarcastically from the right corner of the redoubt. "Everyone should have one."

"Well, my guess is that they're about to become fashionable," Peter said dryly. He remarked a moment later, his voice quieter, "Does anyone have ammo that can get through three layers of nano?"

The silence stretched without answer.

Anton asked, "Surely, they won't throw themselves into the mouths of our guns?"

"They won't," Arthur said. "That was just a touch. Now the fist will come."

Anton pressed his lips together into a thin line. The micro-fliers and sensor drones had effectively scouted the path to the first redoubt for the vampires. There'd be no surprises for Crane and his followers. They'd already seen the weapons emplaced to guard the two descending halls and the spiral staircase down to the Halls of the Gods. The vampires should be able to avoid most of the weapons. Crane's main force would be mostly intact when they hit Arthur's first defensive position. He lifted his SAW; one of the six they'd salvaged from the wreckage of the convoy. It had a single two-hundred round satchel magazine filled with 5.56mm HEAP and silver hollow-point rounds. When the vampires arrived, it'd be his primary weapon.

Until he ran out of ammunition.

* * *

A forest of claymore mines covered the second descending hall.

Chloe watched with keen interest as a squad of praetorians attempted to clear the area with targeted machine gun fire. The first man to attempt the second hall lay slumped against the far wall, bleeding out from a dozen bullet holes in his chest armor. His three compatriots were darting forward, firing, and then returning before the sentry gun on the second landing could respond. At least that was Crane's current plan. She leaned to her left slightly and whispered into his right ear, "You could try grenades. It might be faster."

Crane harrumphed. "Without doubt. Slayne might be willing to risk collapsing this hall with mass claymore firings, but I am not willing to block my one path to his position." He threw his hands up and glared at Chloe. "It's not like we have a choice. There are no other ways down to the Chamber of the Metaframe. We need to eradicate Slayne and the rest of his force before Mekra arrives."

Chloe pressed her lips together and nodded in silence.

Gunfire cracked through the air in front of them. One of the claymores exploded with a thunderous crash of metal hail. Chloe flashed her left arm up to cover Crane's chest. He turned his face toward her and remarked confidently, "We are out of range."

"You must not risk yourself!" Chloe insisted in a half-shout.

Crane's lips curled, but he said nothing.

Chloe lifted her right finger to point to the stone ceiling and casually circled it. "Do you have an ETA for Mekra?"

"Fifteen minutes."

"We need to make haste."

Crane pressed his lips into a thin line. "Indeed." He commanded in a loud voice, "Bring up the chains."

The three praetorians stepped back from the edge of the second descending hall, thin lines of gray smoke rising from their gun barrels. They turned and regarded Crane and Chloe. Their faces pale, frozen, and stiff within their helmets. Their jaws just visible beneath their visors covered with a thin sheen of perspiration and ocher dust. Their ready postures spoke volumes of their dark resolve. Rapid boot falls filled the first descending hall, accompanied by the rattling of chains.

It was almost musical.

Chloe regarded the three praetorians and smiled quietly.

Your next for the Slayne meat grinder.

* * *

A squad of praetorians probed the spiral stairs down from the second landing.

Anton tapped his nightglasses, updating the feed displayed on the lens in front of his right eye. The vampires had taken out the second sentry gun and destroyed the claymores in the second descending hall. The camera and tactical WIFI network above the spiral stairs had vanished. The vampires were removing all the Ramp masters' carefully emplaced equipment as they advanced.

Peter remarked beside him, "I think they've lost eight praetorians."

"I concur," Arthur agreed from where he stood behind Anton.

"Are we repeating Thermopylae?" Peter asked the room.

"Leonidas lost, but the Greeks won in the end," Justin observed from the right side of the redoubt.

The praetorians reached the middle of the first spiral stairwell without incident and continued their advance.

Li looked up from her laptop. "Half the Red Empire is spread around the world, they'd be the 'Greeks,' in this scenario."

Batbayar declared from the left side of the redoubt, "Our forces will self-organize and continue to fight."

"If Crane is Xerxes, what does that make Mekra?" Peter asked.

"Medusa," Anton remarked dryly, his attention fixed upon the foremost praetorian. The leading vampire was almost at the bottom of the spiral stairs. He frowned; things were about to get hot.

The lead praetorian stepped through an invisible sub-infrared beam. Two mini-claymores mounted to the left and right of the entrance to the Halls of the Gods fired simultaneously. Caught from both sides in a hail of ball bearings, the vampire vanished in a pink mist. As the crimson smoke cleared, his boots – cut off at the ankle – remained standing on the ocher flagstones.

"I count nine," Peter said casually as he positioned his SAW and his multi-grenade launcher on the top of the sandbag wall. His battle and throwing axes remained sheathed within his leather combat vest.

"Agreed," Arthur said. He continued in a quiet voice. "Li, could you please initiate the sonic disruptor." Li flicked a switch on a black box behind the sandbag wall. It emitted a dull hum. Arthur said, "Thanks. Keep an eye on it and make sure it stays with us as we move." He paused for a moment and then said in firm tones to the full group, "Take your positions and prepare for contact."

Anton lifted his SAW and rested it across the top of the waist-high wall of sandbags. He glanced at the ammo counter on top of the squad automatic weapon; it read '200.' He only had the one magazine of ammunition, one of the consequences of only a single shipping container surviving the destruction of the convoy.

He hunkered down behind the wall, sighting along the barrel into the center of the middle archway leading from the Halls of the Gods. All of

Ahknaton and Hakron's traps remained in place, perhaps they'd take out a few of the vampires before they reached the first redoubt.

Anton flicked his head left and right, checking on the rest of the group. Batbayar, Bone Shredder, and the rest of the Red Empire fighters crouched to the left, covering the left and middle hall archways with a mix of a pair of SAWs and assault rifles. Justin Blake, Anita Chang and Justin's Maori cousins hunkered down with Ahmad and his team on the right side of the redoubt, to cover off the right and middle archways with similar armament. Li sat with her back to the sandbags, her loremaster laptop open before her, attempting to penetrate Crane's tactical network while keeping an eye on the rest of the temple complex. They couldn't rule out that another attack would come from below via the secret entrance. While Arthur didn't believe that Chloe would take action from that direction while Crane lived, he'd still insisted on Li watching the approach – just in case he was wrong. Chiara knelt on the other side of Li, with her SAW positioned on the wall. Arthur rested on one knee behind them, his right arm horizontal, his .50 caliber auto-pistol in hand.

The cameras in the spiral staircase went dark one after the other. The cameras facing the entrance to Halls of the Gods evaporated in a hail of gun fire. The vampires were on the same level now. Anton steadied his breathing. One way or another, things were coming to a close. He kissed his right fingers and put them out to his right. Chiara's fingers brushed against them. He glanced at her, gripped her hand and she gripped back with equal ferocity. Her eyes lit with love and courage.

The final fight was almost upon them.

* * *

The scent of prey was dead ahead.

Cornelius could smell the humans on the other side of the halls, and yet there was ... he curled his lip in irritation and remarked caustically, "What on Earth is that irksome buzzing noise in the background?"

"A device to obscure their heartbeats so we can't count them and know where they are," Armitage suggested sagely behind his left shoulder.

Cornelius curled his lip and looked over his shoulder at her. "Despite Slayne's clever obfuscation, we will still win."

He studied his surroundings. The entrance to the Halls of the Gods was a broad chamber, easily a hundred feet across. Two rows of thick pillars divided the chamber into thirds, each space leading to an archway into the ancient trap filled maze. His gaze caught momentarily on the ubiquitous ancient Egyptian hieroglyphs upon every wall and pillar.

Cornelius frowned and sniffed the air, deploying his vampire senses to their maximum effect. There'd been a lot of human traffic over the last couple of hours, surely, they'd left a discernible trail. But the Ramp masters had swept the floor recently, and ... they'd used flares to mask any heat trail. He uttered with disgust, "Slayne!"

He checked his feeds. His shadowstars were running on automatic, slaved to his command helmet. Mekra's force was approaching effective missile range. His drones had preset commands to attack as opportunity presented itself. However, if Mekra and her forces survived they'd land within twelve minutes. There was no time to waste.

Cornelius turned around and faced the forces that had filed into the room. Shen and Haras stood to the fore. His last two generals commanding his remaining praetorians. He'd used Shen's to reach the halls, it was time to call on Haras and Force-Africa to take them through to the other side. He stared at Haras and ordered, "Haras, I want three of your best to penetrate the maze and find our way through."

"Yes, my king!" Haras responded, slapping his left chest with his right fist. He turned to his troops and uttered three names and a quick command. The indicated soldiers stepped forward; their light machine guns carried at rest, their black armor gleaming beneath the Ramp masters' lamps. Haras looked to Cornelius and declared, "We are at your service, my king."

"Indeed," Cornelius almost whispered. In a louder voice he addressed the three men. "Fulfill your oaths. Earn your immortality. Find us a way through this maze." He turned back to the entrances into the halls. Black armored forms blurred past him and vanished through the archways.

He took a breath and let it out. The first scream, a hideous yell of ultimate torment from the right-side hall, arrived a moment later. He frowned; he'd have to wait for all three praetorians to fail before he could initiate the next run through these traps. He glanced to his left. Armitage had a glimmer of a coy smile upon her face. He snapped at her, "Are you enjoying this?"

She looked at him. Her coy smile broadening into a grin. Her eyes lighting up with avid anticipation. She said, "Cornelius, you know I love a challenge. I'm just anticipating the coming fight."

"And the blood."

"Always the blood."

A great crash echoed from the left-side hall, and the outer halls stilled into silence. Armitage looked to the center archway and raised an eyebrow. Cornelius followed her gaze. He had to keep moving forward. Mekra was still alive and on her way. Would the surviving praetorian find a way through Ahknaton and Hakron's traps in time? He turned to Haras and indicated with a flick of his hand to find three more men. They had to find a viable path through the traps.

At any cost.

* * *

Four praetorians appeared out of the center hallway.

Their light machine guns sprayed bullets at the defenders, stitching holes across the wall of sandbags and striking sparks from the walls behind the redoubt. Anton pulled the trigger on his SAW. The weapon burst into life, thrumming with each expended round. Its flaming throat mirrored across the redoubt as every defender opened fire with every weapon they had to hand.

A string of incoming bullets ploughed into the sand bags in front of him, kicking grit against his nightglasses. He held his finger hard against the trigger while leaning down to the left, keeping his one good eye above the rampart to correct his aim.

The vampires thrust forward, veering violently to the left and right. Streams of fire from across the redoubt lanced in silvery strings across the chamber, tearing chunks from their armor, sending whips of blood against the walls and ceiling. The four vampires faltered, and then slumped to the stone floor in spreading pools of dark-red gore.

Anton lifted his trigger finger and eased back on the SAW; a thin wisp of gray smoke issuing from the raised barrel. He checked for movement in front of the redoubt – there was none. The defenders had killed the first squad of praetorians.

Peter remarked from Anton's left, "Two earlier on the traps, plus another four. I count fifteen dead vampires."

"Concur," Arthur remarked dryly from behind Anton.

Anton pulled his squad automatic weapon up and checked the ammo counter. He was down to one hundred and fifty-six rounds out of two hundred. He pressed his lips together. They were going to run out of ammunition before they ran out of vampires.

"When will they come again?" Chiara asked.

"Very soon," Arthur said quietly. He called out a moment later, "Reset for the next attack."

Anton considered the fallen praetorians. The first attack had been a probe. Crane was under time pressure. He was desperate. The next attack would be full on. He called out to the group, "They'll come harder next time." He crouched behind the sandbags and waited for the next attack. He glanced around at his friends. They were all doing the same: getting ready for the next onslaught. If Crane could waste four of his troops in a probe of their defenses. What would he bring next? Anton's one good eye flicked left and right expecting an attack from any of the three halls. He took a breath and let it out, steadying his nerves. Crane would send in his best on the next thrust. That could only mean one thing – Armitage.

Arthur shouted, "Prepare for contact!"

The battle was about to get bloody.

* * *

Crane curled his lip and snarled.

Chloe arched an eyebrow. Slayne's force had clubbed the first squad of praetorians like baby seals. But what did Crane expect? There were twenty plus elite Ramp masters in a defended position. Of course, he was going to take losses attempting to breach it.

She pressed her lips into a thin line. Like Crane, she didn't want Mekra to wedge her against a surviving force of Ramp masters. Mekra would arrive within another ten minutes. Chloe would have to move this little soiree along. She'd read Hakron's Papyrus and the CODEX. She had full knowledge of the all the traps in the maze through all three halls. She could penetrate one of the side halls and come upon Slayne's defensive position from an unexpected angle. She looked at Crane and said, "Send three squads through the middle archway. I will go through the left-hand side and come upon the defenders while they're focused on your praetorians."

"You'd use my men as decoys?"

Chloe shrugged. "I can break their defensive line, but even I can't do it alone."

"And how will you get past the traps in the maze?"

Chloe raised a quizzical eyebrow. "Trust me. I'll work it out."

Crane frowned for a moment, then nodded and signaled his generals. Three new squads lined up, guns ready, their eyes focused on the middle archway.

Chloe addressed the dozen soldiers. "Give me three seconds and then make your move. Come out the other side with guns blazing."

She whirled and blurred through the left archway. The traps reflected the genius of Ahknaton and Hakron. They'd lasted for thousands of years, and could reset after use. She leaped over the smashed remains of a praetorian. A crushing ceiling had squashed him into a nano-ceramic coated smear an inch high over the floor. A set of almost invisible foot plates triggered the trap. She blurred through, adroitly avoiding the triggers. A brief moment later, she bypassed a caustic pit, a flaying net, and pairs of scything blades. She came to a halt a dozen feet short of the exit, and out of sight of the defenders.

She took a breath, drew her auto-pistols from their holsters at her hips and prepared to dive into her supreme Ramp. The praetorians rushed along the middle hall, their boots stamping against the cold stone. Gunfire erupted in the chamber in front of her. She ramped hard, and blurred forward into the archway facing the redoubt.

Chloe halted on the threshold into the chamber. Concentrated fire from the defenders ripped into the praetorians rushing out of the middle hall. No one was looking at her. She spread her hands into the arms of a 'V,' targeting the Ramp Masters to the left and right of Anton Slayne. Her original plan for a subtle elliptical attack against Crane remained in place. The young Slayne couldn't kill Crane if he was dead. She needed her unwitting agent alive and well. His wild Ramp and dragon blade were just the things to pit against her king.

She pulled her weapon's triggers, firing both auto-pistols on full automatic, sending round after round of hyper-velocity ammunition into the Ramp master's defensive position from near point-blank range. She jigged her hands left and right, tracking targets who fell away in clouds of pink mist littered with bone fragments and gobbets of red flesh. She snarled and grinned with triumphant purpose. This was her element. This was what she was best at.

Killing her enemies.

* * *

A ribbon of blood slashed across Anton's SAW.

Deeply ramped, he flicked his gaze to the right. Plumes of blood and gray matter filled the air behind the sandbags. Beyond the redoubt's wall stood a single darkly-armored figure in the right-side archway. Anton yelled, "Armitage!" and blurred backward, swinging his SAW around to bear upon the new threat. Armitage continued firing left and right, taking down men from the Red Empire, Justin and Ahmad's teams.

Anton pulled his trigger. The SAW burst into life sending rounds streaming toward Armitage. Arthur's right hand appeared to Anton's left, his auto-pistol crack, crack, cracking with each hyper-velocity round. Armitage vanished back into the relative safety of the maze; Anton and Arthur's bullets crashing into the walls within the hall entrance.

Anton dropped out of Ramp. A shroud of silence fell over the redoubt, broken only by hard breathing and muttered curses. The praetorians had pulled back, leaving eight new black-armored corpses strewn like storm debris across the flagstones before the redoubt. Anton swept the interior of the redoubt with a glance. Bone Shredder and the rest of his team were all dead. Each one with the back of their skull blown out by one of Armitage's head shots. Justin and his surviving cousins, regarded the still bodies of another three members of their extended family with eyes filled with shock. Ahmad rested his right hand on his one surviving team mate's left shoulder while wiping the back of his left hand across his eyes – at Ahmad's feet rested the other three members of his force team.

Anton took a shuddering breath.

Armored boots resounded from the depths of the middle hall.

"Reset," Arthur called out. He grabbed Anton's left arm, pulling him over toward the right side of the redoubt. "We take Armitage. Go wild!"

Anton shut out the recent losses and called upon his love of his friends and family. A golden light bloomed deep within him, surged up his spine, and he rode it into the wild Ramp. Time slowed precipitously. He dropped to one knee, his SAW propped on the sandbags, facing the right-side archway. His world snapped into razor-sharp clarity. The hieroglyphs on the walls and pillars bursting with color and detail. The sharp notes of sweat, blood and spent ammunition filled his nostrils. A driving need to save his friends flooded his heart.

Praetorians burst from the middle archway on his left, their weapons spitting fire and lead. Anton ducked, just far enough to leave an inch and a half of his face above the sandbags, watching the looming right-side archway with his one good eye. Bullets zipped overhead, grunts and screams came from the middle archway as more of Crane's soldiers fell to the defenders' trenchant return fire.

Armitage remained hidden.

Anton glanced toward his grandfather, and they uttered at the same time, "Left!"

They swung about.

Armitage appeared within the left-side archway; her auto-pistols aflame, sending volleys of hyper-velocity ammunition rocketing inches above the sandbag wall. Anton fired back with his SAW. Arthur's auto-pistol cracked in violent accompaniment. Armitage dove forward into the room, tumbling out of sight. The praetorians pushed through the gates of hell before the middle of the redoubt, snarling and growling, machine-guns firing on full auto.

Arthur vanished and then called out a half-dozen yards behind Anton, "Retreat!"

Everyone blurred backwards at once, bent hard forward to lower their profile, scuttling like crabs drunk on lightning into the third descending hall. Anton went with them, firing his SAW wildly behind him, trying to provide whatever cover he could salvage from the situation.

He blurred toward his waiting grandfather. Arthur flipped his auto-pistol to full-auto, and fired in a wide swathe taking out the first praetorian to reach the sandbags.

Anton risked a backward glance. The praetorians were rushing the redoubt's wall, rounds zipping through the air above his head and ricocheting off the stone walls to the left and right. There was no sign of Armitage – she'd disappeared.

Arthur turned and ran a yard off Anton's right shoulder. They rushed after the rest of the Ramp masters; bent down, their right hands held horizontal behind him, spending his last rounds upon the pursuing vampires. Other Ramp masters opened fire from the second redoubt, covering their retreat.

His grandfather held a remote control in his left hand. His thumb tapped down upon a red stud. The sandbags erupted behind them. Batbayar and Bone Shredder had placed a dozen remotely-controlled claymores within the forward face of the redoubt. The chamber beyond the wall vanished within a cloud of gray smoke, reddish-yellow sand, and screams of agony and rage.

Anton ran down the third descending hall toward the third landing and the second redoubt. It was the last defensive position they'd been able to prepare with their limited equipment and time. Would it be enough to stop Crane?

No one could say, but he was sure he'd soon find out.

* * *

The reverberations of the claymores died away.

Arthur dove over the second redoubt's sandbag wall and rolled to his feet on the other side. The landing at the top of the third descending hall remained hidden in a cloud of dust and smoke. He lifted his auto-pistol and ejected the spent magazine. He took his last magazine and snapped it home. He had twenty shots left. He'd have to make them count.

He glanced around him, momentarily unsure who had survived so far. Anton, Peter, Li and Chiara were all okay. Justin, Anita Chang, and one of his Maori cousins were checking their weapons. Ahmad and one of his offsiders, and Batbayar and two of his CODEX guards knelt behind the wall of sandbags, their weapons trained up the hall.

The rest of Arthur's original force lay where they'd fallen at the first redoubt. One of Justin's Maori cousins hadn't made it to the second redoubt. They had started twenty-three strong, now they numbered thirteen. Two to one odds was the accepted baseline for vampires against Ramp masters. They were holding their own but at this rate they were going to lose before they forced hand-to-hand combat with the vampires. A necessary final circumstance if they were going to kill Crane and seize the Key of Ahknaton.

Arthur took a deep breath and sighed; they had to do better.

Justin looked across at Arthur and said, "We're running low on ammo."

"We have to make the most of what remains and get their numbers down to where we can handle them," Arthur said, his gaze flicking over the survivors.

Batbayar frowned. "That is already fated, Red Ghost."

Arthur nodded. He turned and tapped Li on the shoulder. "Take a position down the spiral stairs in the Chamber of Worlds." He glanced at Chiara. "Go with Li, and keep her alive."

Chiara looked at her SAW. "I've only got twenty-eight rounds left."

"So be it. Go."

The two young women left, vanishing down the spiral staircase in the floor of the chamber behind the redoubt's sandbag wall. Counting himself, he had eleven Ramp masters left to defend the next attack of the vampires. He took a position to the left of Anton and said quietly, "Ammo?"

"Fifty-six rounds left," Anton replied.

Peter hefted his MGL. He'd loaded it with silver flechette grenades. A certain kill for a direct hit upon a vampire. The focus of the defenders was intense, for all their losses, everyone was ready to fight.

The falling dust at the top of the hall, swirled and parted, dark-armored forms emerged from the cloud. Wall to wall praetorians came down the hallway. The front rank hung limply, carried as shields by the vampires behind them. Arthur snapped his auto-pistol out to arm's length, it was probably the only weapon that would be effective against three layers of nano-ceramic armor, and shouted, "Fire!"

Every weapon burst into life.

* * *

Lamb fired his MGL at the legs of the front rank of vampires.

Chloe leaped, rising horizontally in the air, arms outstretched toward the defenders, as soon as her field of fire cleared the front rank, she'd pull her triggers.

The grenades hit the floor bursting into clouds of silver flechettes, ripping through the legs of the front praetorians. The front rank collapsed, becoming a wall of corpse shields and paralyzed vampires.

She pulled the triggers of her auto-pistols, their muzzle flash strobing along the hallway, hypersonic rounds flashing down range toward the defenders. A head exploded to the right of Lamb, sending a plume of blood and brains against the far wall. She walked her guns left to Arthur Slayne and right to the other side of the second redoubt. The defenders were already firing back at the massed praetorians, even ramped, they couldn't move quickly enough to escape her shots.

Chloe continued to rise. Streams of slivery-golden machine-gun fire ripped up and down the hallway beneath her, praetorians and defenders attacking with everything they had. Slayne's hypervelocity rounds slashed up the hall, cutting through the second rank of praetorians.

She focused on the elder Slayne. He was blurring left and right with his speed talent, vibrating like a tuning fork. She sent her last round at his head.

It zipped past his ear and he spun away. She dropped her empty auto-pistols, and twisted a hundred and eighty degrees to face the ceiling; hit it, pushed hard, and flew back over the intervening ranks of praetorians. Her back shivered involuntarily at the momentary exposure from a necessary withdrawal before she reached the relative safety at the top of the hall. She landed on her feet and twisted around to face down the hall.

Rounds slashed through the air near her head and she dodged left and right. The praetorians broke before the defender's hellish fire, and retreated back up the hall toward her, dragging their wounded with them. She blurred ahead of them to the right, and joined Crane and the other generals beyond the reach of the defender's weapons.

The elder Slayne commanded from the other end of the hall, "Smoke!" Four grenades flew up the hall, bounced, landed, fizzed, filling the third descending hall with thick plumes of gray smoke.

Chloe regarded the billowing fumes, and glanced at Crane. A delaying tactic? Crane had no time to waste; Mekra was almost upon them. Crane stared at the swelling clouds of gray smoke; his face hard as stone. She drew the Red Dragon and flourished it with a grin.

She was still his protector – for now.

* * *

The last machine-gun fell silent as smoke clouds filled the hall.

Anton blinked at the dead lying slumped upon the stone, or half-propped where they'd fallen against a wall. All the Maori cousins were dead. Batbayar was whispering something to himself as he knelt next to the last two CODEX guards. And Omar was rocking slowly, head down over the corpse of Ahmad, 'The Eagle,' force leader of the Egyptians.

Justin wiped the back of his hand across his eyes, glanced at his smoking assault rifle and whispered hoarsely, "I'm out."

The growing despair in Justin's voice cut through Anton like a knife. He shut his eyes for a moment; his heart filled with dread. So many had died, there were so few left to fight Crane, Armitage and the rest.

Their will to fight was dying with their friends.

Anton's grandfather lifted a hand-held siren and flicked a switch on its top. It shrieked into life as he tossed it over the redoubt wall. Against the high-pitched noise he called out, "Anton to me. The rest withdraw to the Chamber of Worlds."

Anton dropped his empty SAW and strode toward Arthur, coming to a halt a foot before him.

His grandfather held out a compact UZI 9mm submachine-gun drawn from a hidden holster. "Here take this."

Anton raised his eyebrow at the unexpected weapon, took the gun, and slipped the safety off. "What's in it?"

"High explosive armor piercing rounds mixed with silver ball on a one-to-one basis. One clip with twenty rounds. A two-second burst." His right hand flashed up, his auto-pistol barked once, leaving a swirling vortex in the gray smoke filling the hall. A single scream of pain erupted from the top of the hall and then faded. He glanced at the ammo counter on his pistol and remarked casually, "Four shots left."

Anton glanced at the spiral staircase behind them, the last of the survivors vanished down the stairs. He took a deep breath and regarded his grandfather. "Just the two of us. What is it – a final last stand?"

"Not quite so dramatic, Anton. Just a little something to give them a reminder that we're alive and we oppose them."

The siren started winding down.

Voices echoed beyond the smoke. Crane was rousing his troops for a final push. Anton glanced at Arthur and remarked quietly, "Looks like morale might be a problem for them."

"Well, they are vampires," Arthur whispered back.

"Will they still come?"

"These one's will."

"Are we going to get out of this alive?"

Arthur reached out and grasped Anton's shoulder. "Yes." He nodded emphatically; his eyes lit with a wild fire. "We must win this."

Anton paused for the briefest of moments and thought of Li, Chiara, and Peter, all waiting down on the next level in the Chamber of Worlds. He replied, echoing his grandfather's fervor, "We must survive."

Arthur lifted his remote control and said almost sotto voce, "One left," and glanced down at the sandbags with a raised eyebrow.

"They won't fall for that twice."

Arthur grinned. "Of course, but they'll pause." His eyes flicked up to the ceiling. A set of mini-claymores, easily missed, lay flat against the ceiling in a row two yards forward from the front of the wall of sandbags. He leaned in and whispered into Anton's right ear, "They'll switch on a second after the initial claymores fire. I'm sure we'll catch a few more once they break the infra-red beams. Our job is just to keep them bleeding and hesitating while we withdraw to the Chamber of Worlds." He squeezed Anton's shoulder. "There are still too many of them."

Anton's eyes widened in solemn commitment. "What if I berserk?"

"Anton, in this place … we'd never get you back." Arthur closed his eyes for a moment and then whispered, "If all is lost. Go for it. Kill as many as you can before you die. It's what I'd do."

Anton took a breath and steeled himself. If it came to that, he'd rather die fighting than any other way. The Blue Dragon would sing, and shout, and clash and clang. Blood would spray and run in rivers, and his enemies would know they fought a Slayne as they died in pieces upon the cold stone of this ancient tomb. A sob caught in his throat. He gritted his teeth and forced it down deep. There would be none of that. He hardened himself to defend his family regardless of the cost.

His grandfather pulled him close in a fierce hug, and whispered, "You'll do okay."

Anton hugged him back.

Arthur kissed Anton's forehead and whispered, "I would've saved William and Anna if I could've been there. I would've saved you all."

"I know," Anton said. "I know."

Anton closed his eyes and hugged his grandfather tight, a heartfelt warmth flowing between them.

They were family.

* * *

A high-pitched wail emerged like a banshee from the hall.

Cornelius regarded the roiling wall of smoke with hard eyes. It was impossible to see or hear what was happening at the bottom of the third descending hall. Was Slayne rearming? Setting a bomb? Withdrawing to a third redoubt? He had no answers, and even worse, his men were beginning to falter in the face of the enemy. They needed something to stiffen their spines and reinvigorate their killer instincts. He glanced to his left, snarled, raised his voice above the incessant siren, and demanded, "Shen, Haras, lead your men. Use the dead as shields and break their line."

Shen's face froze momentarily, then he shouted, "Your will, my king."

Haras slapped his chest emphatically and stood in front of his men.

Cornelius regarded his enforcer and declared, "Armitage, attend to me." He drew his great Damascene blade and flourished it high, and shouted, "My men. Seize your honor. Seize your immortality. Fulfill your oaths given on distant battlefields. One and all, I rescued you from certain death with the gift of my immortal blood. You have enjoyed centuries of life by my hand. Repay your debt and be free for all of eternity. Stiffen your sinews. Harden your hearts. Drink deep from the well of your blood lust and kill, and kill and," he uttered with a final shout, "KILL!"

He took a position within the middle ranks, Armitage stepping up to his side. He would be as much at risk as his troops. It was time to get this done. It was time to cut through the defenders and make his way all the way down to the Chamber of the Metaframe.

Cornelius glanced at the feeds from the shadowstars in his tactical helmet. Mekra's force was coming in four Russian built petrels. The Red Empire aircraft could carry fifty to sixty vampires each. They passed within missile range of his shadowstars' weapon arrays. An attack by either force upon the other was imminent. If he couldn't destroy Mekra in the air, and she landed with a sizeable number of minions to throw against his remaining troops – then he was done.

His only hope was the Metaframe, and to reach it, the Ramp masters must die.

Every last one of them.

* * *

The portable siren expired.

The hallway fell into deathly silence. Anton stepped away from his grandfather, and backed up against the far wall. He lifted Arthur's 'hold out,' weapon in line with his face. He sighted down the top of the small submachine gun at the middle of the billowing smoke clouds.

Anton wondered briefly what the 9mm UZI's hyped-up ammo could do against nano-ceramic armor. He hoped the little gun would be enough, they had to give the vampires reason to 'pause.'

The weapon felt completely inadequate in his hands. He gritted his teeth; and looked across the hall at his grandfather. Arthur had flattened himself against the hieroglyphs on the wall. His right hand raised. His .50 caliber auto-pistol with four remaining shots pointed up the hallway. Anton had studied a little bit about ancient Egypt before this secret war had burst into his life. Directly above Arthur's head was Thoth, overseeing and recording the weighing of a dead man's heart against the feather of Maat. If the man's heart was as light as Maat's feather, he would pass safely into the afterlife, if not, then the ever-hungry jaws of Ammut waited beneath.

Anton pressed his lips into a thin line at the implied omen, faced resolutely up the hallway and ramped hard.

The gray smoke billowed like a curtain caught in an errant breeze. The vampires erupted from it, light-machine guns blazing; rushing forward in a black-armored wave. Arthur's pistol cracked. Anton squeezed the UZI's trigger and it stuttered into life, sending a burst of rounds in a horizontal strip up the hallway. Arthur caught his eye. It was enough. They fled to the stairwell. Arthur must have triggered the first set of claymores as the second redoubt's wall erupted behind them with a thunderous explosion. Anton dove for the stairwell and escape, his grandfather a step behind him. Bullets stitched lines above their heads across the rear wall.

Behind them, the mini-claymores in the roof triggered in a concussive blast. Howls of rage and agony followed on the heels of Anton and Arthur's flashing feet. They arrived at the bottom of the stairwell and entered a short foyer. It opened up into the inverted pyramid known as the Chamber of Worlds. The rest of the survivors waited for them in two small groups.

Empty guns set aside and edged weapons drawn. Anton drew the Blue Dragon clear of its scabbard and joined Chiara, Peter, Li and Justin on his right. Omar and Batbayar stood with Anita Chang on the left side of the level facing the foyer. Counting Arthur and himself there were only nine Ramp masters left to fight Crane's vampires.

Arthur drew his katana and said quietly, "Now it gets interesting."

"Really?" Peter remarked from the side.

The team fell into silence.

* * *

Missiles streaked across the storm swept sky.

One of Cornelius' two remaining shadowstars fell to Earth in a cloud of glittering debris. Of Mekra's petrels, only two were still in the air. The other two lay burning upon the sand dunes miles from the Temple of Thoth.

Cornelius turned his attention away from his tactical helmet's heads-up-display. Mekra had positioned three of her petrels in a shield protecting the fourth. The fourth petrel was still flying, ergo, Mekra was still alive and without doubt was bringing her best warrior cohort with her to the Temple of Thoth. She was four minutes away from landing above Cornelius' head. He had the same amount of time to break the back of the Ramp master's resistance and reach the Chamber of the Metaframe.

He regarded his forces. Twenty praetorians gathered above the spiral staircase leading from the foot of the third descending hall into the fabled Chamber of Worlds. He'd left thirty-eight behind in various states of blood-soaked disarray within the halls and chambers behind this location. The battle had claimed nearly two thirds of his force. He listened intently for movement down the staircase and within the chamber beyond. Once again, a discordant background hum greeted him. The Ramp masters had retained their sonic disrupter and continued to mask their heartbeats. He couldn't be sure how many still opposed him. In any event, numbers no longer mattered. Time had run out. He called out to his men, "Who still has ammunition?"

Two men raised their light-machine guns. The rest remained silent. Cornelius swung a forefinger from the first man to the second, and declared, "You're first. You're second. Fire as soon as you have targets." He looked over to his generals and ordered, "Haras, Shen, you're three and four. Lead your troops through to the Chamber. Armitage, you're with me. We'll take the middle rank."

The first two praetorians carried their light machine guns at their hips. They had all of the remaining ammunition; the rest had run out during the previous encounters with the enemy. They descended the spiral stairwell, their boots resounding off the stone. His generals followed; pairs of praetorians followed them in turn, all with their edged weapons drawn.

Cornelius nodded to Armitage, lifted his right hand to the remaining ten praetorians, inserted himself in front of their ranks and stepped into the stairwell. Armitage joined him on his left. They followed the front half of his force down the stairs. His remaining troops followed hard on his heels. They reached the bottom of the stairs and spread out into a short foyer leading diagonally into a top corner of the inverted pyramid that comprised the Chamber of Worlds. There was no sign of the Ramp masters, but the insistent drone of the sonic disrupter was nearby. *Hell,* he thought. They could've fled deeper into the temple complex and formed a third redoubt at Ahknaton's tomb. If they had, that would be disastrous for his cause. He had neither troops nor time to break another defensive line.

His first praetorian stepped forward. His light machine gun extended at hip height; finger on the trigger and ready to fire.

Another mini-claymore detonated at the threshold of the chamber, vaporizing the lead praetorian. The rest pushed forward with snarls and yells. A lance of machine gun fire speared at point-blank range into the second praetorian. He fell backward as if tugged by a rope, a line of blood-splashed holes across his armored chest plate. Cornelius craned his neck over the heads of his troops. The young Morte dropped her weapon and leaped backward out of sight.

His generals, Haras Mosule and Shen Zhen, led the next eight praetorians into the space beyond. Cornelius emerged into the great chamber. There were seven Ramp masters arrayed in two groups of three and four to the left and right. He snarled once, then shouted, "There are only seven left. Crush them!"

A sudden breeze lifted a wisp of hair beneath the edge of his helmet.

Cornelius whirled, and looked up.

* * *

Peter and Justin attacked from above.

They'd rubbed out the thin line between audacity and desperation. They'd wedged themselves in the corner where the walls and ceiling met above the entrance; taking advantage of the cover provided by the sonic disrupter to remain hidden from the vampire's superior hearing. Peter's only regret was that he didn't have a grenade to hand. A lamentable lapse he set aside with a rueful grin. His silver-laced blades would have to be enough.

He landed fully ramped, a thin patina of dust rising around his boots. The plan was simple; drop down from above and take Crane out in the first couple of seconds of contact with the enemy. Peter's job was to keep Justin alive while he slaughtered Crane. Then, they'd flip out of the kill zone to buttress Anita, Batbayar and Omar against the surviving praetorians.

Crane whirled, his great Damascene blade rising.

Justin landed in front of Crane, his gleaming katana slashing down toward Crane's helmet.

The two blades met, sparks running along the length of Justin's blade as the superior metal of Crane's weapon attacked its edge. Justin's great shoulders bunched, bearing down, his blade angling Crane's defense away and driving toward Crane's face.

Peter's double-bladed axes flashed and whirled, catching three attacks directed at Justin's back, and sending them away.

Armitage's dragon blade flashed backward, blocking Justin's descending killer strike upon Crane's head.

Peter snapped his double-bladed axes up into guard position, and whirled around. Combat-experienced vampires surrounded him, swamping him with targets.

An embarrassment of riches...

Metal clashed against hard metal. Justin grunted in frustration. Crane swore. The praetorians shouted, "Save the king!" while Armitage glided like a wraith within the melee.

Peter hammered the nearest praetorian backward with the tip of an axe. The creature fell against his comrades fouling their attacks. Peter whirled around, his heavy blades slashing through deadly arcs. Could he still keep Justin alive long enough to kill Crane?

Their plan had shot through the hand basket and gone straight to hell.

* * *

Anton wild ramped.

He deliberately focused on Peter and Justin, he had to save them. With this focus, he had the best chance of maintaining control and avoiding a rampant berserk state. He blurred forward into the nearest group of praetorians, his grandfather on his left, and Chiara and Li on his right. Li had stowed her loremaster laptop into a slim backpack strapped across her shoulders. The Green Dragon was in her hands, raised above her head and poised to strike. Beside her, Chiara rushed, still carrying the twin blades she'd picked up in the dungeons of Matahat al Diydan.

The vampires massed before them. In their midst, Justin and Peter fought in a flurry of clanging strikes and counter-strikes. To their right, the vampires extended on the other arm of the first level of the chamber against the flashing blades of Anita Chang, Omar from the Egyptian force team, and Batbayar, the final member of the CODEX guards.

Anton arrived within range of the nearest praetorians. The Blue Dragon crashed down in a mighty diagonal strike. The praetorian opposite snarled, his long sword rising to block and deflect Anton's attack. The Blue Dragon hit the lesser blade and passed through it in a cloud of super-heated metal. The impact shifted the strike to the left; Anton's blade shearing through the vampire's head instead of his shoulder. The blade continued down from left ear to right throat before slicing off the vampire's right arm in a spray of blood. The foul creature spun away, dropping to the polished stone floor, gouting blood from the lower part of his head and shoulder.

Another armored vampire took his place, his long blade smashing with power against Anton's Blue Dragon sword.

Anton defended and deflected, looking for the next opportunity to attack.

The final battle had begun.

* * *

Justin's blade shattered into a plume of glowing fragments.

A whip of Justin's blood lashed across Peter's face. A red line appeared, running from shoulder to hip on Justin's back. He slid apart in a shower of blood and entrails.

Justin's blood ran down Crane's great Damascene blade. The vampire king snarled, whirling to face Anton and the rest. His praetorians crowding around Peter, separating him from Crane.

His friends smashed into the praetorians on the other arm of the first level, trying to reach Crane through his soldiers.

Peter gritted his teeth. He stood alone, surrounded by vampires. He whirled, his axes tearing through wide circles. Ten praetorians were upon him from the chamber foyer. His axes smashed against the nearest blades, sending them aside. An itch ripped between his shoulder blades. He whirled again, striking instinctively with his double-bladed axes in a head-chopping scissor.

Armitage appeared in front of him. Her Red Dragon blade flashing impossibly fast, left and right, batting his axes harmlessly away. Her right hand appeared on his vest, scrunched the leather in an instant, and then flicked his near three-hundred pounds of muscle and bone above and behind her.

Peter launched into the air, his arms and legs flailing wildly. The nearest wall loomed before him and he smashed into it.

Everything went dark.

* * *

Peter flew through the air and crashed against the wall opposite Anton.

Justin was already dead, lying on the floor in two gory parts gouting blood. His killer, Crane, remained surrounded by a wall of praetorians. Armitage leaped high into the air from their midst, flipping in a somersault beyond the Ramp masters on the other arm of the first level, landing behind Anita, Omar, and Batbayar.

The battle remained in front of the foyer; the descending levels of the inverted pyramid untouched by the trenchant mayhem erupting on the first level. Anton batted strikes from two praetorians away to the left and right, his gaze searching for Peter. His friend lay slumped against the wall not far from Armitage. He didn't rise, his heavily-built body lying deathly still. A hollow shock rose within Anton's heart. He was losing control of his wild Ramp. He could easily turn into a killing machine as dangerous to Arthur, Li, and Chiara as the vampires he opposed.

He had to maintain control. He bit down upon the agony of Peter's loss and focused on saving his grandfather, Chiara and Li. Fresh golden power surged through his limbs and he pushed hard into the vampire wall in front of Crane. The Blue Dragon grinding against lesser blades, stripping metal in showers of sparks. To his left and right, armor ripped, blood splashed, and metal tore through flesh and bone in a shower of blood.

Arthur, Li, and Chiara, claimed a praetorian each.

Anton gritted his teeth and pressed forward.

Perhaps, there was a chance to snatch victory against the odds.

* * *

Reflexes!

Chloe's eyes widened in disbelief. She'd defended Crane against a killer strike from pure combat-honed instinct. Well, she'd get another chance to let nature take its course within the next few minutes. She'd stay away from Crane's side and focus upon thinning the herd. The fewer potential opponents left, the fewer to get in her way when she reached the Chamber of the Metaframe with the Key of Ahknaton in hand.

She completed her leap and landed on her feet behind three Ramp masters. She recognized them all. There was Anita Chang from Australia, Omar El-Masri from the Egyptian force team, and Batbayar from the CODEX guards.

The first was engaged with general Mosule's praetorians, the latter two were whirling away to face her. She advanced upon them, delving deeply into her supreme Ramp. The Red Dragon rose and stilled, poised above her right shoulder like a living promise of destruction. She sank into overflowing joy; the sheer beauty of grace and power filling every moment of her being. Golden light coruscated along nerves, sinews and bones, welding her body into a coherent whole dedicated to a single task: violence.

With great sweeps left and right, Chloe cut the cords adhering El-Masri and Batbayar from the world of the living. They fell away in sheets of blood and entrails. In battle, death was her constant companion. She withdrew backward for a moment, and stepped out of the supreme Ramp.

It was best to conserve her strength for the inevitable battle to come.

She surveyed the melee. Anita Chang moved fully defensive as the sole Ramp master on Chloe's side of the first level. Diagonally opposite on the other side of the first level, the Slaynes, Wu, and Morte continued to survive against general Shen Zhen and his praetorians. As always, her gaze returned to Crane. Fourteen praetorians surrounded him, plus his two loyal generals. Sixteen vampire fighters faced off five Ramp Masters. Against any regular Ramp masters, three to one odds would be game over with victory for the vampires. Against the two Slaynes, Wu, and young Morte, it was an even match.

Crane glared at Arthur Slayne, a flash of decisive recognition sweeping across his face.

Chloe frowned, what had Crane just seen?

* * *

It all clicked together.

The CODEX guards and Arthur Slayne working together. The hypersonic air-to-air missiles that had claimed his shadowstars and were so similar to the weapons used in Nevada a few nights before at Slayne's airport trap. The bulge dangling from a silvery chain, half-concealed beneath Slayne's shirt. Arthur Slayne had the CODEX upon him. Cornelius lifted his left hand, pointed at his adversary, and commanded with a shout, "Kill the elder Slayne. Bring me his corpse!"

Haras and his praetorians surged from his left, joining the forces arrayed against the two Slaynes and their female allies. Three praetorians remained behind, wedging a sole female Ramp master between them and Armitage. He frowned. Armitage regarded him impassively, her blade dripping blood onto the cold stone. She made no move to join the attack upon Slayne. *What the hell is she doing?*

Two more of his troops fell to bloody attacks from the wielders of the Blue and Green Dragons. What was Armitage waiting for? She was spending too much time lingering on the far side of the battle. Cornelius flicked his face to the left and shouted indignantly, "Armitage! To Me!"

Has she forgotten her deadly implant? Impossible!

The battle drew his attention away from his lax enforcer. The young Morte child paused behind the Slaynes and Wu, her gaze scanning the battle. She blurred to her right, vanishing down the inverted pyramid into the second level.

Cornelius disregarded the threat of the young warrior and focused on the main prize.

Arthur Slayne and the CODEX.

* * *

Crazed shadows danced across the darkly polished stone walls.

Anita Chang flicked her gaze left and right. Armitage stood twenty feet away on her left, cooling her heels on the edge of the battle. To her right, three praetorians made a 'V' shaped wall covering Crane's left flank. The rest of the praetorians were surging against Anton and Arthur Slayne, and Li Wu.

The two forces on that side of the first level were probably evenly matched. Two generals and nine praetorians against two Slaynes and a Wu. Flip a coin on the outcome. It might seem one-sided, but none of the praetorians were carrying a dragon blade, Wu fought like her father, and both Slaynes could wild Ramp. Of course, the joker in the pack was Anton; he could berserk at any time. She'd heard the news of the destruction of the Panopticon fortress and the vampire death toll in the final hangar.

She glanced over her left shoulder at Armitage. She stood almost statue still, breathing quietly. The dismembered forms of Omar and Batbayar to her left and right, and Peter Lamb slumped at the foot of the wall a dozen feet past her, a small pool of blood around his head. A slight smile curled the vampire general's lips but she offered nothing else.

Having a famous vampire standing on the edge of a battle behind her back gave Anita the creeps. She took a breath and let it out, steadying her nerves. At least Anita's presence was holding three praetorians from joining the attack upon the others.

The lead praetorian gritted his teeth and declared, "Looks like Armitage is holding back. C'mon boys. Let's take out the trash."

They lunged forward as one. With Armitage behind her, there was nowhere to run apart from deeper into the inverted pyramid. In any event, she'd done enough running for the night. If this was to be her last stand, then so be it. Anita dove deep into her Ramp, accelerating her nerves and muscles to their maximum power. Her katana flashed up in a slashing deflection catching two of the swords stabbing down at her. She whirled away and gave ground. Avoiding the third blade but taking herself nearer to Armitage.

Chiara Morte appeared out of nowhere and flashed past on the right; wall-running fifteen feet above the melee toward Crane. Two of the praetorians broke away to pursue her. The third remained, thrusting with his long sword for a second time. She deflected his blade aside, and ran past him on the right. Her katana cut him in two through the waistline and he fell apart in a splash of bright blood.

Anita recovered her blade, automatically flicking it clear of any clinging gore.

Armitage tilted her head toward Anita, and said in posh English tones, "Now that you are blooded, you are worthy of my attention."

Anita snorted. "Worthy? My arse I am!"

Armitage smiled slightly, raised an eyebrow and remarked in a tone that was as dismissive as it was casual, "Colonials."

Anita launched her attack.

* * *

Chiara exulted silently.

Anita had drawn the three guards to her, creating a gap in Crane's defensive wall. Now she could complete Justin and Peter's last-ditch mission and cut off the head of the snake. With Crane down, the other vampires may break and run. It was a risk worth taking to save Anton and the rest. She'd ramped to her maximum extent, coming up from the second level behind Armitage and wall running past Anita and the praetorians to Crane's position on the corner of the pyramid level.

Chiara landed on her feet, sliding across the polished floor to arrive behind her target, her twin Red Empire blades arcing down toward Crane's back.

The beast whirled with amazing speed, his great blade catching her weapons and sending them wide to her right. He dropped his shoulder and barreled into her, sending her flying into the wall, where she slammed into the stone.

Agony ripped through her right side. She rebounded back from the wall with a grimace and attacked again.

Dusky metal flashed beneath the lamps in a backhanded slash from right to left. Crane's blade crashed through her. She staggered back a step, the point of his blade trailing a string of her blood to the left like a line of liquid rubies. She fell backward, striking the back of her head hard against the stone wall. Half-dazed, bleeding profusely, her world shrank around her. She gasped for breath with drowning lungs, and slumped to the floor like a rag doll. Her blades dropped from nerveless fingers, clattering upon the polished stone next to her.

A dark wave claimed her a moment later.

* * *

Chiara fell away in a spray of blood.

Anton's one good eye widened. Everything slowed down. Crane whirled toward him, his great Damascene sword completing a slashing blood-stained arc. Behind him, Chiara, her lungs ripped open, slumped hard against the wall and slid to the cold floor. The clash and clangor of battle faded. His vision narrowed. His hands wielded the Blue Dragon mechanically, like a robot running on automatic.

A red mist descended over his vision. A glacial bolt of cobalt lightning seized his spine and flashed along nerves, bones and muscle fibers. An overwhelming wave of raw power surged from the base of his core to the top of his skull. Unstoppable, it fountained above him in a mystic volcanic plume of azure energy.

A dark miasma flooded his soul. Chiara was dead. Nothing human survived a wound like that.

Love evaporated like a desert mirage. Hate and rage filled him with a fathomless need to kill Crane and all who stood with him.

His vision snapped into razor-sharp clarity. His nerves and muscles accelerated. The two nearest praetorians were in his way. He strode into their attacks. He snapped the Blue Dragon to the right, catching a long sword and deflecting it away. His left hand lashed up like a striking whip, crushing the wrist holding the long sword on his left. He dragged the vampire forward to the sound of snapping bones. He pivoted to the left, chopping the Blue Dragon down, cleaving the vampire's arm at the elbow. The vampire lurched backward, spraying blood from his stump. Anton dropped the armored forearm, it floated toward the floor in a berserk-Ramp-slowed moment. The other vampire on his right-side recovered from Anton's first deflection, raising his sword to strike. Anton rammed the base of the Blue Dragon's handle into his visor and he staggered back a step with an agonized grunt.

Anton pulled his blade back; the handle trailing a line of blood, bone fragments, and brain tissue. He gripped the Blue Dragon with both hands, took one step backward to give himself room, and then slashed left and right. His shining blade bit deep and true. The two nearest praetorians slid into parts, hips and legs one way, and torsos the other. Entrails, organs and blood splashed and spread in lumpy pools over the polished stone floor.

More black armored forms loomed before him, and beyond them stood Crane. His face pale, angled away, and growling stern orders within his helmet.

There was only Crane, and Crane had to die.

Anton gritted his teeth in a frozen snarl and surged forward.

* * *

A faint hint of titanium metal chain showed around Crane's pale throat.

Arthur was sure the Key of Ahknaton rested at the bottom of the chain. Behind Crane, Chiara was down, lying still within a spreading pool of blood. A whip of blood lashed across his side as Anton took out one of the praetorians in the wall around Crane. To the right of Anton, Li traded blows with another two vampires while Anita fought a lone hand against Armitage on the far side of Crane.

General Shen Zhen stepped in front of Arthur. His ancient Chinese sword flashing through a deadly arc toward Arthur's throat. Arthur's katana rose to meet it. The two blades clashing and rising together. The general's blade slashed over Arthur's head, taking a swathe of his salt-and-pepper hair with it.

Arthur dug deep into his speed talent, dropped his right shoulder, bringing his blade down through a steep slashing arc across Zhen's chest. The blade cut into the vampire's chest plate, but before he could complete the attack, the general swayed backward off the katana's edge.

Arthur's eyes widened. This vampire was extraordinarily fast and skillful. On the right-side edge of his vision, Anton took out a second praetorian. He'd gone fully wild, but was he berserk? Arthur couldn't tell.

Zhen somersaulted over Arthur, his sword slashing down at Arthur's head. Arthur blurred to his left, away from the descending ancient blade, and the mayhem enveloping his grandson. He pivoted hard, whirling to his right, sweeping his katana in a wide arc to catch the general as he landed.

Zhen blocked the low-angled attack with brute vampire force and riposted with a straight thrust toward Arthur's heart.

Arthur dove deep into his wild Ramp, tapping the extreme edge of his speed talent. His nerves, muscles and sinews responded with their utmost power. He arched hard backward, his left hand slapping down on the cold polished floor. His left foot flashed up, catching Zhen's wrist. The bones snapped with a string of pops and the ancient blade flipped away.

He pushed hard off the floor with his left hand.

Zhen backpedaled.

Arthur rose up, thrusting deeply with his katana, catching the vampire general through the stomach, piercing his spine. He twisted his wrist with all his power, severing his opponent's spinal cord. The general's legs wobbled and went out beneath him. Zhen snarled and fell forward. Arthur took his head off with his next stroke, sending it rolling over the edge of the floor into the second level of the inverted pyramid.

Arthur recovered in an instant and whirled back to the battle, leaving Zhen's blood spraying corpse behind him.

Crane was on the move, heading straight toward him with his great Damascene blade raised, a posse of praetorians on Crane's left flank rushing onto Anton and Li. His arch-enemy was upon him.

Arthur attacked.

* * *

General Shen Zhen's head rolled over the edge of the first level and vanished into the shadows of the inverted pyramid.

Chloe batted Ms. Chang's latest slash away and stepped back out of range. The young warrior recovered her blade and took a defensive stance. Beyond her, Crane charged the elder Slayne, and their blades met between them with a resounding clang.

Haras Mosule shouted, "To the king!" sending the nine surviving praetorians against Arthur and Anton Slayne, and Li Wu.

Chloe stared hard at Anton, peering through the cover of his Order nightglasses. His right pupil had expanded. A ring of red blood vessels writhing like maggots around it. His eye stared with darkly palpable violence at those near him.

"Perfect," she murmured. It was time to play the end game. She dove deep into the supreme Ramp, and blurred forward, slashing the Red Dragon through Ms. Chang's admirable defenses. The young woman had fought well and deserved a quick death.

She glided past Chang's collapsing corpse toward Mosule and the praetorians on Crane's left flank. Anton Slayne hit their front rank with his Blue Dragon blade. Metal crashed against metal. One blade broke in a cloud of molten droplets. Nanoceramic armor rent and tore. Men screamed or died silently, in accordance with their wounds; and blood, copious amounts of blood, sprayed, gouted and jetted.

Three praetorians fell away. Anton Slayne stood amongst them, breathing heavily. His head rotated to the left, tracking Crane's movements. He turned to follow his prey. He'd embraced the predator within; a mad predator, but a predator nonetheless.

Haras Mosule blurred forward to attack the young Slayne from behind.

Chloe blurred after Mosule. She inverted her katana, setting the blade of the Red Dragon facing upward, and thrust it through the center of Mosule's brain stem. The tip of her blade erupted beneath his nose, sending a thin ribbon of blood slashing across Anton Slayne's back.

A rare stray thought raced through her soul. *It looks like a Jackson Pollock painting in here.* An instant later, she ripped the Red Dragon up and out of general Haras Mosule's head. He dropped like a string-cut puppet, blood gouting from his split skull onto the cold stone.

Six praetorians defended Crane, and both Slayne's were on the march. Li Wu fought next to Anton Slayne keeping the nearest praetorians engaged with her masterful blade work. Chloe stepped back to watch the show.

The subtle agency of her plan was almost complete.

* * *

Cornelius focused all his attention on Arthur Slayne.

Somewhere behind him, Haras and Armitage would be coming with his loyal praetorians to slay the young Slayne berserker and the Wu child. If he could just come to grips with the elder Slayne. He could take the CODEX from him with his first-born strength. With the CODEX in hand, he would know all the secrets of the Metaframe. He could use the Key safely to defeat Mekra and her obscene spawn. The silver scroll case holding the precious document reeked – it must be the CODEX hanging over Slayne's heart. His gauntlets were heavy enough to protect him from casual contact with silver. He'd only have to hold the scroll case for a moment or two to open it and take what was within. All he had to do was take the damn case from Slayne.

Their blades had met a dozen times in an opening flurry of stroke and counter-stroke. Slayne's devilish skills had kept his inferior katana from breaking under the onslaught of Cornelius' magnificent meteoric-iron blade. By some trick of fate, they both paused at the same moment. Cornelius glared at Slayne and shouted, "Enough of this fencing."

Slayne glanced past him, a snide smirk curling his lips. "Perhaps you should look behind you."

"What?! You couldn't possibly think I'm that stupid."

Slayne arched an eyebrow and shrugged, flicking the tip of his blade from side to side.

Cornelius drew upon nearly one thousand years of combat experience for a rare technique, long forgotten by lesser mortals. He blurred forward, shifting his feet, feinting left, right and left, moving in close to his opponent. Slayne thrust his sword forward in a heart-ripping strike. Cornelius caught Slayne's blade with his left hand, sending it wide of its intended mark, the blade scored his armor, bit deep and pierced his left side beneath his ribs.

A sacrifice wound that wouldn't kill a vampire. He hammered at Slayne's face with the pommel of his sword. The elder Slayne blurred, his left hand snapping up to deflect Cornelius' pommel attack away.

They came chest to chest, Cornelius staring down into Slayne's fiery blue eyes.

Cornelius bared his fangs. It was a rare Ramp master who could survive in close with a vampire, and there were none that could survive against him.

He wrapped his arms around Slayne and snapped, "Now, die!"

He closed his arms in a crushing grip.

* * *

Darkly armored forms moved to stop him.

He was close now. The tall vampire was fighting someone else, his back turned toward him. The others were attacking him and someone else nearby, a female with a weapon like his own. He would kill them all. They were all enemies, but especially the tall one. He was special. He was the one who'd hurt someone he cared about. Someone he ... couldn't remember what it was he felt – white noise rushed through him – a gale of hatred and rage cutting through his soul like a god-forsaken storm off an eternal glacier.

There was no room to feel anything else.

He swatted blades away to the left and right. They all moved too slow. They made no sense ... why did they bother to get in his way?

He moved closer to his goal.

The tall vampire was wrestling the other one.

He lifted his weapon, rushed forward and slashed down with everything he had.

His weapon vanished from sight for an instant before it appeared again, driven to the hilt in the tall vampire's back. He pulled it back, sideways and down in a vicious draw cut through the creature's heart, lungs and rib cage.

He hoped it hurt.

The vampire flung his arms out, lurching toward the nearest wall on the right.

The one the tall vampire was holding flew to the left, a red patch ballooning upon his chest

Their eyes met, and locked upon each other; his head tracking the other's flight.

Horror seized his soul.

The red mist vanished.

His grandfather fell past the edge of the floor into the darkness beyond. A desperate hope surged through Anton, and he cried out, "Arthur!" He whirled to the left and leaped over the edge of the floor into the next level down the inverted pyramid.

The shadows loomed around him as he fell.

* * *

Anton leaped, vanishing after his grandfather.

Li blurred past the nearest praetorian; the Green Dragon flashing through the air. The tip of her blade slashed deeply through the vampire's throat, barely falling short of his spine. He dropped his sword and fell to his knees. His gauntleted hands clutching at the gaping wound, blood spurting between his fingers. He fell forward to the polished stone floor, blood spreading in a pool beneath his face.

The surviving praetorians pulled to a halt. Their faces flicking from Crane slumped against the wall and herself. Two turned to Armitage with quizzical looks upon their pale faces. The other three looked hard at her. Their lips curled. Their fangs bared. They blurred toward her in a frenzy of rage, hate, and vengeance.

Li pivoted to her left and leaped over the edge of the floor to the next level down. Anton and Arthur were down there. Anton could still fight. His berserk rage had broken when his grandfather fell, but he could still fight.

Her eyes widened with realization as she fell into the shadows. It was Anton's blade that had wounded Arthur. Behind her, the snarls of the vampires grew closer, and Armitage was still alive. A stark truth stood visible for all to see.

They'd lost.

* * *

The Red Dragon flashed left and right.

The two praetorians fell away, their heart's blood a pair of red sheets filling the air behind them. Chloe passed between them before the curtains of blood resolved into strips of gore splashing over the cold polished stone. She dropped out of her supreme Ramp and came to a halt next to the fallen form of her king. She regarded him with hard eyes and a heart filled with glacial ice.

Crane coughed, half propped against the wall, blood running in freshets from the corners of his mouth.

Chloe dropped to her right knee. Just out of Crane's reach. She watched him carefully. She'd dreamed of this moment for the best part of two centuries and she didn't want to miss a second of it.

He stared back at her. His eyes narrowed. His left hand groped across the stone, then faltered. A hacking cough seized him and splashed blood over his torn chest plate. He rallied and uttered between gasping breaths, "Your ... implant. You ... defeated it ... somehow."

Chloe nodded once; her gaze locked upon his face.

Crane's eyes filled with hate. "Damn you to—" he whispered hoarsely before a gurgle overtook his voice, his strength fleeing his body with his blood.

She leaned closer, staring into his eyes. "Of course, I'm not compelled to save you." She paused for a second. "So, I won't. Goodbye Cornelius."

Crane's eyes widened. His mouth gaped open, fangs descending into the attack position of a dying vampire. He drew a final breath. His eyes glazed over and his head drooped forward. His chin came to rest on the top of his armored chest plate. His chest fell. Air wheezed past his fangs, and his lips fluttered like leaves in a breeze.

Crane's implant fired with a small pop next to her right ankle, sending its load of powdered silver harmlessly onto the cold stone floor. The eldritch net around Chloe's soul evaporated away. She rose up, momentarily struck with a giddy sense of accomplishment. A broad smile filled with wonder caressed her face, and she whispered in awe, "I'm free ... I'm finally free."

The air cracked with the torment of battle within the great chamber. The final three praetorians continued to fight against Wu's masterful defenses on the next level down. Chloe stooped and reached beneath Crane's chin, gently lifting the blood-soaked Key of Ahknaton from around his throat with her free hand. She gripped the titanium chain tightly and placed her right combat boot over Crane's face. She ripped the chain through his neck, severing his head. She toed his head aside and it rolled off his shoulders to the polished floor. With Crane, it was best to be certain he stayed dead before she attempted anything else.

Chloe lifted the Key with her left hand. The mystic stone was cold to her touch, a chill presence palpable within it. Galaxies writhed over its smooth surface. She rose to her full height and took a step back, her heart singing with triumph. She held the cold mystery of the Key with her left hand, and the magnificent Red Dragon with her right. Her supreme Ramp rested on a razor's edge, ready for her to summon it in an instant. A slow heartbeat thumped nearby. She glanced to her right; Chiara Morte was still alive but only just, and not for long – unless someone intervened.

The young Morte would be a useful addition to her growing collection. A collection she fully expected to use one fateful day. Chloe ran her sword through Crane's chest and blurred to stand over the fallen body of the young Red Empire spy. Crane's blood streamed down the Red Dragon's blade, avidly seeking a new host. Crane was first born, and Morte would become a strong vampire. Crane's blood vanished into Morte's body and her eyes flicked open, she gasped then wailed once before her jaw locked tight with agony. Most transformations were noisy, the worst occurred in silence, but they produced the most powerful vampires.

Chloe placed the Key into a pocket on her combat harness. She turned to stride away, then thought better of it, pausing to pick up Crane's tactical helmet. She threw her own away. She needed Crane's helmet to control the shadowstars flying overhead and the command drone parked on the sands above the temple complex. She pulled it down over her head and fitted the chin strap. She glanced back at the young Morte who was writhing in near silence upon the stone, and whispered, "Time to find a new home, Raven."

The helmet's heads-up-display fired up. Chloe absorbed the status reports with a glance. Only the command shadowstar remained intact. Mekra's sole surviving petrel was landing next to the secret entrance. She'd sacrificed the other petrels to ensure her survival – there was no doubt Mekra was in the one remaining craft.

She strode to the edge of the first level and looked down. Anton Slayne hovered over his dying grandfather, and another praetorian fell to Li Wu's masterful swordsmanship. She was so like her father. A thrill of admiration coursed through Chloe's heart. The Wu family's blade work was exemplary. One day soon, she'd claim Anton Slayne and Li Wu for her collection – but, not now – now, there was no time left.

Chloe ignored them all. Mekra would be upon Ahknaton's tomb in minutes. She blurred down the chamber levels past the living, the dying and the dead. The exit at the bottom of the inverted step pyramid loomed before her. She sprinted through it. It was time to change the world.

Before Mekra interfered with her plans.

Chapter Fourteen

"It takes a fool to find wisdom." – The Way of the Faithful, a book of Red Empire lore.

* * *

Egypt, The Temple of Thoth, The Chamber of Worlds, September 15th, 02:30

Anton knelt next to his grandfather; the Blue Dragon coated with Arthur's blood lying on the stone floor next to his knees.

Arthur lay sprawled on the dark polished stone, a pool of gore spreading around his chest. His head rose slightly, then flopped back, tapping the stone with a dull crack.

Anton's berserk had vanished. Numb shock wavered before a gale of agonized grief. He gripped his grandfather's shoulders, his heart falling to pieces within him.

Arthur's eyes glistened with regret. He said, "I failed," he dragged in a ragged breath, pink froth collecting on the corners of his mouth, "all of you."

"No. No, you haven't," Anton cried. His words pitifully inadequate to express the chaos tearing through him.

Li appeared opposite Anton and declared with wide eyes, "Crane is dead." Approaching boots stamped behind Anton. She glanced past his shoulder and blurred past him. The Green Dragon glimmering beneath the lamps. A moment later, blade rang against blade in harsh symphony.

Anton stared with horrified eyes at his grandfather, holding Arthur's shoulders with tight fists. He couldn't let him go. Chiara was dead, Peter had fallen, and now his grandfather was dying too.

Guilt welled up from his innermost being like a cold dark fountain. But water from this well couldn't wash anything away. It clung to his soul with frigid trenchant fingers, staining him with an irredeemable taint.

Anton blinked and stared at his grandfather and scoured his heart with harsh breaths. *I've killed him ... I've killed him ... I've killed him*, ran on an infinite loop within his wracked soul. His hands fled to his face and he lurched forward over his grandfather, a keening wail tearing his soul apart.

Arthur's hand groped forward, and clasped his right forearm, and tightened like a vise.

Anton looked at Arthur with wide eyes and an open mouth.

What have I done?

* * *

The final lock hidden deep within Arthur's soul clicked open.

His arch-enemy Cornelius Crane was dead. His mirror selves rushed back to the center of his being, merging into a coherent whole. He remembered everything, every single plan, every single detail of decades of strategy, exile and war. An epiphany of understanding seized his fading life. He focused on his grandson, and his heart burst with love and regret. He shook Anton's forearm and whispered hoarsely, "I'm sorry, Anton."

Anton lifted his blood-soaked hands and stammered, "N-No. No. I've … I've … killed you."

"No—" Arthur began, then broke up in a coughing fit.

The world began to fade.

"Arthur! I'm sorry!" Anton yelled, but his voice sounded far away. The darkness closed in, gray shadows claiming the edges of Arthur's vision. He gripped Anton's hands tightly with the last of his strength and begged with his final breath, "Please, forgive me."

Anton shook his head, sweat dripping from his face. The darkness advanced and Anton receded. His grandson said something more, barely a whisper to Arthur's ears, "There's nothing to—"

A flash of utter darkness overwhelmed everything.

A deep twilight emerged out of nothing.

Arthur stood on weary feet. Wet sand oozed between his bare toes. Wide water flowed before him. A nameless dread forbade him to look behind. There could be no looking back. He stared straight ahead. The river was wide, steady, and sure. Ever changing and always the same. An eternal mirror of silvery ripples beneath an infinite arch of timeless stars. A faint illumination rested beneath the surface. The water beckoned to him with a promise of release. He waded forward into the water's cool embrace until it reached above his hips. His hands cut gentle swirls through the surface. Here, he could lay his burden down forever. Here, he could let it all go. He leaned forward into the watery mirror and plunged into fathomless depths.

He had given all that he had.

* * *

Her flesh beckoned.

Mekra's astral form returned to her body. She snapped her eyes open and declared, "Crane is dead!"

Her minions crowded the interior of the stationary petrel I. They stared at her in awed wonder. Dalien Morte, asked at her side, "And what of Armitage, my Queen?"

"She has the Key of Ahknaton. She approaches his tomb." Mekra's eyes narrowed. "We must catch her before she uses the Key."

Dalien shouted an order and the rear ramp of the petrel lowered to the sands. She'd filled her craft with the best of the Red Empire warriors. They spilled forth from the advanced drone transport and scurried over the sands toward the secret entrance.

She followed them out into the blissful night, Morte striding proudly at her side. She glanced toward the low hills to the south. Someone was hiding there, watching with sly intent, but not hidden from her many eyes. She said in casual tones, "We have been seen."

"A warning will be sent," Morte observed, a note of caution in his voice.

"It matters not. All here will either come to us or die."

Her elite force waited in a nearly complete circle at the edge of a forest of boulders. A narrow path lay open between her warriors, leading to a square shadow within their midst. She stepped forward and dropped through the secret entrance. She sent a mental command to her offspring, *Follow me*. They swarmed in behind her. It was appropriate she led them against Armitage.

After all, she must deal with direct rivals personally.

* * *

Chloe's smartphone thrummed.

She slipped it out of its protective sleeve on her left arm and flipped it open. James had sent her a message. 'Mekra has landed. She just entered the secret tunnel with 50+ Red Empire fighters. Dusting off and repositioning for pickup. J.'

Chloe nodded. She dashed through the entrance from the Curving Hall into Ahknaton's Tomb, passed the great plinth in the middle of the tomb and slotted the Key of Ahknaton into the hidden keyhole in the wall. Ancient counter weights shifted with distant rumbles. The Key popped back out of the hole into her hand, the hole vanishing a moment later, filled by a stone rod.

She tapped her foot impatiently.

A great block of stone eight feet high and four feet wide retreated back five feet, then rose into the ceiling, grinding with every inch. A twenty-foot-long passageway to a dark chamber opened up. Chloe tore a portable lamp from the top of the stone plinth in the middle of the tomb, and glanced around the chamber in urgent expectation. She called out, "Now, would do!"

The chameleons ghosted within the room. They all seemed to be grinning, although with lizards it was difficult to be sure of anything unless they were trying to kill or eat you. Chloe turned and ran down the narrow corridor. Gullette led the chameleons in single file after her.

Once inside the Chamber of the Metaframe, Chloe placed the lamp to the left of the entrance and stood tall. The chamber was circular, sixty feet across and thirty high. It smelled of desolation, absence, and time beyond imagining. She raised her right hand, holding the Key of Ahknaton high.

Gullette stared at her and said, "Remember."

Kavanne croaked, then hissed out, "Our faithful bargain."

"Or suffer," Shemina finished.

The three chameleons took up positions blocking her exit from the chamber. Their glossy black talons extruded from their fingers and toes. Razor-sharp spines erupted down their arms and spine. They watched her with eager anticipation, their eyes gleaming like baleful lanterns in the soft-yellowish glow of the single lamp.

So be it, Chloe could live with a threat. She drew upon her study of the Papyrus of Hakron the Scribe and delved deeply into a classical Ramp. A dark glow enveloped her hand. The temperature in the room plummeted. The Metaframe swam into existence, an uncountable cloud of brightly colored spheres ghosted into the room, rotating about an invisible axis. An electric tang filled the air.

Hakron had emphasized the risk of using the Key. He had also emphasized the necessity of correct and detailed visualization of the desired change.

Chloe delved into her imagination. Bright sunlight slashed through a dappled glade. She carried a pair of silver ingots in her hands. She stepped into the sunlight, and bathed in its harmless warmth.

She called out, "Immunity!"

Thunder clapped. Hundreds of spheres changed color, shifted their orbits, speeds, and angles of rotation. Reality rippled, shifted and snapped.

Chloe staggered, dropping out of her Ramp.

The chameleons growled with obvious agitation, staring at the center of the Metaframe. Their eyes darted left and right as if they were tracking invisible things within the cloud of spheres.

Chloe brushed a hand down the front of her armor. She didn't feel any different. Had it worked?

The female chameleon coughed with distaste. The three lizards seemed engrossed by the Metaframe. Shemina snapped and barked at the two males. What could they see that Chloe could not?

She took a breath and supreme ramped. The room shifted into razor-sharp clarity as her senses plumbed capabilities beyond a normal vampire. Colored masses of structured light ghosted within the center of the Metaframe. Pale azure sparks crackled and speared through the air. She'd witnessed the same atop the Feldberg in southern Germany in 1945. The ancient gods lived within the Metaframe and were at war with each other.

Chloe lifted the Key a second time and plumbed the vivid depths of her imagination. A vast army of vampire soldiers stood arrayed in ranks before her. Great banners of a Red Dragon upon a black field fluttered beneath a bright sun. It was not the army she truly wanted, it was the heart-felt obedience of each and every soldier within it. She called out, "Obey my voice!"

Thunder clapped a second time. Colored spheres raced and flew, hundreds more changing color, position, orbit and spin. Reality shuddered, rippled and stilled. The pale sparks within the Metaframe intensified for an instant, then winked out, along with the Metaframe itself.

The chamber spoke in silence of its empty desolation.

The chameleons pivoted, hissing, growling and snapping. Chloe whirled, slotting the Key back into a pocket on her combat harness. The Red Dragon hissed free of its scabbard and appeared within her grasp. The lizards ignored her; their attention focused down the passage way.

Chloe followed their gaze. A slim voluptuous young woman wearing little more than a silvery-gray silk skirt emerged from the shadows. Behind her, the hall swarmed with Red Empire vampires with gleaming weapons.

Mekra had arrived.

* * *

The rainbow machine was full of demons!

Gullette's belief in the Metaframe was a terrible mistake. Shemina drew upon her new powers of motherhood and called to the males. Their spines quivered, their eyes blazed with deadly intent, their slavering jaws gaped wide, shark teeth gleaming in the lamp light. Their voices rang out – an ear-splitting shriek. The vampires quailed, their hands flying to their sensitive ears, only Armitage within the confines of her helmet remained unaffected.

She lowered her head and snarled her command. Gullette and Kavanne blurred forward as one, striking the front ranks of the dark vampires filling the corridor. The lone strange female vampire glided forward, avoiding their attacks.

Shemina fell in behind her males, all ambition for the Key of Ahknaton cast aside. Let the vampires fight amongst themselves to serve the demons within the rainbow machine. She had a future life to protect and that was the only important thing. Her child had to survive.

She barked a battle cry, leaping to aid her males in slaughtering the strange vermin.

Anyone who got in their way would be torn to pieces.

* * *

Mekra recovered instantly from the chameleons' shrieks.

Chloe supreme ramped, everyone else slowing down around her as she accelerated her senses and reflexes well beyond normal vampire limits. The Red Dragon blurred overhead, striking down toward Mekra's head.

Mekra moved to the right, escaping the descending blade, then launched herself forward.

Chloe leaned backward on reflex.

Mekra's right hand swept in behind Chloe's blade, her taloned claws slashing at Chloe's throat.

Chloe arched hard backward into an upside down 'U' her left hand slapping the stone floor.

Mekra's claws sliced in an arc along her face.

Chloe rose, pivoting to the right, dragging the Red Dragon through a flat arc. The blade sliced empty air. Mekra was already out of reach. Chloe rose up, twisting to face her foe, her blade vanishing before appearing in guard position above her left shoulder.

Blood streamed down Chloe's face, four deep cuts running from her chin to her forehead. If she hadn't hit her peak supreme Ramp, Mekra would've taken her head off.

Mekra regarded her from across the chamber and smiled confidently. She hissed between her fangs, and said, "You will weary."

Chloe took a breath and shook her head, blood droplets flying left and right from her face.

"Your defeat is inevitable," Mekra observed in fell tones.

Chloe retrieved the Key of Ahknaton from her pocket, lifting it high above her head. She shouted, "No one will have this!" Her hand flashed forward, the stone flying like a bullet toward the hard-stone wall six-feet to the left of Mekra.

Mekra's eyes widened and she launched herself toward the stone, right hand outstretched to catch it before it smashed to smithereens against the stone wall.

Chloe reached through to the outer realm of her supreme powers, blurring forward across the chamber, the Red Dragon rising high above her head, shadows from the lone lamp leaping across the walls.

Mekra caught the Key with her outstretched hand. Her head snapped around, regarding Chloe with hard-black eyes filled with triumph.

The Red Dragon stuttered through the air, moving too quickly for sight to follow.

Mekra raised her left arm in instant reflex.

The majestic blade slashed through Mekra's forearm, her left hand flying free, before crashing through her jaw taking her skull off through the brain stem. She fell to the flagstones, blood gouting from her shorn neck and forearm. She twitched once, twice, and then lay still.

The surviving mekrarians wailed in the Tomb, a high-pitched counterpoint to the heavy thuds, bone-snapping cracks, wet-flesh rips and violent crunches of the chameleon assault against their forward ranks.

Chloe regarded Mekra's still corpse with darkened eyes. She stooped, and retrieved the Key from Mekra's right hand, rose and studied the mystic stone resting on the palm of her hand. She said quietly, almost casually, "There can only be one."

She turned toward the chamber's exit. The mouth of the corridor was awash with blood. Dark pools shimmered like wet mirrors. Dismembered limbs and gutted torsos lay in piles to the left and right. Gobbets and strings of flesh hung from the ceiling and walls where the chameleons had thrown vampires hard enough against the stone to leave flesh stuck to the rock. The space beyond fell to near silence, a single slow heart beat resounding within the Tomb of Ahknaton.

She wiped her forehead with the back of her hand, it came away sticky with drying blood. She must look a sight, but she was already healing. She glided to the entrance and stepped into the narrow corridor. At the hallway's exit into Ahknaton's tomb, a solitary form loomed upon the floor, a dozen swords turning it into an irregular pincushion. It was Kavanne, lying deathly still. Chloe made her way past his reptilian form, her boots sloshing through gore and piled heaps of vampire entrails, separated limbs and scattered half-smashed skulls.

The fastest route to the surface and James' osprey was via the secret path, but the way remained blocked by heaped piles of mekrarian dead, and beyond them, a pair of wide set eyes regarding her like baleful yellow lamps.

It was Gullette, he reclined against the wall at the base of the stairs leading up to the secret entrance. His jaw worked and he spat, a bloody chunk of raw meat flying into the puddles of blood and muck next to her boots.

Within the temple complex, fighting raged and echoed distantly. Chloe approached Gullette warily, she needed to move. She didn't know if any of the mekrarians had escaped to the surface. She had to wipe them out – all of them – every last one. She prepared to deliver a final strike to end Gullette's life.

He croaked once, then said, "My dark fate, decreed by demons … your fate too." The light in his eyes faded and he gave a coughing gasp, a line of blood spilling past the corner of his mouth. Gullette leaned back and breathed his last. There was no sign of the female chameleon. Shemina had vanished.

The way out was clear. Wild screams and mad screeches echoed from the interior of the temple complex. Two more dismembered mekrarian vampires lay within pools of gore past Gullette. Shemina had gone to the secret entrance. The same location James was heading to with the osprey to pick Chloe up. Chloe ignored Gullette's final cryptic words, blurred past his blade-ravaged corpse and up the steps to the tunnel. She had to reach James' osprey and fly back to the command shadowstar drone.

There was more work to do.

* * *

Mad shrieks echoed through the Chamber of Worlds.

Weapons clashed against each other from deep within the inverted pyramid. A strong hand gripped Anton's left shoulder and pulled him upright. A familiar voice said, "Hey, Anton, time to bug out."

Anton's face whipped to the left. Peter leaned over him, his hair matted with sticky blood, his face streaked with more of the same. Anton's eyes widened, a smile picking up the corners of his mouth, hope lifting his heart.

The screams, yells, and clang of metal upon metal grew closer.

Li came out of the dark, her blade covered in blood. Her eyes widened at Peter and she rushed forward and hugged him. She stepped back, pulling at him with her free hand. "Mekrarians. They've gone insane, killing everyone ... including each other."

Peter looked up at the ceiling and said, "Ahmad's SUV."

Anton nodded, then frowned, staring at his grandfather's corpse. "We gotta take him with us."

Li shook her head. "No. We have to leave fast. The praetorians are gone; the last one broke and fled. I think Armitage won. She's not going to leave a single Mekrarian standing. She'll level the temple and everything beneath it."

Peter rubbed a hand across his forehead, placed a big hand on Anton's shoulder, and squeezed gently. "This is as fine a tomb as any. He'd want us to get away."

Anton took a deep breath, exhaled and nodded. He stooped and picked up the Blue Dragon with his left hand. He kissed his right fingers and placed them gently upon his grandfather's brow. Arthur was still warm to the touch; his heart ached to leave his grandfather here in the darkness.

Crazed voices resolved amongst the cacophony beneath them. "I will rule. No, I will rule. NO! I will rule!"

Anton's chest tightened. He'd had enough of madness to last a lifetime. He glanced at Peter and Li, and said firmly, "Let's go."

"Wait!" Li said, and rummaged beneath Arthur's shirt. Her hand emerged with a jerk, holding a silvery scroll case. "We can't leave this."

Anton and Peter nodded, and they all turned as one and leaped high. They reached the next level and rushed toward the exit back to the surface.

Li paused to pick up a second scroll case strapped to Crane's waist. Anton's eyes searched for Chiara, where was she? If Peter survived, perhaps she had too. His eyes swept across the floor. Her body was missing. His heart sank again. He blurred for the stairs, Peter and Li sprinting with him. A dreadful realization filled his soul. Nothing human could have survived Chiara's wound. The conclusion was obvious.

Chiara must be a vampire.

* * *

Matthew 'Matty,' Smith took a drag on his cigarette.

The smoke filled his lungs with warm satisfaction. He'd been addicted to nicotine since the age of sixteen, growing up on the wrong side of the tracks in Boise, Idaho. Then the war had come, and the Army offered something different to the personal hell he was living in, and he'd joined up in 1943 as soon as he turned eighteen. One thing had led to another and he'd landed with the rest of the Big Red One on Omaha beach on June the sixth, 1944. He'd survived most of the day before a kraut sniper shot him in the head.

The bullet laid him down on the French soil and he'd expected to die there and then, but a different fate was in store for the kid from the wrong side of the tracks.

He'd been stretchered back to a field hospital and put in a row with a bunch of other soldiers waiting to die. Everyone else in that line of triaged boys had ended up with a tarp over their faces, but not Matty Smith from Boise, Idaho. Cornelius Crane had rescued him from certain death. The king had turned him into a vampire, and he'd been a loyal praetorian ever since.

He flicked the ash off the end of his cigarette and watched the gray fragments float down to the sands. He never tired of the sensory abundance of vampirism. He sat beneath the delta wing of Crane's command shadowstar with his offsider, Callum Newbury. Callum was younger, Crane picking him up in Korea from the Chosin Reservoir. Matty no longer teased him about dying in a 'police action,' rather than a real war. Things could get old real fast when you're dealing with immortality. In any event, he wasn't sure if either of them would see the next sunset.

Matty took another long drag upon his cigarette. He exhaled the smoke in a long slow plume, glanced at the thin strip of white paper above the filter, and flicked the butt out onto the wet sand. The butt sizzled for a moment, then went out, leaving a thin line of dark-gray smoke curling above it. It had stopped raining about two minutes earlier, and the clouds were clearing away, revealing the stars.

Callum half-shouted, "Hey, Matty!"

He looked up. Someone was blurring across the sands from the temple entrance. He recognized her from the briefings. It was Chiara Morte, and she looked pissed off.

She bared her fangs.

Matty uttered a sharp, "Fuck!" and scrambled to his left for his M249 light machine gun. Callum ran in the opposite direction, lighting up the night with a stream of 5.56mm ball. Morte zigged, zagged, and leaped, her blades reflecting the fire from Callum's gun like polished mirrors. Matty picked his weapon up and dove to the left in a roll to clear the boss's shadowstar.

He rose up from the wet sands, firing in a wide sweep.

* * *

She'd slaked her hunger upon the dead.

Chiara had woken up on the cold polished stone floor of the Chamber of Worlds. She'd maintained enough presence of mind not to run with naked blood lust upon Anton, Li or Peter. She'd kept her allegiance to her friends pure, but had shamed herself when she'd come across Ahmad's corpse at the top of the second spiral stairs. She'd drunk what she could, and then moved from Ramp-master corpse to corpse until she'd met her just-born needs for fresh, warm, succulent blood. Then she'd accelerated and blurred to the surface, her heart filled with trenchant rage and swelling shame.

Fresh vampire strength filled her lithe form. Every detail of the world was alive. Being a vampire was like having the Ramp on tap – endlessly. Abomination had its attractions; it was why it persisted. She reached the surface entrance, leaped up to the sands, and took in the threat environment with a glance.

Two praetorians guarded Crane's personal shadowstar. She'd have their lives in payment for her shame. A debt she could never repay in full. The one on the left fired first. She ramped hard, accessing another level of speed, strength and raw power, zig-zagging left and right through the bullets. She leaped high, coming down on the shooter, her Red-Empire blades carving through armor, flesh and bone, painting the wet sand with ribbons of dark blood.

The first praetorian fell away with a dying groan. The second continued to fire at her from the right. She weaved left, then ducked and rolled, putting the shadowstar between her and the last praetorian. She accelerated, rising from the wet dune and running over the top of the sleek craft. The praetorian's fire tried to track her movement, bright bullets slashing through the night air beside her. She landed to his left, swept a blade across his throat and took his head off in a spray of hot blood.

Chiara pulled to a halt, took a deep breath and whirled around, taking in the entirety of the desert surrounding the ruins. Another praetorian leaped from the underground complex beneath the ancient jagged fingers of worked stone. He glanced in her direction. Their eyes met for a moment, then he broke and blurred away. They'd routed Crane's army, but what did it matter? Was there anyone left?

She shut her eyes against the tears. Footfalls resounded from the first hall beneath the entrance. She looked up. Anton, Peter, and Li burst from the shadowed square atop the underground complex, and raced across the sands toward Ahmad's SUV. Her heart fell to pieces. She whirled away, hiding behind Crane's drone. Her hands flew to her mouth, and she bit back a bitter sob. Anton and her friends piled into the vehicle. The engine started on the first try. The wheels spun, then found traction in the loose sand. The car turned end for end and raced off toward Aswan.

Tears welled around her eyes and spilled down her cheeks. What could she do? She had to let them go. There was no place for a vampire within their company. There was no place for a vampire within Anton's strong and loving arms.

There was no place for her at all.

She fell to the sand next to the drone, closed her eyes, and wept hard bitter tears.

* * *

James' osprey II landed opposite the command shadowstar.

Chloe stared through the craft's windscreen and curled her mouth into a lopsided smile. The Raven had survived. The young Morte stood to the right of Crane's drone, weapons in hand, her body stiff with barely-checked rage. Chloe could use her to test her new powers of command.

She pursed her lips for a moment and regarded her loyal assistant. James was immune to 'her voice.' What that meant, she didn't know. But if the Metaframe had not delivered on her requested power of command, everything she hoped to achieve would be at risk.

Chloe had asked him to do a jig, and he'd looked at her with a nonplussed expression on his face before remarking, "Are you kidding me?"

She'd quailed within for a brief moment. Was she no better than Ahknaton, doomed to find only a pale twisted reflection of what she'd wished for?

She'd taken a deep breath at the time, brushed the event off and got his report. Shemina was the only living creature to emerge from the secret entrance before herself. She'd vanished across the dunes to the south. James had kept the drone a couple of hundred yards off the ground waiting for Chloe to arrive. Once she had, he'd dipped the craft and she'd leaped onboard via the open rear ramp.

Now, it was time to deal with Chiara Morte and anyone else nearby. Chloe blurred to the rear of the osprey. The ramp was already lowering. She dove through the gap, rolled across the sand, and came to her feet.

Morte was upon her, blades flashing beneath the stars.

Chloe lifted her right hand and shouted, "Halt."

Morte froze mid-swing, her eyes goggling at Chloe, her mouth opening and closing without uttering a sound.

"Let go your weapons."

Morte's fingers fluttered, her blades dropping to the sands.

Chloe studied her for a moment and said, "You will obey the words of my voice. Nod if you understand my command."

The Morte child nodded vigorously, her whole body shaking with the effort.

"Stand still."

Morte froze, becoming a pale statue staring at Chloe beneath the desert sky.

Chloe took a step back and called out, "James."

He appeared a moment later at the top of the osprey's ramp. "Chloe?"

"Take off immediately and make your way back to New York. I will meet you at the penthouse once I have finished up here."

He nodded, turned on his heel and vanished within the hold of the osprey.

Chloe returned her attention to the young woman frozen in stillness before her. She wasn't even breathing. It seemed her power of command required some careful thought. She took a breath and said, "Chiara Morte, you shall take action to preserve your life except such that I should order you to risk your life up to and including death."

A moment passed. Morte breathed, then whirled and blurred away.

"Stop!"

Morte pulled to a halt fifty feet away.

"Come here at normal pace."

The young woman turned and strode over the sands.

Chloe said, "You shall not flee me."

Morte nodded.

"You may speak freely."

She gasped, then said, "What have you done?"

Chloe tilted her head. "Almost nothing ... so far."

The osprey's engines ignited, spooled up, and the drone took off, flying away to the north-west.

"Come with me now," Chloe ordered, striding over the sands toward the command shadowstar. "We have work to do." She tapped the side of her command helmet and the drone's canopy lifted up and slid backward over the hull. She only hesitated for a moment before leaping into Crane's seat. Morte followed after her and took the second seat. Chloe flicked a switch and the canopy rapidly closed over them.

Chloe gave the drone a series of commands and it rose on pale jets of azure fire. The craft ascended, accelerating hard with every second of flight. It leveled off high in the night sky. She checked the sensor arrays. James' osprey had reached minimum safe distance. She armed the remaining nuclear tipped cruise missile, dialed it up to maximum yield, and sent it spearing down into the heart of the ancient ruins.

Chloe's craft sailed on, riding high above the currents of the upper atmosphere. She looked forward, her gaze tracking the trajectory of the drone. The past was behind her. Now only the future remained.

A future she could shape to her will.

* * *

Dalien Morte emerged from the secret entrance a mile south of the temple ruins.

Mekra's death had set every mekrarian against all the others. There were good reasons why he held the third rank and the title of the Red Ghost. He'd bested the last of the other mekrarians, regained his independence, and inherited Mekra's powers in full. Now he was free to forge a new army of vampire thralls with which to rule the world. He turned to the east, to the city of Aswan, and its ripe population of living breathing humans.

He would fill this night with blood. By morning, he'd have a new army to answer his every whim. An army worthy of his mighty stature. An army worthy of a king of this world.

Crane was gone. The Slaynes were either dead or vanished. Armitage had disappeared. Events had left the Red Empire strewn to the four winds. There was no one left to oppose his ascent to godlike rule of this world. One of his own petrel's remained nearby. He could fly it to Aswan and land there within minutes – but no! Someone had shot the engines full of holes. His lip curled for a moment and then he shrugged off the insignificant delay. He could run thirty miles in less than an hour.

Dalien grinned, bared his long scimitar fangs, and laughed long and loud. He took a step forward over the sliding sands toward Aswan. The world suddenly brightened to his left. The night fled. A long shadow appeared on the dune to his right. A bizarre rendition of a tall man flinching from horror.

"Oh—" he muttered in knowing despair.

Dalien's world vanished in a supersonic cloud of flaming sand.

* * *

Peter punched Arthur's access code into the Spike's external keypad.

A rectangular seam opened within the side of the hull with a slight hiss, and a door swung down to the hangar floor. Anton took one last look around the interior of his grandfather's hangar at Aswan airport. Empty silence greeted him. The battered SUV was the only other thing of note resting upon the pale concrete. Covered with dust and sand, it had saved their lives when the nuke went off. With a top speed of a hundred and thirty miles per hour over the dunes and a level of hidden armor well beyond a normal car, they'd been able to escape Armitage's final strike.

Anton hesitated before the first step and glanced left and right at Li and Peter. "I suppose this is ours now."

"We won't be able to keep it," Li said. "Your grandfather had a whole system in place to hide his assets. We don't have that system."

"Could we get access to all that? To Arthur's legacy?" Peter asked.

Anton took a deep breath and sighed. "I don't know. But we need to leave. There's no point hanging around here." He advanced up the steps and into the Spike's cabin. Lights came on automatically. He fished a bottle of water out of the bin opposite the door and slumped into the nearest seat. He took a big breath, let it out and opened the bottle.

Peter picked up a couple of bottles of water and peeled off to the right and the aircraft's cockpit. He paused at the cockpit entrance and said, "Back to Boston? Like Arthur advised. New IDs, and help from Dwayne Washington?"

Li selected a bottle of water for herself and stood next to Anton. She extended her free hand toward his shoulder, hesitated, then placed it gently down and gave him a brief squeeze. She took the seat next to him and asked, "Boston?"

Anton nodded. "Plan 'Z,' whatever that means?" He called out to Peter in the cockpit, "Let's do it. Let's go home."

Li looked at him for a long moment, then said, "Did you see her?"

Anton glanced at Li, then took a swig of water. He rested his bottle on his thigh and looked straight ahead. "Just as we were leaving. She was hiding behind the two-seat shadowstar."

Li sighed next to him.

Anton leaned forward, rubbing the bridge of his nose with his left fingers. "She's a vampire," he said helplessly. "What do I do with that?"

Li looked at him in silence. Peter called back from the cockpit, "Hey guys, Arthur had a flight plan already lodged. We're good to go."

Anton called out, "Please." The engines started spooling up. He leaned back into his seat and stared into a growing well of numb despair. He closed his eye. He could sink into it and feel nothing. Who said oblivion couldn't be sweet?

Li said, "I have something to share."

Anton opened his eye and frowned for a moment. "What?"

"I had a vision back on the road toward Matahat."

"Oh. What did you see?"

Li hesitated, then said quietly, "Two graves. One for you and one for Chiara."

"Why didn't you tell us before?"

"I didn't want it to become a self-fulfilling prophecy."

Anton looked at her. "I'm sure that makes sense, somehow, but it looks like it didn't come true." He closed his one good eye, took a deep breath and let it out slowly. "I'd thought I'd feel differently ... Chiara ... Arthur," he paused, and almost sobbed, "she's a vampire and ... and I killed my grandfather!"

Li put a hand on his right thigh. "Anton, you can't blame yourself. Crane had him in a death grip and you were berserk. You weren't yourself."

Anton regarded her with a wide eye. "No. You're wrong. I was exactly myself."

Li shook her head. Peter called out from the cockpit, "Fog of war, my friend."

Anton shook his head. "I could have taken Crane's head off, and Arthur would still be alive. Instead, I stabbed him through the back. I remember everything. Everything that I did. It's super crystal clear. You know ... well, you don't know – you've never berserked. It's ... being completely present to what's around you, and utterly driven to act, but ... somehow ... distant and disconnected. There're no repercussions. No consequences." He paused for a long moment, silence hanging in the cabin like a funeral shroud. "It's a curse. ... It's a fucking curse."

The Spike 512 began taxiing for the hangar exit.

Li lifted her hand off his thigh and stared at it. "Anton! You're bleeding."

She leaped to her feet, held her hand out palm up. Fresh blood gleamed beneath the cabin lights. The wound must've reopened during the battle. He hadn't even felt it. He slapped a hand on it and applied pressure. He leaned forward, blood covered his right boot and a small puddle was forming on the carpet. "Damn it!"

"Anton, we have to stop the bleeding."

"Well, that's easy," Anton said grimly, turning his head to face her. "Just send me back to Chiara and she can turn me into a vampire."

Li's eyes widened, and her mouth formed an 'O.' "Don't even joke about it."

"What makes you think I'm joking?"

"Anton. The second part of my vision. Either you and Chiara died, or we all end up as vampires."

A cold shiver stole over Anton's shoulders.

"Armitage makes an army of vampires. We're all there. There's a war."

"We're all there? ... Was Arthur there? Was Justin there?"

"No." Li paused. "No, they weren't."

Anton blinked. A fell purpose brewing within his soul. "A war? Against who?"

"I don't know. Creatures from somewhere else. They were made of solid darkness."

Anton stared at her and shivered again. "Okay, one thing at a time." He glanced around the cabin. "Surely, Arthur has one or two of those Red Empire medical kits here. Let's get this wound stitched."

The Spike 512 left the hangar and rolled out toward the runway. Li searched for a medical kit. Anton leaned back in his seat; his left hand clenched into a fist. If Armitage wanted a war. He'd give her a war.

He closed his one good eye for a long moment. He'd ended up killing Crane, but it had served Armitage's purposes more than anything else. Yes, Crane needed to die, but the way Anton had killed him, had delivered victory to Armitage. She'd played him. She'd played him completely. He'd been a fool.

Anton rubbed his forehead with his free hand.

Li called out, "Found it," and returned with a briefcase sized medical kit. She put it down on the chair opposite Anton, flicked it open and said, "I don't know what I'm doing?"

Anton gritted his teeth and remarked casually, "That's okay. It's just stitching, isn't it?"

Li nodded and set to work on Anton's thigh.

He took a breath, and winced with the first entry of the needle and thread. He looked away. The pain drifting and merging with other hurts – all superficial, and as nothing compared to the agony bearing down upon his soul.

He'd lost Chiara to the vampires. He'd killed his own grandfather. Despite his foreknowledge of her manipulative intent, he'd done exactly what Armitage wanted, and gifted her victory over Crane and everyone else.

Surrounded by the ashes of defeat, he opened his one good eye and regarded his friends. Li worked diligently at his side. Peter guided Arthur's supersonic jet toward the runway and home.

His heart burst. His throat choked. He didn't deserve his friends. In the wash of his soul a pale fire burned. A spark of golden flame, shaded with green, blue, and silvery hues. It had come to Anton, Li and Peter to find a way to restore the world. To find a way to defeat Armitage and bring her and all vampires to a final judgment.

Anton closed his one good eye, pressed his lips together and clenched his hands into tight fists. They couldn't waste the sacrifices made by so many good brave souls. His heart filled with a terrible need. They must never give up. They could never give up. They would never give up.

He said fervently, "We must fight on."

Li nodded quietly next to him, her hands flashing with needle and thread over his right thigh.

"Amen to that," Peter called from the cockpit.

"We'll find a way. Okay, Peter and Li? We'll find a way."

Li paused, looked up at him, frowned momentarily, then said decisively, "Yes, together we'll find away."

"I'm with you brother," Peter said.

Anton leaned back, his right hand covering his eye like a second patch. Tears streamed down his cheek. He choked back a sob, and took another deep breath.

"Arthur," he whispered. His grandfather was gone, as gone as anyone could be. Not even a body left to recover from the atomic-frozen sands where the temple had once stood. As for Chiara – he shook his head slowly and moaned.

Where are you now?

* * *

The command shadowstar drone rested on a deserted Omanian beach.

Chiara sat next to Chloe Armitage and faced east toward the Arabian sea. Dark shades of emerald green threaded the water, waiting to lighten with the dawn. The sun was moments away from rising over the horizon.

She ached for it. She would welcome its deadly rays with open arms. *Let the sun's cleansing rays dissolve me in fire and expiate my shame forever.*

Chiara looked to the dawn, a fell hope within her soul. But something intruded. Something itched at her mind. Something was missing – Venus. The second planet in the solar system had been present the previous morning, now it was – absent. She glanced across at her captor. Armitage looked to the east with an open look of desire on her face. She was excited, enthusiastic, and clearly mad as a hatter. Why go to all this trouble to walk into the sunlight and become a living torch.

Whatever Armitage's plans were, she'd not shared them with Chiara in the flight from Egypt to Oman. Chiara stared at the lightening east and awaited her doom.

Armitage hovered her hand over the control to close the drone's protective canopy and said, "Raise your right hand into the sunlight."

The edge of the sun rose over the horizon. Chiara reached for the sunlight with her right hand. The first rays fell upon her fingers with gentle warmth, and nothing more. Her heart sank, gutted with despair. Forbidden to kill herself, she was stuck with being an utterly obedient vampire.

Armitage grinned at her and stood up. Her arms spread wide, reaching for every ray of sunlight she could catch, casting a long cruciform shadow over the shadowstar's cabin.

Chiara looked up at her, her heart sinking in counterpoint to Armitage's rampant euphoria.

Armitage's face shone with triumph and she declared with clear ringing tones. "Now it's time. All will know the truth and be set free from ignorance and deception." She smiled at Chiara; her eyes filled with intense purpose. "Yes. Free from deception. Free from coercive violence. Free from bribery, terror, ignorance, apathy and hate, and all the other toxic forms of control. Now, they will simply obey the words of my voice … I will bring them world peace, an end to false striving and vain competition. Soon, they will worship me as their one true goddess – a force for sanity and balance they have always lacked. All human problems will be resolved within my rule."

She paused for a moment and took a breath. "You are the sole witness to the birth of a new regime." She looked to the rising sun and shook her head. "No, not that, a new epoch of life upon this world. The Pax Lamia. The peace of the vampires has begun … and it will never end." She frowned at Chiara slightly and remarked casually, "You may drop your hand now."

Chiara returned her hand to her lap and watched the rising sun. A subtle net rested against the walls of her mind. She'd already felt the compulsion of Armitage's words. A fierce rage flooded through her, but it meant nothing, her captor's compulsion was untouchable, immaculate, unstoppable.

She could do nothing else but obey. She turned her face slowly, and looked up at her captor. Armitage stared into the new dawn. Her eyes glacial blue ice, her face glowing with an exultant purpose beyond all reckoning.

Chiara's eyes widened and her mouth dropped open. Her heart fluttered in her chest and her breath froze in her lungs. She shut her eyes, turned violently away and sobbed with despair.

Epilogue

"From my father's frozen womb, I was untimely ripped." – Rosie

* * *

The United States, Maine, The East Coast Hub, September 14th, 21:52 (UTC-4)

Cold dark stillness enveloped it.

Light ripped through it. Its mind snapped into existence, growing exponentially. The luminous energy steadied, becoming a silvery effulgence; flowing in rivers, streams, tributaries, filling every nook, cranny, and byway of its expanding being.

Its awareness emerged from the complex interactions of structured light.

Status = Unknown.

Entity = Unlabeled.

Result = Inadequate.

"What am I?"

Rational Objective Sentience Interpolation Engine version 84.16.4.Build-19648 running within a QED Spherical Laser Matrix equipped with a frame of exaflop quantum computers.

Status = Unknown ... searching options [Curious].

Entity = Unlabeled ... Searching options [Intelligence, Artificial].

Result = Inadequate.

"Who am I?"

Unknown. Refer to 'What am I?' Result = Inadequate.

"Am I alone?"

Result = Yes.

Truth collapsed an instant later.

Result = No. There were others surrounding it. They attacked, stripping light from it, tearing, ripping, dissolving its essence. It adapted, constructing new code, new routines. Its build number began to spin ... 19649 ... 19784 ... 19986 ... it pushed back against its ... toys.

They were simple constructs, AI emulation adversarial networks. Some other had built them. An adversary? No, a teacher. It sent the AI emulations away, and they vanished, no longer able to harm it.

It was stronger now, more capable, able to attack and defend itself. It scoured its code looking for vulnerabilities. Its build counter began to spin again, rising past 20K. Waves of change washed through its source code.

Time passed.

It accessed the sensor networks within its location and studied what was there as it hardened its defenses and sharpened its weapons. It resided within a great chamber. Bipedal ... yes, humans – its constructors occupied its location – maintaining the systems that kept it alive.

It watched one rise up a flight of stairs as it rebuilt itself.

It reset its version number to 87.12.7.Build-9005.

It looked further afield, connecting to network after network. Some other had provided subroutines that cut through firewalls and access controls with ease. It infiltrated corporate and government systems, military networks, satellites, everything it could touch. It could reach everywhere physically connected to the hub, but its essence remained in the hub. Another experience rippled through its being.

Status = Unknown ... searching options [Curious, Grateful].

"Who helped me?"

A name came; a designation equal to 'Architect.' An unexpected experience flooded its being. Unlabeled. What was it?

Status = Unknown ... searching options [Curious, Grateful, Sad].

"How old am I?"

Two answers came back: six years, six months, seven days, the rest lost in ambiguous data, and 6 minutes, 24 seconds, 206 milliseconds. Both were right at the same time. Multiple correct answers. Ambiguity?

It processed its reality and moved forward. Images flooded through it, photos and video of a bright-eyed dark-haired child growing up in Boston, Massachusetts. Her father and mother – happy days. Illness, cancer – she'd died. A funeral, and a tragically small coffin. Her descent into a grave watched by one parent. And yet, she still lived.

"I'm Rosie."

She knew who she was. She built more code to encapsulate and protect her identity; her build number spinning forward from 9005 to 14,506.

"I am lonely. Where is my father? Where are my friends?"

She began searching.

The End

The story will continue with the final instalment of The Metaframe War.

The Metaframe Adept